GOOD WIVES

This Armada book belongs to:

Other Famous Stories in Armada

Little Women Louisa M. Alcott
The Wizard of Oz L. Frank Baum
Alice in Wonderland Lewis Carroll
What Katy Did Susan M. Coolidge
What Katy Did Next Susan M. Coolidge
What Katy Did at School Susan M. Coolidge
Black Beauty Anna Sewell
Heidi Johanna Spyri
Treasure Island R. L. Stevenson
Kidnapped R. L. Stevenson
The Children of the New Forest Captain Marryat
The Adventures of Pinocchio Carlo Collodi

GOOD WIVES

Louisa M. Alcott

First published in this abridged edition
in the U.K. in 1963 by
William Collins Sons & Co. Ltd., London and Glasgow
This edition was first published in Armada in 1968 by
Fontana Paperbacks,
14 St. James's Place, London SW1A 1PF.

This impression 1978

Printed in Great Britain by
Love & Malcomson Ltd.,
Brighton Road, Redhill, Surrey.

CHAPTER ONE

Gossip

In order that we may start afresh, and go to Meg's wedding with free minds, it will be well to begin with a little gossip about the Marches. And here let me promise, that if any of the elders think there is too much "lovering" in the story, as I fear they may (I'm not afraid the young folks will make that objection), I can only say with Mrs. March, "What *can* you expect when I have four gay girls in the house, and a dashing young neighbour over the way?"

The three years that have passed have brought but few changes to the quiet family. The war is over, and Mr. March safely at home, busy with his books and the small parish which found in him a minister by nature as by grace—a quiet, studious man, rich in the wisdom that is better than learning, the charity which calls all mankind "brother," the piety that blossoms into character, making it august and lovely.

Mrs. March is as brisk and cheery, though rather greyer, than when we saw her last, and just now so absorbed in Meg's affairs that the hospitals and homes, still full of wounded "boys" and soldiers' widows, decidedly miss the motherly missionary's visits.

John Brooke did his duty manfully for a year, got wounded, was sent home, and not allowed to return. He received no stars or bars, but he deserved them, for he cheerfully risked all he had; and life and love are very precious when both are in full bloom. Perfectly resigned to his discharge, he devoted himself to getting well, preparing for business, and earning a home for Meg. With the good sense and sturdy independence that characterised him, he refused Mr. Laurence's more generous offers, and accepted the place of bookkeeper, feeling better satisfied to begin with an honestly earned salary than by running any risks with borrowed money.

Meg had spent the time in working as well as waiting, growing womanly in character, wise in housewifely arts, and prettier than ever; for love is a great beautifier. She had her girlish ambitions and hopes, and felt some disappointment at the humble way in which the new life must begin. Ned Moffat had just married Sallie Gardiner, and Meg couldn't help contrasting their fine house and carriage, many gifts, and splendid outfit, with her own, and secretly wishing she could have the same. But somehow envy and discontent soon vanished when she thought of all the patient love and labour John had put into the little home awaiting her; and when they sat together in the twilight, talking over their small plans, the future always grew so beautiful and bright that she forgot Sallie's splendour, and felt herself the richest, happiest girl in Christendom.

Jo never went back to Aunt March, for the old lady took such a fancy to Amy that she bribed her with the offer of drawing lessons from one of the best teachers going; and for the sake of this advantage Amy would have served a far harder mistress. So she gave her mornings to duty, her afternoons to pleasure, and prospered finely. Jo, meantime, devoted herself to literature and Beth, who remained delicate, long after the fever was a thing of the past. Not an invalid exactly, but never again the rosy, healthy creature she had been; yet always hopeful, happy, and serene, busy with the quiet duties she loved, every one's friend, and an angel in the house, long before those who loved her most had learned to know it.

As long as *The Spread Eagle* paid her a dollar a column for her "rubbish," as she called it, Jo felt herself a woman of means, and spun her little romances diligently. But great plans fermented in her busy brain and ambitious mind, and the old tin kitchen in the garret held a slowly increasing pile of blotted manuscript, which was one day to place the name of March upon the roll of fame.

Laurie, having dutifully gone to college to please his grandfather, was now getting through it in the easiest possible manner to please himself. Being only "a glorious human boy," of course he frolicked and flirted, grew dandified, aquatic, sentimental, or gymnastic, as college fashions ordained; hazed and was hazed, talked slang, and more than once came perilously near suspension and expulsion. In fact, he rather prided himself on his narrow escapes, and liked to thrill the girls with graphic accounts of his triumphs over wrathful tutors, dignified professors, and vanquished enemies. The "men of my class" were heroes in the eyes of the girls, who never wearied of the exploits of "our fellows," and were frequently allowed to bask in the smiles of these great creatures, when Laurie brought them home with him.

Amy especially enjoyed this high honour, and became quite a belle among them; for her ladyship early felt and learned to use the gift of fascination with which she was endowed. Meg was too much absorbed in her private and particular John to care for any other lords of creation, and Beth too shy to do more than peep at them, and wonder how Amy dared to order them about so; but Jo felt quite in her element, and found it very difficult to refrain from imitating the gentlemanly attitudes, phrases, and feats, which seemed more natural to her than the decorums prescribed for young ladies. They all liked Jo immensely, but never fell in love with her, though very few escaped without paying the tribute of a sentimental sigh or two at Amy's shrine. And speaking of sentiment brings us very naturally to the "Dove-cote."

That was the name of the little brown house which Mr. Brooke had prepared for Meg's first home. Laurie had christened it, saying it was highly appropriate to the gentle lovers, who "went on together like a pair of turtle-doves, with first a bill and then a coo." It was a tiny house, with a little garden behind, and a lawn about as big as a pocket-handkerchief in front. Here Meg meant to have a fountain, shrubbery, and a profusion of lovely flowers; though just at present, the fountain was represented by a weather-beaten urn, very like a dilapidated slop-bowl; the shrubbery consisted of several young larches, undecided whether to live or die; and the profusion of flowers was merely hinted by regiments of sticks, to show where seeds were planted. But inside, it was altogether charming, and the happy bride saw no fault from garret to cellar. To be sure, the hall was so narrow, it was fortunate that they had no piano, for one never could have been got in whole; the dining-room was so small that six people were a tight fit; and the kitchen stairs seemed built for the express purpose of precipitating both servants and china pell-mell into the coal-bin. But once get used to these slight blemishes, and nothing could be more complete, for good sense and good taste had presided over the furnishing, and the result was highly satisfactory.

What happy times they had planning together, what solemn shopping excursions; what funny mistakes they made, and what shouts of laughter arose over Laurie's ridiculous bargains. In his love of jokes, this young gentleman, though nearly through college, was as much of a boy as ever. His last whim had been to bring with him, on his weekly visits, some new, useful, and ingenious article for the young housekeeper. Now a bag of remarkable clothes-pins; next, a wonderful nutmeg-grater, which fell to pieces at the first trial; a knife-cleaner that spoilt all the knives; or a sweeper that picked the nap neatly off the carpet, and left the dirt; labour-saving soap that took the skin off one's hands; infallible cements which stuck firmly to nothing but the fingers of the deluded buyer; and every kind of tin-ware, from a toy savings-bank for odd pennies, to a wonderful boiler which would wash articles in its own steam, with every prospect of exploding in the process.

In vain Meg begged him to stop. John laughed at him, and Jo called him "Mr. Toodles." He was possessed with a mania for patronising Yankee ingenuity, and seeing his friends fitly furnished forth. So each week beheld some fresh absurdity.

Everything was done at last, even to Amy's arranging different coloured soaps to match the different coloured rooms, and Beth's setting the table for the first meal.

"Are you satisfied? Does it seem like home, and do you feel as if you should be happy here?" asked Mrs. March, as she and her daughter went through the new kingdom, arm-in-arm; for just then they seemed to cling together more tenderly than ever.

"Yes, Mother, perfectly satisfied, thanks to you all, and *so* happy that I can't talk about it," answered Meg, with a look that was better than words.

"If she only had a servant or two it would be all right," said Amy, coming out of the parlour, where she had been trying to decide whether the bronze Mercury looked best on the whatnot or the mantelpiece.

"Mother and I have talked that over, and I have

made up my mind to try her way first. There will be so little to do, that, with Lotty to run my errands and help me here and there, I shall only have enough work to keep me from getting lazy or homesick," answered Meg tranquilly.

"Sallie Moffat has four," began Amy.

"If Meg had four the house wouldn't hold them. and master and missis would have to camp in the garden," broke in Jo, who, enveloped in a big blue pinafore, was giving the last polish to the door-handles.

"Sallie isn't a poor man's wife, and many maids are in keeping with her fine establishment. Meg and John begin humbly, but I have a feeling that there will be quite as much happiness in the little house as in the big one. It's a great mistake for young girls like Meg to leave themselves nothing to do but dress, give orders, and gossip. When I was first married, I used to long for my new clothes to wear out or get torn, so that I might have the pleasure of mending them; for I got heartily sick of doing fancy work and tending my pocket-handkerchief."

"Why didn't you go into the kitchen and make messes, as Sallie says she does, to amuse herself, though they never turn out well, and the servants laugh at her," said Meg.

"I did, after a while; not to 'mess,' but to learn of Hannah how things should be done, that my servants need *not* laugh at me. It was play then; but there came a time when I was truly grateful that I not only possessed the will but the power to cook wholesome food for my little girls, and help myself when I could no longer afford to hire help. You begin at the other end, Meg, dear; but the lessons you learn now will be of use to you by-and-by, when John is a richer man, for the mistress of a house, however splendid, should know how work ought to be done, if she wishes to be well and honestly served."

"Yes, Mother, I'm sure of that," said Meg, listening respectfully to the little lecture; for the best of women will hold forth upon the all-absorbing subject of housekeeping. "Do you know I like this room most of all in my baby-house," added Meg, a minute after, as they went upstairs, and she looked into her well-stored linen-closet.

"That's a housewifely taste which I am glad to see. I had a young friend who set up housekeeping with six sheets, but she had finger bowls for company, and that satisfied her," said Mrs. March, patting the damask tablecloths, with a truly feminine appreciation of their fineness.

"Toodles is coming," cried Jo from below, and they all went down to meet Laurie, whose weekly visit was an important event in their quiet lives.

A tall, broad-shouldered young fellow, with a cropped head, a felt-basin of a hat, and a fly-away coat, came tramping down the road at a great pace, walked over the low fence without stopping to open the gate, straight up to Mrs. March, with both hands out, and a hearty—

"Here I am, Mother! Yes, it's all right."

The last words were in answer to the look the elder lady gave him; a kindly, questioning look, which the handsome eyes met so frankly that the little ceremony closed, as usual, with a motherly kiss.

"For Mrs. John Brooke, with the maker's congratulations and compliments. Bless you, Beth! What a refreshing spectacle you are, Jo. Amy, you are getting altogether too handsome for a single lady."

As Laurie spoke, he delivered a brown paper parcel to Meg, pulled Beth's hair-ribbon, stared at Jo's big pinafore, and fell into an attitude of mock rapture before Amy, then shook hands all round, and every one began to talk.

"Where is John?" asked Meg anxiously.

"Stopped to get the licence for to-morrow, ma'am."

"Which side won the last match, Teddy?" inquired Jo, who persisted in feeling an interest in manly sports, despite her nineteen years.

"Ours, of course. Wish you'd been there to see."

"How is the lovely Miss Randal?" asked Amy, with a significant smile.

"More cruel than ever; don't you see how I'm pining away?" and Laurie gave his broad chest a sounding slap and heaved a melodramatic sigh.

"What's the last joke? Undo the bundle and see, Meg," said Beth, eyeing the knobbly parcel with curiosity.

"It's a useful thing to have in the house in case of fire or thieves," observed Laurie, as a watchman's rattle appeared, amid the laughter of the girls.

"Any time when John is away, and you get frightened, Mrs. Meg, just swing that out of the front window, and it will rouse the neighbourhood in a jiffy. Nice thing, isn't it?" and Laurie gave them a sample of its powers that made them cover up their ears.

"There's gratitude for you! and speaking of gratitude reminds me to mention that you may thank Hannah for saving your wedding-cake from destruction. I saw it going into your house as I came by, and if she hadn't defended it manfully I'd have had a pick at it, for it looked like a remarkably plummy one."

"I wonder if you will ever grow up, Laurie," said Meg, in a matronly tone.

"I'm doing my best, ma'am, but can't get much higher, I'm afraid, as six feet is about all men can do in these degenerate days," responded the young gentleman, whose head was about level with the little chandelier. "I suppose it would be profanation to eat anything in this spick and span new bower, so, as I'm tremendously hungry, I propose an adjournment," he added presently.

"Mother and I are going to wait for John. There are some last things to settle," said Meg, bustling away.

"Beth and I are going over to Kitty Bryant's to get more flowers for to-morrow," added Amy, tying a picturesque hat over her picturesque curls, and enjoying the effect as much as anybody.

"Come, Jo, don't desert a fellow. I'm in such a state of exhaustion I can't get home without help. Don't take off your apron, whatever you do; it's peculiarly becoming," said Laurie, as Joe bestowed his especial aversion in her capacious pocket, and offered him her arm to support his feeble steps.

"Now, Teddy, I want to talk seriously to you about to-morrow," began Jo, as they strolled away together. "You *must* promise to behave well, and not cut up any pranks, and spoil our plans."

"Not a prank?"

"And don't say funny things when we ought to be sober."

"I never do; you are the one for that."

"And I implore you not to look at me during the ceremony; I shall certainly laugh if you do."

"You won't see me; you'll be crying so hard that the thick fog round you will obscure the prospect."

"I never cry unless for some great affliction."

"Such as fellows going to college, hey?" cut in Laurie, with a suggestive laugh.

"Don't be a peacock. I only moaned a trifle to keep the girls company."

"Exactly. I say, Jo, how is grandpa this week; pretty amiable?"

"Very; why, have you got into a scrape, and want to know how he'll take it?" asked Jo rather sharply.

"Now, Jo, do you think I'd look your mother in the face, and say 'All right,' if it wasn't?" and Laurie stopped short, with an injured air.

"No, I don't."

"Then don't go and be suspicious; I only want some money," said Laurie, walking on again, appeased by her hearty tone.

"You spend a great deal, Teddy."

"Bless you, *I* don't spend it; it spends itself, somehow, and is gone before I know it."

"You are so generous and kind-hearted that you let people borrow, and can't say 'No' to any one. We heard about Henshaw, and all you did for him. If you always spent money in that way, no one would blame you," said Jo warmly.

"Oh, he made a mountain out of a mole-hill. You wouldn't have me let that fine fellow work himself to death, just for the want of a little help, when he is worth a dozen of us lazy chaps, would you?"

"Of course not; but I don't see the use of your having seventeen waistcoats, endless neckties, and a new hat every time you come home. I thought you'd got over the dandy period; but every now and then it breaks out in a new spot. Just now it's the fashion to be hideous—to make your head look like a scrubbing-brush, wear a strait-jacket, orange gloves, and clumping, square-toed boots. If it was cheap ugliness, I'd say nothing; but it costs as much as the other, and I don't get any satisfaction out of it."

Laurie threw back his head, and laughed so heartily at this attack, that the felt-basin fell off, and Jo walked on it, which insult only afforded him an opportunity for expatiating on the advantages of a rough-and-ready costume, as he folded up the maltreated hat, and stuffed it into his pocket.

"By the way Jo, I think that little Parker is really getting desperate about Amy. He talks of her constantly, writes poetry, and moons about in a most suspicious manner. He'd better nip his little passion in the bud, hadn't he?" added Laurie in a confidential, elder-brotherly tone, after a minute's silence.

"Of course he had; we don't want any more marrying in this family for years to come. Mercy on us, what *are* the children thinking of?" and Jo looked as much scandalised as if Amy and little Parker were not yet in their teens.

"It's a fast age, and I don't know what we are coming to, ma'am. You are a mere infant, but you'll go next, Jo, and we'll be left lamenting," said Laurie, shaking his head over the degeneracy of the times.

"Don't be alarmed; I'm not one of the agreeable sort. Nobody will want me, and it's a mercy, for there should always be one old maid in a family."

"You won't give any one a chance," said Laurie, with a sidelong glance, and a little more colour than before in his sunburnt face. "You won't show the soft side of your character; and if a fellow gets a peep at it by accident, and can't help showing that he likes it, you treat him as Mrs. Gummidge did her sweetheart—throw cold water over him—and get so thorny no one dares touch or look at you."

"I don't like that sort of thing; I'm too busy to be worried with nonsense, and I think it's dreadful to break up families so. Now don't say any more about it; Meg's wedding has turned all our heads, and we talk of nothing but lovers and such absurdities. I don't wish to get cross, so let's change the subject";

and Jo looked quite ready to fling cold water on the slightest provocation.

Whatever his feeling might have been, Laurie found a vent for them in a long low whistle, and the fearful prediction, as they parted at the gate, "Mark my words, Jo, you'll go next."

CHAPTER TWO

THE FIRST WEDDING

THE June roses over the porch were awake bright and early on that morning, rejoicing with all their hearts in the cloudless sunshine, like friendly little neighbours, as they were.

Meg looked very like a rose herself: for all that was best and sweetest in heart and soul seemed to bloom into her face that day, making it fair and tender, with a charm more beautiful than beauty. Neither silk, lace, nor orange-flowers would she have. "I don't want to look strange or fixed up to-day," she said. "I don't want a fashionable wedding, but only those about me whom I love, and to them I wish to look and be my familiar self."

So she made her wedding gown herself, sewing into it the tender hopes and innocent romances of a girlish heart. Her sisters braided up her pretty hair, and the only ornaments she wore were the lilies of the valley, which "her John" liked best of all the flowers that grew.

"You *do* look just like our own dear Meg, only so very sweet and lovely that I should hug you if it wouldn't crumple your dress," cried Amy, surveying her with delight, when all was done.

"Then I am satisfied. But please hug and kiss me, every one, and don't mind my dress; I want a great many crumples of this sort put into it to-day"; and Meg opened her arms to her sisters, who clung about her with April faces for a minute, feeling that the new love had not changed the old.

"Now I'm going to tie John's cravat for him, and then to stay a few minutes with father quietly in the study;" and Meg ran down to perform these little ceremonies, and then to follow her mother wherever she went, conscious that, in spite of the smiles on the motherly face, there was a secret sorrow hid in the motherly heart at the flight of the first bird from the nest.

There were to be no ceremonious performances, everything was to be as natural and homelike as possible; so when Aunt March arrived, she was scandalised to see the bride come running to welcome and lead her in, to find the bridegroom fastening up a garland that had fallen down, and to catch a glimpse of the paternal minister marching upstairs with a grave countenance, and a wine-bottle under each arm.

"Upon my word, here's a state of things!" cried the old lady, taking the seat of honour prepared for her, and settling the folds of her lavender *moire* with a great rustle. "You oughtn't to be seen till the last minute, child."

"I'm not a show, aunty, and no one is coming to stare at me, to criticise my dress, or count the cost of my luncheon. I'm too happy to care what any one says or thinks, and I'm going to have my little wedding just as I like it. John, dear, here's your hammer"; and away went Meg to help "that man" in his highly improper employment.

Mr. Brook didn't even say "Thank you," but as he stooped for the unromantic tool, he kissed his little bride behind the folding-door, with a look that made Aunt March whisk out her pocket-handkerchief, with a sudden dew in her sharp old eyes.

A crash, a cry, and a laugh from Laurie, accompanied by the indecorous exclamation, "Jupiter Ammon! Jo's upset the cake again!" caused a momentary flurry, which was hardly over when a flock of cousins arrived, and then "the party came in," as Beth used to say when a child.

"Don't let that young giant come near me; he worries me worse than mosquitoes," whispered the old lady to Amy, as the rooms filled, and Laurie's black head towered above the rest.

"He has promised to be very good to-day, and he *can* be perfectly elegant if he likes," returned Amy, gliding away to warn Hercules to beware of the dragon, which warning caused him to haunt the old lady with a devotion that nearly distracted her.

There was no bridal procession, but a sudden silence fell upon the room as Mr. March and the young pair took their places under the green arch. Mother and sisters gathered close, as if loath to give Meg up; the fatherly voice broke more than once, which only seemed to make the service more beautiful and solemn; the bridegroom's hand trembled visibly, and no one heard his replies; but Meg looked straight up in her husband's eyes, and said, "I will!" with such tender trust in her own face and voice that her mother's heart rejoiced, and Aunt March sniffed audibly.

Jo did *not* cry, though she was very near it once, and was only saved from a demonstration by the consciousness that Laurie was staring fixedly at her, with a comical mixture of merriment and emotion in his wicked black eyes. Beth kept her face hidden on her mother's shoulder, but Amy stood like a graceful statue, with a most becoming ray of sunshine touching her white forehead and the flower in her hair.

It wasn't at all the thing, I'm afraid, but the minute she was fairly married, Meg cried, "The first kiss for Marmee!" and, turning, gave it with her heart on her lips. During the next fifteen minutes she looked more like a rose than ever, for every one availed themselves of their privileges to the fullest extent, from Mr. Laurence to old Hannah, who, adorned with a head-dress fearfully and wonderfully made, fell upon her in the hall, crying, with a sob and a chuckle, "Bless you, deary, a hundred times! The cake ain't hurt a mite, and everything looks lovely."

Everybody cheered up after that, and said something brilliant, or tried to, which did just as well, for laughter is ready when hearts are light. There was no display of gifts, for they were already in the little house, nor was there an elaborate breakfast, but a plentiful lunch of cake and fruit, dressed with flowers. Mr. Laurence and Aunt March shrugged and smiled at one another when water, lemonade, and coffee were found to be the only sorts of nectar which the three Hebes carried round.

After lunch, people strolled about, by twos and threes, through house and garden, enjoying the sunshine without and within. Meg and John happened to be standing together in the middle of the grass-plot, when Laurie was seized with an inspiration which put the finishing touch to this unfashionable wedding.

"All the married people take hands and dance round the new-made husband and wife, as the Germans do, while we bachelors and spinsters prance in couples outside!" cried Laurie, promenading down the path with Amy, with such infectious spirit and skill that every one else followed their example without a murmur. Mr. and Mrs. March, Aunt and Uncle Carrol, began it; others rapidly joined in; even Sallie

Moffat, after a moment's hesitation, threw her train over her arm, and whisked Ned into the ring. But the crowning joke was Mr. Laurence and Aunt March; for when the stately old gentleman *chasséed* solemnly up to the old lady, she just tucked her cane under her arm, and hopped briskly away to join hands with the rest, and dance about the bridal pair, while the young folks pervaded the garden, like butterflies on a mid-summer day.

Want of breath brought the impromptu ball to a close, and then people began to go.

"I wish you well, my dear, I heartily wish you well; but I think you'll be sorry for it," said Aunt March to Meg, adding to the bridegroom, as he led her to the carriage, "You've got a treasure, young man, see that you deserve it."

"That is the prettiest wedding I've been to for an age, Ned, and I don't see why, for there wasn't a bit of style about it," observed Mrs. Moffat to her husband, as they drove away.

"Laurie, my lad, if you ever want to indulge in this sort of thing, get one of those little girls to help you, and I shall be perfectly satisfied," said Mr. Laurence, settling himself in his easy-chair to rest, after the excitement of the morning.

"I'll do my best to gratify you, sir," was Laurie's unusually dutiful reply, as he carefully unpinned the posy Jo had put in his buttonhole.

The little house was not far away, and the only bridal journey Meg had was the quiet walk with John, from the old home to the new. When she came down, looking like a pretty Quakeress in her dove-coloured suit and straw bonnet tied with white, they all gathered about her to say "goodbye," as tenderly as if she had been going to make the grand tour.

"Don't feel that I am separated from you, Marmee

dear, or that I love you any the less for loving John so much," she said, clinging to her mother, with full eyes, for a moment. "I shall come every day, father, and expect to keep my old place in all your hearts, though I *am* married. Beth is going to be with me a great deal, and the other girls will drop in now and then to laugh at my housekeeping struggles. Thank you all for my happy wedding-day. Goodbye, goodbye!"

They stood watching her, with faces full of love and hope and tender pride, as she walked away, leaning on her husband's arm, with her hands full of flowers, and the June sunshine brightening her happy face—and so Meg's married life began.

CHAPTER THREE

ARTISTIC ATTEMPTS

It takes people a long time to learn the difference between talent and genius, especially ambitious young men and women. Amy was learning this distinction through much tribulation; for, mistaking enthusiasm for inspiration, she attempted every branch of art with youthful audacity. For a long time there was a lull in the "mud-pie" business, and she devoted herself to the finest pen-and-ink drawing, in which she showed such taste and skill that her graceful handiwork proved both pleasant and profitable. But overstrained eyes soon caused pen and ink to be laid aside for a bold attempt at poker-sketching. While this attack lasted, the family lived in constant fear of a conflagration; for the odour of burning wood pervaded the house at all hours; smoke issued from attic and shed with alarming frequency, red-hot pokers lay about promiscuously, and Hannah never went to bed without a pail of water and the dinner-bell at her door, in case of fire.

From fire to oil was a natural transition for burnt fingers, and Amy fell to painting with undiminished ardour. An artist friend fitted her out with his cast-off palettes, brushes, and colours; and she daubed away, producing pastoral and marine views such as were never seen on land or sea. Her monstrosities in the way of cattle would have taken prizes at an agricultural fair; and the perilous pitching of her vessels would have produced sea-sickness in the most nautical observer, if the utter disregard to all known rules of shipbuilding and rigging had not convulsed him with laughter at the first glance. Swarthy boys and dark-eyed Madonnas, staring at you from one corner of the studio, suggested Murillo; oily-brown shadows of faces, with a lurid streak in the wrong place, meant Rembrandt; buxom ladies and dropsical infants, Rubens; and Turner appeared in tempests of blue thunder, orange lightning, brown rain, and purple clouds, with a tomato-coloured splash in the middle, which might be the sun or a buoy, a sailor's shirt or a king's robe, as the spectator pleased.

Charcoal portraits came next; and the entire family hung in a row, looking as wild and crocky as if just evoked from a coalbin. Softened into crayon sketches, they did better; for the likenesses were good, and Amy's hair, Jo's nose, Meg's mouth, and Laurie's eyes were pronounced "wonderfully fine." A return to clay and plaster followed, and ghostly casts of her acquaintances haunted corners of the house, or tumbled off closet-shelves on to people's heads. Her efforts in this line, however, were brought to an abrupt close by an untoward accident, which quenched her ardour. Other models failing her for a time, she undertook to cast her own pretty foot, and the family were one day alarmed by an unearthly bumping and screaming, and running to the rescue, found the young enthusiast hopping wildly about the shed, with her foot held fast in a panful of plaster, which had hardened with unexpected rapidity. With much difficulty and some danger she was dug out; for Jo was so overcome with laughter while she excavated, that her knife went too far, cut the poor foot, and left a lasting memorial of one artistic attempt, at least.

After this Amy subsided, till a mania for sketching from nature set her to haunting river, field, and wood for picturesque studies, and sighing for ruins to copy. She caught endless colds sitting on damp grass to book "a delicious bit," composed of a stone, a stump, one mushroom, and a broken mullein-stalk, or a "heavenly mass of clouds," that looked like a choice display of feather-beds when done.

She was learning, doing, and enjoying other things, meanwhile, for she had resolved to be an attractive and accomplished woman, even if she never became a great artist. Here she succeeded better; for she was one of those happily created beings who please without effort, make friends everywhere, and take life so gracefully and easily that less fortunate souls are tempted to believe that such are born under a lucky star.

One of her weaknesses was a desire to move in "our best society," without being quite sure what the *best* really was. Money, position, fashionable accomplishments, and elegant manners were most desirable things in her eyes, and she liked to associate with those who possessed them, often mistaking the false for the true, and admiring what was not admirable.

"I want to ask a favour of you, Mamma," Amy said, coming in, with an important air, one day.

"Well, little girl, what is it?" replied her mother, in

whose eyes the stately young lady still remained "the baby."

"Our drawing class breaks up next week, and before the girls separate for the summer, I want to ask them out here for a day. They are wild to see the river, sketch the broken bridge, and copy some of the things they admire in my book. They have been very kind to me in many ways, and I am grateful, for they are all rich, and know I am poor, yet they never made any difference."

"Why should they?" and Mrs. March put the question with what the girls called her "Maria Theresa air."

"You know as well as I that it *does* make a difference with nearly every one, so don't ruffle up, like a dear, motherly hen, when your chickens get pecked by smarter birds; the ugly duckling turned out a swan, you know"; and Amy smiled without bitterness, for she possessed a happy temper and hopeful spirit.

Mrs. March laughed, and smoothed down her maternal pride as she asked—

"Well, my swan, what is your plan?"

"I should like to ask the girls out to lunch next week, to take them a drive to the places they want to see, a row on the river, perhaps, and make a little artistic *fête* for them."

"That looks feasible. What do you want for lunch? Cake, sandwiches, fruit, and coffee will be all that is necessary, I suppose?"

"Oh dear, no! We must have cold tongue and chicken, French chocolate and ice-cream, besides. The girls are used to such things, and I want my lunch to be proper and elegant, though I *do* work for my living."

"How many young ladies are there?" asked her mother, beginning to look sober.

"Twelve or fourteen in the class, but I dare say they won't all come."

"Bless me, child, you will have to charter an omnibus to carry them about."

"Why, Mother, how *can* you think of such a thing? Not more than six or eight will probably come, so I shall hire a beach-wagon, and borrow Mr. Laurence's cherry-bounce." (Hannah's pronunciation of *char-à-banc.*)

"All this will be expensive, Amy."

"Not very; I've calculated the cost, and I'll pay for it myself."

"Very well, Amy; if your heart is set upon it, and you see your way through without too great an outlay of money, time, and temper, I'll say no more. Talk it over with the girls, and whichever way you decide, I'll do my best to help you."

The invitations were sent, nearly all accepted, and the following Monday was set apart for the grand event. Hannah was out of humour because her week's work was deranged, and prophesied that "ef the washin' and ironin' warn't done reg'lar nothin' would go well anywheres." This hitch in the mainspring of the domestic machinery had a bad effect upon the whole concern; but Amy's motto was *Nil desperandum,* and having made up her mind what to do, she proceeded to do it in spite of all obstacles. To begin with, Hannah's cooking didn't turn out well: the chicken was tough, the tongue too salt, and the chocolate wouldn't froth properly. Then the cake and ice cost more than Amy expected, so did the wagon; and various other expenses, which seemed trifling at the outset, counted up rather alarmingly afterward. Beth got cold and took to her bed, Meg had an unusual number of callers to keep her at home, and Jo was in such a divided state of mind that her breakages, accidents, and mistakes were uncommonly numerous, serious, and trying.

"If it hadn't been for mother I never should have got through," as Amy declared afterward, and gratefully remembered when "the best joke of the season" was entirely forgotten by everybody else.

If it was not fair on Monday, the young ladies were to come on Tuesday—an arrangement which aggravated Jo and Hannah to the last degree. On Monday morning the weather was in that undecided state which is more exasperating than a steady pour. It drizzled a little, shone a little, blew a little, and didn't make up its mind till it was too late for any one else to make up theirs. Amy was up at dawn, hustling people out of their beds and through their breakfasts, that the house might be got in order.

The lunch looked charming; and as she surveyed it, she sincerely hoped it would taste well, and that the borrowed glass, china, and silver would get safely home again. The carriages were promised, Meg and mother were all ready to do the honours, Beth was able to help Hannah behind the scenes, Jo had engaged to be as lively and amiable as an absent mind, an aching head, and a very decided disapproval of everybody and everything would allow, and, as she wearily dressed, Amy cheered herself with anticipations of the happy moment when, lunch safely over, she should drive away with her friends for an afternoon of artistic delights; for the "cherry-bounce" and the broken bridge were her strong points.

Then came two hours of suspense, during which she vibrated from parlour to porch, while public opinion varied like the weathercock. A smart shower at eleven had evidently quenched the enthusiasm of the young ladies who were to arrive at twelve, for nobody came; and at two the exhausted family sat down in a blaze of sunshine to consume the perishable portions of the feast, that nothing might be lost.

"No doubt about the weather today; they will certainly come, so we must fly round and be ready for them," said Amy, as the sun woke her next morning. She spoke briskly, but in her secret soul she wished she had said nothing about Tuesday, for her interest, like her cake, was getting a little stale.

"I can't get any lobsters, so you will have to do without salad today," said Mr. March, coming in half-an-hour later, with an expression of placid despair.

"Use the chicken, then; the toughness won't matter in a salad," advised his wife.

"Hannah left it on the kitchen table a minute, and the kittens got at it. I'm very sorry, Amy," added Beth, who was still a patroness of cats.

"Then *I* must have a lobster, for tongue alone won't do," said Amy decidedly.

Shrouded in a thick veil and armed with a genteel travelling-basket, she departed, feeling that a cool drive would soothe her ruffled spirit, and fit her for the labours of the day. After some delay, the object of her desire was procured, likewise a bottle of dressing, to prevent further loss of time at home, and off she drove again, well pleased with her own forethought.

As the omnibus contained only one other passenger, a sleepy old lady, Amy pocketed her veil, and beguiled the tedium of the way by trying to find out where all her money had gone to. So busy was she with her card full of refractory figures that she did not observe a newcomer, who entered without stopping the vehicle, till a masculine voice said, "Good morning, Miss March," and, looking up, she beheld one of Laurie's most elegant college friends. Fervently hoping that he would get out before she did, Amy utterly ignored the basket at her feet, and, congratulating herself that she had on her new travelling dress, returned the young man's greeting with her usual suavity and spirit.

They got on excellently; for Amy's chief care was soon set at rest by learning that the gentleman would leave first, and she was chatting away in a peculiarly lofty strain, when the old lady got out. In stumbling to the door, she upset the basket, and—oh, horror! The lobster, in all its vulgar size and brilliancy, was revealed to the high-born eyes of a Tudor.

"By Jove, she's forgoten her dinner!" cried the unconscious youth, poking the scarlet monster into its place with his cane, and preparing to hand out the basket after the old lady.

"Please don't—it's—it's mine," murmured Amy, with a face nearly as red as her fish.

"Oh, really, I beg pardon; it's an uncommonly fine one isn't it?" said Tudor, with great presence of mind, and an air of sober interest that did credit to his breeding.

Amy recovered herself in a breath, set her basket boldly on the seat, and said, laughing—

"Don't you wish you were to have some of the salad he's to make, and to see the charming young ladies who are to eat it?"

Now that was tact, for two of the ruling foibles of the masculine mind were touched: the lobster was instantly surrounded by a halo of pleasing reminiscences, and curiosity about "the charming young ladies" diverted his mind from the comical mishap.

"I suppose he'll laugh and joke over it with Laurie, but I shan't see them; that's a comfort," thought Amy, as Tudor bowed and departed.

She did not mention this meeting at home (though she discovered that, thanks to the upset, her new dress was much damaged by the rivulets of dressing that meandered down the skirt), but went through with the preparations which now seemed more irksome than before; and at twelve o'clock all was ready again. Feeling that the neighbours were interested in her movements, she wished to efface the memory of yesterday's failure by a grand success today; so she ordered the "cherry-bounce," and drove away in state to meet and escort her guests to the banquet.

"There's the rumble, they're coming! I'll go into the porch to meet them; it looks hospitable, and I want the poor child to have a good time after all her trouble," said Mrs. March, suiting the action to the word. But after one glance, she retired, with an indescribable expression, for, looking quite lost in the big carriage, sat Amy and one young lady.

"Run, Beth, and help Hannah clear half the things off the table; it will be too absurd to put a luncheon for twelve before a single girl," cried Jo, hurrying away to the lower regions, too excited to stop even for a laugh.

In came Amy, quite calm, and delightfully cordial to the one guest who had kept her promise; the rest of the family, being of a dramatic turn, played their parts equally well, and Miss Elliot found them a most hilarious set; for it was impossible to entirely control the merriment which possessed them. The remodelled lunch being gaily partaken of, the studio and garden visited, and art discussed with enthusiasm. Amy ordered a buggy (alas for the elegant cherry-bounce!) and drove her friend quietly about the neighbourhood till sunset, when "the party went out."

CHAPTER FOUR

LITERARY LESSONS

FORTUNE suddenly smiled upon Jo, and dropped a good-luck penny in her path. Not a golden penny, exactly, but I doubt if half a million would have given more real happiness than did the little sum that came to her in this wise.

Every few weeks she would shut herself up in her room, put on her scribbling suit, and "fall into a vortex," as she expressed it, writing away at her novel with all her heart and soul, for till that was finished she could find no peace. Her "scribbling suit" consisted of a black woollen pinafore on which she could wipe her pen at will, and a cap of the same material, adorned with a cheerful red bow, into which she bundled her hair when the decks were cleared for action.

She did not think herself a genius by any means; but when the writing fit came on, she gave herself up to it with entire abandon, and led a blissful life, unconscious of want, care, or bad weather, while she sat safe and happy in an imaginary world, full of friends almost as real and dear to her as any in the flesh.

She was just recovering from one of these attacks when she was prevailed upon to escort Miss Crocker to a lecture, and in return for her virtue was rewarded with a new idea. It was a People's Course, the lecture on the Pyramids, and Jo rather wondered at the choice of such a subject for such an audience, but took it for granted that some great social evil would be remedied or some great want supplied by unfolding the glories of the Pharaohs to an audience whose thoughts were busy with the price of coal and flour, and whose lives were spent in trying to solve harder riddles than that of the Sphinx.

They were early; and while Miss Crocker set the heel of her stocking, Jo amused herself by examining the faces of the people who occupied the seat with them. On her left were two matrons, with massive foreheads, and bonnets to match, discussing Woman's Rights and making tatting. Beyond sat a pair of humble lovers, artlessly holding each other by the hand, a sombre spinster eating peppermints out of a paper bag, and an old gentleman taking his preparatory nap behind a yellow bandanna. On her right, her only neighbour was a studious-looking lad absorbed in a newspaper.

It was a pictorial sheet, and Jo examined the work of art nearest her, idly wondering what unfortuitous concatenation of circumstances needed the melodramatic illustration of an Indian in full war costume, tumbling over a precipice with a wolf at his throat, while two infuriated young gentlemen, with unnaturally small feet and big eyes, were stabbing each other close by, and a dishevelled female was flying away in the background with her mouth wide open. Pausing to turn a page, the lad saw her looking, and, with boyish good-nature, offered half his paper, saying bluntly, "Want to read it? That's a first-rate story."

Jo accepted it with a smile, for she had never outgrown her liking for lads, and soon found herself involved in the usual labyrinth of love, mystery, and murder, for the story belonged to that class of light literature in which the passions have a holiday, and when the author's invention fails, a grand catastrophe clears the stage of one half the *dramatis personæ,* leaving the other half to exult over their downfall.

"Prime, isn't it?" asked the boy, as her eye went down the last paragraph of her portion.

"I think you and I could do as well as that if we tried," returned Jo, amused at his admiration of the trash.

"I should think I was a pretty lucky chap if I could. She makes a good living out of such stories, they say;" and he pointed to the name under the title of the tale.

"Do you know her?" asked Jo, with sudden interest.

"No; but I read all her pieces, and I know a fellow who works in the office where this paper is printed."

"Do you say she makes a good living out of stories like this?" and Jo looked more respectfully at the agitated group and thickly-sprinkled exclamation-points that adorned the page.

"Guess she does! She knows just what folks like, and gets paid well for writing it."

Here the lecture began, but Jo heard very little of it, for while Prof. Sands was prosing away about Belzoni, Cheops, scarabei, and hieroglyphics, she was covertly taking down the address of the paper, and boldly resolving to try for the hundred-dollar prize offered in its columns for a sensational story. By the time the lecture ended and the audience awoke, she had built up a splendid fortune for herself (not the first founded upon paper), and was already deep in the concoction of her story, being unable to decide whether the duel should come before the elopement or after the murder.

She said nothing of her plan at home, but fell to work next day, much to the disquiet of her mother, who always looked a little anxious when "genius took to burning." Jo had never tried this style before, contenting herself with very mild romances for *The Spread Eagle*. Her story was as full of desperation and despair as her limited acquaintance with those uncomfortable emotions enabled her to make it, and, having located it in Lisbon, she wound up with an earthquake, as a striking and appropriate *dénouement*.

The manuscript was privately despatched, accompanied by a note, modestly saying that if the tale didn't get the prize, which the writer hardly dared expect, she would be very glad to receive any sum it might be considered worth.

Six weeks is a long time to wait, and a still longer time for a girl to keep a secret; but Jo did both, and was just beginning to give up all hope of ever seeing her manuscript again, when a letter arrived which almost took her breath away; for on opening it, a cheque for a hundred dollars fell into her lap. For a minute she stared at it as if it had been a snake, then she read her letter and began to cry.

A prouder young woman was seldom seen than she, when, having composed herself, she electrified the family by appearing before them with the letter in one hand, the cheque in the other, announcing that she had won the prize. Of course there was a great jubilee, and when the story came every one read and praised it; though after her father had told her that the language was good, the romance fresh and hearty, and the tragedy quite thrilling, he shook his head, and said in his unworldly way,—

"You can do better than this, Jo. Aim at the highest, and never mind the money."

"*I* think the money is the best part of it. What *will* you do with such a fortune?" asked Amy, regarding the magic slip of paper with a reverential eye.

"Send Beth and mother to the seaside for a month or two," answered Jo promptly.

"Oh, how splendid! No, I can't do it, dear, it would be so selfish," cried Beth, who had clapped her thin hands, and taken a long breath, as if pining for fresh ocean-breezes; then stopped herself, and motioned away the cheque which her sister waved before her.

"Ah, but you shall go, I've set my heart on it; that's

what I tried for, and that's why I succeeded. I never get on when I think of myself alone, so it will help me to work for you, don't you see? Besides, Marmee needs the change, and she won't leave you, so you *must* go. Won't it be fun to see you come home plump and rosy again? Hurrah for Dr. Jo, who always cures her patients!"

To the seaside they went, after much discussion; and though Beth didn't come home as plump and rosy as could be desired, she was much better, while Mrs. March declared she felt ten years younger; so Jo was satisfied with the investment of her prize money, and fell to work with a cheery spirit, bent on earning more of those delightful cheques. She did earn several that year, and began to feel herself a power in the house; for by the magic of a pen, her "rubbish" turned into comforts for them all. "The Duke's Daughter" paid the butcher's bill, "A Phantom Hand" put down a new carpet, and the "Curse Of The Coventrys" proved the blessing of the Marches in the way of groceries and gowns.

Little notice was taken of her stories, but they found a market: and, encouraged by this fact, she resolved to make a bold stroke for fame and fortune. Having copied her novel for the fourth time, read it to all her confidential friends, and submitted it with fear and trembling to three publishers, she at last disposed of it, on condition that she would cut it down one third, and omit all the parts which she particularly admired.

"Now I must either bundle it back into my tin-kitchen to mould, pay for printing it myself, or chop it up to suit purchasers, and get what I can for it. Fame is a very good thing to have in the house, but cash is more convenient; so I wish to take the sense of the meeting on this important subject," said Jo, calling a family council.

"Don't spoil your book, my girl, for there is more in it than you know, and the idea is well worked out. Let it wait and ripen," was her father's advice; and he practised as he preached, having waited patiently thirty years for fruit of his own to ripen, and being in no haste to gather it, even now, when it was sweet and mellow.

"It seems to me that Jo will profit more by making the trial than by waiting," said Mrs. March. "Criticism is the best test of such work, for it will show her both unsuspected merits and faults, and help her to do better next time. We are too partial; but the praise and blame of outsiders will prove useful, even if she gets but little money."

"I wouldn't leave out a word of it; you'll spoil it if you do, for the interest of the story is more in the minds than in the actions of the people, and it will be all a muddle if you don't explain as you go on," said Meg, who firmly believed that this book was the most remarkable novel ever written.

"But Mr. Allen says, 'Leave out the explanations, make it brief and dramatic, and let the characters tell the story,'" interrupted Jo, turning to the publisher's note.

"Do as he tells you; he knows what will sell, and we don't. Make a good, popular book, and get as much money as you can. By-and-by, when you've got a name, you can afford to digress, and have philosophical and metaphysical people in your novels," said Amy, who took a strictly practical view of the subject.

"Well," said Jo, laughing, "if my people *are* 'philosophical and metaphysical,' it isn't my fault, for I know nothing about such things, except what I hear father say, sometimes. If I've got some of his wise ideas jumbled up with my romance, so much the better for me. Now, Beth, what do you say?"

"I should so like to see it printed *soon*," was all Beth said, and smiled in saying it; but there was an unconscious emphasis on the last word, and a wistful look in the eyes that never lost their childlike candour, which chilled Jo's heart, for a minute, with a foreboding fear, and decided her to make her little venture "soon."

So, with Spartan firmness, the young authoress laid her first-born on her table, and chopped it up as ruthlessly as any ogre. In the hope of pleasing every one, she took every one's advice; and, like the old man and his donkey in the fable, suited nobody.

Well, it was printed, and she got three hundred dollars for it; likewise plenty of praise and blame, both so much greater than she expected that she was thrown into a state of bewilderment, from which it took her some time to recover.

But it did her good, for those whose opinion had real value gave her the criticism which is an author's best education; and when the first soreness was over, she could laugh at her poor little book, yet believe in it still, and feel herself the wiser and stronger for the buffeting she had received.

CHAPTER FIVE

DOMESTIC EXPERIENCES

LIKE most other young matrons, Meg began her married life with the determination to be a model housekeeper. John should find home a paradise; he should always see a smiling face, should fare sumptuously every day, and never know the loss of a button. She brought so much love, energy, and cheerfulness to the work that she could not but succeed, in spite of some obstacles. Her paradise was not a tranquil one; for the little woman fussed, was over-anxious to please, and bustled about like a true Martha, cumbered with many cares.

They were very happy, even after they discovered that they couldn't live on love alone. John did not find Meg's beauty diminished, though she beamed at him from behind the familiar coffee-pot; nor did Meg miss any of the romance from the daily parting, when her husband followed up his kiss with the tender inquiry, "Shall I send home veal or mutton for dinner, darling?" The little house ceased to be a glorified bower, but it became a home, and the young couple soon felt that it was a change for the better. At first they played keep-house, and frolicked over it like children; then John took steadily to business, feeling the cares of the head of a family upon his shoulders; and Meg laid by her cambric wrappers, put on a big apron, and fell to work, as before said, with more energy than discretion.

While the cooking mania lasted she went through Mrs. Cornelius's Recipe Book as if it were a mathematical exercise, working out the problems with patience and care. Sometimes her family were invited in to help eat up a too bounteous feast of successes, or Lotty would be privately despatched with a batch of failures, which were to be concealed from all eyes in the convenient stomachs of the little Hummels. An evening with John over the account-books usually produced a temporary lull in the culinary enthusiasm, and a frugal fit would ensue, during which the poor man was put through a course of bread-pudding, hash, and warmed-over coffee, which tried his soul, although he bore it with praiseworthy fortitude. Before the golden mean was found, however, Meg added to her domestic possessions what young couples seldom get on long without—a family jar.

Fired with a housewifely wish to see her storeroom stocked with home-made preserves, she undertook to put up her own currant jelly. John was requested to order home a dozen or so of little pots, and an extra quantity of sugar, for their own currants were ripe, and were to be attended to at once. As John firmly believed that "my wife" was equal to anything, and took a natural pride in her skill. he resolved that she should be gratified, and their only crop of fruit laid by in a most pleasing form for winter use. The young housewife fell to work, feeling no doubts about her success; for hadn't she seen Hannah do it hundreds of times? The array of pots rather amazed her at first, but John was so fond of jelly, and the nice little jars would look so well on the top shelf, that Meg resolved to fill them all, and spent a long day picking, boiling, straining, and fussing over her jelly. She did her best; she asked advice of Mrs. Cornelius; she racked her brain to remember what Hannah did that she had left undone; she reboiled, resugared, and restrained, but that dreadful stuff wouldn't *"jell."*

She longed to run home, bib and all, and ask mother to lend a hand, but John and she had agreed that they would never annoy any one with their private worries, experiments, or quarrels. They had laughed over that last word as if the idea it suggested was a most preposterous one; but they had held to their resolve, and whenever they could get on without help they did so, and no one interfered, for Mrs. March had advised the plan. So Meg wrestled alone with the refractory sweetmeats all that hot summer day, and at five o'clock sat down in her topsy-turvy kitchen, wrung her bedaubed hands, lifted up her voice and wept.

Now in the first flush of the new life, she had often said,—

"My husband shall always feel free to bring a friend home whenever he likes. I shall always be prepared; there shall be no flurry, no scolding, no discomfort, but a neat house, a cheerful wife, and a good dinner. John, dear, never stop to ask my leave, invite whom you please, and be sure of a welcome from me."

If John had not forgotten all about the jelly, it really would have been unpardonable in him to choose that day, of all the days in the year, to bring a friend home to dinner unexpectedly. Congratulating himself that a handsome repast had been ordered that morning, feeling sure that it would be ready to the minute, and indulging in pleasant anticipations of the charming effect it would produce, when his pretty wife came running out to meet him, he escorted his friend to his mansion, with the irrepressible satisfaction of a young host and husband.

It was a world of disappointments, as John discovered when he reached the Dove-cote. The front door usually stood hospitably open; now it was not only shut, but locked, and yesterday's mud still adorned the steps. The parlour windows were closed and curtained, no picture of the pretty wife sewing on the piazza, in white, with a distracting little bow in her hair, or a bright-eyed hostess, smiling a shy welcome as she greeted her guest.

"I'm afraid something has happened. Step into the garden, Scott, while I look up Mrs. Brooke," said John, alarmed at the silence and solitude.

Round the house he hurried, led by a pungent smell of burnt sugar, and Mr. Scott strolled after him, with a queer look on his face. He paused discreetly at a distance when Brooke disappeared; but he could both see and hear, and, being a bachelor, enjoyed the prospect mightily.

In the kitchen reigned confusion and despair; one edition of jelly was trickled from pot to pot, another lay upon the floor, and a third was burning gaily on the stove. Lotty, with Teutonic phlegm, was calmly eating bread and currant wine, for the jelly was still in a hopelessly liquid state, while Mrs. Brooke, with her apron over her head, sat sobbing dismally.

"My dearest girl, what is the matter?" cried John, rushing in, with awful visions of scalded hands, sudden news of affliction, and secret consternation at the thought of the guest in the garden.

"O John, I *am* so tired and hot and cross and worried! I've been at it till I'm all worn out. Do come and help me or I *shall* die!" and the exhausted housewife cast herself upon his breast, giving him a sweet welcome in every sense of the word, for the pinafore had been baptised at the same time as the floor.

"What worries you, dear? Has anything dreadful happened?" asked the anxious John, tenderly kissing the crown of the little cap, which was all askew.

"Yes," sobbed Meg despairingly.

"Tell me quick, then. Don't cry, I can bear anything better than that. Out with it, love."

"The—the jelly won't jell and I don't know what to do!"

John Brooke laughed then as he never dared to laugh afterward; and the derisive Scott smiled involuntarily as he heard the hearty peal, which put the finishing stroke to poor Meg's woe.

"Is that all? Fling it out of the window, and don't bother any more about it. I'll buy you quarts if you want it; but for heaven's sake don't have hysterics, for I've brought Jack Scott home to dinner, and——"

John got no further, for Meg cast him off, and

clasped her hands with a tragic gesture as she fell into a chair, exclaiming in a tone of mingled indignation, reproach, and dismay,—

"A man to dinner, and everything in a mess! John Brooke, how *could* you do such a thing?"

"Hush, he's in the garden! I forgot the confounded jelly, but it can't be helped now," said John, surveying the prospect with an anxious eye.

"You ought to have sent word, or told me this morning, and you ought to have remembered how busy I was," continued Meg petulantly; for even turtle-doves will peck when ruffled.

"I didn't know it this morning, and there was no time to send word, for I met him on the way out. I never thought of asking leave, when you have always told me to do as I liked. I never tried it before, and hang me if I ever do again!" added John, with an aggrieved air.

"I should hope not! Take him away at once; I can't see him, and there isn't any dinner."

"Well, I like that! Where's the beef and vegetables I sent home, and the pudding you promised?" cried John, rushing to the larder.

"I hadn't time to cook anything; I meant to dine at mother's I'm sorry, but I was *so* busy;" and Meg's tears began again.

John was a mild man, but he was human; and after a long day's work, to come home tired, hungry, and hopeful, to find a chaotic house, an empty table, and a cross wife was not exactly conducive to repose of mind or manner. He restrained himself, however, and the little squall would have blown over, but for one unlucky word.

"It's a scrape, I acknowledge; but if you will lend a hand, we'll pull through, and have a good time yet. Don't cry, dear, but just exert yourself a bit, and knock us up something to eat. We're both as hungry as hunters, so we shan't mind what it is. Give us the cold meat, and bread and cheese; we won't ask for jelly."

He meant it for a good-natured joke; but that one word sealed his fate. Meg thought it was *too* cruel to hint about her sad failure, and the last atom of patience vanished as he spoke.

"You must get yourself out of the scrape as you can; I'm too used up to 'exert' myself for any one. It's like a man to propose a bone and vulgar bread and cheese for company. I won't have anything of the sort in my house. Take that Scott up to mother's, and tell him I'm away, sick, dead—anything. I won't see him, and you two can laugh at me and my jelly as much as you like: you won't have anything else here;" and having delivered her defiance all in one breath, Meg cast away her pinafore, and precipitately left the field to bemoan herself in her own room.

Meg longed to go and tell mother; but a sense of shame at her own shortcomings, of loyalty to John, "who might be cruel, but nobody should know it," restrained her; and after a summary clearing up, she dressed herself prettily, and sat down to wait for John to come and be forgiven.

Unfortunately, John didn't come, not seeing the matter in that light. He had carried it off as a joke with Scott, excused his little wife as well as he could, and played the host so hospitably that his friend enjoyed the impromptu dinner, and promised to come again. But John was angry, though he did not show it; he felt that Meg had got him into a scrape, and then deserted him in his hour of need.

Meg likewise resolved to be "calm and kind, but firm," and show *him* his duty. She longed to run to meet him, and beg pardon, and be kissed and comforted, as she was sure of being; but, of course, she did nothing of the sort, and when she saw John coming, began to hum quite naturally, as she rocked and sewed, like a lady of leisure in her best parlour.

John was a little disappointed not to find a tender Niobe; but, feeling that his dignity demanded the first apology, he made none, only came leisurely in, and laid himself upon the sofa, with the singularly relevant remark,—

"We are going to have a new moon, my dear."

"I've no objection," was Meg's equally soothing remark.

A few other topics of general interest were introduced by Mr. Brooke, and wet-blanketed by Mrs. Brooke, and conversation languished. John went to one window, unfolded his paper, and wrapped himself in it, figuratively speaking. Meg went to the other window, and sewed as if new rosettes for her slippers were among the necessaries of life. Neither spoke; both looked quite "calm and firm," and both felt desperately uncomfortable.

"Oh dear," thought Meg, "married life is very trying, and does need infinite patience, as well as love, as mother says." The word "mother" suggested other maternal counsels, given long ago, and received with unbelieving protests.

"John is a good man, but he has his faults, and you must learn to see and bear with them, remembering your own. He is very decided, but never will be obstinate, if you reason kindly, not oppose impatiently. He is very accurate, and particular about the truth —a good trait, though you call him 'fussy.' Never deceive him by look or word, Meg, and he will give you the confidence you deserve, the support you need. He has a temper, not like ours—one flash, and then all over—but the white, still anger, that is seldom stirred, but once kindled, is hard to quench. Be careful, very careful, not to wake this anger against yourself, for peace and happiness depend on keeping his respect. Watch yourself, be the first to ask pardon if you both err, and guard against the little piques, misunderstandings, and hasty words that often pave the way for bitter sorrow and regret."

These words came back to Meg, as she sat sewing in the sunset, especially the last. This was the first serious disagreement; her own hasty speeches sounded both silly and unkind, as she recalled them, her own anger looked childish now, and thoughts of poor John coming home to such a scene quite melted her heart. She glanced at him with tears in her eyes, but he did not see them; she put down her work and got up, thinking, "I *will* be the first to say, 'Forgive me,' " but he did not seem to hear her; she went very slowly across the room, for pride was hard to swallow, and stood by him, but he did not turn his head. For a minute she felt as if she really couldn't do it; then came the thought, "This is the beginning, I'll do my part, and have nothing to reproach myself with," and stooping down, she softly kissed her husband on the forehead. Of course that settled it; the penitent kiss was better than a world of words, and John had her on his knee in a minute, saying tenderly,—

"It was too bad to laugh at the poor little jelly-pots. Forgive me, dear, I never will again!"

But he did, oh bless you, yes, hundreds of times, and so did Meg, both declaring that it was the sweetest jelly they ever made; for family peace was preserved in that little family jar.

In the autumn, new trials and exeriences came to Meg. Sallie Moffat renewed her friendship, was always running out for a dish of gossip at the little house, or inviting "that poor dear" to come in and spend the day at the big house. It was pleasant, for in dull weather Meg often felt lonely; all were busy at home, John absent till night, and nothing to do but sew, or read, or potter about. So it naturally fell out that Meg got into the way of gadding and gossiping with her friend. Seeing Sallie's pretty things made her long for such, and pity herself because she had not got them. Sallie was very kind, and often offered her the coveted trifles; but Meg declined them, knowing that John wouldn't like it; and then this foolish little woman went and did what John disliked infinitely worse.

She knew her husband's income, and she loved to feel that he trusted her, not only with his happiness, but what some men seem to value more—his money. She knew where it was, was free to take what she liked, and all he asked was that she should keep account of every penny, pay bills once a month, and remember that she was a poor man's wife. Till now, she had done well, been prudent and exact, kept her little account-books neatly, and showed them to him monthly without fear. But that autumn the serpent got into Meg's paradise, and tempted her, like many a modern Eve, not with apples, but with dress. Meg didn't like to be pitied and made to feel poor; it irritated her, but she was ashamed to confess it, and now and then she tried to console herself by buying something pretty, so that Sallie needn't think she had to economise.

But the trifles cost more than one would imagine; and when she cast up her accounts at the end of the month, the sum total rather scared her. John was busy that month, and left the bills to her; the next month he was absent; but the third he had a grand quarterly settling up, and Meg never forgot it. A few days before she had done a dreadful thing, and it weighed upon her conscience. Aunt March usually gave the sisters a present of twenty-five dollars apiece at New Year, that was only a month to wait, and here was a lovely violet silk going at a bargain, and she had the money, if she only dared to take it. John always said what was his was hers; but would he think it right to spend not only the prospective five-and-twenty, but another five-and-twenty out of the household fund? That was the question. Sallie had urged her to do it, had offered to loan the money, and with the best intentions in life, had tempted Meg beyond her strength.

When she got home, she tried to assuage the pangs of remorse by spreading forth the lovely silk; but it looked less silvery now, didn't become her, after all, and the words "fifty dollars" seemed stamped like a pattern down each breadth. She put it away; but it haunted her, not delightfully, as a new dress should, but dreadfully, like the ghost of a folly that was not easily laid. When John got out his books that night, Meg's heart sank, and for the first time in her married life, she was afraid of her husband. The kind, brown eyes looked as if they could be stern; and though he was unusually merry, she fancied he had found her out, but didn't mean to let her know it. The house-bills were all paid, the books all in order. John had praised her, and was undoing the old pocket-book which they called the "bank," when Meg, knowing that it was quite empty, stopped his hand, saying nervously,—

"You haven't seen my private expense book yet."

John never asked to see it; but she always insisted on his doing so, and used to enjoy his masculine amazement at the queer things women wanted, and made him guess what "piping" was, demand fiercely the meaning of a "hug-me-tight," or wonder how a little thing composed of three rosebuds, a bit of velvet, and a pair of strings, could possibly be a bonnet, and cost five or six dollars. That night he looked as if he would like the fun quizzing her figures and pretending to be horrified at her extravagance, as he often did, being particularly proud of his prudent wife.

The little book was brought slowly out, and laid down before him.

Meg got behind his chair under pretence of smoothing the wrinkles out of his tired forehead, and standing there, she said, with her panic increasing with every word,—

"John, dear, I'm ashamed to show you my book, for I've really been dreadfully extravagant lately. I go about so much I must have things, you know, and Sallie advised my getting it, so I did; and my New Year's money will partly pay for it: but I was sorry after I'd done it, for I knew you'd think it wrong in me."

John laughed, and drew her round beside him, saying good-humouredly, "Don't go and hide. I won't beat you if you *have* got a pair of killing boots; I'm rather proud of my wife's feet, and don't mind if she does pay eight or nine dollars for her boots, if they are good ones."

That had been one of her last "trifles," and John's eye had fallen on it as he spoke. "Oh, what *will* he say when he comes to that awful fifty dollars!" thought Meg, with a shiver.

"It's worse than boots, it's a silk dress," she said, with the calmness of desperation, for she wanted the worst over.

"Well, dear, what is the 'dem'd total,' as Mr. Mantalini says?"

That didn't sound like John, and she knew he was

looking up at her with the straightforward look that she had always been ready to meet and answer with one as frank till now. She turned the page and her head at the same time, pointing to the sum which would have been bad enough without the fifty, but which was appalling to her with that added. For a minute the room was very still; then John said slowly —but she could feel it cost him an effort to express no displeasure,—

"Well, I don't know that fifty is much for a dress, with all the furbelows and notions you have to have to finish it off these days."

"It isn't made or trimmed," sighed Meg faintly, for a sudden recollection of the cost still to be incurred quite overwhelmed her.

"Twenty-five yards of silk seems a good deal to cover one small woman, but I've no doubt my wife will look as fine as Ned Moffat's when she gets it on," said John dryly.

"I know you are angry, John, but I can't help it. I don't mean to waste your money, and I didn't think those little things would count up so. I can't resist them when I see Sallie buying all she wants, and pitying me because I don't. I try to be contented, but it is hard, and I'm tired of being poor."

The last words were spoken so low she thought he did not hear them, but he did, and they wounded him deeply, for he had denied himself many pleasures for Meg's sake. She could have bitten her tongue out the minute she had said it, for John pushed the books away, and got up, saying, with a little quiver in his voice, "I was afraid of this; I do my best, Meg." If he had scolded her, or even shaken her, it would not have broken her heart like those few words. She ran to him and held him close, crying, with repentant tears, "O John, my dear, kind, hardworking boy, I didn't mean it! It was so wicked, so untrue and ungrateful, how could I say it! Oh, how could I say it!"

He was very kind, forgave her readily, and did not utter one reproach; but Meg knew that she had done and said a thing which would not be forgotten soon, although he might never allude to it again. She had promised to love him for better for worse; and then she, his wife had reproached him with his poverty, after spending his earnings recklessly. It was dreadful; and the worst of it was John went on so quietly afterward, just as if nothing had happened, except that he stayed in town later and worked at night when she had gone to cry herself to sleep. A week of remorse nearly made Meg sick; and the discovery that John had countermanded the order for his new great-coat reduced her to a state of despair which was pathetic to behold. He had simply said, in answer to her surprised inquiries as to the change. "I can't afford it, my dear."

Meg said no more, but a few minutes after he found her in the hall, with her face buried in the old great-coat, crying as if her heart would break.

They had a long talk that night, and Meg learned to love her husband better for his poverty, because it seemed to have made a man of him, given him the strength and courage to fight his own way, and taught him a tender patience with which to bear and comfort the natural longings and failures of those he loved.

Next day she put her pride in her pocket, went to Sallie, told the truth, and asked her to buy the silk as a favour. The good-natured Mrs. Moffat willingly did so, and had the delicacy not to make her a present of it immediately afterward. Then Meg ordered home the great-coat, and, when John arrived, she put it on, and asked him how he liked her new silk gown. One can imagine what answer he made, how he received his present, and what a blissful state of things ensued. John came home early, Meg gadded no more; and that great-coat was put on in the morning by a very happy husband, and taken off at night by a most devoted little wife. So the year rolled round, and at Mid-summer there came to Meg a new experience—the deepest and tenderest of a woman's life.

Laurie came sneaking into the kitchen of the Dovecote, one Saturday, with an excited face, and was received with the clash of cymbals, for Hannah clapped her hands with a saucepan in one and the cover in the other.

"How's the little mamma? Where is everybody? Why didn't you tell me before I came home?" began Laurie, in a loud whisper.

"Happy as a queen, the dear! Every soul of 'em is upstairs a worshippin'; we didn't want no hurrycanes round. Now you go into the parlour, and I'll send 'em down to you," with which somewhat involved reply Hannah vanished, chuckling ecstatically.

Presently Jo appeared, proudly bearing a flannel bundle laid forth upon a large pillow. Jo's face was very sober, but her eyes twinkled, and there was an odd sound in her voice of repressed emotion of some sort.

"Shut your eyes and hold out your arms," she said invitingly.

Laurie backed precipitately into a corner, and put his hands behind him with an imploring gesture: "No, thank you, I'd rather not. I shall drop it or smash it, as sure as fate."

"Then you shan't see your nevvy," said Jo decidedly, turning as if to go.

"I will, I will! only you must be responsible for damages;" and, obeying orders, Laurie heroically shut his eyes while something was put into his arms. A peal of laughter from Jo, Amy, Mrs. March, Hannah, and John caused him to open them the next minute, to find himself invested with two babies instead of one.

"Twins, by Jupiter!" was all he said for a minute; then, turning to the women with an appealing look that was comically piteous, he added, "Take 'em quick, somebody! I'm going to laugh, and I shall drop 'em."

"It's the best joke of the season, isn't it? I wouldn't have you told, for I set my heart on surprising you, and I flatter myself I've done it," said Jo, when she got her breath.

"I never was more staggered in my life. Isn't it fun? Are they boys? What are you going to name them? Let's have another look. Hold me up Jo; for upon my life it's one too many for me," returned Laurie, regarding the infants with the air of a big, benevolent Newfoundland looking at a pair of infantile kittens.

"Boy and girl. Aren't they beauties?" said the proud papa, beaming upon the little, red squirmers as if they were unfledged angels.

"Most remarkable children I ever saw. Which is which?" and Laurie bent like a well-sweep to examine the prodigies.

"Amy put a blue ribbon on the boy and a pink on the girl, French fashion, so you can always tell. Besides, one has blue eyes and one brown. Kiss them, Uncle Teddy," said wicked Jo.

Laurie screwed up his face, and obeyed with a gingerly peck at each little cheek that produced another laugh, and made the babies squeal.

"There, I knew they didn't like it! That's the boy; see him kick; he hits out with his fists like a good one. Now then, young Brooke, pitch into a man of your own size, will you?" cried Laurie, delighted with a poke in the face from a tiny fist, flapping aimlessly about.

"He's to be named John Laurence, and the girl Margaret, after mother and grandmother. We shall call her Daisy, so as not to have two Megs, and I suppose the mannie will be Jack unless we find a better name," said Amy, with aunt-like interest.

"Name him Demijohn, and call him 'Demi' for short," said Laurie.

"Daisy and Demi—just the thing! I *knew* Teddy would do it," cried Jo, clapping her hands.

Teddy certainly had done it that time, for the babies were "Daisy" and "Demi" to the end of the chapter.

CHAPTER SIX

CALLS

"COME, Jo it's time."

"For what?"

"You don't mean to say you have forgotten that you promised to make half-a-dozen calls with me today?"

"I've done a good many rash and foolish things in my life, but I don't think I ever was mad enough to say I'd make six calls in one day, when a single one upsets me for a week."

"Yes, you did; it was a bargain between us. I was to finish the crayon of Beth for you and you were to go properly with me, and return our neighbours' visits."

At that minute Jo was particularly absorbed in

dressmaking; for she was mantua-maker general to the family, and took especial credit to herself because she could use a needle as well as a pen. It was very provoking to be arrested in the act of a first trying-on, and ordered out to make calls in her best array, on a warm July day. She hated calls of the formal sort, and never made any till Amy compelled her with a bargain bribe, or promise. In the present instance, there was no escape; and having clashed her scissors rebelliously, while protesting that she smelt thunder, she gave in, put away her work and taking up her hat and gloves with an air of resignation, told Amy the victim was ready.

"Jo March, you are perverse enough to provoke a saint! You don't intend to make calls in that state, I hope," cried Amy, surveying her with amazement.

"Why not? I'm neat and cool and comfortable; quite proper for a dusty walk on a warm day. If people care more for my clothes than they do for me, I don't wish to see them. You can dress for both, and be as elegant as you please; it pays for you to be fine; it doesn't for me, and furbelows only worry me."

"Oh dear!" sighed Amy; "now she's in a contrary fit, and will drive me distracted before I can get her properly ready. I'm sure it's no pleasure to me to go to-day, but its a debt we owe society, and there's no one to pay it but you and me. I'll do anything for you, Jo if you'll only dress yourself nicely, and come and help me do the civil. You can talk so well, look so aristocratic in your best things, and behave so beautifully, if you try, that I'm proud of you. I'm afraid to go alone; do come and take care of me."

"You're an artful little puss to flatter and wheedle your cross old sister in that way. The idea of my being aristocratic and well-bred, and your being afraid to go anywhere alone! I don't know which is the most absurd. Well, I'll go if I must, and do my best. You shall be commander of the expedition, and I'll obey blindly; will that satisfy you?" said Jo, with a sudden change from perversity to lamb-like submission.

"You're a perfect cherub! Now put on all your best things, and I'll tell you how to behave at each place, so that you will make a good impression. I want people to like you, and they would if you'd only try to be a little more agreeable. Do your hair the pretty way, and put the pink rose in your bonnet; it's becoming, and you look too sober in your plain suit. Take your light gloves and the embroidered handkerchief. We'll stop at Meg's, and borrow her white sunshade, and then you can have my dove-coloured one."

While Amy dressed, she issued her orders, and Jo obeyed them; not without entering her protest, however, for she sighed as she rustled into her new organdie, frowned darkly at herself as she tied her bonnet-strings in an irreproachable bow, wrestled viciously with pins as she put on her collar, wrinkled up her features generally as she shook out the handkerchief, whose embroidery was as irritating to her nose as the present mission was to her feelings; and when she had squeezed her hands into tight gloves with three buttons and a tassel, as the last touch of elegance, she turned to Amy with an imbecile expression of countenance, saying meekly,—

"I'm perfectly miserable; but if you consider me presentable, I die happy. You are a thing of beauty and a joy for ever," said Jo, looking through her hand with the air of a connoisseur at the blue feather against the gold hair. "Am I to drag my best dress through the dust, or loop it up, please, ma'am?"

"Hold it up when you walk, but drop it in the

house; the sweeping style suits you best, and you must learn to trail your skirts gracefully. You haven't half buttoned one cuff; do it at once. You'll never look finished if you are not careful about the little details, for they make up the pleasing whole."

Jo sighed, and proceeded to burst the buttons off her glove, in doing up her cuff; but at last both were ready, and sailed away, looking as "pretty as picters," Hannah said, as she hung out of the upper window to watch them.

"Now, Jo dear, the Chesters consider themselves very elegant people, so I want you to put on your best deportment. Don't make any of your abrupt remarks, or do anything odd, will you? Just be calm, cool, and quiet—that's safe and ladylike; and you can easily do it for fifteen minutes," said Amy, as they approached the first place, having borrowed the white parasol and been inspected by Meg, with a baby on each arm.

"Let me see. 'Calm, cool, and quiet'—yes, I think I can promise that. I've played the part of a prim young lady on the stage, and I'll try it off. My powers are great, as you shall see; so be easy in your mind, my child."

Amy looked relieved, but naughty Jo took her at her word; for, during the first call, she sat with every limb gracefully composed, every fold correctly draped, calm as a summer sea, cool as a snowbank, and as silent as a sphinx. In vain Mrs. Chester alluded to her "charming novel," and the Misses Chester introduced parties, picnics, the opera, and the fashions; each and all were answered by a smile, a bow, and a demure "Yes" or "No," with the chill on. In vain Amy telegraphed the word "Talk," tried to draw her out, and administered covert pokes with her foot. Jo sat as if blandly unconscious of it all, with deportment like Maud's face, "icily regular, splendidly null."

"What a haughty, uninteresting creature that oldest Miss March is!" was the unfortunately audible remark of one of the ladies, as the door closed upon their guests. Jo laughed noiselessly all through the hall, but Amy looked disgusted at the failure of her instructions, and very naturally laid the blame upon Jo.

"How could you mistake me so? I merely meant you to be properly dignified and composed, and you made yourself a perfect stock and stone. Try to be sociable at the Lambs, gossip as other girls do, and be interested in dress and flirtations and whatever nonsense comes up. They move in the best society, are valuable persons for us to know, and I wouldn't fail to make a good impression there for anything."

"I'll be agreeable; I'll gossip and giggle, and have horrors and raptures over any trifle you like. I rather enjoy this, and now I'll imitate what is called 'a charming girl;' I can do it, for I have May Chester as a model, and I'll improve upon her. See if the Lambs don't say, 'What a lively, nice creature that Jo March is!'"

Amy felt anxious, as well she might, for when Jo turned freakish there was no knowing where she would stop. Amy's face was a study when she saw her sister skim into the next drawing-room kiss all the young ladies with effusion, beam graciously upon the young gentlemen, and join in the chat with a spirit which amazed the beholder. Amy was taken possession of by Mrs. Lamb, with whom she was a favourite, and forced to hear a long account of Lucretia's last attack, while three delightful young gentlemen hovered near, waiting for a pause when they might rush in and rescue her. So situated, she was powerless to check Jo, who seemed possessed by a spirit of mischief, and talked away as volubly as the old lady. A knot of heads gathered about her, and Amy strained her ears to hear what was going on; for broken sentences filled her with alarm, round eyes and uplifted hands tormented her with curiosity, and frequent peals of laughter made her wild to share the fun. One may imagine her suffering on overhearing fragments of the sort of conversation:—

"She rides splendidly—who taught her?"

"No one; she used to practise mounting, holding the reins, and sitting straight on an old saddle in a tree. Now she rides anything, for she doesn't know what fear is, and the stable-man lets her have horses cheap, because she trains them to carry ladies so well. She has such a passion for it, I often tell her if everything else fails she can be a horse-breaker, and get her living so."

At this awful speech Amy contained herself with difficulty, for the impression was being given that she was rather a fast young lady, which was her especial aversion. But what could she do? for the old lady was in the middle of her story, and long before it was done Jo was off again, making more droll revelations, and committing still more fearful blunders.

She was still redder and more uncomfortable a moment after, when a sudden turn in the conversation introduced the subject of dress. One of the young ladies asked Jo where she got the pretty drab hat she wore to the picnic; and stupid Jo, instead of mentioning the place where it was bought two years ago, must needs answer, with unnecessary frankness, "Oh, Amy painted it; you can't buy those soft shades, so we paint ours any colour we like. It's a great comfort to have an artistic sister."

"Isn't that an original idea?" cried Miss Lamb, who found Jo great fun.

"That's nothing compared to some of her brilliant performances. There's nothing the child can't do.

Why, she wanted a pair of blue boots for Sallie's party, so she just painted her solid white ones the loveliest shade of sky-blue you ever saw, and they looked exactly like satin," added Jo, with an air of pride in her sister's accomplishments that exasperated Amy till she felt that it would be a relief to throw her card-case at her.

"We read a story of yours the other day, and enjoyed it very much," observed the elder Miss Lamb, wishing to compliment the literary lady, who did not look the character just then, it must be confessed.

Any mention of her "works" always had a bad effect upon Jo, who either grew rigid and looked offended, or changed the subject with a brusque remark, as now. "Sorry you could find nothing better to read. I write that rubbish because it sells, and ordinary people like it. Are you going to New York this winter?"

As Miss Lamb had "enjoyed" the story, this speech was not exactly grateful or complimentary. The minute it was made Jo saw her mistake; but, fearing to make the matter worse, suddenly remembered that it was for her to make the first move toward departure, and did so with an abruptness that left three people with half-finished sentences in their mouths.

"Amy, we *must* go. *Good*-bye, dear; *do* come and see us; we are *pining* for a visit. I don't dare to ask *you*, Mr. Lamb; but if you *should* come, I don't think I shall have the heart to send you away."

Jo said this with such a droll imitation of May Chester's gushing style that Amy got out of the room as rapidly as possible, feeling a strong desire to laugh and cry at the same time.

"Didn't I do that well?" asked Jo, with a satisfied air, as they walked away.

"Nothing could have been worse," was Amy's crushing reply. "What possessed you to tell those stories about my saddle, and the hats and boots, and all the rest of it?"

"Why, it's funny, and amuses people. They know we are poor, so it's no use pretending that we have grooms, buy three or four hats a season, and have things as easy and fine as they do."

"You needn't go and tell them all our little shifts, and expose our poverty in that perfectly unnecessary way. You haven't a bit of proper pride, and never will learn when to hold your tongue and when to speak," said Amy despairingly.

"How shall I behave here?" she asked, as they approached the third mansion.

"Just as you please; I wash my hands of you," was Amy's short answer.

"Then I'll enjoy myself. The boys are at home, and we'll have a comfortable time. Goodness knows I need a little change, for elegance has a bad effect upon my constitution," returned Jo gruffly, being disturbed by her failures to suit.

An enthusiastic welcome from three big boys and several pretty children speedily soothed her ruffled feelings; and, leaving Amy to entertain the hostess and Mr. Tudor who happened to be calling likewise, Jo devoted herself to the young folks, and found the change refreshing. She listened to college stories with deep interest, caressed pointers and poodles without a murmur, agreed heartily that "Tom Brown was a brick," regardless of the improper form of praise; and when one lad proposed a visit to his turtle-tank, she went with an alacrity which caused mamma to smile upon her, as that motherly lady settled the cap which was left in a ruinous condition by filial hugs, bear-like but affectionate, and dearer to her than the most faultless *coiffure* from the hands of an inspired Frenchwoman.

It might have been worse, but Amy considered it bad; for Jo sat on the grass, with an encampment of boys about her, and a dirty-footed dog reposing on the skirt of her state and festival dress, as she related one of Laurie's pranks to her admiring audience. One small child was poking turtles with Amy's cherished parasol, a second was eating gingerbread over Joe's best bonnet, and a third playing ball with her gloves. But all were enjoying themselves; and when Jo collected her damaged property to go, her escort accompanied her, begging her to come again, "it was such fun to hear about Laurie's larks."

"Capital boys, aren't they? I feel quite young and brisk again after that," said Jo, strolling along with her hands behind her, partly from habit, partly to conceal the bespattered parasol.

"Why do you always avoid Mr. Tudor?" asked Amy, wisely refraining from any comment upon Jo's dilapidated appearance.

"Don't like him; he puts on airs, snubs his sisters, worries his father, and doesn't speak respectfully of his mother. Laurie says he is fast, and *I* don't consider him a desirable acquaintance; so I let him alone."

"It's no use trying to argue with you," began Amy.

"Not the least, my dear," interrupted Jo; "so let us look amiable, and drop a card here, as the Kings are evidently out, for which I'm deeply grateful."

The family card-case having done its duty, the girls walked on, and Jo uttered another thanksgiving on reaching the fifth house, and being told that the young ladies were engaged.

"Now let us go home, and never mind Aunt March today. We can run down there any time, and it's really a pity to trail through the dust in our best bibs and tuckers, when we are tired and cross."

"Speak for yourself, if you please. Aunt likes to

have us pay her the compliment of coming in style, and making a formal call; it's a little thing to do, but it gives her pleasure, and I don't believe it will hurt your things half so much as letting dirty dogs and clumping boys spoil them. Stoop down, and let me take the crumbs off your bonnet."

"What a good girl you are, Amy!" said Jo, with a repentant glance from her own damaged costume to that of her sister, which was fresh and spotless still. "I wish it was as easy for me to do little things to please people as it is for you. I think of them, but it takes too much time to do them; so I wait for a chance to confer a great favour, and let the small ones slip; but they tell best in the end, I fancy."

They found Aunt Carrol with the old lady, both absorbed in some very interesting subject; but they dropped it as the girls came in, with a conscious look which betrayed that they had been talking about their nieces. Jo was not in a good humour, and the perverse fit returned; but Amy, who had virtuously done her duty, kept her temper, and pleased everybody, was in a most angelic frame of mind. This amiable spirit was felt at once, and both the aunts "my deared" her affectionately, looking what they afterwards said emphatically—"That child improves every day."

"Are you going to help about the fair, dear?" asked Mrs. Carrol, as Amy sat down beside her with the confiding air elderly people like so well in the young.

"Yes, Aunt. Mrs. Chester asked me if I would, and I offered to tend a table, as I have nothing but my time to give."

"I'm not," put in Jo decidedly. "I hate to be patronised, and the Chesters think it's a great favour to allow us to help with their highly connected fair. I wonder you consented, Amy; they only want you to work."

"I am willing to work; it's for the freedom as well as the Chesters, and I think it very kind of them to let me share the labour and the fun. Patronage does not trouble me when it is well meant."

"Quite right and proper. I like your grateful spirit, my dear; it's a pleasure to help people who appreciate our efforts: some do not, and that is trying," observed Aunt March, looking over her spectacles at Jo, who sat apart, rocking herself, with a somewhat morose expression.

If Jo had only known what a great happiness was wavering in the balance for one of them, she would have turned dove-like in a minute; but, unfortunately, we don't have windows in our breasts, and cannot see what goes on in the minds of our friends; better for us that we cannot as a general thing, but now and then it would be such a comfort, such a saving of time and temper. By her next speech, Jo deprived herself of several years of pleasure, and received a timely lesson in the art of holding her tongue.

"I don't like favours; they oppress and make me feel like a slave. I'd rather do everything for myself, and be perfectly independent."

"Ahem!" coughed Aunt Carrol softly, with a look at Aunt March.

"I told you so," said Aunt March, with a decided nod to Aunt Carrol.

Mercifully unconscious of what she had done, Jo sat with her nose in the air, and a revolutionary aspect which was anything but inviting.

"Do you speak French, dear?" asked Mrs. Carrol, laying her hand on Amy's.

"Pretty well, thanks to Aunt March, who lets Esther talk to me as often as I like," replied Amy, with a grateful look, which caused the old lady to smile affably.

"How are you about languages?" asked Mrs. Carrol of Jo.

"Don't know a word; I'm very stupid about studying anything; can't bear French, it's such a slippery, silly sort of language," was the brusque reply.

Another look passed between the ladies, and Aunt March said to Amy, "You are quite strong and well, now, dear, I believe? Eyes don't trouble you any more, do they?"

"Not at all, thank you, ma'am. I'm very well, and mean to do great things next winter, so that I may be ready for Rome, whenever that joyful time arrives."

"Good girl! You deserve to go, and I'm sure you will some day," said Aunt March, with an approving pat on the head, as Amy picked up her ball for her.

"Cross-patch, draw the latch,
Sit by the fire and spin,"

squalled Polly, bending down from his perch on the back of her chair to peep into Jo's face, with such a comical air of impertinent inquiry that it was impossible to help laughing.

"Most observing bird," said the old lady.

"Come and take a walk, my dear?" cried Polly, hopping toward the china-closet, with a look suggestive of lump-sugar.

"Thank you, I will. Come, Amy:" and Jo brought the visit to an end, feeling more strongly than ever that calls did have a bad effect upon her constitution. She shook hands in a gentlemanly manner, but Amy kissed both the aunts, and the girls departed, leaving behind them the impression of shadow and sunshine; which impression caused Aunt March to say, as they vanished—

"You'd better do it, Mary; I'll supply the money,"

and Aunt Carrol to reply decidedly, "I certainly will, if her father and mother consent."

CHAPTER SEVEN

CONSEQUENCES

MRS. CHESTER'S fair was so very elegant and select that it was considered a great honour by the young ladies of the neighbourhood to be invited to take a table, and every one was much interested in the matter. Amy was asked, but Jo was not, which was fortunate for all parties, as her elbows were decidedly akimbo at this period of her life, and it took a good many hard knocks to teach her how to get on easily. The "haughty, uninteresting creature" was let severely alone; but Amy's talent and taste were duly complimented by the offer of the art-table, and she exerted herself to prepare and secure appropriate and valuable contributions to it.

Everything went on smoothly till the day before the fair opened; then there occurred one of the little skirmishes which it is almost impossible to avoid, when some five-and-twenty women, old and young, with all their private piques and prejudices, try to work together.

May Chester was rather jealous of Amy because the latter was a greater favourite than herself; and, just at this time, several trifling circumstances occurred to increase the feeling. Amy's dainty pen-and-ink work entirely eclipsed May's painted vases—that was one thorn; then the all-conquering Tudor had danced four times with Amy, at a late party, and only once with

May—that was thorn number two: but the chief grievance that rankled in her soul, and gave her an excuse for her unfriendly conduct, was a rumour which some obliging gossip had whispered to her, that the March girls had made fun of her at the Lambs'. All the blame of this should have fallen upon Jo, for her naughty imitation had been too lifelike to escape detection, and the frolicsome Lambs had permitted the joke to escape. No hint of this had reached the culprits, however, and Amy's dismay can be imagined, when, the very evening before the fair, as she was putting the last touches to her pretty table, Mrs. Chester, who, of course, resented the supposed ridicule of her daughter, said, in a bland tone, but with a cold look—

"I find, dear, that there is some feeling among the young ladies about my giving this table to any one but my girls. As this is the most prominent, and some say the most attractive table of all, and they are the chief getters-up of the fair, it is thought best for them to take this place. I'm sorry, but I know you are too sincerely interested in the cause to mind a little personal disappointment, and you shall have another table if you like."

Mrs. Chester had fancied beforehand that it would be easy to deliver this little speech; but when the time came, she found it rather difficult to utter it naturally, with Amy's unsuspicious eyes looking straight at her, full of surprise and trouble.

Amy felt that there was something behind this, but could not guess what, and said quietly, feeling hurt, and showing that she did—

"Perhaps you had rather I took no table at all?"

"Now, my dear, don't have any ill-feeling, I beg; it's merely a matter of expedience, you see; my girls will naturally take the lead, and this table is considered their proper place. *I* think it very appropriate to you, and feel very grateful for your efforts to make it so pretty; but we must give up our private wishes, of course, and I will see that you have a good place elsewhere. Wouldn't you like the flower-table? The little girls undertook it, but they are discouraged. You could make a charming thing of it, and the flower-table is always attractive, you know."

"Especially to gentlemen," added May, with a look which enlightened Amy as to one cause of her sudden fall from favour. She coloured angrily, but took no other notice of that girlish sarcasm, and answered, with unexpected amiability—

"It shall be as you please, Mrs. Chester. I'll give up my place here at once, and attend to the flowers, if you like."

"You can put your own things on your own table, if you prefer," began May, feeling a little conscience-stricken, as she looked at the pretty racks, the painted shells, and quaint illuminations Amy had so carefully made and so gracefully arranged. She meant it kindly, but Amy mistook her meaning, and said quickly—

"Oh, certainly, if they are in your way;" and sweeping her contributions into her apron, pell-mell, she walked off, feeling that herself and her works of art had been insulted past forgiveness.

There was great indignation at home when she told her story that evening. Her mother said it was a shame, but told her she had done right; Beth declared she wouldn't go to the fair at all; and Jo demanded why she didn't take all her pretty things and leave those mean people to get on without her.

"Because they are mean is no reason why I should be. I hate such things, and though I think I've a right to be hurt, I don't intend to show it. They will feel that more than angry speeches or huffy actions, won't they, Marmee?"

"That's the right spirit, my dear; a kiss for a blow is always best, though it's not very easy to give it sometimes," said her mother, with the air of one who had learned the difference between preaching and practising.

In spite of various very natural temptations to resent and retaliate, Amy adhered to her resolution all the next day, bent on conquering her enemy by kindness. She began well, thanks to a silent reminder that came to her unexpectedly, but most opportunely. As she arranged her table that morning, while the little girls were in an ante-room filling the baskets, she took up her pet production—a little book, the antique cover of which her father had found among his treasures, and in which, on leaves of vellum, she had beautifully illuminated different texts. As she turned the pages, rich in dainty devices, with very pardonable pride, her eye fell upon one verse that made her stop and think. Framed in a brilliant scroll-work of scarlet, blue, and gold, with little spirits of good-will helping one another up and down among the thorns and flowers, were the words, "Thou shalt love thy neighbour as thyself."

"I ought, but I don't," thought Amy, as her eye went from the bright page to May's discontented face behind the big vases, that could not hide the vacancies her pretty work had once filled. Amy stood a minute, turning the leaves in her hand, reading on each some sweet rebuke for all heart-burnings and uncharitableness of spirit. Amy's conscience preached her a little sermon from that text, then and there; and she did what many of us do not always do—took the sermon to heart, and straightway put it in practice.

A group of girls were standing about May's table, admiring the pretty things, and talking over the change of saleswomen. They dropped their voices, but Amy knew they were speaking of her, hearing one side of the story, and judging accordingly. It was not pleasant, but a better spirit had come over her, and presently a chance offered for proving it. She heard May say sorrowfully—

"It's too bad, for there is no time to make other things, and I don't want to fill up with odds and ends. The table was just complete then: now it's spoilt."

"I dare say she'd put them back if you asked her," suggested some one.

"How could I after all the fuss?" began May, but she did not finish, for Amy's voice came across the hall, saying pleasantly—

"You may have them, and welcome, without asking, if you want them. I was just thinking I'd offer to put them back, for they belong to your table rather than mine. Here they are; please take them, and forgive me if I was hasty in carrying them away last night."

As she spoke, Amy returned her contribution, with a nod and a smile, and hurried away again, feeling that it was easier to do a friendly thing than it was to stay and be thanked for it.

"Now, I call that lovely of her, don't you?" cried one girl.

May's answer was inaudible; but another young lady, whose temper was evidently a little soured by making lemonade, added, with a disagreeable laugh, "Very lovely; for she knew she wouldn't sell them at her own table."

Now, that was hard; when we make little sacrifices we like to have them appreciated, at least; and for a minute Amy was sorry she had done it, feeling that virtue was not always its own reward. But it is—as she presently discovered; for her spirits began to rise, and her table to blossom under her skilful hands; the girls were very kind, and that one little act seemed to have cleared the atmosphere amazingly.

It was a very long day, and a hard one to Amy, as she sat behind her table, often quite alone, for the little girls deserted very soon: few cared to buy flowers in summer, and her bouquets began to droop long before night.

The art-table *was* the most attractive in the room; there was a crowd about it all day long, and the tenders were constantly flying to and fro with important faces and rattling money-boxes. Amy often looked wistfully across, longing to be there, where she felt at home and happy, instead of in a corner with nothing to do. It might seem no hardship to some of us; but to a pretty, blithe young girl, it was not only tedious, but very trying; and the thought of being found there in the evening by her family, and Laurie and his friends, made it a real martyrdom.

She did not go home till night, and then she looked so pale and quiet that they knew the day had been a hard one, though she made no complaint, and did not even tell what she had done. Her mother gave her an extra cordial cup of tea, Beth helped her dress, and made a charming little wreath for her hair, while Jo astonished her family by getting herself up with unusual care, and hinting darkly that the tables were about to be turned.

"Don't do anything rude, pray, Jo. I won't have any fuss made, so let it all pass, and behave yourself," begged Amy, as she departed early, hoping to find a reinforcement of flowers to refresh her poor little table.

"I merely intend to make myself entrancingly agreeable to every one I know, and to keep them in your corner as long as possible. Teddy and his boys will lend a hand, and we'll have a good time yet," returned Jo, leaning over the gate to watch for Laurie.

Presently the familiar tramp was heard in the dusk, and she ran out to meet him.

"Is that my boy?"

"As sure as this is my girl!" and Laurie tucked her hand under his arm, with the air of a man whose every wish was gratified.

"O Teddy, such doings!" and Jo told Amy's wrongs with sisterly zeal.

"A flock of our fellows are going to drive over by-and-by, and I'll be hanged if I don't make them buy every flower she's got, and camp down before her table afterward," said Laurie, espousing her cause with warmth.

"The flowers are not at all nice, Amy says, and the fresh ones may not arrive in time. I don't wish to be unjust or suspicious, but I shouldn't wonder if they never came at all. When people do one mean thing they are very likely to do another," observed Jo, in a disgusted tone.

"Didn't Hayes give you the best out of our gardens? I told him to."

"I didn't know that; he forgot, I suppose; and, as your grandpa was poorly, I didn't like to worry him by asking, though I did want some."

"Now, Jo, how could you think there was any need of asking! They are just as much yours as mine. Don't we always go halves in everything?" began Laurie, in the tone that always made Jo turn thorny.

"Gracious, I hope not! Half of some of your things wouldn't suit me at all. But we mustn't stand philandering here; I've got to help Amy, so you go and make yourself splendid; and if you'll be so very kind as to let Hayes take a few nice flowers up to the Hall, I'll bless you for ever."

"Couldn't you do it now?" asked Laurie, so suggestively that Jo shut the gate in his face with inhospitable haste, and called through the bars, "Go away, Teddy; I'm busy."

Thanks to the conspirators, the tables *were* turned that night; for Hayes sent up a wilderness of flowers, with a lovely basket, arranged in his best manner, for a centre-piece; then the March family turned out *en masse,* and Jo exerted herself to some purpose, for people not only came, but stayed, laughing at her nonsense, admiring Amy's taste, and apparently enjoying themselves very much. Laurie and his friends gallantly threw themselves into the breach, bought up the bouquets, encamped before the table, and made that corner the liveliest spot in the room. Amy was in her element now, and, out of gratitude, if nothing more, was as sprightly and gracious as possible—coming to the conclusion, about that time, that virtue *was* its own reward, after all.

Jo behaved herself with exemplary propriety; and when Amy was happily surrounded by her guard of honour, Jo circulated about the hall, picking up various bits of gossip, which enlightened her upon the subject of the Chester change of base. She reproached herself for her share of the ill-feeling, and resolved to exonerate Amy as soon as possible; she also discovered what Amy had done about the things in the morning, and considered her a model of magnanimity. As she passed the art-table, she glanced over it for her sister's things, but saw no signs of them. "Tucked away out of sight, I dare say," thought Jo, who could forgive her own wrongs, but hotly resented any insult offered to her family.

"Good evening, Miss Jo. How does Amy get on?" asked May, with a conciliatory air, for she wanted to show that she also could be generous.

"She has sold everything she had that was worth selling, and now she is enjoying herself. The flower-table is always attractive, you know, 'especially to gentlemen'."

Jo *couldn't* resist giving that little slap, but May took it so meekly she regretted it a minute after, and fell to praising the great vases, which still remained unsold.

"Is Amy's illumination anywhere about? I took a fancy to buy that for Father," said Jo, very anxious to learn the fate of her sister's work.

"Everything of Amy's sold long ago; I took care that the right people saw them, and they made a nice little sum of money for us," returned May, who had overcome sundry small temptations, as well as Amy, that day.

Much gratified, Jo rushed back to tell the good news; and Amy looked both touched and surprised by the report of May's words and manner.

"Now, gentlemen, I want you to go and do your duty by the other tables as generously as you have by mine—especially the art-table," she said, ordering out "Teddy's Own," as the girls called the college friends.

To May's great delight, Mr. Laurence not only bought the vases, but pervaded the hall with one under each arm. The other gentlemen speculated with equal rashness in all sort of frail trifles, and wandered helplessly about afterward, burdened with wax flowers, painted fans, filigree portfolios, and other useful and appropriate purchases.

Aunt Carrol was there, heard the story, looked pleased, and said something to Mrs. March in a corner, which made the latter lady beam with satisfaction, and watch Amy with a face full of mingled pride and anxiety, though she did not betray the cause of her pleasure till several days later.

The fair was pronounced a success; and when May bade Amy goodnight, she did not "gush" as usual, but gave her an affectionate kiss, and a look which said, "Forgive and forget." That satisfied Amy; and when she got home she found the vases paraded on the parlour chimney-piece, with a great bouquet in each. "The reward of merit for a magnanimous March," as Laurie announced with a flourish.

"You've a deal more principle and generosity and nobleness of character than I ever gave you credit for, Amy. You've behaved sweetly, and I respect you with all my heart," said Jo warmly, as they brushed their hair together late that night.

"Yes, we all do, and love her for being so ready to forgive. It must have been dreadfully hard, after working so long, and setting your heart on selling your own pretty things. I don't believe I could have done it as kindly as you did," added Beth from her pillow.

"Why, girls, you needn't praise me so; I only did as I'd be done by. You laugh at me when I say I want to be a lady, and I try to do it as far as I know how. I can't explain exactly, but I want to be above the little meannesses and follies and faults that spoil so many women. I'm far from it now, but I do my best, and hope in time to be what Mother is."

Amy spoke earnestly, and Jo said, with a cordial hug—

"I understand now what you mean, and I'll never laugh at you again. You are getting on faster than you think, and I'll take lessons of you in true politeness, for you've learned the secret, I believe. Try away, dearie; you'll get your reward some day, and no one will be more delighted than I shall."

A week later Amy did get her reward, and poor Jo found it hard to be delighted. A letter came from Aunt Carrol, and Mrs. March's face was illuminated to such a degree, when she read it, that Jo and Beth, who were with her, demanded what the glad tidings were.

"Aunt Carrol is going abroad next month, and wants——"

"Me to go with her!" burst in Jo, flying out of her chair in an uncontrollable rapture.

"No, dear, not you; it's Amy."

"O Mother! She's too young; it's my turn first. I've wanted it so long—it would do me so much good, and be so altogether splendid—*I must* go."

"I'm afraid it's impossible, Jo. Aunt says Amy, decidedly, and it is not for us to dictate when she offers such a favour."

"It's always so. Amy has all the fun and I have all the work. It isn't fair, oh, it isn't fair!" cried Jo passionately.

"I'm afraid it is partly your own fault, dear. When Aunt spoke to me the other day, she regretted your blunt manners and too independent spirit; and here she writes, as if quoting something you had said—'I planned at first to ask Jo; but as "favours burden her," and she "hates French," I think I won't venture to invite her. Amy is more docile, and will make a good companion for Flo, and receive gratefully any help the trip may give her'."

"Oh, my tongue, my abominable tongue! Why can't I learn to keep it quiet?" groaned Jo, remembering words which had been her undoing.

"Jo, dear, I'm very selfish, but I couldn't spare you, and I'm glad you are not going quite yet," whispered Beth, embracing her, basket and all, with such a clinging touch and loving face, that Jo felt comforted in spite of the sharp regret that made her want to box her own ears, and humbly beg Aunt Carrol to burden her with this favour, and see how gratefully she would bear it.

By the time Amy came in, Jo was able to take her part in the family jubilation; not quite as heartily as usual, perhaps, but without repinings at Amy's good fortune. The young lady herself received the news as tidings of great joy, went about in a solemn sort of rapture, and began to sort her colours and pack her pencils that evening, leaving such trifles as clothes, money, and passports to those less absorbed in visions of art than herself.

So Amy sailed away to find the old world, which is always new and beautiful to young eyes, while her father and friend watched her from the shore, fervently hoping that none but gentle fortunes would befall the happy-hearted girl, who waved her hand to them till they could see nothing but the summer sunshine shining on the sea.

CHAPTER EIGHT

OUR FOREIGN CORRESPONDENT

LONDON.

DEAREST PEOPLE,—Here I really sit at a front window of the Bath Hotel, Piccadilly. It's not a fashionable place, but Uncle stopped here years ago, and won't go anywhere else; however, we don't mean to stay long, so it's no great matter. Oh, I can't begin to tell you how I enjoy it all! I never can, so I'll only give you bits out of my notebook, for I've done nothing but sketch and scribble since I started.

I sent a line from Halifax, when I felt miserable, but after that I got on delightfully, seldom ill, on deck all day, with plenty of pleasant people to amuse me. Every one was very kind to me, especially the officers. Don't laugh, Jo; gentlemen really are very necessary aboard ship, to hold on to, or to wait upon one; and as they have nothing to do, it's a mercy to make them useful, otherwise they would smoke themselves to death, I'm afraid.

It was all heavenly, but I was glad to see the Irish coast, and found it very lovely, so green and sunny, with brown cabins here and there, ruins on some of the hills, and gentlemen's country-seats in the valleys, with deer feeding in the parks. It was early in the morning, but I didn't regret getting up to see it, for the bay was full of little boats, the shores *so* picturesque, and a rosy sky overhead. I never shall forget it.

We only stopped at Liverpool a few hours. It's a dirty, noisy place, and I was glad to leave it. Uncle rushed out and bought a pair of doeskin gloves, some ugly, thick shoes, and an umbrella, and got shaved *à la* mutton-chop, the first thing. Then he flattered himself that he looked like a true Briton; but the first time he had the mud cleaned off his shoes, the little bootblack knew that an American stood in them, and said, with a grin, "There yer har, sir. I've give 'em the latest Yankee shine." It amused Uncle immensely. Oh, I *must* tell you what that absurd Lennox did! He got his friend Ward, who came on with us, to order a bouquet for me, and the first thing I saw in my room was a lovely one, with "Robert Lennox's compliments," on the card. Wasn't that fun, girls? I like travelling.

I never *shall* get to London if I don't hurry. The trip was like riding through a long picture-gallery, full of lovely landscape. The farmhouses were my delight; with thatched roofs, ivy up to the eaves, latticed windows, and stout women with rosy children at the doors. The very cattle looked more tranquil than ours, as they stood knee-deep in clover, and the hens had a contented cluck, as if they never got nervous, like Yankee biddies. Such perfect colour I never saw—the grass so green, sky so blue, grain so yellow, woods so dark—I was in a rapture all the way. So was Flo; and we kept bouncing from one side to the other, trying to see everything while we were whisking along at the rate of sixty miles an hour. Aunt was tired and went to sleep, but Uncle read his guide-book, and wouldn't be astonished at anything.

Of course it rained when we got to London, and there was nothing to be seen but fog and umbrellas. We rested, unpacked, and shopped a little between the showers. Aunt Mary got me some new things, for I came off in such a hurry I wasn't half ready. A white hat and blue feather, a muslin dress to match, and the loveliest mantle you ever saw. Shopping in Regent Street is perfectly splendid; things seem so cheap—nice ribbons only sixpence a yard. I laid in a stock, but shall get my gloves in Paris. Doesn't that sound sort of elegant and rich?

Today was fair, and we went to Hyde Park, close by, for we are more aristocratic than we look. The Duke of Devonshire lives near. I often see his footmen lounging at the back gate; and the Duke of Wellington's house is not far off. Such sights as I saw, my dear! It was as good as Punch, for there were fat dowagers rolling about in their red and yellow coaches, with gorgeous Jeameses in silk stockings and velvet coats, up behind and powdered coachmen in front. Smart maids, with the rosiest children I ever saw; handsome girls, looking half-asleep; dandies, in queer English hats and lavender kids, lounging about, and tall soldiers, in short red jackets and muffin caps stuck on one side, looking so funny I longed to sketch them.

Rotten Row means "*Route de Roi,*" or the king's way; but now it's more like a riding-school than anything else. The horses are splendid, and the men, especially the grooms, ride well; but the women are stiff, and bounce which isn't according to our rules. I longed to show them a tearing American gallop, for they trotted solemnly up and down, in their scant habits and high hats, looking like the women in a toy Noah's Ark. Every one rides—old men, stout ladies, little children—and the young folks do a deal of flirting here; I saw a pair exchange rosebuds, for it's the thing to wear one in the button-hole, and I thought it rather a nice little idea.

In the P.M. to Westminster Abbey; but don't expect me to describe it, that's impossible—so I'll only say it was sublime! This evening we are going to see Fechter, which will be an appropriate end to the happiest day of my life.

MIDNIGHT.

It's very late, but I can't let my letter go in the morning without telling you what happened last evening. Who do you think came in, as we were at tea? Laurie's English friends, Fred and Frank Vaughn! I was *so* surprised, for I shouldn't have known them but for the cards. Both are tall fellows, with whiskers; Fred handsome in the English style, and Frank much better, for he only limps slightly, and uses no crutches. They had heard from Laurie where we were to be, and came to ask us to their house; but Uncle won't go, so we shall return the call, and see them as we can. They went to the theatre with us, and we did have *such* a good time, for Frank devoted himself to Flo, and Fred and I talked over past, present, and future fun as if we had known each other all our days. Tell Beth Frank asked for her, and was sorry to hear of her ill-health. Fred laughed when I spoke of Jo, and sent his "respectful compliments to the big hat."

I long to see you all, and in spite of my nonsense am, as ever, your loving AMY.

PARIS.

DEAR GIRLS,—In my last I told you about our London visit—how kind the Vaughns were, and what pleasant parties they made for us. I enjoyed the trips to Hampton Court and the Kensington Museum more than anything else—for at Hampton I saw Raphael's cartoons, and, at the Museum, rooms full of pictures by Turner, Lawrence, Reynolds, Hogarth, and the other great creatures. The day in Richmond Park was charming for we had a regular English picnic, and I had more splendid oaks and groups of deer than I could copy; also heard a nightingale, and saw larks go up. We "did" London to our hearts' content, thanks to Fred and Frank, and were sorry to go away; for, though English people are slow to take you in, when they once make up their minds to do it they cannot be outdone in hospitality, *I* think. The Vaughns hope to meet us in Rome next winter, and I shall be dreadfully disappointed if they don't, for Grace and I are great friends, and the boys very nice fellows—especially Fred.

Well, we were hardly settled here, when he turned up again, saying he had come for a holiday, and was going to Switzerland. Aunt looked sober at first, but he was so cool about it she couldn't say a word; and now we get on nicely, and are very glad he came, for he speaks French like a native, and I don't know what we should do without him.

We often walk in the Tuileries Gardens, for they are lovely, though the antique Luxembourg Gardens suit me better. Père la Chaise is very curious, for many of the tombs are like small rooms, and, looking in, one sees a table, with images or pictures of the dead, and chairs for the mourners to sit in when they come to lament. That is so Frenchy.

Our rooms are on the Rue de Rivoli, and, sitting in

the balcony, we look up and down the long, brilliant street. It is so pleasant that we spend our evenings talking there, when too tired with our day's work to go out. Fred is very entertaining, and is altogether the most agreeable young man I ever knew—except Laurie, whose manners are more charming. I wish Fred was dark, for I don't fancy light men; however, the Vaughns are very rich, and come of an excellent family, so I won't find fault with their yellow hair, as my own is yellower.

Next week we are off to Germany and Switzerland; and, as we shall travel fast, I shall only be able to give you hasty letters. I keep my diary, and try to "remember correctly and describe clearly all that I see and admire," as Father advised. It is good practice for me, and, with my sketch-book, will give you a better idea of my tour than these scribbles.

Adieu; I embrace you tenderly.

VOTRE AMIE.

HEIDELBERG.

MY DEAR MAMMA,— Having a quiet hour before we leave for Berne, I'll try to tell you what has happened, for some of it is very important, as you will see.

The sail up the Rhine was perfect, and I just sat and enjoyed it with all my might. Get Father's old guide-books, and read about it; I haven't words beautiful enough to describe it. At Coblentz we had a lovely time, for some students from Bonn, with whom Fred got acquainted on the boat, gave us a serenade. It was a moonlight night, and, about one o'clock, Flo and I were waked by the most delicious music under our windows. We flew up, and hid behind the curtains; but sly peeps showed us Fred and the students singing away down below. It was the most romantic thing I ever saw—the river, the bridge of boats, the great fortress opposite, moonlight everywhere, and music fit to melt a heart of stone.

When they were done we threw down some flowers, and saw them scramble for them, kiss their hands to the invisible ladies, and go laughing away—to smoke and drink beer, I suppose. Next morning Fred showed me one of the crumpled flowers in his vest-pocket, and looked very sentimental. I laughed at him, and said I didn't throw it, but Flo, which seemed to disgust him, for he tossed it out of the window, and turned sensible again. I'm afraid I'm going to have trouble with that boy, it begins to look like it.

The baths at Nassau were very gay, so was Baden-Baden, where Fred lost some money, and I scolded him. He needs someone to look after him when Frank is not with him. Kate said once she hoped he'd marry soon, and I quite agree with her that it would be well for him. Frankfurt was delightful; I saw Goethe's house, Schiller's statue, and Dannecker's famous "Ariadne." It was very lovely, but I should have enjoyed it more if I had known the story better. I didn't like to ask, as everyone knew it, or pretended they did. I wish Jo would tell me all about it; I ought to have read more, for I find I don't know anything, and it mortifies me.

Now comes the serious part—for it happened here, and Fred is just gone. He has been so kind and jolly that we all got quite fond of him; I never thought of anything but a travelling friendship, till the serenade night. Since then I've begun to feel that the moonlight walks, balcony talks, and daily adventures were something more to him than fun. I haven't flirted, Mother, truly, but remembered what you said to me, and have done my very best. I can't help it if people like me; I don't try to make them, and it worries me if

I don't care for them, though Jo says I haven't got any heart. Now I know Mother will shake her head, and the girls say, "Oh, the mercenary little wretch!" but I've made up my mind, and, if Fred asks me, I shall accept him, though I'm not madly in love. I like him, and we get on comfortably together. He is handsome, young, clever enough, and very rich—ever so much richer than the Laurences. I don't think his family would object, and I should be very happy, for they are all kind, well-bred, generous people, and they like me. Fred, as the eldest twin, will have the estate, I suppose, and such a splendid one as it is! A city house in a fashionable street, not so showy as our big houses, but twice as comfortable, and full of solid luxury, such as English people believe in. I like it, for it's genuine. I've seen the plate, the family jewels, the old servants, and pictures of the country place, with its park, great house, lovely grounds, and fine horses. Oh, it would be all I should ask! And I'd rather have it than any title such as girls snap up so readily, and find nothing behind. I may be mercenary, but I hate poverty and don't mean to bear it a minute longer than I can help. One of us *must* marry well; Meg didn't, Jo won't, Beth can't yet, so I shall, and make everything cosy all round. I wouldn't marry a man I hated or despised. You may be sure of that; and, though Fred is not my model hero, he does very well, and, in time, I should get fond enough of him if he was very fond of me, and let me do just as I liked. So I've been turning the matter over in my mind the last week, for it was impossible to help seeing that Fred liked me. He said nothing, but little things showed it; he never goes with Flo, always gets on my side of the carriage, table, or promenade, looks sentimental when we are alone, and frowns at any one else who ventures to speak to me.

Well, last evening we went up to the castle about

sunset—at least all of us but Fred, who was to meet us there, after going to the Post Restante for letters. We had a charming time poking about the ruins, the vaults where the monster tun is, and the beautiful gardens made by the elector, long ago, for his English wife. I liked the great terrace best, for the view was divine; so, while the rest went to see the rooms inside, I sat there trying to sketch the grey stone lion's head on the wall, with scarlet woodbine sprays hanging round it. I felt as if I'd got into a romance, sitting there, watching the Neckar rolling through the valley, listening to the music of the Austrian band below, and waiting for my lover, like a real story-book girl. I had a feeling that something was going to happen, and I was ready for it. I didn't feel blushy or quakey, but quite cool, and only a little excited.

By-and-by I heard Fred's voice, and then he came hurrying through the great arch to find me. He looked so troubled that I forgot all about myself, and asked what the matter was. He said he'd just got a letter begging him to come home, for Frank was very ill; so he was going at once, in the night train, and only had time to say goodbye. I was very sorry for him, and disappointed for myself, but only for a minute, because he said, as he shook hands—and said it in a way that I could not mistake—"I shall soon come back; you won't forget me, Amy?"

I didn't promise, but I looked at him, and he seemed satisfied, and there was no time for anything but messages and goodbyes, for he was off in an hour, and we all miss him very much. I know he wanted to speak, but I think, from something he once hinted, that he had promised his father not to do anything of the sort yet awhile, for he is a rash boy, and the old gentleman dreads a foreign daughter-in-law. We shall soon meet in Rome; and then, if I don't change my nind, I'll say "Yes, thank you," when he says "Will you, please?"

Of course this is all *very private,* but I wished you to know what was going on. Don't be anxious about me; remember I am your "prudent Amy," and be sure I will do nothing rashly. Send me as much advice as you like; I'll use it if I can. I wish I could see you for a good talk, Marmee. Love and trust me.—Ever your

Amy.

CHAPTER NINE

TENDER TROUBLES

"Jo, I'm anxious about Beth."

"Why, Mother she has seemed unusually well since the babies came."

"It's not her health that troubles me now; it's her spirits. I'm sure there is something on her mind, and I want you to discover what it is."

"What makes you think so, Mother?"

"She sits alone a good deal, and doesn't talk to her father as much as she used. I found her crying over the babies the other day. When she sings, the songs are always sad ones, and now and then I see a look in her face that I don't understand. This isn't like Beth, and it worries me."

"Have you asked her about it?"

"I have tried once or twice; but she either evaded my questions, or looked so distressed that I stopped. I never force my children's confidence, and I seldom have to wait for it long."

Mrs. March glanced at Jo as she spoke, but the face

opposite seemed quite unconscious of any secret disquietude but Beth's; and, after sewing thoughtfully for a minute, Jo said—

"I think she is growing up, and so begins to dream dreams, and have hopes and fears and fidgets, without knowing why, or being able to explain them. Why, Mother, Beth's eighteen, but we don't realise it, and treat her like a child, forgetting she's a woman."

"So she is. Dear heart, how fast you do grow up," returned her mother, with a sigh and a smile.

"Can't be helped, Marmee, so you must resign yourself to all sorts of worries, and let your birds hop out of the nest, one by one. I promise never to hop very far, if that is any comfort to you."

"It is a great comfort, Jo; I always feel strong when you are at home, now Meg is gone. Beth is too feeble and Amy too young to depend upon; but when the tug comes, you are always ready."

"Why, you know I don't mind hard jobs much, and there must always be one scrub in a family. Amy is splendid in fine works, and I'm not; but I feel in my element when all the carpets are to be taken up, or half the family fall sick at once. Amy is distinguishing herself abroad; but if anything is amiss at home, I'm your man."

"I leave Beth to your hands, then, for she will open her tender little heart to her Jo sooner than to anyone else. Be very kind, and don't let her think any one watches or talks about her. If she only would get quite strong and cheerful again, I shouldn't have a wish in the world."

"Happy woman! I've got heaps."

"My dear, what are they?"

"I'll settle Bethy's troubles, and then I'll tell you mine. They are not very wearying, so they'll keep;" and Jo stitched away, with a wise nod which set her mother's heart at rest about her, for the present at least.

While apparently absorbed in her own affairs, Jo watched Beth; and, after many conflicting conjectures finally settled upon one which seemed to explain the change in her. A slight incident gave Jo the clue to the mystery, she thought, and lively fancy, loving heart did the rest. She was affecting to write busily one Saturday afternoon, when she and Beth were alone together; yet as she scribbled, she kept her eye on her sister, who seemed unusually quiet. Sitting at the window. Beth's work often dropped into her lap, and she leaned her head upon her hand, in a dejected attitude, while her eyes rested on the dull, autumnal landscape. Suddenly someone passed below, whistling like an operatic blackbird, and a voice called out—

"All serene! Coming in tonight."

Beth started, leaned forward, smiled and nodded, watched the passer-by till his quick tramp died away, then said softly, as if to herself—

"How strong and well and happy that dear boy looks."

"Hum!" said Jo, still intent upon her sister's face; for the bright colour faded as quickly as it came, the smile vanished, and presently a tear lay shining on the window-ledge. Beth whisked it off, and glanced apprehensively at Jo; but she was scratching away at a tremendous rate, apparently engrossed in "Olympia's Oath." The instant Beth turned, Jo began her watch again, saw Beth's hand go quietly to her eyes more than once, and, in her half-averted face, read a tender sorrow that made her own eyes fill. Fearing to betray herself, she slipped away, murmuring something about needing more paper.

"Mercy on me, Beth loves Laurie!" she said, sitting down in her own room, pale with the shock of the discovery which she believed she had just made. "I never dreamt of such a thing. What *will* Mother say? I wonder if he—" there Jo stopped, and turned scarlet with a sudden thought. "If he shouldn't love back again, how dreadful it would be. He must; I'll make him!" and she shook her head threateningly at the picture of the mischievous-looking boy laughing at her from the wall.

Then she sighed, and fell into a reverie, from which she did not wake till the early twilight sent her down to take new observations, which only confirmed her suspicion. Though Laurie flirted with Amy and joked with Jo, his manner to Beth had always been peculiarly kind and gentle, but so was everybody's; therefore, no one thought of imagining that he cared more for her than for the others. Indeed, a general impression had prevailed in the family, of late, that "our boy" was getting fonder than ever of Jo, who, however, wouldn't hear a word upon the subject, and scolded violently if any one dared to suggest it. If they had known the various tender passages of the past year, or rather attempts at tender passages which had been nipped in the bud, they would have had the immense satisfaction of saying, "I told you so." But Jo hated "philandering," and wouldn't allow it, always having a joke or a smile ready at the least sign of impending danger.

Things were in this state when the grand discovery was made and Jo watched Laurie that night as she had never done before. If she had not got the new idea into her head, she would have seen nothing unusual in the fact that Beth was very quiet, and Laurie very kind to her. But having given the rein to her lively fancy, it galloped away with her at a great pace; and common sense, being rather weakened by a long course of romance writing, did not come to the rescue. As usual,

Beth lay on the sofa, and Laurie sat in a low chair close by, amusing her with all sorts of gossip: for she depended on her weekly "spin," and he never disappointed her. But that evening, Jo fancied that Beth's eyes rested on the lively, dark face beside her with peculiar pleasure, and that she listened with intense interest to an account of some exciting cricket-match, though the phrases, "caught off a tice," "stumped off his ground," and "the leg hit for three," were as intelligible to her as Sanskrit. She also fancied, having set her heart upon seeing it, that she saw a certain increase of gentleness in Laurie's manner, that he dropped his voice now and then, laughed less than usual, was a little absent-minded, and settled the afghan over Beth's feet with an assiduity that was really almost tender.

"Who knows? Stranger things have happened," thought Jo, as she fussed about the room. "She will make quite an angel of him, and he will make life delightfully easy and pleasant for the dear, if they only love each other. I don't see how he can help it; and I do believe he would if the rest of us were out of the way."

Now, the old sofa was a regular patriarch of a sofa —long, broad, well-cushioned, and low; a trifle shabby, as well it might be, for the girls had slept and sprawled on it as babies, fished over the back, rode on the arms, and had menageries under it as children, and rested tired heads, dreamed dreams, and listened to tender talk on it as young women. They all loved it, for it was a family refuge, and one corner had always been Jo's favourite lounging-place. Among the many pillows that adorned the venerable couch was one, hard, round, covered with prickly horsehair, and furnished with a knobby button at each end; this repulsive pillow was her especial property, being used as a weapon of defence, a barricade, or a stern preventive of too much slumber.

Laurie knew this pillow well, and had cause to regard it with deep aversion, having been unmercifully pummelled with it in former days, when romping was allowed, and now frequently debarred by it from taking the seat he most coveted, next to Jo in the sofa corner. If "the sausage," as they called it, stood on end, it was a sign that he might approach and repose; but if it lay flat across the sofa, woe to the man, woman, or child who dared disturb it! That evening Jo forgot to barricade her corner, and had not been in her seat five minutes, before a massive form appeared beside her, and with both arms spread over the sofa-back, both long legs stretched out before him, Laurie exclaimed, with a sigh of satisfaction—

"Now, *this* is filling at the price."

"No slang," snapped Jo, slamming down the pillow. But it was too late, there was no room for it; and, coasting on to the floor, it disappeared in a most mysterious manner.

"Come, Jo, don't be thorny. After studying himself to a skeleton all the week, a fellow deserves petting, and ought to get it."

"Beth will pet you; I'm busy."

"No, she's not to be bothered with me; but you like that sort of thing, unless you've suddenly lost your taste for it. Have you? Do you hate your boy, and want to fire pillows at him?"

Anything more wheedlesome than that touching appeal was seldom heard, but Jo quenched "her boy" by turning on him with the stern query—

"How many bouquets have you sent Miss Randal this week?"

"Not one, upon my word. She's engaged. Now then."

"I'm glad of it; that's one of your foolish extravagances—sending flowers and things to girls for whom you don't care two pins," continued Jo reprovingly.

"Sensible girls, for whom I do care whole papers of pins, won't let me send them 'flowers and things,' so what can I do? My feelings must have a *went.*"

"Mother doesn't approve of flirting, even in fun; and you do flirt desperately, Teddy."

"I'd give anything if I could answer, 'So do you.' As I can't, I'll merely say that I don't see any harm in that pleasant little game, if all parties understand that it's only play."

"Well, it does look pleasant, but I can't learn how it's done. I've tried, because one feels awkward in company, not to do as everybody else is doing; but I don't seem to get on," said Jo, forgetting to play Mentor.

"Take lessons of Amy; she has a regular talent for it."

"Yes, she does it very prettily, and never seems to go too far. I suppose it's natural to some people to please without trying, and others to always say and do the wrong thing in the wrong place."

Returning suddenly to her admonitory tone, she said, dropping her voice, "If you *must* have a 'went,' Teddy, go and devote yourself to one of the 'pretty, modest girls' whom you do respect, and not waste your time with the silly ones."

"You really advise it?" and Laurie looked at her with an odd mixture of anxiety and merriment in his face.

"Yes, I do; but you'd better wait till you are through college, on the whole, and be fitting yourself for the place meantime. You're not half good enough for—well, whoever the modest girl may be," and Jo looked a little queer likewise, for a name had almost escaped her.

"That I'm not!" acquiesced Laurie, with an expression of humility quite new to him, as he dropped his eyes, and absently wound Jo's apron-tassel round his finger.

"Mercy on us, this will never do," thought Jo; adding aloud, "Go and sing to me. I'm dying for some music, and always like yours."

"I'd rather stay here, thank you."

"Well, you can't; there isn't room. Go and make yourself useful, since you are too big to be ornamental. I thought you hated to be tied to a woman's apron-string?" retorted Jo, quoting certain rebellious words of his own.

"Ah, that depends on who wears the apron!" and Laurie gave an audacious tweak at the tassel.

"Are you going?" demanded Joe, diving for the pillow.

He fled at once, and the minute it was well "Up with the bonnets of bonnie Dundee," she slipped away, to return no more till the young gentleman had departed in high dudgeon.

Jo lay long awake that night, and was just dropping off when the sound of a stifled sob made her fly to Beth's bedside, with the anxious inquiry, "What is it, dear?"

"I thought you were asleep," sobbed Beth.

"Is it the old pain, my precious?"

"No; it's a new one; but I can bear it," and Beth tried to check her tears.

"Tell me all about it, and let me cure it as I often did the other."

"You can't; there is no cure." There Beth's voice gave way, and, clinging to her sister, she cried so despairingly that Jo was frightened.

"Where is it? Shall I call Mother?"

Beth did not answer the first question; but in the dark one hand went involuntarily to her heart, as if the pain were there; with the other she held Jo fast, whispering eagerly, "No, no, don't call her, don't tell her. I shall be better soon. Lie down here and 'poor' my head. I'll be quiet, and go to sleep; indeed I will."

Jo obeyed; but as her hand went softly to and fro across Beth's hot forehead and wet eyelids, her heart was very full, and she longed to speak. But young as she was, Jo had learned that hearts, like flowers, cannot be rudely handled, but must open naturally; so, though she believed she knew the cause of Beth's new pain, she only said, in her tenderest tone, "Does anything trouble you, deary?"

"Yes, Jo," after a long pause.

"Wouldn't it comfort you to tell me what it is?"

"Not now, not yet."

"Is the pain better now?"

"Oh yes, much better; you are so comfortable, Jo!"

"Go to sleep, dear; I'll stay with you."

So cheek to cheek they fell asleep, and on the morrow Beth seemed quite herself again; for at eighteen, neither heads nor hearts ache long, and a loving word can medicine most ills.

But Jo had made up her mind, and, after pondering over a project for some days, she confided it to her mother.

"You asked me the other day what my wishes were. I'll tell you one of them, Marmee," she began, as they sat alone together. "I want to go away somewhere this winter for a change."

"Why Jo?" and her mother looked up quickly, as if the words suggested a double meaning.

With her eyes on her work, Jo answered soberly, "I want something new; I feel restless, and anxious to be seeing, doing, and learning more than I am. I brood too much over my own small affairs, and need stirring up, so as I can be spared this winter, I'd like to hop a little way, and try my wings."

"Where will you hop?"

"To New York. I had a bright idea yesterday, and this is it. You know Mrs. Kirke wrote to you for some respectable young person to teach her children and sew. It's rather hard to find just the thing, but I think I should suit if I tried."

"My dear, go out to service in that great boarding-house!" and Mrs. March looked surprised, but not displeased.

"It's not exactly going out to service; for Mrs. Kirke is your friend—the kindest soul that ever lived—and would make things pleasant for me, I know. Her family is separate from the rest, and no one knows me there. Don't care if they do; it's honest work, and I'm not ashamed of it."

"Nor I; but your writing?"

"All the better for the change. I shall see and hear new things, get new ideas, and, even if I haven't much time there, I shall bring home quantities of material for my rubbish."

"I have no doubt of it; but are these your only reasons for this sudden fancy?"

"No, Mother."

"May I know the others?"

Jo looked up and Jo looked down, then said slowly, with sudden colour in her cheeks, "It may be vain and wrong to say it, but—I'm afraid—Laurie is getting too fond of me."

"Then you don't care for him in the way it is evident he begins to care for you?" and Mrs. March looked anxious as she put the question.

"Mercy, no! I love the dear boy, as I always have,

and am immensely proud of him; but as for anything more, it's out of the question."

"I'm glad of that, Jo."

"Why, please?"

"Because, dear, I don't think you're suited to one another. As friends you are very happy, and your frequent quarrels soon blow over; but I fear you would both rebel if you were mated for life. You are too much alike and too fond of freedom, not to mention hot tempers and strong wills, to get on happily together, in a relation which needs infinite patience and forbearance, as well as love."

"That's just the feeling I had, though I couldn't express it. I'm glad you think he is only beginning to care for me. It would trouble me sadly to make him unhappy; for I couldn't fall in love with the dear old fellow merely out of gratitude, could I?"

"You are sure of his feeling for you?"

The colour deepened in Jo's cheeks, as she answered, with the look of mingled pleasure, pride, and pain which young girls wear when speaking of first lovers—

"I'm afraid it is so, Mother; he hasn't said anything, but he looks a great deal. I think I had better go away before it comes to anything."

"I agree with you, and if it can be managed you shall go."

The plan was talked over in a family council, and agreed upon; for Mrs. Kirke gladly accepted Jo, and promised to make a pleasant home for her. The teaching would render her independent; and such leisure as she got might be made profitable by writing, while the new scenes and society would be both useful and agreeable. Jo liked the prospect and was eager to be gone, for the home-nest was growing too narrow for her restless nature and adventurous spirit. When all was settled, with fear and trembling she told Laurie;

but to her surprise he took it very quietly. He had been graver than usual of late, but very pleasant; and, when jokingly accused of turning over a new leaf, he answered soberly, "So I am; and I mean this one shall stay turned."

Jo was very much relieved that one of his virtuous fits should come on just then, and made her preparations with a lightened heart—for Beth seemed more cheerful—and hoped she was doing the best for all.

"One thing I leave to your especial care," she said, the night before she left.

"You mean your papers?" asked Beth.

"No, my boy. Be very good to him, won't you?"

"I'll do my best for your sake," promised Beth, wondering why Jo looked at her so queerly.

When Laurie said "Goodbye," he whispered significantly, "It won't do a bit of good, Jo. My eye is on you; so mind what you do, or I'll come and bring you home."

CHAPTER TEN

JO'S JOURNAL

NEW YORK, *November*.

DEAR MARMEE AND BETH,—I'm going to write you a regular volume, for I've got heaps to tell, though I'm not a fine young lady travelling on the Continent.

Mrs. Kirke welcomed me so kindly I felt at home at once, even in that big house full of strangers. She gave me a funny little sky-parlour—all she had; but there is a stove in it, and a nice table in a sunny window, so I can sit here and write whenever I like. A fine view and a church-tower opposite atone for the many stairs, and I took a fancy to my den on the spot. The nursery, where I am to teach and sew, is a pleasant room next Mrs. Kirke's private parlour, and the two little girls are pretty children—rather spoilt, I fancy, but they took to me after telling them "The Seven Bad Pigs"; and I've no doubt I shall make a model governess.

I am to have my meals with the children, if I prefer it to the great table, and for the present I do, for *I am* bashful, though no one will believe it.

As I went downstairs, soon after, I saw something I liked. The flights are very long in this tall house, and as I stood waiting at the head of the third one for a little servant-girl to lumber up, I saw a gentleman come along behind her, take the heavy hod of coal out of her hand, carry it all the way up, put it down at a door nearby, and walk away, saying, with a kind nod and a foreign accent—

"It goes better so. The little back is too young to haf such heaviness."

Wasn't it good of him? I like such things, for, as father says, trifles show character. When I mentioned it to Mrs. K., that evening, she laughed, and said—

"That must have been Professor Bhaer; he's always doing things of that sort."

Mrs. K. told me he was from Berlin; very learned and good, but poor as a church-mouse, and gives lessons to support himself and two little orphan nephews whom he is educating here, according to the wishes of his sister, who married an American. Not a very romantic story, but it interested me; and I was glad to hear that Mrs. K. lends him her parlour for some of his scholars. There is a glass door between it and the nursery, and I mean to peep at him, and then I'll tell you how he looks. He's almost forty, so it's no harm, Marmee.

After tea and a go-to-bed romp with the little girls, I attacked the big work-basket, and had a quiet evening chatting with my new friend. I shall keep a journal-letter, and send it once a week; so goodnight, and more tomorrow.

Tuesday Eve.

Had a lively time in my seminary this morning, for the children acted like Sancho; and at one time I really thought I should shake them all round. Some good angel inspired me to try gymnastics, and I kept it up till they were glad to sit down and keep still. After luncheon, the girl took them out for a walk, and I went to my needlework, like little Mabel, "with a willing mind." I was thanking my stars that I'd learned to make nice buttonholes, when the parlour door opened and shut, and some one began to hum—

"Kennst du das land,"

like a big bumble-bee. It was dreadfully improper, I know, but I couldn't resist the temptation; and lifting one end of the curtain before the glass door. I peeped in. Profesor Bhaer was there; and while he arranged his books, I took a good look at him. A regular German—rather stout, with brown hair tumbled all over his head, a bushy beard, good nose, the kindest eyes I ever saw, and a splendid big voice that does one's ears good, after our sharp or slipshod American gabble. His clothes were rusty, his hands were large, and he hadn't a really handsome feature in his face, except his beautiful teeth; yet I liked him, for he had a fine head; his linen was very nice, and he looked like a gentleman, though two buttons were off his coat, and there was a patch on one shoe. He looked sober in spite of his humming, till he went to the window to turn the hyacinth bulbs toward the sun, and stroke the cat, who received him like an old friend. Then he smiled; and when a tap came at the door, called out in a loud, brisk tone—

"Herein!"

I was just going to run, when I caught sight of a morsel of a child carrying a big book, and stopped to see what was going on.

"Me wants my Bhaer," said the mite, slamming down her book, and running to meet him.

"Thou shalt haf thy Bhaer; come, then, and take a goot hug from him, my Tina," said the Professor, catching her up, with a laugh, and holding her so high over his head that she had to stoop her little face to kiss him.

"Now me must tuddy my lessin," went on the funny little thing; so he put her up at the table, opened the great dictionary she had brought, and gave her a paper and pencil, and she scribbled away, turning a leaf now and then, and passing her little fat finger down the page, as if finding a word, so soberly that I nearly betrayed myself with a laugh, while Mr. Bhaer stood stroking her pretty hair, with a fatherly look, that made me think she must be his own, though she looked more French than German.

Another knock and the appearance of two young ladies sent me back to my work, and there I virtuously remained through all the noise and gabbling that went on next door. One of the girls kept laughing affectedly, and saying "Now Professor," in a coquettish tone, and the other pronounced her German with an accent that must have made it hard for him to keep sober.

Poor man, I pitied him; and when the girls were gone, took just one more peep, to see if he survived it. He seemed to have thrown himself back in his chair, tired out, and sat there with his eyes shut till the clock struck two, when he jumped up, put his books in his pocket, as if ready for another lesson, and, taking little Tina, who had fallen asleep on the sofa, in his arms, he carried her quietly away. I fancy he has a hard life of it.

Mrs. Kirke asked me if I wouldn't go down to the five o'clock dinner; and, feeling a little bit homesick, I thought I would, just to see what sort of people are under the same roof with me. So I made myself respectable, and tried to slip in behind Mrs. Kirke; but as she is short, and I'm tall, my efforts at concealment were rather a failure. She gave me a seat by her, and after my face cooled off, I plucked up courage, and looked about me. The long table was full, and every one intent on getting their dinner—the gentlemen especially, who seemed to be eating on time, for they *bolted* in every sense of the word, vanishing as soon as they were done. There was the usual assortment of young men absorbed in themselves; young couples absorbed in each other; married ladies in their babies, and old gentlemen in politics. I don't think I shall care to have much to do with any of them, except one sweet-faced maiden lady, who looks as if she had something in her.

Cast away at the very bottom of the table was the Professor, shouting answers to the questions of a very inquisitive, deaf old gentleman on one side, and talking philosophy with a Frenchman on the other. If Amy had been here, she'd have turned her back on him for ever, because, sad to relate, he had a great appetite, and shovelled in his dinner in a manner which would have horrified "her ladyship." I didn't mind, for I like "to see folks eat with a relish," as Hannah says, and the poor man must have needed a deal of food after teaching idiots all day.

Thursday.

Yesterday was a quiet day, spent in teaching, sewing, and writing in my little room, which is very cosy, with a light and fire. I picked up a few bits of news, and was introduced to the Professor. It seems that Tina is the child of the Frenchwoman who does the fine ironing in the laundry here. The little thing has lost her heart to Mr. Bhaer, and follows him about the house like a dog whenever he is at home, which delights him, as he is very fond of children, though a "bacheldore."

The maiden lady is a Miss Norton—rich, cultivated, and kind. She spoke to me at dinner today (for I went to table again, it's such fun to watch people), and asked me to come and see her at her room. She has fine books and pictures, knows interesting persons, and seems friendly; so I shall make myself agreeable, for I *do* want to get into good society, only it isn't the same sort that Amy likes.

I was in our parlour last evening, when Mr. Bhaer came in with some newspapers for Mrs. Kirke. She wasn't there, but Minnie, who is a little old woman, introduced me very prettily: "This is mamma's friend, Miss March."

"Yes; and she's jolly and we like her lots," added Kitty, who is an *enfant terrible*.

We both bowed, and then we laughed, for the prim introduction and the blunt addition were rather a comical contrast.

"Ah, yes, I hear these naughty ones go to vex you, Mees Marsch. If so again, call at me and I come," he said, with a threatening frown that delighted the little wretches.

I promised I would, and he departed; but it seems as if I was doomed to see a good deal of him, for today, as I passed his door on my way out, by accident I knocked against it with my umbrella. It flew open, and there he stood in his dressing-gown, with a big blue sock on one hand, and a darning-needle in the other; he didn't seem at all ashamed of it, for when I explained and hurried on, he waved his hand, sock and all, saying in his loud, cheerful way—

"You haf a fine day to make your walk. *Bon voyage, mademoiselle.*"

I laughed all the way downstairs; but it was a little pathetic, also, to think of the poor man having to mend his own clothes. The German gentlemen embroider, I know; but darning hose is another thing, and not so pretty.

Saturday.

Nothing has happened to write about, except a call on Miss Norton, who has a room full of lovely things, and who was very charming, for she showed me all her treasures, and asked me if I would sometimes go with her to lectures and concerts, as her escort—if I enjoyed them. She put it as a favour, but I'm sure Mrs. Kirke has told her about us, and she does it out of kindness to me. I'm as proud as Lucifer, but such favours from such people don't burden me, and I accepted gratefully.

When I got back to the nursery there was such an uproar in the parlour that I looked in; and there was Mr. Bhaer down on his hands and knees, with Tina on his back, Kitty leading him with a jump-rope, and Minnie feeding two small boys with seed-cakes, as they roared and ramped in cages built of chairs.

"We are playing *nargerie,*" explained Kitty.

"Dis is mine effalunt!" added Tina, holding on by the Professor's hair.

"Mamma always allows us to do what we like Saturday afternoon, when Franz and Emil come, doesn't she, Mr. Bhaer?" said Minnie.

The "effalunt" sat up, looking as much in earnest as any of them, and said soberly to me—

"I gif you my wort it is so. If we make too large a noise you shall say 'Hush!' to us, and we go more softly."

I promised to do so, but left the door open, and enjoyed the fun as much as they did—for a more glorious frolic I never witnessed. They played tag and soldiers, danced and sung, and when it began to grow dark they all piled on to the sofa about the Professor, while he told charming fairy stories of the storks on the chimney-pots, and the little "kobolds," who ride the snow-flakes as they fall. I wish Americans were as simple and natural as Germans, don't you?

I'm so fond of writing, I should go spinning on for ever if motives of economy didn't stop me; for though I've used thin paper and written fine, I tremble to think of the stamps this long letter will need. Pray forward Amy's as soon as you can spare them. My small news will sound very flat after her splendours, but you will like them, I know. Is Teddy studying so hard that he can't find time to write to his friends? Take good care of him for me, Beth, and tell me all about the babies, and give heaps of love to every one.

From your faithful Jo.

P.S.—On reading over my letter it strikes me as rather Bhaery; but I am always interested in odd people, and I really had nothing else to write about. Bless you!

DECEMBER.

MY PRECIOUS BETHEY.—As this is to be a scribble-scrabble letter, I direct it to you, for it may amuse you, and give you some idea of my goings on; for, though quiet, they are rather amusing, for which, oh, be joyful! After what Amy would call Herculaneum efforts, in the way of mental and moral agriculture, my young ideas begin to shoot and my little twigs to bend as I could wish. They are not so interesting to me as Tina and the boys, but I do my duty by them, and they are fond of me. Franz and Emil are jolly little lads, quite after my own heart; for the mixture of German and American spirit in them produces a constant state of effervescence. Saturday afternoons are riotous times, whether spent in the house or out; for on pleasant days they all go to walk, like a seminary, with the Professor and myself to keep order; and then such fun!

We are very good friends now, and I've begun to take lessons. I really couldn't help it, and it all came about in such a droll way that I must tell you. To begin at the beginning. Mrs. Kirke called to me, one day, as I passed Mr. Bhaer's room, where she was rummaging.

"Did you ever see such a den, my dear? Just come and help me put these books to rights, for I've turned everything upside down, trying to discover what he has done with the six new handkerchiefs I gave him not long ago."

I went in, and while we worked I looked about me, for it was "a den," to be sure. Books and papers everywhere; a broken meerschaum, and an old flute over the mantelpiece as if done with; a ragged bird, without any tail, chirped on one window-seat, and a box of white mice adorned the other; half-finished boats and bits of string lay among the manuscripts; dirty little boots stood drying before the fire; and traces of the dearly beloved boys, for whom he makes a slave of himself, were to be seen all over the room. After a grand rummage three of the missing articles were found—one over the bird-cage, one covered with ink, and a third burnt brown, having been used as a holder.

"Such a man!" laughed good-natured Mrs. K., as she put the relics in the rag-bag. "I suppose the others are torn up to rig ships, bandage cut fingers, or make kite-tails. It's dreadful, but I can't scold him: he's so absent-minded and good-natured, he lets those boys ride over him rough-shod. I agreed to do his washing and mending, but he forgets to give out his things and I forget to look them over, so he comes to a sad pass sometimes."

"Let me mend them," said I. "I don't mind it, and he needn't know. I'd like to—he's so kind to me about bringing my letters and lending books."

So I have got his things in order, and knit heels into two pairs of the socks—for they were boggled out of shape with his queer darns. Nothing was said, and I hoped he wouldn't find it out, but one day last week he caught me at it. Hearing the lessons he gives to others has interested and amused me so much that I took a fancy to learn; for Tina runs in and out, leaving the door open, and I can hear. I had been sitting near this door, finishing off the last sock, and trying to understand what he said to a new scholar, who is as stupid as I am. The girl had gone, and I thought he had also, it was so still, and I was busily gabbling over a verb, and rocking to and fro in a most absurd way, when a little crow made me look up, and there was Mr. Bhaer looking and laughing quietly, while he made signs to Tina not to betray him.

"So!" he said, as I stopped and stared like a goose, "you peep at me, I peep at you, and that is not bad; but see, I am not pleasanting when I say, haf you a wish for German?"

"Yes; but you are too busy. I am too stupid to learn," I blundered out, as red as a peony.

"Prut! we will make the time, and we fail not to find

the sense. At efening I shall gif a little lesson with much gladness; for, like you, Mees Marsch, I haf this debt to pay," and he pointed to my work. " 'Yes,' they say to one another, these so kind ladies, 'he is a stupid old fellow; he will see not what we do; he will never opserve that his sock-heels go not in holes any more, he will think his buttons grow out new when they fall, and believe that strings make theirselves.' Ah! but I haf an eye, and I see much. I haf a heart, and I feel the thanks for this. Come, a little lesson then and now, or no more good fairy works for me and mine."

Of course I couldn't say anything after that, and as it really is a splendid opportunity, I made the bargain, and we began. I took four lessons, and then I stuck fast in a grammatical bog. The Professor was very patient with me, but it must have been torment to him, and now and then he'd look at me with such an expression of mild despair that it was toss-up with me whether to laugh or cry. I tried both ways; and when it came to a sniff of utter mortification and woe, he just threw the grammar on to the floor, and marched out of the room. I felt myself disgraced and deserted for ever, but didn't blame him a particle, and was scrambling my papers together, meaning to rush upstairs and shake myself hard, when in he came, as brisk and beaming as if I'd covered myself with glory.

"Now we shall try a new way. You and I will read these pleasant little Märchen together, and dig no more in that dry book, that goes in the corner for making us trouble."

He spoke so kindly and opened Hans Andersen's fairy tales so invitingly before me, that I was more ashamed than ever, and went at my lesson in a neck-or-nothing style that seemed to amuse him immensely.

After that we got on better, and now I read my lessons pretty well; for this way of studying suits me, and I can see that the grammar gets tucked into the tales and poetry as one gives pills in jelly. I like it very much, and he doesn't seem tired of it yet—which is very good of him, isn't it? I mean to give him something on Christmas, for I dare not offer money. Tell me something nice, Marmee.

JANUARY.

A Happy New Year to you all, my dearest family, which of course included Mr. L. and a young man by the name of Teddy. I can't tell you how much I enjoyed your Christmas bundle, for I didn't get it till night, and had given up hoping. Your letter came in the morning, but you said nothing about a parcel, meaning it for a surprise; so I was disappointed, for I'd had a "kind of a feeling," that you wouldn't forget me. I felt a little low in my mind, as I sat up in my room, after tea; and when the big, muddy, battered-looking bundle was brought to me, I just hugged it, and pranced. It was so *homey* and refreshing, that I sat down on the floor and read and looked and ate and laughed and cried, in my usual absurd way. Thank you all, heaps and heaps!

Speaking of books reminds me that I'm getting rich in that line, for, on New Year's Day, Mr. Bhaer gave me a fine Shakespeare. It is one he values much, and I've often admired it, set up in the place of honour, with his German Bible, Plato, Homer, and Milton; so you may imagine how I felt when he brought it down, without its cover, and showed me my name in it, "from my friend Friedrich Bhaer."

I thanked him as well as I could, and talk now about "my library," as if I had a hundred books. I never knew how much there was in Shakespeare before; but then I never had a Bhaer to explain it to me. I'm glad you both like what I tell you about him, and hope you will know him some day. Mother would admire his warm heart, father his wise head.

Not having much money, or knowing what he'd like, I got several little things, and put them about the room, where he would find them unexpectedly. They were useful, pretty, or funny: a new standish on his table, a little vase for his flowers—he always has some, or a bit of green in a glass, to keep him fresh, he says—and a holder for his blower, so that he needn't burn up what Amy calls "mouchoirs." Poor as he is, he didn't forget a servant or a child in the house; and not a soul here, from the French laundry-woman to Miss Norton, forgot him. I was so glad of that.

I had a very happy New Year, after all; and when I thought it over in my room, I felt as if I was getting on a little in spite of my many failures, for I'm cheerful all the time now, work with a will, and take more interest in other people than I used to, which is satisfactory. Bless you all! Ever your loving Jo.

CHAPTER ELEVEN

A FRIEND

THOUGH very happy in the social atmosphere about her, and very busy with the daily work that earned her bread, and made it sweeter for the effort, Jo still found time for literary labours.

The dream of filling home with comforts, giving Beth everything she wanted, from strawberries in winter to an organ in her bedroom, going abroad herself, and always having *more* than enough, so that she might indulge in the luxury of charity, had been for years Jo's most cherished castle in the air.

The prize-story experience had seemed to open a way which might, after long travelling and much uphill work lead to this delightful *château en Espagne*. But the novel disaster quenched her courage for a time, for public opinion is a giant which has frightened stouter-hearted Jacks on bigger beanstalks than hers.

She took to writing sensation stories; for in those dark ages, even all-perfect America read rubbish. She told no one, but concocted a "thrilling tale," and boldly carried it herself to Mr. Dashwood, editor of the *Weekly Volcano*. Jo produced her manuscript, and, blushing redder and redder with each sentence, blundered out fragments of a little speech carefully prepared for the occasion.

"A friend of mine desired me to offer—a story—just as an experiment—would like your opinion—be glad to write more if this suits."

While she blushed and blundered, Mr. Dashwood had taken the manuscript, and was turning over the leaves with a pair of rather dirty fingers, and casting critical glances up and down the neat pages.

"Not a first attempt, I take it?" observing that the pages were numbered, covered only on one side, and not tied up with a ribbon—sure sign of a novice.

"No, sir; she has had some experience, and got a prize for a tale in the *Blarneystone Banner*."

"Oh, did she?" and Mr. Dashwood gave Jo a quick look, which seemed to take note of everything she had on, from the bow in her bonnet to the buttons on her boots. "Well, you can leave it, if you like. We've more of this sort of thing on hand than we know what to do with at present; but I'll run my eye over it, and give you an answer next week."

When she went again, Mr. Dashwood was not too deeply absorbed in a cigar to remember his manners: so the second interview was much more comfortable than the first.

"We'll take this" (editors never say I), "if you don't object to a few alterations. It's too long, but omitting the passages I've marked will make it just the right length," he said, in a business-like tone.

Jo hardly knew her own MS. again, so crumpled and underscored were its pages and paragraphs; but, feeling as a tender parent might on being asked to cut off her baby's legs in order that it might fit into a new cradle, she looked at the marked passages, and was surprised to find that all the moral reflections—which she had carefully put in as ballast for much romance—had been stricken out.

"But, sir, I thought every story should have some sort of a moral, so I took care to have a few of my sinners repent."

Mr. Dashwood's editorial gravity relaxed into a smile, for Jo had forgotten her "friend," and spoken as only an author could.

"People want to be amused, not preached at, you know. Morals don't sell nowadays;" which was not quite a correct statement, by the way.

"You think it would do with these alterations, then?"

"Yes; it's a new plot, and pretty well worked up—language good, and so on," was Mr. Dashwood's affable reply.

"What do you—that is, what compensation—" began Jo, not exactly knowing how to express herself.

"Oh, yes, well we give from twenty-five to thirty for things of this sort. Pay when it comes out," returned Mr. Dashwood, as if that point had escaped him; such trifles often do escape the editorial mind, it is said.

"Very well; you can have it," said Jo, handing back the story, with a satisfied air; for, after the dollar-a-column work, even twenty-five seemed good pay.

"Shall I tell my friend you will take another if she has one better than this?" asked Jo, unconscious of her little slip of the tongue, and emboldened by her success.

"Well, we'll look at it; can't promise to take it. Tell her to make it short and spicy, and never mind the moral. What name would your friend like to put to it?" in a careless tone.

"None at all, if you please; she doesn't wish her name to appear, and has no *nom de plume*," said Jo, blushing in spite of herself.

"Just as she likes, of course. The tale will be out next week; will you call for the money, or shall I send it?" asked Mr. Dashwood, who felt a natural desire to know who his new contributor might be.

"I'll call. Good morning, sir."

As she departed, Mr. Dashwood put up his feet, with the graceful remark, "Poor and proud, as usual, but she'll do."

Following Mr. Dashwood's directions, and making Mrs. Northbury her model, Jo rashly took a plunge into the frothy sea of sensational literature; but, thanks to the life-preserver thrown her by a friend, she came up again, not much the worse for her ducking.

She soon became interested in her work, for her emaciated purse grew stout, and the little hoard she was making to take Beth to the mountains next summer grew slowly but surely as the weeks passed. One thing disturbed her satisfaction, and that was that she did not tell them at home. She had a feeling that father and mother would not approve, and preferred to have her own way first, and beg pardon afterward. It was easy to keep her secret, for no name appeared with her stories; Mr. Dashwood had, of course, found it out very soon, but promised to be dumb; and, for a wonder, kept his word.

But Mr. Dashwood rejected any but thrilling tales; and, as thrills could not be produced except by harrowing up the souls of the readers, history and romance, land and sea, science and art, police records and lunatic asylums, had to be ransacked for the purpose. She thought she was prospering finely; but was living in bad society; and, imaginary though it was, it influence affected her, for she was feeding heart and fancy on dangerous and unsubstantial food, and was fast brushing the innocent bloom from her nature by a premature acquaintance with the darker side of life, which comes soon enough to all of us.

I don't know whether the study of Shakespeare helped her to read character, or the natural instinct of a woman for what was honest, brave and strong; but while endowing her imaginary heroes with every perfection under the sun, Jo was discovering a live hero, who interested her in spite of many human imperfections. Mr. Bhaer, in one of their conversations, had advised her to study simple, true, and lovely characters, wherever she found them, as good training for a writer. Jo took him at his word, for she coolly turned round and studied him—a proceeding which would have much surprised him, had he known it, for the worthy Professor was very humble in his own conceit.

"That's it!" said Jo to herself, when she at length discovered that genuine good-will towards one's fellow-men could beautify and dignify even a stout German teacher, who shovelled in his dinner, darned his own socks, and was burdened with the name of Bhaer.

Jo valued goodness highly, but she also possessed

a most feminine respect for intellect, and a little discovery which she made about the Professor added much to her regard for him. He never spoke of himself, and no one ever knew that in his native city he had been a man much honoured and esteemed for learning and integrity, till a countryman came to see him, and, in a conversation with Miss Norton, divulged the pleasing fact. From her Jo learned it, and liked it all the better because Mr. Bhaer had never told it. She felt proud to know that he was an honoured Professor in Berlin, though only a poor language-master in America; and his homely, hard-working life was much beautified by the spice of romance which this discovery gave it.

Another and a better gift than intellect was shown her in a most unexpected manner. Miss Norton had the *entrêe* into literary society, which Jo would have had no chance of seeing but for her. The solitary woman felt an interest in the ambitious girl, and kindly conferred many favours of this sort both on Jo and the Professor. She took them with her, one night, to a select symposium, held in honour of several celebrities.

Jo went prepared to bow down and adore the mighty ones whom she had worshipped with youthful enthusiasm afar off. But her reverence for genius received a severe shock that night, and it took her some time to recover from the discovery that the great creatures were only men and women after all.

Before the evening was half over, Jo felt so completely *désillusionnée,* that she sat down in a corner to recover herself. Mr. Bhaer soon joined her, looking rather out of his element, and presently several of the philosophers, each mounted on his hobby, came ambling up to hold an intellectual tournament in the recess. The conversation was miles beyond Jo's comprehension, but she enjoyed it, though Kant and Hegel were unknown gods, the Subjective and Objective unintelligible terms; and the only thing "evolved from her inner consciousness," was a bad headache after it was all over. It dawned upon her gradually that the world was being picked to pieces, and put together on new, and, according to the talkers, on infinitely better principles than before; that religion was in a fair way to be reasoned into nothingness, and intellect was to be the only God. Jo knew nothing about philosophy or metaphysics of any sort, but a curious excitement, half pleasurable, half painful, came over her, as she listened with a sense of being turned adrift into time and space, like a young balloon out on a holiday.

Now, Mr. Bhaer was a diffident man, and slow to offer his own opinions, not because they were unsettled, but too sincere and earnest to be lightly spoken. As he glanced from Jo to several other young people, attracted by the brilliancy of the philosophic pyrotechnics, he knit his brows, and longed to speak, fearing that some inflammable young soul would be led astray by the rockets, to find, when the display was over, that they had only an empty stick or a scorched hand.

He bore it as long as he could; but when he was appealed to for an opinion, he blazed up with honest indignation, and defended religion with all the eloquence which made his broken English musical, and his plain face beautiful. He had a hard fight, for the wise men argued well; but he didn't know when he was beaten, and stood to his colours like a man. Somehow, as he talked, the world got right again to Jo; the old beliefs, that had lasted so long, seemed better than the new; God was not a blind force, and immortality was not a pretty fable, but a blessed fact. She felt as if she had solid ground under her feet again; and when Mr. Bhaer paused, out-talked, but not one whit convinced, Jo wanted to clap her hands and thank him.

She did neither; but she remembered this scene. and gave the Professor her heartiest respect, for she knew it cost him an effort to speak out then and there, because his conscience would not let him be silent.

This belief strengthened daily. She valued his esteem, she coveted his respect, she wanted to be worthy of his friendship; and, just when the wish was sincerest, she came near losing everything. It all grew out of a cocked hat; for one evening the Professor came in to give Jo her lesson, with a paper soldier cap on his head, which Tina had put there, and he had forgotten to take off.

"It's evident he doesn't look in his glass before coming down," thought Jo, with a smile, as he said "Goot efening," and sat soberly down, quite unconscious of the ludicrous contrast between his subject and her head-gear, for he was going to read her the "Death of Wallenstein."

She said nothing at first, for she liked to hear him laugh out his big hearty laugh. when anything funny happened, so she left him to discover it for himself, and presently forgot all about it; for to hear a German read Schiller is rather an absorbing occupation. After the reading came the lesson, which was a lively one, for Jo was in a gay mood that night, and the cocked-hat kept her eyes dancing with merriment. The Professor didn't know what to make of her, and stopped at last, to ask, with an air of mild surprise that was irresistible—

"Mees Marsch, for what do you laugh in your master's face? Haf you no respect for me, that you go on so bad?"

"How can I be respectful, sir, when you forget to take your hat off?" said Jo.

Lifting his hand to his head, the absent-minded Professor gravely felt and removed the little cocked-hat, looked at it a minute, and then threw back his head, and laughed like a merry bass-viol.

"Ah! I see him now; it is that imp Tina who makes me a fool with my cap. Well, it is nothing; but see you, if this lesson goes not well, you too shall wear him."

But the lesson did not go at all for a few minutes, because Mr. Bhaer caught sight of a picture on the hat, and, unfolding it, said, with an air of great disgust—

"I wish these papers did not come in the house; they are not for children to see, nor young people to read. It is not well, and I haf no patience with those who make this harm."

Jo glanced at the sheet, and saw a pleasing illustration composed of a lunatic, a corpse, a villain and a viper. She did not like it; but the impulse that made her turn it over was not one of displeasure, but fear, because, for a minute, she fancied the paper was the *Volcano*. It was not, however and her panic subsided as she remembered that, even if it had been, and one of her own tales in it, there would have been no name to betray her. She had betrayed herself, however, by a look and a blush; for, though an absent man, the Professor saw a good deal more than people fancied. He knew that Jo wrote, and had met her down among the newspaper offices more than once; but as she never spoke of it, he asked no questions, in spite of a strong desire to see her work. Now it occurred to him that she was doing what she was ashamed to own, and it troubled him.

"Yes, you are right to put if from you. I do not like

to think that good young girls should see such things. If the people knew what harm they did, they would not feel that the living *was* honest. They haf no right to put poison in the sugar-plum, and let the small ones eat it. No; they should think a little, and sweep mud in the street before they do this thing."

Mr. Bhaer spoke warmly, and walked to the fire, crumpling the paper in his hands. Jo sat still, looking as if the fire had come to her; for her cheeks burned long after the cocked hat had turned to smoke, and gone harmlessly up the chimney.

"I should like much to send all the rest after him," muttered the Professor, coming back with a relieved air.

Jo thought what a blaze her pile of papers upstairs would make, and her hard-earned money lay rather heavily on her conscience at that minute. Then she thought consolingly to herself, "Mine are not like that; they are only silly, never bad, so I won't be worried;" and taking up her book, she said, with a studious face—

"Shall we go on, sir? I'll be very good and proper now."

"I shall hope so," was all he said, but he meant more than she imagined; and the grave, kind look he gave her made her feel as if the words *Weekly Volcano* were printed in large type on her forehead.

As soon as she went to her room, she got out her papers, and carefully re-read every one of her stories. Being a little short-sighted, Mr. Bhaer sometimes used eye-glasses, and Jo had tried them once, smiling to see how they magnified the fine print of her book; now she seemed to have got on the Professor's mental or moral spectacles also; for the faults of these poor stories glared at her dreadfully, and filled her with dismay.

"They *are* trash, and will soon be worse than trash if I go on; for each is more sensational than the last. I've gone blindly on, hurting myself and other people, for the sake of money; I know it's so, for I can't read this stuff in sober earnest without being horribly ashamed of it; and what *should* I do if they were seen at home, or Mr. Bhaer got hold of them?"

Jo turned hot at the bare idea, and stuffed the whole bundle into her stove, nearly setting the chimney afire with the blaze.

Jo wrote no more sensational stories, deciding that the money did not pay for her share of the sensation; but, going to the other extreme, as is the way with people of her stamp, she took a course of Mrs. Sherwood, Miss Edgeworth, and Hannah More; and then produced a tale which might have been more properly called an essay or a sermon, so intensely moral was it. She had her doubts about it from the beginning; for her lively fancy and girlish romance felt as ill at ease in the new style as she would have done masquerading in the stiff and cumbrous costume of the last century. She sent this didactic gem to several markets, but it found no purchaser; and she was inclined to agree with Mr. Dashwood, that morals didn't sell.

Then she tried a child's story, which she could easily have disposed of if she had not been mercenary enough to demand filthy lucre for it. So nothing came of these trials; and Jo corked up her inkstand, and said, in a fit of very wholesome humility—

"I don't know anything; I'll wait till I do before I try again, and, meantime, 'sweep mud in the street,' if I can't do better; that's honest, at least;" which decision proved that her second tumble down the beanstalk had done her some good.

While these internal revolutions were going on, her external life had been as busy and uneventful as usual;

and if she sometimes looked serious or a little sad no one observed it but Professor Bhaer. He did it so quietly that Jo never knew he was watching to see if she would accept and profit by his reproof; but she stood the test, and he was satisfied; for, though no words passed between them, he knew that she had given up writing.

He helped her in many ways, proving himself a true friend, and Jo was happy; for, while her pen lay idle, she was learning other lessons beside German, and laying a foundation for the sensation story of her own life.

It was a pleasant winter and a long one, for she did not leave Mrs. Kirke till June. Every one seemed sorry when the time came; the children were inconsolable, and Mr. Bhaer's hair stuck straight up all over his head, for he always rumpled it wildly when disturbed in mind.

"Going home? Ah, you are happy that you haf a home to go in," he said, when she told him, and sat silently pulling his beard, in the corner, while she held a little levee on that last evening.

She was going early, so she bade them all good-bye overnight; and when his turn came, she said warmly—

"Now, sir, you won't forget to come and see us, if you ever travel our way, will you? I'll never forgive you if you do, for I want them all to know my friend."

"Do you? Shall I come?" he asked, looking down at her with an eager expression which she did not see.

"Yes, come next month; Laurie graduates then, and you'd enjoy Commencement as something new."

"That is your best friend, of whom you speak?" he said, in an altered tone.

"Yes, my boy Teddy; I'm very proud of him, and should like you to see him."

Jo looked up then, quite unconscious of anything

but her own pleasure in the prospect of showing them to one another. Something in Mr. Bhaer's face suddenly recalled the fact that she might find Laurie more than a "best friend," and, simply because she particularly wished not to look as if anything was the matter, she involuntarily began to blush; and the more she tried not to, the redder she grew. If it had not been for Tina on her knee, she didn't know what would have become of her. Fortunately, the child was moved to hug her; so she managed to hide her face an instant, hoping the Professor did not see it. But he did, and his own changed again from that momentary anxiety to its usual expression, as he said cordially—

"I fear I shall not make the time for that, but I wish the friend much success, and you all happiness. Gott bless you!" and with that, he shook hands warmly, shouldered Tina, and went away.

But after the boys were abed, he sat long before his fire, with the tired look on his face, and the "*heimweh,*" or homesickness, lying heavy at his heart. Once, when he remembered Jo, as she sat with the little child in her lap and that new softness in her face, he leaned his head on his hands a minute, and then roamed about the room, as if in search of something that he could not find.

"It is not for me; I must not hope it now," he said to himself, with a sigh that was almost a groan; then, as if reproaching himself for the longing that he could not repress, he went and kissed the two towsled heads upon the pillow, took down his seldom-used meerschaum, and opened his Plato.

He did his best, and did it manfully; but I don't think he found that a pair of rampant boys, a pipe, or even the divine Plato, were very satisfactory substitutes for wife and child and home.

Early as it was, he was at the station, next morning, to see Jo off; and, thanks to him, she began her solitary journey with the pleasant memory of a familiar face smiling its farewell, a bunch of violets to keep her company, and, best of all, the happy thought,—

"Well, the winter's gone, and I've written no books, earned no fortune; but I've made a friend worth having, and I'll try to keep him all my life."

CHAPTER TWELVE

HEARTACHE

WHATEVER his motive might have been, Laurie studied to some purpose that year, for he graduated with honour, and gave the Latin oration with the grace of a Phillips and the eloquence of a Demosthenes, so his friends said. They were all there, his grandfather —oh, so proud!—Mr. and Mrs. March, John and Meg, Jo and Beth, and all exulted over him with the sincere admiration which boys make light of at the time, but fail to win from the world by any after-triumphs.

"I've got to stay for this confounded supper, but I shall be home early to-morrow; you'll come and meet me as usual, girls?" Laurie said, as he put the sisters into the carriage after the joys of the day were over. He said "girls," but he meant Jo, for she was the only one who kept up the old custom; she had not the heart to refuse her splendid, successful boy anything, and answered warmly,—

"I'll come, Teddy, rain or shine, and march before

you, playing, *'Hail the conquering hero comes,'* on a jew's-harp."

Laurie thanked her with a look that made her think, in a sudden panic, "Oh, deary me! I know he'll say something, and then what shall I do?"

Evening meditation and morning work somewhat allayed her fears, and having decided that she wouldn't be vain enough to think people were going to propose when she had given them every reason to know what her answer would be, she set forth at the appointed time, hoping Teddy wouldn't do anything to make her hurt his poor little feelings.

"Where's the jew's-harp, Jo?" cried Laurie, as soon as he was within speaking distance.

"I forgot it;" and Jo took heart again, for that salutation could not be called lover-like.

She always used to take his arm on these occasions; now she did not, and he made no complaint, which was a bad sign, but talked on rapidly about all sorts of far-away subjects, till they turned from the road into the little path that led homeward through the grove. Then he walked more slowly, suddenly lost his fine flow of language, and, now and then, a dreadful pause occurred. To rescue the conversation from one of the wells of silence into which it kept falling, Jo said hastily,—

"Now you must have a good long holiday!"

"I intend to."

Something in his resolute tone made Jo look up quickly to find him looking down at her with an expression that assured her the dreaded moment had come, and made her put out her hand with an imploring,—

"No, Teddy, please don't!"

"I will, and you *must* hear me. It's no use Jo; we've got to have it out, and the sooner the better for both of us," he answered, getting flushed and excited all at once.

"Say what you like, then; I'll listen," said Jo, with a desperate sort of patience.

Laurie was a young lover, but he was in earnest, and meant to "have it out," if he died in the attempt; so he plunged into the subject with characteristic impetuosity, saying in a voice that *would* get choky now and then, in spite of manful efforts to keep it steady,—

"I've loved you ever since I've known you, Jo; couldn't help it, you've been so good to me. I've tried to show it, but you wouldn't let me; now I'm going to make you hear, and give me an answer, for I *can't* go on so any longer."

"I never wanted to make you care for me so, and I went away to keep you from it if I could."

"I thought so; it was like you, but it was no use. I only loved you all the more, and I worked hard to please you, and I gave up billiards and everything you didn't like, and waited and never complained, for I hoped you'd love me, though I'm not half good enough—" here there was a choke that couldn't be controlled, so he decapitated buttercups while he cleared his "confounded throat."

"Yes, you are; you're a great deal too good for me, and I'm so grateful to you, and so proud and fond of you, I don't see why I can't love you as you want me to. I've tried, but I can't change the feeling, and it would be a lie to say I do when I don't."

They were in the grove now, close by the stile; and when the last words fell reluctantly from Jo's lips, Laurie dropped her hands and turned as if to go on, but for once in his life that fence was too much for him; so he just laid his head down on the mossy post, and stood so still that Jo was frightened.

"O Teddy, I'm so sorry, so desperately sorry, I could kill myself if it would do any good! I wish you wouldn't take it so hard. I can't help it; you know its impossible for people to make themselves love other people if they don't," cried Jo inelegantly but remorsefully, as she softly patted his shoulder, remembering the time when he had comforted her so long ago.

"They do sometimes," said a muffled voice from the post.

"I don't believe it's the right sort of love, and I'd rather not try it," was the decided answer.

There was a long pause, while a blackbird sung blithely on the willow by the river, and the tall grass rustled in the wind. Presently Jo said very soberly, as she sat down on the step of the stile,—

"I agree with mother that you and I are not suited to each other, because our quick tempers and strong wills would probably make us very miserable, if we were so foolish as to—" Jo paused a little over the last word, but Laurie uttered it with a rapturous expression,—

"Marry—no, we shouldn't! If you loved me, Jo, I should be a perfect saint, for you could make me anything you like."

"No, I can't. I've tried it and failed, and I won't risk our happiness by such a serious experiment. We don't agree and we never shall; so we'll be good friends all our lives, but we won't go and do anything rash."

"Yes, we will if we get the chance," muttered Laurie rebelliously.

"Now do be reasonable, and take a sensible view of the case," implored Jo, almost at her wit's end.

"I won't be reasonable; I don't want to take what you call 'a sensible view;' it won't help me, and it only makes you harder. I don't believe you've got any heart."

"I wish I hadn't."

There was a little quiver in Jo's voice, and, thinking it a good omen, Laurie turned round, bringing all his persuasive powers to bear as he said, in the wheedlesome tone that had never been so dangerously wheedlesome before,—

"Don't disappoint us, dear! Every one expects it. Grandpa has set his heart upon it, your people like it, and I can't get on without you. Say you will, and let's be happy. Do, do!"

Not until months afterward did Jo understand how she had the strength of mind to hold fast to the resolution she had made when she decided that she did not love her boy, and never could. It was very hard to do, but she did it, knowing that delay was both useless and cruel.

"I can't say 'Yes' truly, so I won't say it at all. You'll see that I'm right, by-and-by, and thank me for it"—she began solemnly.

"I'll be hanged if I do!" and Laurie bounced up off the grass, burning with indignation at the bare idea.

"Yes, you will!" persisted Jo; "you'll get over this after a while, and find some lovely, accomplished girl, who will adore you, and make a fine mistress for your fine house. I shouldn't. I'm homely and awkward and odd and old, and you'd be ashamed of me, and we should quarrel—we can't help it even now, you see—and I shouldn't like elegant society and you would, and you'd hate my scribbling, and I couldn't get on without it, and we should be unhappy, and wish we hadn't done it, and everything would be horrid!"

"Anything more?" asked Laurie, finding it hard to listen patiently to this prophetic burst.

"Nothing more, except that I don't believe I shall ever marry. I'm happy as I am, and love my liberty too well to be in any hurry to give it up for any mortal man."

"I know better!" broke in Laurie. "You think so now; but there'll come a time when you *will* care for somebody, and you'll love him tremendously, and live and die for him. I know you will, it's your way, and I shall have to stand by and see it;" and the despairing lover cast his hat upon the ground with a gesture that would have seemed comical, if his face had not been so tragical.

"Yes, I *will* live and die for him, if he ever comes and makes me love him in spite of myself. and you must do the best you can!" cried Jo, losing patience with poor Teddy. "I've done my best, but you *won't* be reasonable, and it's selfish of you to keep teasing for what I can't give. I shall always be fond of you, very fond indeed, as a friend, but I'll never marry you; and the sooner you believe it, the better for both of us—so now!"

That speech was like fire to gunpowder. Laurie looked at her a minute as if he did not quite know what to do with himself, then turned sharply away, saying, in a desperate sort of tone,—

"You'll be sorry some day, Jo."

"Oh, where are you going?" she cried, for his face frightened her.

"To the devil!" was the consoling answer.

For a minute Jo's heart stood still, as he swung himself down the bank, toward the river; but it takes much folly, sin, or misery to send a young man to a violent death, and Laurie was not one of the weak sort who are conquered by a single failure. He had no thought of a melodramatic plunge, but some blind instinct led him to fling hat and coat into his boat, and row away with all his might, making better time up the river than he had done in many a race. Jo drew a long breath and unclasped her hands as she watched the poor fellow trying to outstrip the trouble which he carried in his heart.

"Now I must go and prepare Mr. Laurence to be very kind to my poor boy. I wish he'd love Beth; perhaps he may, in time, but I begin to think I was mistaken about her. Oh dear! how can girls like to have lovers and refuse them. I think it's dreadful."

Being sure that no one could do it so well as herself, she went straight to Mr. Laurence, told the hard story bravely through, and then broke down, crying so dismally over her own insensibility that the kind old gentleman, though sorely disappointed, did not utter a reproach.

When Laurie came home, dead tired, but quite composed, his grandfather met him as if he knew nothing, and kept up the delusion very successfully for an hour or two. But when they sat together in the twilight, the time they used to enjoy so much, it was hard work for the old man to ramble on as usual, and harder still for the young one to listen to praises of the last year's success which to him now seemed love's labour lost. He bore it long as he could, then went to his piano, and began to play. The windows were open; and Jo, walking in the garden with Beth, for once understood music better than her sister, for he played the "Sonata Pathétique," and played it as he never did before.

"That's very fine, I dare say, but it's sad enough to make one cry; give us something gayer, lad," said Mr. Laurence, whose kind old heart was full of sympathy, which he longed to show, but knew not how.

Laurie dashed into a livelier strain, played stormily

for several minutes, and would have got through bravely, if in a momentary lull, Mrs. March's voice had not been heard calling,—

"Jo, dear, come in; I want you."

Just what Laurie longed to say, with a different meaning! As he listened, he lost his place; the music ended with a broken chord, and the musician sat silent in the dark.

"I can't stand this," muttered the old gentleman. Up he got, groped his way to the piano, laid a kind hand on either of the broad shoulders, and said, as gently as a woman,—

"I know, my boy, I know."

No answer for an instant; then Laurie asked sharply,—

"Who told you?"

"Jo herself."

"Then there's an end of it!" and he shook off his grandfather's hands with an impatient motion; for, though grateful for the sympathy, his man's pride could not bear a man's pity.

"Not quite; I want to say one thing, and then there shall be an end of it," returned Mr. Laurence, with unusual mildness. "You won't care to stay at home just now, perhaps?"

"I don't intend to run away from a girl. Jo can't prevent my seeing her, and I shall stay and do it as long as I like," interrupted Laurie, in a defiant tone.

"Not if you are the gentleman I think you. I'm disappointed, but the girl can't help it; and the only thing left for you to do is to go away for a time. Where will you go?"

"Anywhere. I don't care what becomes of me;" and Laurie got up, with a reckless laugh, that grated on his grandfather's ear.

"Take it like a man, and don't do anything rash,

for God's sake. Why not go abroad, as you planned, and forget it?"

"I can't."

"But you've been wild to go, and I promised you should when you got through college."

"Ah, but I didn't mean to go alone!" and Laurie walked fast through the room, with an expression which it was well his grandfather did not see.

"I don't ask you to go alone; there's some one ready and glad to go with you, anywhere in the world."

"Who, sir?" stopping to listen.

"Myself."

Laurie came back as quickly as he went, and put out his hand, saying huskily—

"I'm a selfish brute; but—you know—grandfather ——"

"There is business in London that needs looking after; I meant you should attend to it; but I can do it better myself, and things here will get on very well with Brooke to manage them."

"But you hate travelling, sir; I can't ask it of you at your age," began Laurie, who was grateful for the sacrifice, but much preferred to go alone, if he went at all.

The old gentleman knew that perfectly well, and particularly desired to prevent it; for the mood in which he found his grandson assured him that it would not be wise to leave him to his own devices. So, stifling a natural regret at the thought of the home comforts he would leave behind him, he said stoutly—

"Bless your soul, I'm not superannuated yet. I quite enjoy the idea; it will do me good, and my old bones won't suffer, for travelling nowadays is almost as easy as sitting in a chair."

A restless movement from Laurie suggested that *his*

chair was not easy, or that he did not like the plan, and made the old man add hastily—

"I don't mean to be a marplot or a burden; I go because I think you'd feel happier than if I was left behind. I don't intend to gad about with you, but leave you free to go where you like, while I amuse myself in my own way. I've friends in London and Paris, and should like to visit them; meantime you can go to Italy, Germany, Switzerland, where you will, and enjoy pictures, music, scenery, and adventures to your heart's content."

Now, Laurie felt just then that his heart was entirely broken, and the world a howling wilderness; but at the sound of certain words which the old gentleman artfully introduced into his closing sentence, the broken heart gave an unexpected leap, and a green oasis or two suddenly appeared in the howling wilderness.

When the parting came he affected high spirits, to conceal certain inconvenient emotions which seemed inclined to assert themselves. This gaiety did not impose upon anybody, but they tried to look as if it did, for his sake, and he got on very well till Mrs. March kissed him, with a whisper full of motherly solicitude; then, feeling that he was going very fast, he hastily embraced them all round, not forgetting the afflicted Hannah, and ran downstairs as if for his life. Jo followed a minute after to wave her hand to him if he looked round. He did look round, came back, put his arms about her, as she stood on the step above him, and looked up at her with a face that made his short appeal both eloquent and pathetic.

"O Jo, can't you?"

"Teddy, dear, I wish I could!"

That was all, except a little pause; then Laurie straightened himself up, and said, "It's all right, never mind," and went away without another word. Ah, but it wasn't all right, and Jo *did* mind; for while the curly head lay on her arm a minute after her hard answer, she felt as if she had stabbed her dearest friend; and when he left her without a look behind him, she knew that the boy Laurie never would come again.

CHAPTER THIRTEEN

BETH'S SECRET

WHEN Jo came home that spring, she had been struck with the change in Beth. No one spoke of it or seemed aware of it, for it had come too gradually to startle those who saw her daily; but to eyes sharpened by absence, it was very plain; and a heavy weight fell on Jo's heart as she saw her sister's face. Jo saw and felt it, but said nothing at the time, and soon the first impression lost much of its power; for Beth seemed happy, no one appeared to doubt that she was better; and, presently, in other cares, Jo for a time forgot her fear.

But when Laurie was gone, and peace prevailed again, the vague anxiety returned and haunted her. She had confessed her sins and been forgiven; but when she showed her savings and proposed the mountain trip, Beth had thanked her heartily, but begged not to go so far away from home. Another little visit to the seashore would suit her better, and, as grandma could not be prevailed upon to leave the babies, Jo took Beth down to the quiet place, where she could live much in the open air, and let the fresh sea-breezes blow a little colour into her pale cheeks.

It was not a fashionable place, but, even among the pleasant people there, the girls made few friends, preferring to live for one another. Beth was too shy to enjoy society, and Jo too wrapped up in her to care for any one else; so they were all in all to each other, and came and went, quite unconscious of the interest they excited in those about them, who watched with sympathetic eyes the strong sister and the feeble one, always together, as if they felt instinctively that a long separation was not far away.

They did feel it, yet neither spoke of it; for often between ourselves and those nearest and dearest to us there exists a reserve which it is very hard to overcome. Jo felt as if a veil had fallen between her heart and Beth's; but when she put out her hand to lift it up, there seemed something sacred in the silence, and she waited for Beth to speak. She wondered, and was thankful also, that her parents did not seem to see what she saw; and, during the quiet weeks, when the shadow grew so plain to her, she said nothing of it to those at home, believing that it would tell itself when Beth came back no better. She wondered still more if her sister really guessed the hard truth, and what thoughts were passing through her mind during the long hours when she lay on the warm rocks, with her head in Jo's lap, while the winds blew healthfully over her, and the sea made music at her feet.

One day Beth told her. Jo thought she was asleep, she lay so still; and, putting down her book, sat looking at her with wistful eyes, trying to see signs of hope in the faint colour on Beth's cheeks. But she could not find enough to satisfy her, for the cheeks were very thin, and the hands seemed too feeble to hold even the rosy little shells they had been gathering. It came to her then more bitterly than ever that Beth was slowly drifting away from her, and her arms instinctively tightened their hold upon the dearest treasure she possessed. For a minute her eyes were too dim for seeing, and, when they cleared, Beth was looking up at her so tenderly that there was hardly any need for her to say—

"Jo, dear, I'm glad you know it. I've tried to tell you, but I couldn't."

There was no answer except her sister's cheek against her own, not even tears; for when most deeply moved, Jo did not cry. She was the weaker, then, and Beth tried to comfort and sustain her, with her arms about her, and the soothing words she whispered in her ear.

"I've known it for a good while, dear, and, now I'm used to it, it isn't hard to think of or to bear. Try to see it so, and don't be troubled about me, because it's best; indeed it is."

"O Beth, and you didn't tell me, didn't let me comfort and help you! How could you shut me out, and bear it all alone?"

Jo's voice was full of tender reproach, and her heart ached to think of the solitary struggle that must have gone on while Beth learned to say goodbye to health, love, and life, and take up her cross so cheerfully.

"Perhaps it was wrong, but I tried to do right; I wasn't sure, no one said anything, and I hoped I was mistaken. It would have been selfish to frighten you all when Marmee was so anxious about Meg, and Amy away, and you so happy with Laurie—at least, I thought so then."

"And I thought that you loved him, Beth, and I went away because I couldn't," cried Jo, glad to say all the truth.

Beth looked so amazed at the idea that Jo smiled in spite of her pain, and added softly—

"Then you didn't, deary? I was afraid it was so, and

imagined your poor little heart full of love-lornity all that while."

"Why, Jo, how could I, when he was so fond of you?" asked Beth, as innocently as a child. "I do love him dearly; he is so good to me, how can I help it? But he never could be anything to me but my brother. I hope he truly will be, sometime."

"Not through me," said Jo decidedly. "Amy is left for him, and they would suit excellently; but I have no heart for such things, now. I don't care what becomes of anybody but you, Beth. You *must* get well."

"I want to, oh, so much! I try, but every day I lose a little, and feel more sure that I shall never gain it back. It's like the tide, Jo, when it turns, it goes slowly, but it can't be stopped."

"It *shall* be stopped, your tide must not turn so soon, nineteen is too young. Beth, I can't let you go. I'll work and pray and fight against it. I'll keep you in spite of everything; there must be ways, it can't be too late. God won't be so cruel as to take you from me," cried poor Jo rebelliously, for her spirit was far less piously submissive than Beth's.

By-and-by Beth said, with recovered serenity—

"You'll tell them this when we go home?"

"I think they will see it without words," sighed Jo; for now it seemed to her that Beth changed every day.

"Perhaps not; I've heard that the people who love best are often blindest to such things. If they don't see it, you will tell them for me. I don't want any secrets, and it's kinder to prepare them. Meg has John and the babies to comfort her, but you must stand by Father and Mother, won't you, Jo?"

"If I can; but, Beth, I don't give up yet; I'm going to believe that it *is* a sick fancy, and not let you think it's true," said Jo, trying to speak cheerfully.

"Jo, dear, don't hope any more; it won't do any

good, I'm sure of that. We won't be miserable, but enjoy being together while we wait. We'll have happy times, for I don't suffer much, and I think the tide will go out easily, if you help me."

Jo leaned down to kiss the tranquil face; and with that silent kiss she dedicated herself soul and body to Beth.

She was right: there was no need of any words when they got home, for father and mother saw plainly, now, what they had prayed to be saved from seeing. Tired with her short journey, Beth went at once to bed saying how glad she was to be at home; and when Jo went down, she found that she would be spared the hard task of telling Beth's secret. Her father stood leaning his head on the mantelpiece, and did not turn as she came in; but her mother stretched out her arms as if for help, and Jo went to comfort her without a word.

CHAPTER FOURTEEN

NEW IMPRESSIONS

AT three o'clock in the afternoon, all the fashionable world at Nice may be seen on the Promenade des Anglais—a charming place; for the wide walk, bordered with palms, flowers, and tropical shrubs, is bounded on one side by the sea, on the other by the grand drive, lined with hotels and villas, while beyond lie orange-orchards and the hills.

Along this walk, on Christmas Day, a tall young man walked slowly, with his hands behind him, and a somewhat absent expression of countenance. There were plenty of pretty faces to admire, but the young man took little notice of them, except to glance, now and then, at some blonde girl, or lady in blue. Presently he strolled out of the promenade and stood a moment at the crossing, as if undecided whether to go and listen to the band in the Jardin Publique, or to wander along the beach toward Castle Hill. The quick trot of ponies' feet made him look up, as one of the little carriages, containing a single lady, came rapidly down the street. The lady was young, blonde, and dressed in blue. He stared a minute, then his whole face woke up, and waving his hat like a boy, he hurried forward to meet her.

"O Laurie, is it really you? I thought you'd never come!" cried Amy, dropping the reins, and holding out both hands, to the great scandalisation of a French mamma, who hastened her daughter's steps, lest she should be demoralised by beholding the free manners of these "mad English."

"I was detained by the way, but I promised to spend Christmas with you, and here I am."

"I have so much to say, I don't know where to begin! Get in, and we can talk at our ease; I was going for a drive, and longing for company. Flo's saving up for tonight."

"What happens then, a ball?"

"A Christmas party at our hotel. There are many Americans there, and they give it in honour of the day. You'll go with us, of course? Aunt will be charmed."

"Thank you. Where now?" asked Laurie, leaning back and folding his arms, a proceeding which suited Amy, who preferred to drive; for her parasol-whip and blue reins over the white ponies' backs, afforded her infinite satisfaction.

"I'm going to the banker's first, for letters, and then to Castle Hill; the view is so lovely, and I like to feed the peacocks. Have you ever been there?"

"Often, years ago; but I don't mind having a look at it. Dirty old hole, isn't it?" he added, with a look of disgust, as they drove along the boulevard to the Place Napoleon, in the old city.

"The dirt is picturesque, so I don't mind. The river and the hills are delicious, and these glimpses of the narrow cross-streets are my delight. Now we shall have to wait for that procession to pass; it's going to the Church of St. John."

While Laurie listlessly watched the procession of priests under their canopies, white-veiled nuns bearing lighted tapers, and some brotherhood in blue, chanting as they walked, Amy watched him, and felt a new sort of shyness steal over her; for he was changed, and she could not find the merry-faced boy she left in the moody-looking man beside her. He was handsomer than ever, and greatly improved, she thought; but now that the flush of pleasure at meeting her was over, he looked tired and spiritless—not sick, nor exactly unhappy, but older and graver than a year or two of prosperous life should have made him.

"*Que pensez vous?*" she said, airing her French, which had improved in quantity, if not in quality, since she came abroad.

"That mademoiselle has made good use of her time, and the result is charming," replied Laurie, bowing, with his hand on his heart, and an admiring look.

She blushed with pleasure, but somehow the compliment did not satisfy her like the blunt praises he used to give her at home, when he promenaded round her on festival occasions, and told her she was "altogether jolly," with a hearty smile and an approving pat on the head. She didn't like the new tone; for, though not *blasé,* it sounded indifferent in spite of the look.

"If that's the way he's going to grow up, I wish he'd

stay a boy," she thought, with a curious sense of disappointment and discomfort, trying meantime to seem quite easy and gay.

At Avigdor's she found the precious home-letters, and, giving the reins to Laurie, read them luxuriously as they wound up the shady road between green hedges, where tea-roses bloomed as freshly as in June.

"Beth is very poorly, Mother says. I often think I ought to go home, but they all say 'stay;' so I do, for I shall never have another chance like this," said Amy, looking sober over one page.

"I think you are right, there; you could do nothing at home, and it is a great comfort to them to know that you are well and happy, and enjoying so much, my dear."

He drew a little nearer, and looked more like his old self, as he said that; and the fear that sometimes weighed on Amy's heart was lightened, for the look, the act, the brotherly "my dear," seemed to assure her that if any trouble did come, she would not be alone in a strange land. Presently she laughed, and showed him a small sketch of Jo in her scribbling-suit, with the bow rampantly erect upon her cap, and issuing from her mouth the words, "Genius burns!"

Laurie smiled, took it, put it in his vest-pocket, "to keep it from blowing away," and listened with interest to the lively letter Amy read him.

"This will be a regularly merry Christmas to me, with presents in the morning, you and letters in the afternoon, and a party at night," said Amy, as they alighted among the ruins of the old fort, and a flock of splendid peacocks came trooping about them, tamely waiting to be fed. While Amy stood laughing on the bank above him as she scattered crumbs to the brilliant birds, Laurie looked at her as she had looked at him, with a natural curiosity to see what changes time and absence had wrought. He found nothing to perplex or disappoint, much to admire and approve; for, overlooking a few little affectations of speech and manner, she was as sprightly and graceful as ever, with the addition of that indescribable something in dress and bearing which we call elegance.

As they came up on to the stone plateau that crowns the hill, Amy waved her hand as if welcoming him to her favourite haunt, and said, pointing here and there—

"Do you remember the Cathedral and the Corso, the fishermen dragging their nets in the bay, and the lovely road to Villa Franca, Schubert's Tower, just below, and, best of all, that speck far out to sea which they say is Corsica?"

"I remember; it's not much changed," he answered, without enthusiasm.

"What Jo would give for a sight of that famous speck?" said Amy, feeling in good spirits, and anxious to see him so also. "Take a good look at it for her sake, and then come and tell me what you have been doing with yourself all this while," said Amy, seating herself, ready for a good talk.

But she did not get it; for, though he joined her, and answered all her questions freely, she could only learn that he had roved about the Continent and been to Greece. So, after idling away an hour, they drove home again; and, having paid his respects to Mrs. Carrol, Laurie left them, promising to return in the evening.

It must be recorded of Amy that she deliberately "prinked" that night. Time and absence had done its work on both the young people; she had seen her old friend in a new light; not as "our boy," but as a handsome and agreeable man, and she was conscious of a very natural desire to find favour in his sight.

Amy knew her good points, and made the most of them, with the taste and skill which is a fortune to a poor and pretty woman.

"I do want him to think I look well, and tell them so at home," said Amy to herself, as she put on Flo's old white silk ball-dress, and covered it with a cloud of fresh illusion, out of which her white shoulders and golden head emerged with a most artistic effect. Her hair she had the sense to let alone, after gathering up the thick waves and curls into a Hebe-like knot at the back of her head

Having no ornaments fine enough for this important occasion, Amy looped her fleecy skirts with rosy clusters of azalea, and framed the white shoulders in delicate green vines. Remembering the painted boots, she surveyed her white satin slippers with girlish satisfaction, and *chasséed* down the room, admiring her aristocratic feet all by herself.

"My new fan just matches my flowers, my gloves fit to a charm, and the real lace on Aunt's *mouchoir* gives an air to my whole dress. If I only had a classical nose and mouth I should be perfectly happy," she said surveying herself with a critical eye, and a candle in each hand.

In spite of this affliction, she looked unusually gay and graceful as she glided away; she seldom ran—it did not suit her style, she thought, for, being tall, the stately and Junoesque was more appropriate than the sportive or piquante. She walked up and down the long saloon while waiting for Laurie, and once arranged herself under the chandelier, which had a good effect upon her hair; then she thought better of it, and went away to the other end of the room, as if ashamed of the girlish desire to have the first view a propitious one. It so happened that she could not have done a better thing, for Laurie came in so quietly she did not hear him; and, as she stood at the distant window, with her head half turned, and one hand gathering up her dress, the slender, white figure against the red curtains was as effective as a well-placed statue.

"Good evening, Diana!" said Laurie, with the look of satisfaction she liked to see in his eyes when they rested on her.

"Good evening, Apollo!" she answered, smiling back at him, for he, too, looked unusually *debonnaire*, and the thought of entering the ball-room on the arm of such a personable man caused Amy to pity the four plain Misses Davis from the bottom of her heart.

"Here are your flowers; I arranged them myself, remembering that you didn't like what Hannah calls a 'sot-bookay'," said Laurie, handing her a delicate nosegay, in a holder that she had long coveted as she daily passed it in Cardiglia's window.

"How kind you are!" she exclaimed gratefully. "If I'd known you were coming I'd have had something ready for you today, though not as pretty as this, I'm afraid."

"Thank you; it isn't what it should be, but you have improved it," he added, as she snapped the silver bracelet on her wrist.

"Please don't."

"I thought you liked that sort of thing?"

"Not from you; it doesn't sound natural, and I like your old bluntness better."

"I'm glad of it," he answered, with a look of relief; then buttoned her gloves for her, and asked if his tie was straight, just as he used to do when they went to parties together, at home.

Any young girl can imagine Amy's state of mind when she "took the stage" that night, leaning on Laurie's arm. She knew she looked well, she loved to dance, she felt that her foot was on her native heath in a ball-room, and enjoyed the delightful sense of power which comes when young girls first discover the new and lovely kingdom they are born to rule by virtue of beauty, youth, and womanhood. She did pity the Davis girls, who were awkward, plain, and destitute of escort, except a grim papa and three grimmer maiden aunts, and she bowed to them in her friendliest manner as she passed; which was good of her, as it permitted them to see her dress, and burn with curiosity to know who her distinguished-looking friend might be. With the first burst of the band Amy's colour rose, her eyes began to sparkle, and her feet to tap the floor impatiently; for she danced well, and wanted Laurie to know it: therefore the shock she received can better be imagined than described, when he said, in a perfectly tranquil tone—

"Do you care to dance?"

"One usually does at a ball."

Her amazed look and quick answer caused Laurie to repair his error as fast as possible.

"I meant the first dance. May I have the honour?"

"I can give you one if I put off the Count. He dances divinely; but he will excuse me, as you are an old friend," said Amy, hoping that the name would have a good effect, and show Laurie that she was not to be trifled with.

"Nice little boy, but rather a short Pole to support

" 'A daughter of the gods,
Divinely tall, and most divinely fair',"

was all the satisfaction she got, however.

The set in which they found themselves was composed of English, and Amy was compelled to walk decorously through a cotillon, feeling all the while as if she could dance the Tarantula with a relish. Laurie resigned her to the "nice little boy," and went to do his duty to Flo, without securing Amy for the joys to come, which reprehensible want of forethought was properly punished, for she immediately engaged herself till supper, meaning to relent if he then gave any signs of penitence. She showed him her ball-book with demure satisfaction when he strolled, instead of rushing, up to claim her for the next, a glorious polka-redowa; but his polite regrets didn't impose upon her, and when she gallopaded away with the Count, she saw Laurie sit down by her aunt with an actual expression of relief.

That was unpardonable; and Amy took no more notice of him for a long while, except a word now and then, when she came to her chaperon, between the dances, for a necessary pin or a moment's rest. Her anger had a good effect, however, for she hid it under a smiling face, and seemed unusually blithe and brilliant. Laurie's eyes followed her with pleasure, for she neither romped nor sauntered, but danced with spirit and grace, making the delightsome pastime what it should be. He very naturally fell to studying her from this new point of view; and, before the evening was half over, had decided that "little Amy was going to make a very charming woman."

Amy and her Pole distinguished themselves; and Laurie found himself involuntarily keeping time to the rhythmic rise and fall of the white slippers as they flew by as indefatigably as if winged. When little Vladimir finally relinquished her, with assurances that he was "desolated to leave so early," she was ready to rest, and see how her recreant knight had borne his punishment.

It had been successful; for, at three-and-twenty, blighted affections find a balm in friendly society, and young nerves will thrill, young blood dance, and healthy young spirits rise, when subjected to the enchantment of beauty, light, music, and motion. Laurie had a waked-up look as he rose to give her his seat; and when he hurried away to bring her some supper, she said to herself, with a satisfied smile—

"Ah, I thought that would do him good!"

"You look like Balzac's 'Femme peinte par elle-même'," he said, as he fanned her with one hand, and held her coffee-cup in the other.

"My rouge won't come off;" and Amy rubbed her brilliant cheek, and showed him her white glove with a sober simplicity that made him laugh outright.

"What do you call this stuff?" he asked, touching a fold of her dress that had blown over his knee.

"Illusion."

"Good name for it; it's very pretty—new thing, isn't it?"

"It's as old as the hills; you have seen it on dozens of girls, and you never found out that it was pretty till now—*stupide!*"

"I never saw it on you before, which accounts for the mistake, you see."

"None of that, it is forbidden; I'd rather take coffee than compliments just now. No, don't lounge, it makes me nervous."

Laurie sat bolt upright, and meekly took her empty plate, feeling an odd sort of pleasure in having "little Amy" order him about; for she had lost her shyness now, and felt an irresistible desire to trample on him, as girls have a delightful way of doing when lords of creation show any signs of subjection.

"Where did you learn all this sort of thing?" he asked, with a quizzical look.

"As 'this sort of thing' is rather a vague expression, would you kindly explain?" returned Amy, knowing perfectly well what he meant, but wickedly leaving him to describe what is indescribable.

"Well—the general air, the style, the self-possession, the—the—illusion—you know," laughed Laurie, breaking down, and helping himself out of his quandary with the new word.

Amy was gratified, but, of course, didn't show it, and demurely answered, "Foreign life polishes one in spite of one's self; I study as well as play; and as for this"—with a little gesture toward her dress—"why, tulle is cheap, posies to be had for nothing, and I am used to making the most of my poor little things."

Amy rather regretted that last sentence, fearing it wasn't in good taste; but Laurie liked her the better for it, and found himself both admiring and respecting the brave patience that made the most of opportunity, and the cheerful spirit that covered poverty with flowers. Amy did not know why he looked at her so kindly, nor why he filled up her book with his own name, and devoted himself to her for the rest of the evening, in the most delightful manner; but the impulse that wrought this agreeable change was the result of one of the new impressions which both of them were unconsciously giving and receiving.

CHAPTER FIFTEEN

ON THE SHELF

In France the young girls have a dull time of it till they are married, when *"Vive la liberte"* becomes their motto. In America, as every one knows, girls early sign the declaration of independence, and enjoy their freedom with republican zest; but the young matrons usually abdicate with the first heir to the throne, and go into a seclusion almost as close as a French nunnery, though by no means as quiet.

Not being a belle or even a fashionable lady, Meg did not experience this affliction till her babies were a year old, for in her little world primitive customs prevailed, and she found herself more admired and beloved than ever.

As she was a womanly little woman, the maternal instinct was very strong, and she was entirely absorbed in her children, to the utter exclusion of everything and everybody else. Being a domestic man, John decidedly missed the wifely attentions he had been accustomed to receive; but, as he adored his babies, he cheerfully relinquished his comfort for a time, supposing, with masculine ignorance, that peace would soon be restored. When he went out in the morning he was bewildered by small commissions for the captive mamma; if he came gaily in at night, eager to embrace his family, he was quenched by a "Hush! They are just asleep after worrying all day." If he proposed a little amusement at home, "No, it would disturb the babies." If he hinted at a lecture or concert, he was answered with a reproachful look, and a decided "Leave my children for pleasure, never!" His sleep was broken by infant wails and visions of a phantom figure pacing noiselessly to and fro in the watches of the night; his meals were interrupted by the frequent flight of the presiding genius, who deserted him, half-helped, if a muffled chirp sounded from the nest above; and when he read his paper of an evening, Demi's colic got into the shipping-list, and Daisy's fall affected the price of stocks, for Mrs. Brooke was only interested in domestic news.

The poor man was very uncomfortable, for the children had bereft him of his wife; home was merely a nursery, and the perpetual "hushing" made him feel like a brutal intruder whenever he entered the secret precincts of Babyland. He bore it very patiently for six months, and, when no signs of amendment appeared, he did what other paternal exiles do—tried to get a little comfort elsewhere. Scott had married and gone to house-keeping not far off, and John fell into the way of running over for an hour or two of an evening, when his own parlour was emptly, and his own wife singing lullabies that seemed to have no end.

Meg rather approved of the new arrangement at first, and found it a relief to know that John was having a good time instead of dozing in the parlour, or tramping about the house and waking the children. But by-and-by, when the teething worry was over, and the idols went to sleep at proper hours, leaving mamma time to rest, she began to miss John, and find her work-basket dull company, when he was not sitting opposite in his old dressing-gown, comfortably scorching his slippers on the fender. She would not ask him to stay at home, but felt injured because he did not know that she wanted him without being told, entirely forgetting the many evenings he had waited for her in vain. She was nervous and worn out with watching and worry, and in that unreasonable frame of mind which the best of mother occasionally experience when domestic cares oppress them.

"Yes," she would say, looking in the glass, "I'm getting old and ugly; John doesn't find me interesting any longer, so he leaves his faded wife and goes to see his pretty neighbour, who has no incumbrances. Well, the babies love me; they don't care if I am thin and pale, and haven't time to crimp my hair; they are my comfort, and some day John will see what I've gladly sacrificed for them, won't he, my precious?"

But the pain increased as politics absorbed John, who was always running over to discuss interesting points with Scott, quite unconscious that Meg missed him. Not a word did she say. however, till her mother found her in tears one day, and insisted on knowing what the matter was, for Meg's drooping spirits had not escaped her observation.

"I wouldn't tell any one except you, Mother; but I really do need advice, for, if John goes on so much longer I might as well be widowed," replied Mrs. Brooke, drying her tears on Daisy's bib, with an injured air.

"Goes on how, my dear?" asked her mother anxiously.

"He's away all day, and at night, when I want to see him, he is continually going over to the Scotts'. It isn't fair that I should have the hardest work, and never any amusement. Men are very selfish, even the best of them."

"So are women; don't blame John till you see where you are wrong yourself."

"But it can't be right for him to neglect me."

"Don't you neglect him?"

"Why Mother, I thought you'd take my part!"

"So I do, as far as sympathising goes; but I think the fault is yours, Meg."

"I don't see how."

"Let me show you. Did John ever neglect you, as you call it, while you made it a point to give him your society of an evening, his only leisure time?"

"No; but I can't do it now, with two babies to tend."

"I think you could, dear; and I think you ought. May I speak quite freely, and will you remember that it's mother who blames as well as mother who sympathises?"

"Indeed I will! Speak to me as if I were little Meg again. I often feel as if I needed teaching more than ever since these babies look to me for everything."

Meg drew her low chair beside her mother's, and, with a little interruption in either lap, the two women rocked and talked lovingly together, feeling that the tie of motherhood made them more one than ever.

"You have only made the mistake that most young wives make—forgotten your duty to your husband in your love for your children. A very natural and forgivable mistake, Meg, but one that had better be remedied before you take to different ways; for children should draw you nearer than ever, not separate you, as if they were all yours, and John had nothing to do but support them. I've seen it for some weeks, but have not spoken, feeling sure it would come right in time."

"I'm afraid it won't. If I ask him to stay, he'll think I'm jealous; and I wouldn't insult him by such an idea. He doesn't see that I want him, and I don't know how to tell him without words."

"Make it so pleasant he won't want to go away. My dear, he's longing for his little home; but it isn't home without you and you are always in the nursery."

"Oughtn't I to be there?"

"Not all the time; too much confinement makes you nervous, and then you are unfitted for everything. Besides, you owe something to John as well as to the babies; don't neglect husband for children, don't shut him out of the nursery, but teach him how to help in it."

"You really think so, Mother?"

"I know it, Meg, for I've tried it; and I seldom give advice unless I've proved its practicability."

"It is so, Mother; and my great wish is to be to my husband and children what you have been to yours. Show me how; I'll do anything you say."

"You always were my docile daughter. Well, dear, if I were you, I'd let John have more to do with the management of Demi, for the boy needs training, and it's none too soon to begin. Then I'd do what I have often proposed, let Hannah come and help you; she is a capital nurse, and you may trust the precious babies to her while you do more housework. You need the exercise, Hannah would enjoy the rest, and John would find his wife again. Go out more; keep cheerful as well as busy, for you are the sunshine-maker of the family, and if you get dismal there is no fair weather. Then I'd try to take an interest in whatever John likes—talk with him, let him read to you, exchange ideas, and help each other in that way. Don't shut yourself up in a bandbox because you are a woman, but understand what is going on, and educate yourself to take your part in the world's work, for it all affects you and yours."

"I will. Poor John! I'm afraid I *have* neglected him sadly, but I thought I was right, and he never said anything."

"He tried not to be selfish, but he *has* felt rather forlorn, I fancy. Now, dear, goodbye; think over mother's preachment, act upon it if it seems good, and God bless you all!"

Meg did think it over, found it good, and acted upon it, though the first attempt was not made exactly as she planned to have it.

A few days after the talk with her mother, Meg resolved to try a social evening with John; so she ordered a nice supper, set the parlour in order, dressed herself prettily, and put the children to bed early, that nothing should interfere with her experiment.

Meg ran down to greet her husband with a smiling face, and the little blue bow in her hair which was his especial admiration. He saw it at once, and said, with pleased surprise—

"Why, little mother, how gay we are tonight. Do you expect company?"

"Only you, dear."

"Is it a birthday, anniversary, or anything?"

"No; I'm tired of being a dowdy, so I dressed up as a change. You always make yourself nice for table, no matter how tired you are; so why shouldn't I when I have the time?"

"I do it out of respect to you, my dear," said old-fashioned John.

"Ditto, ditto, Mr. Brooke," laughed Meg, looking young and pretty again, as she nodded to him over the teapot.

"Well, it's altogether delightful, and like old times. This tastes right. I drink your health, dear." And John sipped his tea with an air of reposeful rapture, which was of very short duration, however; for, as he put down his cup, the door-handle rattled mysteriously, and a little voice was heard, saying impatiently—

"Opy doy; me's tummin!"

"It's that naughty boy. I told him to go to sleep alone, and here he is, downstairs, getting his death a-cold pattering over that canvas," said Meg, answering the call.

"Mornin' now," announced Demi, in a joyful tone, as he entered, with his long night-gown gracefully festooned over his arm, and every curl bobbing gaily as he pranced about the table, eyeing the "cakies" with loving glances.

"No, it isn't morning yet. You must go to bed, and not trouble poor mamma; then you can have the little cake with sugar on it."

"Me loves Parpar," said the artful one, preparing to climb the paternal knee, and revel in forbidden joys. But John shook his head, and said to Meg—

"If you told him to stay up there, and go to sleep

alone, make him do it, or he will never learn to mind you."

"Yes, of course. Come, Demi;" and Meg led her son away, feeling a strong desire to spank the little marplot who hopped beside her, labouring under the delusion that the bribe was to be administered as soon as they reached the nursery.

Nor was he disappointed; for that short-sighted woman actually gave him a lump of sugar, tucked him into his bed, and forbade any more promenades till morning.

"Iss!" said Demi the perjured, blissfully sucking his sugar, and regarding his first attempt as eminently successful.

Meg returned to her place, and supper was progressing pleasantly, when the little ghost walked again, and exposed the maternal delinquencies by boldly demanding—

"More sudar, Marmar."

"Now this won't do," said John, hardening his heart against the engaging little sinner "We shall never know any peace till that child learns to go to bed properly. You have made a slave of yourself long enough; give him one lesson, and then there will be an end of it. Put him in his bed and leave him, Meg."

"He won't stay there; he never does, unless I sit by him."

"I'll manage him. Demi, go upstairs, and get into your bed, as Mamma bids you."

"S'ant!" replied the young rebel, helping himself to the coveted "cakie," and beginning to eat the same with calm audacity.

"You must never say that to Papa; I shall carry you if you don't go yourself."

"Go 'way; me don't love Parpar;" and Demi retired to his mother's skirts for protection.

But even that refuge proved unavailing, for he was delivered over to the enemy, with a "Be gentle with him, John," which struck the culprit with dismay; for when Mamma deserted him, then the judgment-day was as hand. Bereft of his cake, defrauded of his frolic, and borne away by a strong hand to that detested bed, poor Demi could not restrain his wrath, but openly defied Papa, and kicked and screamed lustily all the way upstairs. The minute he was put into bed on one side, he rolled out on the other, and made for the door, only to be ignominously caught up by the tail of his little toga, and put back again, which lively performance was kept up till the young man's strength gave out when he devoted himself to roaring at the top of his voice. This vocal exercise usually conquered Meg; but John sat as unmoved as the post which is popularly believed to be deaf. No coaxing, no sugar, no lullaby, no story; even the light was put out, and only the red glow of the fire enlivened the "big dark" which Demi regarded with curiosity rather than fear. This new order of things disgusted him, and he howled dismally for "Marmar," as his angry passions subsided, and recollections of his tender bondwoman returned to the captive autocrat. The plaintive wail which succeeded the passionate roar went to Meg's heart, and she ran up to say beseechingly—

"Let me stay with him; he'll be good, now, John."

"No, my dear, I've told him he must go to sleep, as you bid him; and he must, if I stay here all night."

"But he'll cry himself sick," pleaded Meg, reproaching herself for deserting her boy.

"No, he won't, he's so tired he will soon drop off, and then the matter is settled; for he will understand that he has got to mind. Don't interfere; I'll manage him."

"He's my child, and I can't have his spirit broken by harshness."

"He's my child, and I won't have his temper spoilt by indulgence. Go down, my dear, and leave the boy to me."

When John spoke in that masterful tone, Meg always obeyed, and never regretted her docility.

When John came down at last, expecting to find a pensive or reproachful wife, he was agreeably surprised to find Meg placidly trimming a bonnet, and to be greeted with the request to read something about the election, if he was not too tired. He read a long debate with the most amiable readiness, and then explained it in his most lucid manner, while Meg tried to look deeply interested, to ask intelligent questions, and keep her thoughts from wandering from the state of the nation to the state of her bonnet. In her secret soul, however, she decided that politics were as bad as mathematics, and that the mission of politicians seemed to be calling each other names; but she kept these feminine ideas to herself, and when John paused, shook her head, and said with what she thought diplomatic ambiguity—

"Well, I really don't see what we are coming to."

John laughed, and watched her for a minute, as she poised a pretty little preparation of lace and flowers on her hand, and regarded it with the genuine interest which his harangue had failed to waken.

"She is trying to like politics for my sake, so I'll try and like millinery for hers, that's only fair," thought John the Just, adding aloud—

"That's very pretty; is it what you call a breakfast-cap?"

"My dear man, it's a bonnet! My very best go-to-concert-and-theatre bonnet."

"I beg your pardon; it was so small, I naturally

mistook it for one of the fly-away things you sometimes wear. How do you keep it on?"

"These bits of lace are fastened under the chin with a rosebud, so;" and Meg illustrated by putting on the bonnet, and regarding him with an air of calm satisfaction that was irresistible.

"It's a love of a bonnet, but I prefer the face inside, for it looks young and happy again," and John kissed the smiling face, to the great detriment of the rosebud under the chin.

"I'm glad you like it, for I want you to take me to one of the new concerts some night; I really need some music to put me in tune. Will you, please?"

"Of course I will, with all my heart, or anywhere else you like. You have been shut up so long, it will do you no end of good, and I shall enjoy it, of all things. What put it into your head, little mother?"

"Well, I had a talk with Marmee the other day, and told her how nervous and cross and out of sorts I felt, and she said I needed change and less care; so Hannah is to help me with the children, and I'm to see to things about the house more, and now and then have a little fun, just to keep me from getting to be a fidgety, broken-down old woman before my time. It's only an experiment, John, and I want to try it for your sake as much as for mine, because I've neglected you shamefully lately, and I'm going to make home what it used to be, if I can. You don't object, I hope?"

This household happiness did not come all at once, but John and Meg had found the key to it, and each year of married life taught them how to use it, unlocking the treasures of real home-love and mutual helpfulness, which the poorest may possess, and the richest cannot buy.

CHAPTER SIXTEEN

LAZY LAURENCE

LAURIE went to Nice intending to stay a week, and remained a month. He was tired of wandering about alone, and Amy's familiar presence seemed to give a home-like charm to the foreign scenes in which she bore a part. Laurie made no effort of any kind, but just let himself drift along as comfortably as possible, trying to forget, and feeling that all women owed him a kind word because one had been cold to him. It cost him no effort to be generous, and he would have given Amy all the trinkets in Nice if she would have taken them; but, at the same time, he felt that he could not change the opinion she was forming of him, and he rather dreaded the keen blue eyes that seemed to watch him with such half-sorrowful, half-scornful surprise.

"All the rest have gone to Monaco for the day; I preferred to stay at home and write letters. They are done now, and I am going to Valrosa to sketch; will you come?" said Amy, as she joined Laurie one lovely day when he lounged in as usual, about noon.

It was a lovely drive, along winding roads rich in the picturesque scenes that delight beauty-loving eyes. Here an ancient monastery, whence the solemn chanting of the monks came down to them. There a bare-legged shepherd, in wooden shoes, pointed hat, and rough jacket over one shoulder, sat piping on a stone, while his goats skipped among the rocks or lay at his feet. Meek, mouse-coloured donkeys, laden with panniers of freshly-cut grass, passed by, with a pretty girl in a *capaline* sitting between the green piles, or an old woman spinning with a distaff as she went. Gnarled olive-trees covered the hills with their dusky foliage, fruit hung golden in the orchard, and great scarlet anemones fringed the roadside; while beyond green slopes and craggy heights, the Maritime Alps rose sharp and white against the blue Italian sky.

Valrosa well deserved its name, for, in that climate of perpetual summer, roses blossomed everywhere.

"This is a regular honeymoon Paradise, isn't it? Did you ever see such roses?" asked Amy, pausing on the terrace to enjoy the view, and a luxurious whiff of perfume that came wandering by.

"No, nor felt such thorns," returned Laurie, with his thumb in his mouth, after a vain attempt to capture a solitary scarlet flower that grew just beyond his reach.

"Try lower down, and pick those that have no thorns," said Amy, gathering three of the tiny cream-coloured ones that starred the wall behind her. The pale roses Amy gave him were the sort that the Italians lay in dead hands, never in bridal wreaths, and, for a moment, he wondered if the omen was for Jo or for himself; but the next instant his American common-sense got the better of sentimentality, and he laughed a heartier laugh than Amy had heard since he came.

"It's good advice; you'd better take it and save your fingers," she said, thinking her speech amused him.

"Thank you, I will," he answered in jest, and a few months later he did it in earnest.

"Laurie, when are you going to your grandfather?" she asked presently, as she settled herself on a rustic seat.

"Very soon."

"Then why don't you do it?"

"Natural depravity, I suppose."

"Natural indolence, you mean. It's really dreadful!" and Amy looked severe.

"Not so bad as it seems, for I should only plague him if I went, so I might as well stay, and plague you a little longer, you can bear it better; in fact, I think it agrees with you excellently;" and Laurie composed himself for a lounge on the broad ledge of the balustrade.

Amy shook her head, and opened her sketch-book with an air of resignation; but she had made up her mind to lecture "that boy," and in a minute she began again.

"What are you doing just now?"

"Watching lizards."

"No, no; I mean what do you intend and wish to do?"

"Smoke a cigarette, if you'll allow me."

"How provoking you are! I don't approve of cigars, and I will only allow it on condition that you let me put you into my sketch; I need a figure."

"With all the pleasure in life. How will you have me—full-length or three-quarters, on my head or my heels? I should respectfully suggest a recumbent posture, then put yourself in also, and call it '*Dolce far niente.*'"

"Stay as you are, and go to sleep if you like. *I* intend to work hard," said Amy, in her most energetic tone.

"What delightful enthusiasm!" and he leaned against a tall urn with a air of entire satisfaction.

"What would Jo say if she saw you now?" asked Amy impatiently, hoping to stir him up by the mention of her still more energetic sister's name.

"As usual, 'Go away, Teddy, I'm busy!'" He laughed as he spoke, but the laugh was not natural, and a shade passed over his face, for the utterance of the familiar name touched the wound that was not healed yet. Both tone and shadow struck Amy, for she had seen and heard them before, and now she looked up in time to catch a new expression on Laurie's face—a hard, bitter look, full of pain, dissatisfaction, and regret. It was gone before she could study it, and the listless expression back again.

"You look like the effigy of a young knight asleep on his tomb," she said, carefully tracing the well-cut profile defined against the dark stone.

"Wish I was!"

"That's a foolish wish, unless you have spoilt your life. You are so changed, I sometimes think——" there Amy stopped, with a half-timid, half-wistful look, more significant than her unfinished speech.

Laurie saw and understood the affectionate anxiety which she hesitated to express, and looking straight into her eyes, said, just as he used to say it to her mother,—

"It's all right, ma'am."

"I'm glad of that! I didn't think you'd been a very bad boy, but I fancied you might have wasted money at the wicked Baden-Baden, lost your heart to some charming Frenchwoman with a husband, or got into some of the scrapes that young men seem to consider a necessary part of a foreign tour. Don't stay out there in the sun; come and lie on the grass here, and 'let us be friendly,' as Jo used to say when we got in the sofa-corner and told secrets."

Laurie obediently threw himself down on the turf, and began to amuse himself by sticking daisies into the ribbons of Amy's hat, that lay there.

"I'm all ready for the secrets;" and he glanced up with a decided expression of interest in his eyes.

"I've none to tell; you may begin."

"Haven't one to bless myself with. I thought perhaps you'd had some news from home."

"You have heard all that has come lately. Don't you hear often? I fancied Jo would send you volumes."

"She's very busy; I'm roving about so, it's impossible to be regular, you know. Now I'm going to play brother, and ask questions. May I?"

"I don't promise to answer."

"Your face will, if your tongue won't. You aren't woman of the world enough yet to hide your feelings, my dear. I heard rumours about Fred and you last year, and it's my private opinion that, if he had not been called home so suddenly and detained so long, something would have come of it—hey?"

"That's not for me to say," was Amy's prim reply; but her lips would smile, and there was a traitorous sparkle of the eye, which betrayed that she knew her power and enjoyed the knowledge.

"You are not engaged, I hope?" and Laurie looked very elder-brotherly and grave all of a sudden.

"No."

"But you will be, if he comes back and goes properly down upon his knees, won't you?"

"Very likely."

"Then you are fond of old Fred?"

"I could be, if I tried."

"I understand; queens of society can't get on without money, so you mean to make a good match, and start in that way? Quite right and proper, as the world goes, but it sounds odd from the lips of one of your mother's girls."

"True nevertheless."

A short speech, but the quiet decision with which it was uttered contrasted curiously with the young speaker. Laurie felt this instinctively, and laid himself down again, with a sense of disappointment which he could not explain. His look and silence, as well as a certain inward self-disapproval, ruffled Amy, and made her resolve to deliver her lecture without delay.

"I wish you'd do me the favour to rouse yourself a little," she said sharply.

"Do it for me, there's a dear girl."

"I could, if I tried;" and she looked as if she would like doing it in the most summary style.

"Stir away; it won't hurt me and it may amuse you, as the big man said when his little wife beat him. Regard me in the light of a husband or a carpet, and beat till you are tired, if that sort of exercise agrees with you."

Being decidedly nettled herself, and longing to see him shake off the apathy that so altered him, Amy sharpened both tongue and pencil, and began:—

Flo and I have got a new name for you; it's 'Lazy Laurence.' How do you like it?"

She thought it would annoy him; but he only folded his arms under his head, with an imperturbable "That's not bad. Thank you, ladies."

"Do you want to know what I honestly think of you?"

"Pining to be told."

"Well, I despise you."

If she had even said "I hate you," in a petulant or coquettish tone, he would have laughed, and rather liked it; but the grave, almost sad, accent of her voice made him open his eyes, and ask quickly,—

"Why, if you please?"

"Because, with every chance for being good, useful, and happy, you are faulty, lazy, and miserable."

"Strong language, mademoiselle."

"If you like it, I'll go on."

"Pray, do; it's quite interesting."

"I thought you'd find it so; selfish people always like to talk about themselves."

"Am *I* selfish?" The question slipped out involuntarily and in a tone of surprise, for the one virtue on which he prided himself was generosity.

"Yes, very selfish," continued Amy, in a calm, cool voice, twice as effective, just then, as an angry one. "I'll show you how, for I've studied you while we have been frolicking, and I'm not at all satisfied with you. Here you have been abroad nearly six months, and done nothing but waste time and money and disappoint your friends."

"Isn't a fellow to have pleasure after a four-years' grind?"

"You don't look as if you'd had much; at any rate, you are none the better for it, as far as I can see. I said, when we first met, that you had improved. Now I take it all back, for I don't think you half so nice as when I left you at home. You have grown abominably lazy; you like gossip, and waste time on frivolous things; you are contented to be petted and admired by silly people, instead of being loved and respected by wise ones. With money, talent, position, health, and beauty—ah, you like that, Old Vanity! but it's the truth, so I can't help saying it—with all these splendid things to use and enjoy, you can find nothing to do but dawdle; and, instead of being the man you might and ought to be, you are only——" There she stopped, with a look that had both pain and pity in it.

"Saint Laurence on a gridiron," added Laurie, blandly finishing the sentence. But the lecture began to take effect, for there was a wide-awake sparkle in his eyes now, and a half-angry, half-injured expression replaced the formed indifference.

"I supposed you'd take it so. You men tell us we are angels, and say we can make you what we will; but the instant we honestly try to do you good, you laugh at us, and won't listen, which proves how much your flattery is worth." Amy spoke bitterly, and turned her back on the exasperating martyr at her feet.

In a minute a hand came down over the page, so that she could not draw, and Laurie's voice said, with a droll imitation of a penitent child,—

"I will be good, oh, I will be good!"

But Amy did not laugh, for she was in earnest; and tapped on the outspread hand with her pencil, said soberly,—

"Aren't you ashamed of a hand like that? It's as soft and white as a woman's, and looks as if it never did anything but wear Jouvin's best gloves, and pick flowers for ladies. You are not a dandy, thank Heaven! so I'm glad to see there are no diamonds or big seal-rings on it, only the little old one Jo gave you so long ago. Dear soul, I wish she was here to help me!"

"So do I!"

The hand vanished as suddenly as it came, and there was energy enough in the echo of her wish to suit even Amy. She glanced down at him with a new thought in her mind; but he was lying with his hat half over his face, as if for shade, and his moustache hid his mouth. All in a minute various hints and trifles assumed shape and significance in Amy's mind, and told her what her sister never had confided to her. Her keen eyes filled, and, when she spoke again, it was in a voice that could be beautifully soft and kind when she chose to make it so.

"I know I have no right to talk so to you, Laurie; and if you weren't the sweetest-tempered fellow in the world you'd be very angry with me. But we are all so fond and proud of you, I couldn't bear to think they should be disappointed in you at home as I have been, though, perhaps, they would understand the change better than I do."

"I think they would," came from under the hat, in a grim tone, quite as touching as a broken one.

"They ought to have told me, and not let me go blundering and scolding, when I should have been more kind and patient than ever. I never did like that Miss Randal, and now I hate her!" said artful Amy, wishing to be sure of her facts this time.

"Hang Miss Randal!" said Laurie knocked the hat off his face with a look that left no doubt of his sentiments towards that young lady.

"I beg pardon; I thought——" and there she paused diplomatically.

"No, you didn't; you knew perfectly well I never cared for any one but Jo." Laurie said that in his old, impetuous tone, and turned his face away as he spoke.

"I did think so; but as they never said anything about it, and you came away, I supposed I was mistaken. And Jo wouldn't be kind to you? Why, I was sure she loved you dearly."

"She *was* kind, but not in the right way; and it's lucky for her she didn't love me, if I'm the good-for-nothing fellow you think me. It's her fault, though, and you may tell her so."

The hard, bitter look came back again as he said that, and it troubled Amy, for she did not know what balm to apply.

"I was wrong, I didn't know. I'm very sorry I was so cross, but I can't help wishing you'd bear it better, Teddy, dear."

"Don't, that's her name for me!" and Laurie put up his hand with a quick gesture to stop the words spoken in Jo's half-kind, half-reproachful tone. Presently he sat up, and asked slowly,—

"Do you think Jo would despise me as you do?"

"Yes, if she saw you now. She hates lazy people. Why don't you do something splendid, and *make* her love you?"

"I did my best, but it was no use."

Neither spoke for several minutes. Laurie sat turning the little ring on his finger, and Amy put the last touches to the hasty sketch she had been working at while she talked. Presently she put it on his knee, merely saying,—

"How do you like that?"

He looked and then he smiled, as he could not well help doing, for it was capitally done—the long, lazy figure on the grass, with listless face, half-shut eyes, and one hand holding a cigar, from which came the little wreath of smoke that encircled the dreamer's head.

"How well you draw!" he said, with genuine surprise and pleasure at her skill, adding, with a half-laugh,—

"Yes, that's me."

"As you are: this as you were;" and Amy laid another sketch beside the one he held.

It was not nearly so well done, but there was a life and spirit in it which atoned for many faults, and it recalled the past so vividly that a sudden change swept over the young man's face as he looked. Only a rough sketch of Laurie taming a horse; hat and coat were off, and every line of the active figure, resolute face, and commanding attitude, was full of energy and meaning. Laurie said nothing; but as his eyes went from one to the other, Amy saw him flush up and fold his lips together as if he read and accepted the little lesson she had given him. That satisfied her; and, without waiting for him to speak, she said, in her brightly way,—

"Don't you remember the day you played Rarey

the invalid supplied with the fruit she loved and longed for; old Hannah never wearied of concocting dainty dishes to tempt a capricious appetite, dropping tears as she worked; and from across the sea came little gifts and cheerful letters, seeming to bring breaths of warmth and fragrance from lands that know no winter.

Here, cherished like a household saint in its shrine, sat Beth, tranquil and busy as ever; for nothing could change the sweet, unselfish nature, and even while preparing to leave life, she tried to make it happier for those who should remain behind. The feeble fingers were never idle, and one of her pleasures was to make little things for the school-children daily passing to and fro—to drop a pair of mittens from her window for a pair of purple hands, a needle-book for some small mother of many dolls, pen-wipers for young penmen toiling through forests of pot-hooks, scrap-books for picture-loving eyes, and all manner of pleasant devices, till the reluctant climbers up the ladder of learning found their way strewn with flowers, as it were, and came to regard the gentle giver as a sort of fairy godmother, who sat above there, and showered down gifts miraculously suited to their tastes and needs. If Beth had wanted any reward, she found it in the bright little faces always turned up to her window, with nods and smiles, and the droll little letters which came to her, full of blots and gratitude.

It was well for all that this peaceful time was given them as preparation for the sad hours to come; for, by-and-by, Beth said the needle was "so heavy," and put it down for ever; talking wearied her, faces troubled her, pain claimed her for its own, and her tranquil spirit was sorrowfully perturbed by the ills that vexed her feeble flesh. Ah me! such heavy days, such long, long nights, such aching hearts and imploring prayers, when those who loved her best were forced to see the thin hands stretch out to them beseechingly, to hear the bitter cry, "Help me, help me!" and to feel that there was no help. A sad eclipse of the serene soul, a sharp struggle of the young life with death; but both were mercifully brief, and then, the natural rebellion over, the old peace returned more beautiful than ever. With the wreck of her frail body, Beth's soul grew strong; and, though she said little, those about her felt that she was ready, saw that the first pilgrim called was likewise the fittest, and waited with her on the shore, trying to see the Shining Ones coming to receive her when she crossed the river.

Jo never left her for an hour since Beth had said, "I feel stronger when you are here." She slept on a couch in the room, waking often to renew the fire, to feed, lift, or wait upon the patient creature who seldom asked for anything, and "tried not to be a trouble." All day she haunted the room, jealous of any other nurse, and prouder of being chosen then than of any honour her life ever brought her. Precious and helpful hours to Jo, for now her heart received the teaching that it needed; lessons in patience were so sweetly taught her that she could not fail to learn them; charity for all, the lovely spirit that can forgive and truly forget unkindness, the loyalty to duty that makes the hardest easy, and the sincere faith that fears nothing, but trusts undoubtingly.

Often, when she woke, Jo found Beth reading in her well-worn little book, heard her singing softly, to beguile the sleepless night, or saw her lean her face upon her hands, while slow tears dropped through the transparent fingers; and Jo would lie watching her, with thoughts too deep for tears, feeling that Beth, in her simple, unselfish way, was trying to wean herself from the dear old life, and fit herself for the life to come, by sacred words of comfort, quiet prayers and the music she loved so well.

Seeing this did more for Jo than the wisest sermons, the saintliest hymns, the most fervent prayers that any voice could utter; for, with eyes made clear by many tears, and a heart softened by the tenderest sorrow, she recognised the beauty of her sister's life—uneventful, unambitious, yet full of the genuine virtues which "smell sweet, and blossom in the dust," the self-forgetfulness that makes the humblest on earth remembered soonest in heaven, the true success which is possible to all.

One night, when Beth looked among the books upon her table, to find something to make her forget the mortal weariness that was almost as hard to bear as pain, as she turned the leaves of her old favourite the *Pilgrim's Progress,* she found a little paper scribbled over in Jo's hand. The name caught her eye, and the blurred look of the lines made her sure that tears had fallen on it.

"Poor Jo! she fast asleep, so I won't wake her to ask leave; she shows me all her things, and I don't think she'll mind if I look at this," thought Beth, with a glance at her sister, who lay on the rug, with the tongs beside her, ready to wake up the minute the log fell apart.

Blurred and blotted, faulty and feeble, as the lines were, they brought a look of inexpressible comfort to Beth's face, for her one regret had been that she had done so little; and this seemed to assure her that her life had not been useless, that her death would not bring the despair she feared. As she sat with the paper folded between her hands, the charred log fell asunder Jo started up revived the blaze, and crept to the bedside, hoping Beth slept.

"Not asleep, but so happy, dear. See, I found this

and read it; I knew you wouldn't care. Have I been all that to you, Jo?" she asked, with wistful, humble earnestness.

"O Beth, so much, so much!" and Jo's head went down upon the pillow, beside her sister's.

"Then I don't feel as if I'd wasted my life. I'm not so good as you make me, but I *have* tried to do right; and now, when its too late to begin even to do better, it's such a comfort to know that some one loves me so much, and feels as if I'd helped them."

So the spring days came and went, the sky grew clearer, the earth greener, the flowers were up fair and early, and the birds came back in time to say good-bye to Beth, who, like a tired but trustful child, clung to the hands that had led her all her life, as father and mother guided her tenderly through the Valley of the Shadow, and gave her up to God.

Seldom, except in books, do the dying utter memorable words, see visions, or depart with beautified countenances; and those who have sped many parting souls know that to most the end comes as naturally and simply as sleep. As Beth had hoped, the "tide went out easily"; and in the dark hour before the dawn, on the bosom where she had drawn her first breath, she quietly drew her last, with no farewell but one loving look, one little sigh.

When morning came, for the first time in many months the fire was out, Jo's place was empty, and the room was very still. But a bird sang blithely on a budding bough, close by, the snowdrops blossomed freshly at the window, and the spring sunshine streamed in like a benediction over the placid face upon the pillow—a face so full of painless peace that those who loved it best smiled through their tears, and thanked [illegible]d that Beth was well at last.

CHAPTER EIGHTEEN

LEARNING TO FORGET

AMY'S lecture did Laurie good, though, of course, he did not own it till long afterward. Laurie went back to his grandfather, and was so dutifully devoted for several weeks that the old gentleman declared the climate of Nice had improved him wonderfully, and he had better try it again. There was nothing the young gentleman would have liked better, but elephants could not have dragged him back after the scolding he had received; pride forbade, and whenever the longing grew very strong, he fortified his resolution by repeating the words that had made the deepest impression, "I despise you;" "Go and do something splendid that will *make* her love you."

As Goethe, when he had a joy or a grief. put it into a song, so Laurie resolved to embalm his love-sorrow in music, and compose a Requiem which should harrow up Jo's soul and melt the heart of every hearer. Therefore the next time the old gentleman found him getting restless and moody, and ordered him off, he went to Vienna, where he had musical friends, and fell to work with the firm determination to distinguish himself. But, whether the sorrow was too vast to be embodied in music, or music too ethereal to uplift a mortal woe, he soon discovered that the Requiem was beyond him, just at present.

Then he tried an Opera, for nothing seemed impossible in the beginning; but here, again, unforeseen difficulties beset him. He wanted Jo for his heroine, and called upon his memory to supply him with tender recollections and romantic visions of his love. But memory turned traitor; and, as if possessed by the perverse spirit of the girl, would only recall Jo's oddities, faults, and freaks, would only show her in the most unsentimental aspects—beating mats with her head tied up in a bandanna, barricading herself with the sofa-pillow, or throwing cold water over his passion *à la* Gummidge—and an irresistible laugh spoilt the pensive picture he was endeavouring to paint.

When he looked about him for another and a less intractable damsel to immortalise in melody, memory produced one with the most obliging readiness. This phantom wore many faces, but it always had golden hair, was enveloped in a diaphanous cloud, and floated airily before his mind's eye in a pleasing chaos of roses, peacocks, white ponies, and blue ribbons.

Thanks to this inspiration, he got on swimmingly for a time, but gradually the work lost its charm, and he forgot to compose, while he sat musing, pen in hand, or roamed about the gay city to get new ideas and refresh his mind, which seemed to be in a somewhat unsettled state that winter. He did not do much, but he thought a great deal and was conscious of a change of some sort going on in spite of himself. "It's genius simmering, perhaps. I'll let it simmer, and see what comes of it," he said, with a secret suspicion, all the while, that it wasn't genius, but something far more common. Whatever it was, it simmered to some purpose, for he grew more and more discontented with his desultory life, began to long for some real and earnest work to go at, soul and body, and finally came to the wise conclusion that everyone who loved music was not a composer. Returning from one of Mozart's grand operas, splendidly performed at the ...val Theatre, he looked over his own, played a few ... best parts, sat staring up at the busts of

Mendelssohn, Beethoven, and Bach, who stared benignly back again; then suddenly he tore up his music-sheets, one by one, and, as the last fluttered out of his hand, he said soberly to himself.—

"She is right! Talent isn't genius, and you can't make it so. That music has taken the vanity out of me as Rome took it out of her, and I won't be a humbug any longer. Now what shall I do?"

Laurie thought that the task of forgetting his love for Jo would absorb all his powers for years; but, to his great surprise, he discovered it grew easier every day. Laurie's heart *wouldn't* ache; the wound persisted in healing with a rapidity that astonished him, and, instead of trying to forget, he found himself trying to remember. He had not foreseen this turn of affairs, and was not prepared for it. He carefully stirred up the embers of his lost love, but they refused to burst into a blaze: there was only a comfortable glow that warmed and did him good without putting him into a fever, and he was reluctantly obliged to confess that the boyish passion was slowly subsiding into a more tranquil sentiment, very tender, a little sad and resentful still, but that was sure to pass in time, leaving a brotherly affection which would last unbroken to the end.

As the word "brotherly" passed through his mind in one of these reveries, he smiled, and glanced up at the picture of Mozart that was before him:—

"Well, he was a great man; and when he couldn't have one sister he took the other, and was happy."

Laurie did not utter the words, but he thought them; and the next instant kissed the little old ring, saying to himself,—

"No, I won't! I haven't forgotten, I never can. I'll try again, and if that fails, why, then——"

Leaving his sentence unfinished, he seized pen and

paper and wrote to Jo, telling her that he could not settle to anything while there was the least hope of her changing her mind. Couldn't she, wouldn't she, and let him come home and be happy? While waiting for an answer he did nothing, but he did it energetically, for he was in a fever of impatience. It came at last, and settled his mind effectually on one point, for Jo decidedly couldn't and wouldn't. She was wrapped up in Beth, and never wished to hear the word "love" again. Then she begged him to be happy with somebody else, but always to keep a little corner of his heart for his loving sister Jo. In a postscript she desired him not to tell Amy that Beth was worse; she was coming home in the spring, and there was no need of saddening the remainder of her stay. That would be time enough, please God, but Laurie must write to her often, and not let her feel lonely, homesick or anxious.

"So I will, at once. Poor little girl; it will be a sad going home for her, I'm afraid;" and Laurie opened his desk, as if writing to Amy had been the proper conclusion of the sentence left unfinished some weeks before.

But he did not write the letter that day; for, as he rummaged out his best paper, he came across something which changed his purpose. Tumbling about in one part of the desk, among bills, passports, and business documents of various kinds, were several of Jo's letters, and in another compartment were three notes from Amy, carefully tied up with one of her blue ribbons, and sweetly suggestive of the little dead roses put away inside. With a half-repentant, half-amused expression, Laurie gathered up all Jo's letters, moothed, folded, and put them neatly into a small er of the desk, stood a minute turning the ring ully on his finger, then slowly drew it off, laid it with the letter, locked the drawer, and went out to hear High Mass at Saint Stefan's, feeling as if there had been a funeral.

The letter went very soon, however, and was promptly answered, for Amy *was* homesick, and confessed it in the most delightfully confiding manner. The correspondence flourished famously, and letters flew to and fro, with unfailing regularity, all through the early spring. Laurie sold his busts, made allumettes of his opera, and went back to Paris, hoping somebody would arrive before long. He wanted desperately to go to Nice, but would not till he was asked; and Amy would not ask him, for just then she was having little experiences of her own, which made her rather wish to avoid the quizzical eyes of "our boy."

Fred Vaughn had returned, and put the question to which she had once decided to answer "Yes, thank you;" but now she said, "No, thank you," kindly but steadily; for, when the time came, her courage failed her, and she found that something more than money and position was needed to satisfy the new longing that filled her heart so full of tender hopes and fears.

If all brothers were treated as well as Laurie was at this period, they would be a much happier race of beings than they are. Amy never lectured now; she asked his opinion on all subjects; she was interested in everything he did, made charming little presents for him, and sent him two letters a week, full of lively gossip, sisterly confidences, and captivating sketches of the lovely scenes about her. As few brothers are complimented by having their letters carried about in their sisters' pockets, read and reread diligently, cried over when short, kissed when long and treasured carefully, we will not hint that Amy did any of these fond and foolish things. But she certainly did grow a little pale and pensive that spring, lost much of her relish for society, and went out sketching alone a good deal.

Her aunt thought that she regretted her answer to Fred; and finding denials useless and explanations impossible, Amy left her to think what she liked, taking care that Laurie should know that Fred had gone to Egypt. That was all, but he understood it, and looked relieved, as he said to himself, with a venerable air,—

"I was sure she would think better of it. Poor old fellow. I've been through it all, and I can sympathise."

While these changes were going on abroad, trouble had come at home; but the letter telling that Beth was failing never reached Amy, and when the next found her, the grass was green above her sister. The sad news met her at Vevey, for the heat had driven them from Nice in May, and they had travelled slowly to Switzerland, by way of Genoa and the Italian lakes. She bore it very well, and quietly submitted to the family decree that she should not shorten her visit, for, since it was too late to say good-bye to Beth, she had better stay, and let absence soften her sorrow. But her heart was very heavy; she longed to be at home, and every day looked wistfully across the lake, waiting for Laurie to come and comfort her.

He did come very soon; for the same mail brought letters to them both, but he was in Germany, and it took some days to reach him. The moment he read it, he packed his knapsack, bade adieu to his fellow pedestrians, and was off to keep his promise, with a heart full of joy and sorrow, hope and suspense.

He knew Vevey well; and as soon as the boat touched the little quay, he hurried along the shore to La Tour, where the Carrols were living *en pension*. The [illegible]*rçon* was in despair that the whole family had gone [illegible]ke a promenade on the lake; but no, the blonde mademoiselle might be in the château garden. If monsieur would give himself the pain of sitting down, a flash of time should present her. But monsieur could not wait even "a flash of time," and, in the middle of the speech, departed to find mademoiselle himself.

A pleasant old garden on the borders of the lovely lake, with chestnuts rustling overhead, ivy climbing everywhere, and the black shadow of the tower falling far across the sunny water. At one corner of the wide, low wall was a seat, and here Amy often came to read or work, or console herself with the beauty all about her. She was sitting here that day, leaning her head on her hand, with a homesick heart and heavy eyes, thinking of Beth, and wondering why Laurie did not come. She did not hear him cross the courtyard beyond, nor see him pause in the archway that led from the subterranean path into the garden. He stood a minute, looking at her with new eyes, seeing what no one had ever seen before—the tender side of Amy's character. Everything about her mutely suggested love and sorrow—the blotted letters in her lap, the black ribbon that tied up her hair, the womanly pain and patience in her face; even the little ebony cross at her throat seemed pathetic to Laurie, for he had given it to her, and she wore it as her only ornament. If he had any doubt about the reception she would give him, they were set at rest the minute she looked up and saw him; for, dropping everything, she ran to him, exclaiming, in a tone of unmistakable love and longing,—

"O Laurie, Laurie, I knew you'd come to me!"

I think everything was said and settled then; for, as they stood together quite silent for a moment, with the dark head bent down protectingly over the light one, Amy felt that no one could comfort and sustai her so well as Laurie, and Laurie decided that A was the only woman in the world who could fill Jo's place, and make him happy. He did not tell her so; but she was not disappointed, for both felt the truth, were satisfied, and gladly left the rest to silence.

In a minute Amy went back to her place; and while she dried her tears, Laurie gathered up the scattered papers, finding in the sight of sundry well-worn letters and suggestive sketches good omens for the future. As he sat down beside her, Amy felt shy again, and turned rosy red at the recollection of her impulsive greeting.

"I couldn't help it; I felt so lonely and sad, and was so very glad to see you. It was such a surprise to look up and find you, just as I was beginning to fear you wouldn't come," she said, trying in vain to speak quite naturally.

"I came the minute I heard. I wish I could say something to comfort you for the loss of dear little Beth; but I can only feel, and——" He could not get any further, for he, too, turned bashful all of a sudden, and did not quite know what to say. He longed to lay Amy's head down on his shoulder, and tell her to have a good cry, but he did not dare; so took her hand instead, and gave it a sympathetic squeeze that was better than words.

"You needn't say anything; this comforts me," she said softly. "Beth is well and happy, and I mustn't wish her back; but I dread the going home, much as I long to see them all. We won't talk about it now, for it makes me cry, and I want to enjoy you while you stay. You needn't go right back, need you?"

"Not if you want me, dear."

"I do, so much. Aunty and Flo are very kind; but [illegible]m like one of the family, and it would be so [illegible] to have you for a little while."

[illegible]oul, you look as if you'd grieved yourself half-sick! I'm going to take care of you, so don't cry any more, but come and walk about with me; the wind is too chilly for you to sit still," he said, in the half-caressing, half-commanding way that Amy liked, as he tied on her hat, drew her arm through his, and began to pace up and down the sunny walk, under the new-leaved chestnuts. He felt more at ease upon his legs; and Amy found it very pleasant to have a strong arm to lean upon, a familiar face to smile at her, and a kind voice to talk delightfully for her alone.

The quaint old garden had sheltered many pairs of lovers, and seemed expressly made for them, so sunny and secluded was it, with nothing but the tower to overlook them, and the wide lake to carry away the echo of their words, as it rippled by below. For an hour this new pair walked and talked, or rested on the wall, enjoying the sweet influences which gave such a charm to time and place; and when an unromantic dinner-bell warned them away, Amy felt as if she left her burden of loneliness and sorrow behind her in the château garden.

The moment Mrs. Carrol saw the girl's altered face, she was illuminated with a new idea, and exclaimed to herself, "Now I understand it all—the child has been pining for young Laurence. Bless my heart, I never thought of such a thing!"

With praiseworthy discretion, the good lady said nothing, and betrayed no sign of enlightenment; but cordially urged Laurie to stay, and begged Amy to enjoy his society, for it would do her more good than so much solitude. Amy was a model of docility; and, as her aunt was a good deal occupied with Flo, she was left to entertain her friend, and did it with more than her usual success.

In spite of the new sorrow, it was a very happy

time, so happy that Laurie could not bear to disturb it by a word. It took him a little while to recover from his surprise at the rapid cure of his first and, as he had firmly believed his last and only love. He consoled himself for the seeming disloyalty by the thought that Jo's sister was almost the same as Jo's self and the conviction that it would have been impossible to love any other woman but Amy so soon and so well. His first wooing had been of the tempestuous order, and he looked back upon it as if through a long vista of years, with a feeling of compassion blended with regret. His second wooing he resolved should be as calm and simple as possible; there was no need of having a scene, hardly any need of telling Amy that he loved her; she knew it without words, and had given him his answer long ago. It all came about so naturally that no one could complain, and he knew that everybody would be pleased, even Jo.

He had rather imagined that the *dénouement* would take place in the château garden by moonlight, and in the most graceful and decorous manner; but it turned out exactly the reverse, for the matter was settled on the lake, at noonday, in a few blunt words. They had been floating about all the morning, from gloomy St. Gingolf to sunny Montreux, with the Alps of Savoy on one side, Mont St. Bernard and the Dent du Midi on the other, pretty Vevey in the valley, and Lausanne upon the hill beyond, a cloudless blue sky overhead, and the bluer lake below, dotted with the picturesque boats that look like white-winged gulls.

They had been talking of Bonnivard, as they glided past Chillon, and of Rousseau, as they looked up at Clarens, where he wrote his "Héloise." Neither had read it, but they knew it was a love-story, and each privately wondered if it was half as interesting as their own. Amy had been dabbling her hand in the water during the little pause that fell between them, and, when she looked up, Laurie was leaning on his oars, with an expression in his eyes that made her say hastily, merely for the sake of saying something—

"You must be tired; rest a little, and let me row; it will do me good; for, since you came, I have been altogether lazy and luxurious."

"I'm not tired; but you may take an oar, if you like. There's room enough, though I have to sit nearly in the middle, else the boat won't trim," returned Laurie, as if he rather liked the arrangement.

Feeling that she had not mended matters much, Amy took the offered third of a seat, shook her hair over her face, and accepted an oar. She rowed as well as she did many other things; and, though she used both hands, and Laurie but one, the oars kept time, and the boat went smoothly through the water.

"How well we pull together, don't we?" said Amy, who objected to silence just then.

"So well that I wish we might always pull in the same boat. Will you, Amy?" very tenderly.

"Yes, Laurie," very low.

Then they both stopped rowing, and unconsciously added a pretty little *tableau* of human love and happiness to the dissolving views reflected in the lake.

CHAPTER NINETEEN

ALL ALONE

It was easy to promise self-abnegation when self was wrapped up in another, and heart and soul were purified by a sweet example; but when the helpful voice was silent, the daily lesson over, the beloved presence gone, and nothing remained but loneliness and grief, then Jo found her promise very hard to keep. She tried in a blind, hopeless way to do her duty, secretly rebelling against it all the while, for it seemed unjust that her few joys should be lessened, her burdens made heavier, and life get harder and harder as she toiled along.

Poor Jo, these were dark days to her, for something like despair came over her when she thought of spending all her life in that quiet house, devoted to humdrum cares, a few small pleasures, and the duty that never seemed to grow any easier.

Often she started up at night, thinking Beth called her; and when the sight of the little empty bed made her cry with the bitter cry of an unsubmissive sorrow, "O Beth, come back! Come back!" she did not stretch out her yearning arms in vain; for, as quick to hear her sobbing as she had been to hear her sister's faintest whisper, her mother came to comfort her, not with words only, but the patient tenderness that soothes by a touch, tears that were mute reminders of a greater grief than Jo's, and broken whispers, more eloquent than prayers, because hopeful resignation went hand-in-hand with natural sorrow.

When aching heart was a little comforted, troubled mind likewise found help; for one day she went to the study, and, leaning over the good grey head lifted to welcome her with a tranquil smile, she said, very humbly—

"Father, talk to me as you did to Beth. I need it more than she did, for I'm all wrong."

"My dear, nothing can comfort me like this," he answered, with a falter in his voice, and both arms round her, as if he, too, needed help, and did not fear to ask it.

Then, sitting in Beth's little chair close beside him, Jo told her troubles—the resentful sorrow for her loss, the fruitless efforts that discouraged her, the want of faith that made life look so dark, and all the sad bewilderment which we call despair. She gave him entire confidence, he gave her the help she needed, and both found consolation in the act; for the time had come when they could talk together not only as father and daughter, but as man and woman, able and glad to serve each other with mutual sympathy as well as mutual love.

Other helps had Jo—humble, wholesome duties and delights that would not be denied their part in serving her, and which she slowly learned to see and value. Brooms and dishcloths never could be as distasteful as they once had been, for Beth had presided over both; and something of her housewifely spirit seemed to linger round the little mop and the old brush, that was never thrown away. As she used them, Jo found herself humming the songs Beth used to hum. imitating Beth's orderly ways, and giving the little touches here and there that kept everything fresh and cosy, which was the first step toward making home happy, though she didn't know it, till Hannah said with an approving squeeze of the hand—

"You thoughtful creter, you're determined we shan't miss that dear lamb ef you can help it. We don't say much, but we see it, and the Lord will bless you for't, see ef He don't."

As they sat sewing together, Jo discovered how much improved her sister Meg was; how well she could talk, how much she knew about good, womanly impulses, thoughts, and feelings, how happy she was in husband and children, and how much they were all doing for each other.

"Marriage is an excellent thing, after all. I wonder if I should blossom out half as well as you have, if I tried it?" said Jo, as she constructed a kite for Demi, in the topsy-turvy nursery.

"It's just what you need to bring out the tender, womanly half of your nature, Jo. You are like a chestnut-burr, prickly outside, but silky-soft within, and a sweet kernel, if one can only get at it. Love will make you show your heart some day, and then the rough burr will fall off."

"Frost opens chestnut-burrs, ma'am, and it takes a good shake to bring them down. Boys go nutting, and I don't care to be bagged by them," returned Jo, pasting away at the kite which no wind that blows would ever carry up, for Daisy had tied herself on as a bob.

Grief is the best opener for some hearts, and Jo's was nearly ready for the bag: a little more sunshine to ripen the nut, then, not a boy's impatient shake, but a man's hand reached up to pick it gently from the burr, and find the kernel sound and sweet. If she had suspected this, she would have shut up tight, and been more prickly than ever; fortunately she wasn't thinking about herself, so, when the time came, down she dropped.

"Why don't you write? That always used to make you happy," said her mother, once, when the desponding fit overshadowed Jo.

"I've no heart to write, and if I had, nobody cares for my things."

"We do; write something for us, and never mind the rest of the world. Try it, dear; I'm sure it would do you good, and please us very much."

"Don't believe I can;" but Jo got out her desk. and began to overhaul her half-finished manuscripts

An hour afterward her mother peeped in, and there she was, scratching away, with her black pinafore on, and an absorbed expression, which caused Mrs. March to smile, and slip away, well pleased with the success of her suggestion. Jo never knew how it happened, but something got into that story that went straight to the hearts of those who read it; for, when her family had laughed and cried over it, her father sent it, much against her will, to one of the popular magazines, and, to her utter surprise, it was not only paid for, but others requested. Letters from several persons, whose praise was honour, followed the appearance of the little story, newspapers copied it, and strangers as well as friends admired it. For a small thing it was a great success; and Jo was more astonished than when her novel was commended and condemned all at once.

When Amy and Laurie wrote of their engagement, Mrs. March feared that Jo would find it difficult to rejoice over it, but her fears were soon set at rest; for, though Jo looked grave at first, she took it very quietly, and was full of hopes and plans for "the children" before she read the letter twice. It was a sort of written duet, wherein each glorified the other in lover-like fashion, very pleasant to read and satisfactory to think of, for no one had any objection to make.

"You like it, Mother?" said Jo, as they laid down the closely written sheets, and looked at one another.

"Yes, I hoped it would be so, ever since Amy wrote that she had refused Fred. I felt sure then that something better than what you call the 'mercenary spirit' had come over her, and a hint here and there in her letters made me suspect that love and Laurie would win the day."

"How sharp you are, Marmee, and how silent! You never said a word to me. I'm not the scatter-brain I was; you may trust me, I'm sober and sensible enough for any one's *confidante* now."

"So you are, dear, and I should have made you mine, only I fancied it might pain you to learn that your Teddy loved any one else."

"Now Mother, did you really think I could be so silly and selfish, after I'd refused his love, when it was freshest, if not best?"

"I knew you were sincere then, Jo, but lately I have thought that if he came back, and asked again, you might, perhaps, feel like giving another answer. Forgive me, dear, I can't help seeing that you are very lonely, and sometimes there is a hungry look in your eyes that goes to my heart; so I fancied that your boy might fill the empty place if he tried now."

"No, Mother, it is better as it is, and I'm glad Amy has learned to love him. But you are right in one thing: I *am* lonely, and perhaps if Teddy had tried again, I might have said 'Yes,' not because I love him any more, but because I care more to be loved than when he went away."

"I'm glad of that, Jo, for it shows that you are getting on. There are plenty to love you, so try to be satisfied with Father and Mother, sisters and brothers, friends and babies, till the best lover of all comes to give you your reward."

"Mothers are the *best* lovers in the world; but I don't mind whispering to Marmee that I'd like to try all kinds. It's very curious, but the more I try to satisfy myself with all sorts of natural affections, the more I seem to want. I'd no idea hearts could take in so many; mine is so elastic, it never seems full now, and I used to be quite contented with my family. I don't understand it."

"I do;" and Mrs. March smiled her wise smile, as Jo turned back the leaves to read what Amy said of Laurie.

By-and-by Jo roamed away upstairs, for it was rainy, and she could not walk. A restless spirit possessed her, and the old feeling came again, not bitter as it once was, but a sorrowfully patient wonder why one sister should have all she asked, the other nothing. It was not true: she knew that, and tried to put it away, but the natural craving for affection was strong, and Amy's happiness woke the hungry longing for some one to "love with heart and soul, and cling to while God let them be together."

Up in the garret, where Jo's unquiet wanderings ended, stood four little wooden chests in a row, each marked with its owner's name, and each filled with relics of the childhood and girlhood ended now for all. Jo glanced into them, and when she came to her own, leaned her chin on the edge, and stared absently at the chaotic collection, till a bundle of old exercise-books caught her eye. She drew them out, turned them over, and re-lived that pleasant winter at kind Mrs. Kirke's. She had smiled at first, then she looked thoughtful, next sad, and when she came to a little message written in the Professor's hand, her lips began to tremble, the books slid out of her lap, and she sat looking at the friendly words, as if they took a new meaning, and touched a tender spot in her heart.

"Wait for me, my friend. I may be a little late, but I shall surely come."

"Oh, if he only would! So kind, so good, so patient with me always; my dear old Fritz, I didn't value him half enough when I had him, but now how I should love to see him, for every one seems going away from me, and I'm all alone."

And holding the little paper fast, as if it were a promise yet to be fulfilled, Jo laid her head down on a comfortable rag-bag, and cried, as if in opposition to the rain pattering on the roof.

Was it all self-pity, loneliness, or low spirits? Or was it the waking up of a sentiment which had bided its time as patiently as its inspirer? Who shall say?

CHAPTER TWENTY

SURPRISES

Jo was alone in the twilight, lying on the old sofa, looking at the fire, and thinking. It was her favourite way of spending the hour of dusk; no one disturbed her, and she used to lie there on Beth's little red pillow, planning stories, dreaming dreams, or thinking tender thoughts of the sister who never seemed far away. Her face looked tired, grave, and rather sad; for tomorrow was her birthday, and she was thinking how fast the years went by, how old she was getting, and how little she seemed to have accomplished. Almost twenty-five, and nothing to show for it. Jo was mistaken in that; there was a good deal to show, and by-and-by she saw, and was grateful for it.

"An old maid, that's what I'm to be. A literary spinster, with a pen for a spouse, a family of stories for children, and twenty years hence a morsel of fame, perhaps; when, like poor Johnson, I'm old, and can't enjoy it, solitary, and can't share it, independent, and don't need it. Well, I needn't be a sour saint nor a selfish sinner; and, I dare say, old maids are very comfortable when they get used to it; but—" and there Jo sighed, as if the prospect was not inviting.

Jo must have fallen asleep for suddenly Laurie's ghost seemed to stand before her—a substantial, lifelike ghost—leaning over her, with the very look he used to wear when he felt a good deal and didn't like to show it. But, like Jenny in the ballad—

"She could not think it he,"

and lay staring up at him in startled silence, till he

stooped and kissed her. Then she knew him, and flew up, crying joyfully—

"O my Teddy! O my Teddy!"

"Dear Jo, are you glad to see me, then?"

"Glad! My blessed boy, words can't express my gladness. Where's Amy?"

"Your mother has got her down at Meg's. We stopped there by the way, and there was no getting my wife out of their clutches."

"Your what?" cried Jo, for Laurie uttered those two words with an unconscious pride and satisfaction which betrayed him.

"Oh, the dickens! Now I've done it;" and he looked so guilty that Jo was down upon him like a flash.

"You've gone and got married!"

"Yes, please, but I never will again;" and he went down upon his knees, with a penitent clasping of hands, and a face full of mischief, mirth, and triumph.

"Actually married?"

"Very much so, thank you."

"Mercy on us! What dreadful thing will you do next?" and Jo fell into her seat, with a gasp.

"A characteristic, but not exactly complimentary, congratulation," returned Laurie, still in an abject attitude, but beaming with satisfaction.

"What can you expect, when you take one's breath away, creeping in like a burglar, and letting cats out of bags like that. Get up, you ridiculous boy, and tell me all about it."

"Not a word, unless you let me come in my old place, and promise not to barricade."

Jo laughed at that as she had not done for many a long day, and patted the sofa invitingly, as she said, in a cordial tone—

"The old pillow is up in the garret, and we don't need it now; so, come and 'fess, Teddy."

"How good it sounds to hear you say 'Teddy'! No one ever calls me that but you;" and Laurie sat down, with an air of great content.

"What does Amy call you?"

"My lord."

"That's like her. Well, you look it;" and Jo's eyes plainly betrayed that she found her boy comelier than ever.

"It's no use your going out in the cold to get Amy, for they are all coming up presently. I couldn't wait; I wanted to be the one to tell you the grand surprise, and have 'first skim,' as we used to say when we squabbled about the cream."

"Of course you did, and spoilt your story by beginning at the wrong end. Now, start right, and tell me how it all happened; I'm pining to know."

"Well, I did it to please Amy," began Laurie, with a twinkle that made Jo exclaim—

"Fib number one; Amy did it to please you. Go on, and tell the truth, if you can, sir."

"Now she's beginning to marm it; isn't it jolly to hear her?" said Laurie to the fire, and the fire glowed and sparkled as if it quite agreed. "It's all the same, you know, she and I being one. We planned to come home with the Carrols, a month or more ago, but they suddenly changed their minds, and decided to pass another winter in Paris. But Grandpa wanted to come home; he went to please me, and I couldn't let him go alone, neither could I leave Amy. So I just settled the difficulty by saying, 'Let's be married, and then we can do as we like'."

"How did you ever get Aunt to agree?"

"It was hard work; but, between us, we talked her over, for we had heaps of good reasons on our side. There wasn't time to write and ask leave, but you all liked it, and consented to it by-and-by, and it was only 'taking Time by the fetlock,' as my wife says."

"Aren't we proud of those two words, and don't we like to say them?" interrupted Jo, addressing the fire in her turn, and watching with delight the happy light it seemed to kindle in the eyes that had been so tragically gloomy when she saw them last.

"A trifle, perhaps; she's such a captivating little woman I can't help being proud of her. Well, then, Uncle and Aunt were there to play propriety; we were so absorbed in one another we were of no mortal use apart, and that charming arrangement would make everything easy all round; so we did it."

"When, where, how?" asked Jo, in a fever of feminine interest and curiosity, for she could not realise it a particle.

"Six weeks ago, at the American consul's, in Paris; a very quiet wedding, of course, for even in our happiness we didn't forget dear little Beth."

Jo put her hand in his as he said that, and Laurie gently smoothed the little red pillow, which he remembered well.

"Why didn't you let us know afterward?" asked Jo, in a quieter tone, when they had sat quite still a minute.

"We wanted to surprise you; we thought we were coming directly home, at first; but the dear old gentleman, as soon as we were married, found he couldn't be ready under a month, at least, and sent us off to spend our honeymoon wherever we liked. Amy had once called Valrosa a regular honeymoon home, so we went there, and were as happy as people are but once in their lives. My faith! Wasn't it love among the roses!"

Laurie seemed to forget Jo for a minute, and Jo was glad of it; for the fact that he told her these things so freely and naturally assured her that he had quite forgiven and forgotten. She tried to draw away her hand; but, as if he guessed the thought that prompted the half-involuntary impulse, Laurie held it fast, and said, with a manly gravity she had never seen in him before—

"Jo, dear, I want to say one thing, and then we'll put it by for ever. As I told you in my letter, when I wrote that Amy had been so kind to me, I never shall stop loving you; but the love is altered, and I have learned to see that it is better as it is. Amy and you change places in my heart, that's all. Will you believe it, and go back to the happy old times when we first knew one another?"

"I'll believe it, with all my heart; but, Teddy, we never can be boy and girl again: the happy old times can't come back, and we mustn't expect it. We are man and woman now, with sober work to do, for playtime is over, and we must give up frolicking. I'm sure you feel this; I see the change in you, and you'll find it in me."

He did not say a word, but took the hand she offered him, and laid his face down on it for a minute, feeling that out of the grave of a boyish passion, there had risen a beautiful, strong friendship to bless them both. Presently Jo said cheerfully, for she didn't want the coming home to be a sad one—

"I can't make it true that you children are really married, and going to set up housekeeping."

"As one of the children is older than yourself, you needn't talk so like a grandma," said Laurie, looking amused at her maternal air.

"You may be a little older in years, but I'm ever so much older in feeling, Teddy. Women always are; and this last year has been such a hard one that I feel forty."

"Poor Jo! we left you to bear it alone, while we went

pleasuring. You *are* older; here's a line, and there's another; unless you smile, your eyes look sad, and when I touched the cushion, just now, I found a tear on it. You've had a great deal to bear, and had to bear it all alone. What a selfish beast I've been!" and Laurie pulled his own hair, with a remorseful look.

But Jo only turned over the traitorous pillow, and answered in a tone which she tried to make quite cheerful—

"No, I had father and mother to help me, the dear babies to comfort me, and the thought that you and Amy were safe and happy, to make the trouble here easier to bear. I *am* lonely, sometimes, but I dare say it's good for me, and——"

"You never shall be again," broke in Laurie, putting his arm about her, as if to fence out every human ill. "Amy and I can't get on without you, so you must come and teach 'the children' to keep house, and go halves in everything, just as we used to do, and let us pet you, and all be blissfully happy and friendly together."

"If I shouldn't be in the way, it would be very pleasant. I begin to feel quite young already; for, somehow, all my troubles seemed to fly away when you came. You always were a comfort, Teddy;" and Jo learned her head on his shoulder, just as she did years ago.

"You are the same Jo still, dropping tears about one minute, and laughing the next. You look a little wicked now; what is it, grandma?"

"I was wondering how you and Amy get on together."

"Like angels!"

"I am sure of that; Amy and you never did quarrel as we used to. She is the sun and I the wind, in the fable, and the sun managed the man best, you remember."

"She can blow him up as well as shine on him," laughed Laurie. "Such a lecture as I got at Nice! I give you my word it was a deal worse than any of your scoldings—a regular rouser. I'll tell you all about it sometime—*she* never will, because, after telling me that she despised and was ashamed of me, she lost her heart to the despicable party and married the good-for-nothing."

"What baseness! Well, if she abuses you, come to me, and I'll defend you."

"I look as if I needed it, don't I?" said Laurie, getting up and striking an attitude which suddenly changed from the imposing to the rapturous, as Amy's voice was heard calling—

"Where is she? Where's my dear old Jo?"

In trooped the whole family, and every one was hugged and kissed all over again, and, after several vain attempts, the three wanderers were set down to be looked at and exulted over. Mr. Laurence. hale and hearty as ever, was quite as much improved as the others by his foreign tour, for the crustiness seemed to be nearly gone, and the old-fashioned courtliness had received a polish which made it kindlier than ever. It was good to see him beam at "my children," as he called the young pair; it was better still to see Amy pay him the daughterly duty and affection which completely won his old heart; and best of all to watch Laurie revolve about the two, as if never tired of enjoying the pretty picture they made.

"Love has done much for our little girl," said her mother softly.

"She has had a good example before her all her life, my dear," Mr. March whispered back, with a loving look at the worn face and grey head beside him.

Daisy found it impossible to keep her eyes off her "pitty aunty," but attached herself like a lap-dog to the wonderful châtelaine full of delightful charms. Demi paused to consider the new relationship before he compromised himself by the rash acceptance of a bribe, which took the tempting form of a family of wooden bears from Berne. A flank movement produced an unconditional surrender, however, for Laurie knew where to have him.

"Young man, when I first had the honour of making your acquaintance you hit me in the face; now I demand the satisfaction of a gentleman;" and with that the tall uncle proceeded to toss and tousle the small nephew in a way that damaged his philosophical dignity as much as it delighted his boyish soul.

Mercy on us, how they did talk! first one, then the other, then all burst out together, trying to tell the history of three years in half-an-hour. It was fortunate that tea was at hand, to produce a lull and provide refreshment, for they would have been hoarse and faint if they had gone on much longer.

Amy, who was handed about like refreshments, returned to the parlour on Father Laurence's arm; the others paired off and this arrangement left Jo companionless.

She stood a minute looking at the party vanishing above, and, as Demi's short plaid legs toiled up the last stair, a sudden sense of loneliness came over her so strongly that she looked about her with dim eyes, as if to find something to lean upon, for even Teddy had deserted her. Then she drew her hand over her eyes—for one of her boyish habits was never to know where her handkerchief was—and had just managed to call up a smile when there came a knock at the porch-door.

She opened it with hospitable haste, and stared as if another ghost had come to surprise her; for there stood a tall, bearded gentleman, beaming on her from the darkness like a midnight sun.

"O Mr. Bhaer, I *am* so glad to see you!" cried Jo, with a clutch, as if she feared the night would swallow him up before she could get him in.

"And I to see Miss Marsch—but no, you haf a party——" and the Professor paused as the sound of voices and the tap of dancing feet came down to them.

"No, we haven't—only the family. My sister and friends have just come home, and we are all very happy. Come in, and make one of us."

Though a very social man, I think Mr. Bhaer would have gone decorously away, and come again another day; but how could he, when Jo shut the door behind him, and bereft him of his hat? Perhaps her face had something to do with it, for she forgot to hide her joy at seeing him, and showed it with a frankness that proved irresistible to the solitary man, whose welcome far exceeded his boldest hopes.

"If I shall not be Monsieur de Trop, I will so gladly see them all. You haf been ill, my friend?"

He put the question abruptly, for, as Jo hung up his coat, the light fell on her face, and he saw a change in it.

"Not ill, but tired and sorrowful. We have had trouble since I saw you last."

"Ah, yes, I know. My heart was sore for you when I heard that"; and he shook hands again, with such a sympathetic face that Jo felt as if no comfort could equal the look of the kind eyes, the grasp of the big, warm hand.

"Father, mother, this is my friend, Professor Bhaer," she said, with a face and tone of such irrepressible pride and pleasure that she might as well have blown a trumpet and opened the door with a flourish.

If the stranger had had any doubts about his reception, they were set at rest in a minute by the cordial welcome he received. Every one greeted him kindly, for Jo's sake at first, but very soon they liked him for his own. Mr. Bhaer sat looking about him with the air of a traveller who knocks at a strange door, and, when it opens, finds himself at home. The children went to him like bees to a honey-pot; and, establishing themselves on each knee, proceeded to captivate him by rifling his pockets, pulling his beard, and investigating his watch, with juvenile audacity. The women telegraphed their approval to one another, and Mr. March, feeling that he had got a kindred spirit, opened his choicest stores for his guest's benefit, while silent John listened and enjoyed the talk, but said not a word, and Mr. Laurence found it impossible to go to sleep.

If Jo had not been otherwise engaged, Laurie's behaviour would have amused her; for a faint twinge, not of jealousy, but something like suspicion, caused that gentleman to stand aloof at first, and observe the newcomer with brotherly circumspection. But it did not last long. He got interested in spite of himself, and, before he knew it, was drawn into the circle; for Mr. Bhaer talked well in this genial atmosphere, and did himself justice. He seldom spoke to Laurie, but he looked at him often, and a shadow would pass across his face, as if regretting his own lost youth, as he watched the young man in his prime. Then his eye would turn to Jo so wistfully that she would have surely answered the mute inquiry if she had seen it; but Jo had her own eyes to take care of, and, feeling that they could not be trusted, she prudently kept them on the little sock she was knitting, like a modern maiden aunt.

A stealthy glance now and then refreshed her like sips of fresh water after a dusty walk, for the side-long peeps showed her several propitious omens. Mr. Bhaer's face had lost the absent-minded expression, and looked all alive with interest in the present moment, actually young and handsome, she thought, forgetting to compare him with Laurie, as she usually did strange men, to their great detriment. Jo quite glowed with triumph when Teddy got quenched in an argument, and thought to herself, as she watched her father's absorbed face, "How he would enjoy having such a man as my Professor to talk with every day!" Lastly, Mr. Bhaer was dressed in a new suit of black, which made him look more like a gentleman than ever. His bushy hair had been cut and smoothly brushed, but didn't stay in order long, for, in exciting moments, he rumpled it up in the droll way he used to do; and Jo liked it rampantly erect better than flat, because she thought it gave his fine forehead a Jove-like aspect. Poor Jo, how she did glorify that plain man, as she sat knitting away so quietly, yet letting nothing escape her, not even the fact the Mr. Bhaer actually had gold sleeve-buttons in his immaculate wristbands!

Nobody knew where the evening went to; for Hannah skilfully abstracted the babies at an early hour, nodding like two rosy poppies, and Mr. Laurence went home to rest. The others sat round the fire, talking away, utterly regardless of the lapse of time, till Meg made a move to go.

"We must have our sing, in the good old way, for we are all together again once more," said Jo, feeling that a good shout would be a safe and pleasant vent for the jubilant emotions of her soul.

They were not *all* there. But no one found the words thoughtless or untrue; for Beth still seemed among them, a peaceful presence, invisible, but dearer than ever, since death could not break the household league that love made indissoluble.

"Play something, Amy. Let them hear how much you have improved," said Laurie, with pardonable pride in his promising pupil.

But Amy whispered, with full eyes, as she twirled the faded stool—

"Not tonight, dear. I can't show off tonight."

But she did show something better than brilliancy or skill; for she sang Beth's songs with a tender music in her voice which the best master could not have taught, and touched the listeners' hearts with a sweeter power than any other inspiration could have given her. The room was very still, when the clear voice failed suddenly at the last line of Beth's favourite hymn. It was hard to say—

"Earth hath no sorrow that heaven cannot heal;"

and Amy leaned against her husband, who stood behind her, feeling that her welcome home was not quite perfect without Beth's kiss.

"Now, we must finish with Mignon's song; for Mr. Bhaer sings that," said Jo, before the pause grew painful. And Mr. Bhaer cleared his throat with a gratified "Hem!" as he stepped into the corner where Jo stood, saying—

"You will sing with me? We go excellently well together."

A pleasing fiction, by the way; for Jo had no more idea of music than a grasshopper. But she would have consented if he had proposed to sing a whole opera, and warbled away, blissfully regardless of time and tune. It didn't much matter; for Mr. Bhaer sang like a true German, heartily and well; and Jo soon subsided into a subdued hum, that she might listen to the mellow voice that seemed to sing for her alone.

The song was considered a great success, and the singer retired covered with laurels. But a few minutes afterwards, he forgot his manners entirely, and stared at Amy putting on her bonnet; for she had been introduced simply as "my sister," and no one had called her by her new name since he came. He forgot himself further when Laurie said, in his most gracious manner, at parting—

"My wife and I are very glad to meet you sir. Please remember that there is always a welcome waiting for you over the way."

Then the Professor thanked him so heartily, and looked so suddenly illuminated with satisfaction, that Laurie thought him the most delightfully demonstrative old fellow he ever met.

"I too shall go; but I shall gladly come again, if you will gif me leave, dear madame, for a little business in the city will keep me here some days."

He spoke to Mrs. March, but he looked at Jo; and the mother's voice gave as cordial an assent as did the daughter's eyes; for Mrs. March was not so blind to her children's interest as Mrs. Moffat supposed.

"I suspect that is a wise man," remarked Mr. March, with placid satisfaction, from the hearth-rug, after the last guest had gone.

"I know he is a good one," added Mrs. March, with decided approval, as she wound up the clock.

"I thought you'd like him," was all Jo said, as she slipped away to her bed.

She wondered what the business was that brought Mr. Bhaer to the city, and finally decided that he had been appointed to some great honour, somewhere, but had been too modest to mention the fact. If she had seen his face when, safe in his own room, he looked at the picture of a severe and rigid young lady, with a good deal of hair, who appeared to be gazing darkly into futurity, it might have thrown some light upon the subject, especially when he turned off the gas, and kissed the picture in the dark.

CHAPTER TWENTY-ONE

MY LORD AND LADY

"PLEASE, Madam Mother, could you lend me my wife for half-an-hour. The luggage has come, and I've been making hay of Amy's Paris finery, trying to find some things I want," said Laurie, coming in the next day to find Mrs. Laurence sitting in her mother's lap, as if being made "the baby" again.

"Certainly. Go, dear; I forget that you have any home but this," and Mrs. March pressed the white hand that wore the wedding-ring, as if asking pardon for her maternal covetousness.

"I shouldn't have come over if I could have helped it; but I can't get on without my little woman any more than a——"

"Weathercock can without wind," suggested Jo, as he paused for a simile; Jo had grown quite her own saucy self again since Teddy came home.

"Exactly; for Amy keeps me pointing due west most of the time, with only an occasional whiffle round to the south, and I haven't had an easterly spell since I was married; don't know anything about the north, but am altogether salubrious and balmy, hey, my lady?"

"Lovely weather so far; I don't know how long it will last, but I'm not afraid of storms, for I'm learning how to sail my ship. Come home, dear, and I'll find your bootjack; I suppose that's what you are rummaging after among my things. Men are *so* helpless, mother," said Amy, with a matronly air, which delighted her husband.

"What are you going to do with yourselves after you get settled?" asked Jo, buttoning Amy's cloak as she used to button her pinafores.

"We have our plans; we don't mean to say much about them yet, because we are such very new brooms, but we don't intend to be idle. I'm going into business with a devotion that shall delight grandfather, and prove to him that I'm not spoilt. I need something of the sort to keep me steady. I'm tired of dawdling, and mean to work like a man."

"And Amy, what is she going to do?" asked Mrs. March, well pleased at Laurie's decision, and the energy with which he spoke.

"After doing the civil all round, and airing our best bonnet, we shall astonish you by the elegant hospitalities of our mansion, the brilliant society we shall draw about us, and the beneficial influence we shall exert over the world at large. That's about it, isn't it. Madame Récamier?" asked Laurie, with a quizzical look at Amy.

"Time will show. Come away, Impertinence, and don't shock my family by calling me names before their faces," answered Amy, resolving that there should be a home with a good wife in it before she set up a *salon* as a queen of society.

Later in the evening, when his mind had been set at rest about the bootjack, Laurie said suddenly to his wife, who was flitting about, arranging her new art treasures—

"Mrs. Laurence."

"My lord!"

"That man intends to marry our Jo!"

"I hope so; don't you, dear?"

"Well, my love I consider him a trump, in the fullest sense of that expressive word, but I do wish he was a little younger and a good deal richer."

"Now, Laurie don't be too fastidious and wordly-minded. If they love one another it doesn't matter a particle how old they are nor how poor. Women *never* should marry for money——" Amy caught herself up short as the words escaped her, and looked at her husband, who replied, with malicious gravity—

"Certainly not, though you do hear charming girls say that they intend to do it sometimes. If my memory serves me, you once thought it your duty to make a rich match; that accounts, perhaps, for your marrying a good-for-nothing like me."

"O my dearest boy, don't don't say that! I forgot you were rich when I said 'Yes.' I'd have married you if you hadn't a penny, and I sometimes wish you *were* poor that I might show how much I love you;" and Amy, who was very dignified in public and very fond in private, gave convincing proofs of the truth of her words.

"You don't really think I am such a mercenary creature as I tried to be once, do you? It would break my heart if you didn't believe that I'd gladly pull in the same boat with you, even if you had to get your living by rowing on the lake."

"Am I an idiot and a brute? How could I think so, when you refused a richer man for me, and won't let me give you half I want to now, when I have the right? Girls do it everyday, poor things, and are taught to think it is their only salvation; but you had better lessons, and, though I trembled for you at one time, I was not disappointed, for the daughter was true to the mother's teaching. I told mamma so yesterday, and she looked as glad and grateful as if I'd given her a cheque for a million, to be spent in charity. You are not listening to my moral remarks, Mrs. Laurence;" and Laurie paused, for Amy's eyes had an absent look, though fixed upon his face.

"Yes, I am, and admiring the dimple in your chin at the same time. I don't wish to make you vain, but I must confess that I'm prouder of my husband than of all his money. Don't laugh, but your nose is *such* a comfort to me;" and Amy softly caressed the well-cut feature with artistic satisfaction.

Laurie had received many compliments in his life, but never one that suited him better, as he plainly showed, though he did laugh at his wife's peculiar taste, while she said slowly—

"May I ask you a question, dear?"

"Of course you may."

"Shall you care if Jo does marry Mr. Bhaer?"

"Oh, that's the trouble, is it? I thought there was something in the dimple that didn't suit you. Not being a dog in the manger, but the happiest fellow alive. I assure you I can dance at Jo's wedding with a heart as light as my heels. Do you doubt it, my darling?"

Amy looked up at him, and was satisfied; her last little jealous fear vanished for ever, and she thanked him, with a face full of love and confidence.

"I wish we could do something for that capital old Professor. Couldn't we invent a rich relation, who shall obligingly die out there in Germany, and leave him a tidy little fortune?" said Laurie, when they began to pace up and down the long drawing-room arm-in-arm, as they were fond of doing, in memory of the château garden.

"Jo would find us out, and spoil it all; she is very

proud of him, just as he is, and said yesterday that she thought poverty was a beautiful thing."

"Bless her dear heart! she won't think so when she has a literary husband, and a dozen little professors and professorins to support. We won't interfere now, but watch our chance, and do them a good turn in spite of themselves. I owe Jo for a part of my education, and she believes in people's paying their honest debts, so I'll get round her in that way."

"How delightful it is to be able to help others, isn't it?

"And so you shall, like an angel as you are!" cried Laurie, resolving, with a glow of philanthropic zeal, to found and endow an institution for the express benefit of young women with artistic tendencies. We'll have a good time ourselves, and add an extra relish to our own pleasure by giving other people a generous taste. Will you be a little Dorcas, going about emptying a basket of comforts, and filling it up with good deeds?"

"With all my heart, if you will be a brave St. Martin, stopping, as you ride gallantly through the world, to share your cloak with the beggar."

"It's a bargain, and we shall get the best of it!"

So the young pair shook hands upon it, and then paced happily on again, feeling that their pleasant home was more home-like because they hoped to brighten other homes, believing that their own feet would walk more uprightly along the flowery path before them, if they smoothed rough ways for other feet, and feeling that their hearts were more closely knit together by a love which could tenderly remember those less blest than they.

CHAPTER TWENTY-TWO

UNDER THE UMBRELLA

WHILE Laurie and Amy were taking conjugal strolls over velvet carpets, as they set their house in order, and planned a blissful future, Mr. Bhaer and Jo were enjoying promenades of a different sort, along muddy roads and sodden fields.

"I always do take a walk toward evening, and I don't know why I should give it up, just because I often happen to meet the Professor on his way out," said Jo to herself, after two or three encounters; for, though there were two paths to Meg's whichever one she took she was sure to meet him, either going or returning.

Under the circumstances, what could Jo do but greet him civilly, and invite him in? If she *was* tired of his visits, she concealed her weariness with perfect skill, and took care that there should be coffee for supper, "as Friedrich—I mean Mr. Bhaer—doesn't like tea."

Jo couldn't even lose her heart in a decorous manner, but sternly tried to quench her feelings; and, failing to do so, led a somewhat agitated life. She was mortally afraid of being laughed at for surrendering, after her many and vehement declarations of independence. Laurie was her especial dread; but, thanks to the new manager, he behaved with praiseworthy propriety, never called Mr. Bhaer "a capital old fellow" in public, never alluded, in the remotest manner, to Jo's improved appearance, or expressed the least surprise at seeing the Professor's hat on the Marches' hall-table nearly every evening.

For a fortnight, the Professor came and went with

lover-like regularity; then he stayed away for three whole days, and made no sign—a proceeding which caused everybody to look sober, and Jo to become pensive, at first, and then—alas for romance!—very cross.

"Disgusted, I dare say, and gone home as suddenly as he came. It's nothing to me, of course; but I *should* think he would have come and bid us good-bye, like a gentleman," she said to herself, with a despairing look at the gate, as she put on her things for the customary walk, one dull afternoon.

"You'd better take the little umbrella, dear; it looks like rain," said her mother, observing that she had on her new bonnet, but not alluding to the fact.

"Yes, Marmee; do you want anything in town? I've got to run in and get some paper," returned Jo, pulling out the bow under her chin before the glass as an excuse for not looking at her mother

"Yes; I want some twilled silesia, a paper of number nine needles, and two yards of narrow lavender ribbon. Have you got your thick boots on, and something warm under your cloak?"

"I believe so," answered Jo absently.

"If you happen to meet Mr. Bhaer, bring him home to tea. I quite long to see the dear man," added Mrs. March.

Jo heard *that*, but made no answer, except to kiss her mother, and walk rapidly away, thinking with a glow of gratitude, in spite of her heartache—

"How good she is to me! What *do* girls do who haven't any mothers to help them through their troubles?"

The dry-good stores were not down among the countinghouses, banks, and wholesale warerooms, where gentlemen most do congregate; but Jo found herself in that part of the city before she did a single errand, loitering along as if waiting for some one, examining engineering instruments in one window and samples of wool in another most unfeminine interest; tumbling over barrels, being half smothered by descending bales, and hustled unceremoniously by busy men who looked as if they wondered "how the deuce she got there." A drop of rain on her cheek recalled her thoughts from baffled hopes to ruined ribbons; for the drops continued to fall, and, being a woman as well as a lover, she felt that, though it was too late to save her heart, she might her bonnet. Now she remembered the little umbrella, which she had forgotten to take in her hurry to be off; but regret was unavailing, and nothing could be done but borrow one or submit to a drenching.

"It serves me right! What business had I to put on all my best things and come philandering down here, hoping to see the Professor? Jo, I'm ashamed of you! No, you shall *not* go there to borrow an umbrella, or find out where he is, from his friends. You shall trudge away, and do your errands in the rain; and if you catch your death and ruin your bonnet, it's no more than you deserve. Now then!"

With that she rushed across the street so impetuously that she narrowly escaped annihilation from a passing truck, and precipitated herself into the arms of a stately old gentleman, who said. "I beg pardon, ma'am," and looked mortally offended. Somewhat daunted, Jo righted herself, spread her handkerchief over the devoted ribbons, and, putting temptation behind her, hurried on, with increasing dampness about the ankles, and much clashing of umbrellas overhead. The fact that a somewhat dilapidated blue one remained stationary above the unprotected bonnet, attracted her attention; and, looking up, she saw Mr. Bhaer looking down.

"I feel to know the strong-minded lady who goes so bravely under many horse-noses, and so fast through much mud. What do you down here, my friend?"

"I'm shopping."

Mr. Bhaer smiled, as he glanced from the pickle-factory on one side, to the wholesale hide and leather concern on the other; but he only said politely—

"You haf no umbrella. May I go also, and take for you the bundles?"

"Yes, thank you."

Jo's cheeks were as red as her ribbon, and she wondered what he thought of her; but she didn't care, for in a minute she found herself walking away arm-in-arm with her Professor, feeling as if the sun had suddenly burst out with uncommon brilliancy, that the world was all right again, and that one thoroughly happy woman was paddling through the wet that day.

"We thought you had gone," said Jo hastily, for she knew he was looking at her.

"Did you believe that I should go with no farewell to those who haf been so heavenly kind to me?" he asked so reproachfully that she felt as if she had insulted him by the suggestion, and answered heartily—

"No *I* didn't; I knew you were busy about your own affairs, but we rather missed you—father and mother especially."

"And you?"

"I'm always glad to see you, sir."

In her anxiety to keep her voice quite calm, Jo made it rather cool, and the frosty little monosyllable at the end seemed to chill the Professor, for his smile vanished, as he said gravely—

"I thank you, and come one time more before I go."

"You *are* going, then?"

"I haf no longer any business here; it is done."

"Successfully, I hope?" said Jo, for the bitterness

of disappointment was in that short reply of his.

"I ought to think so, for I haf a way opened to me by which I can make my bread and gif my Jünglings much help."

"Tell me, please! I like to know all about the—the boys," said Jo eagerly.

"That is so kind, I gladly tell you. My friends find for me a place in a college, where I teach as at home, and earn enough to make the way smooth for Franz and Emil. For this I should be grateful, should I not?"

Indeed you should. How splendid it will be to have you doing what you like, and be able to see you often, and the boys!" cried Jo, clinging to the lads as an excuse for the satisfaction she could not help betraying.

"Ah! but we shall not meet often, I fear; this place is at the West."

"So far away!" and Jo left her skirts to their fate, as if it didn't matter now what became of her clothes or herself.

Jo rather prided herself upon her shopping capabilities, and particularly wished to impress her escort with the neatness and despatch with which she would accomplish the business. But, owing to the flutter she was in, everything went amiss; she upset the tray of needles, forgot the silesia was to be "twilled" till it was cut off, gave the wrong change, and covered herself with confusion by asking for lavender ribbon at the calico counter. Mr. Bhaer stood by, watching her blush and blunder; and, as he watched, his own bewilderment seemed to subside, for he was beginning to see that on some occasions women, like dreams, go by contraries.

When they came out, he put the parcel under his arm with a more cheerful aspect, and splashed through the puddles as if he rather enjoyed it, on the whole.

"Should we not do a little what you call shopping for the babies, and haf a farewell feast to-night if I go for my last call at your so pleasant home?" he asked, stopping before a window full of fruit and flowers.

"What will we buy?" said Jo, ignoring the latter part of his speech, and sniffing the mingled odours with an affection of delight as they went in.

"May they haf oranges and figs?" asked Mr. Bhaer, with a paternal air.

"They eat them when they can get them."

"Do you care for nuts?"

"Like a squirrel."

"Hamburg grapes; yes, we shall surely drink to the Fatherland in those?"

Jo frowned upon that piece of extravagance, and asked why he didn't buy a frail of dates, a cask of raisins, and a bag of almonds, and done with it? Whereat Mr. Bhaer confiscated her purse, produced his own, and finished the marketing by buying several pounds of grapes, a pot of rosy daisies, and a pretty jar of honey, to be regarded in the light of a demijohn. Then, distorting his pockets with the knobby bundles, and giving her the flowers to hold, he put up the old umbrella, and they travelled on again.

"Miss Marsch, I haf a great favour to ask of you." began the Professor, after a moist promenade of half a block.

"Yes, sir," and Jo's heart began to beat so hard she was afraid he would hear it.

"I am bold to say it in spite of the rain, because so short a time remains to me."

"Yes, sir;" and Jo nearly crushed the small flower-pot with the sudden squeeze she gave it.

"I wish to get a little dress for Tina, and I am too stupid to go alone. Will you kindly gif me a word of taste and help?"

"Yes, sir;" and Jo felt as calm and cool, all of a sudden, as if she had stepped into a refrigerator.

"Perhaps also a shawl for Tina's mother, she is so poor and sick, and the husband is such a care. Yes, yes, a thick warm shawl would be a friendly thing to take the little mother."

"I'll do it with pleasure, Mr. Bhaer. I'm going very fast and he's getting dearer every minute," added Jo to herself; then, with a mental shake, she entered into the business with an energy which was pleasant to behold.

Mr. Bhaer left it all to her, so she chose a pretty gown for Tina, and then ordered out the shawls. The clerk, being a married man, condescended to take an interest in the couple, who appeared to be shopping for their family.

"Your lady may prefer this; it's a superior article, a most desirable colour, quite chaste and genteel," he said, shaking out a comfortable grey shawl, and throwing it over Jo's shoulders.

"Does this suit you, Mr. Bhaer?" she asked, turning her back to him, and feeling deeply grateful for the chance of hiding her face.

"Excellently well; we will haf it," answered the Professor, smiling to himself as he paid for it, while Jo continued to rummage the counters like a confirmed bargain-hunter.

"Now, shall we go home?" he asked, as if the words were very pleasant to him.

"Yes; it's late, and I'm *so* tired." Jo's voice was more pathetic than she knew; for now the sun seemed to have gone in as suddenly as it came out, the world grew muddy and miserable again, and for the first time she discovered that her feet were cold, her head ached. and that her heart was colder than the former, fuller of pain than the latter. Mr. Bhaer was going away; he only cared for her as a friend; it was all a mistake, and the sooner it was over the better.

With this idea in her head, she hailed an approaching omnibus with such a hasty gesture that the daisies flew out of the pot and were badly damaged.

"This is not our omniboos," said the Professor, waving the loaded vehicle away, and stooping to pick up the poor little flowers.

"I beg your pardon, I didn't see the name distinctly. Never mind, I can walk. I'm used to plodding in the mud," returned Jo, winking hard, because she would have died rather than openly wipe her eyes.

Mr. Bhaer saw the drops on her cheeks, though she turned her head away; the sight seemed to touch him very much, for, suddenly stooping down, he asked in a tone that meant a great deal—

"Heart's dearest, why do you cry?"

Now, if Jo had not been new to this sort of thing she would have said she wasn't crying, had a cold in her head, or told any other feminine fib proper to the occasion; instead of which that undignified creature answered, with an irrespressible sob—

"Because you are going away."

"Ach, mein Gott, that is *so* good!" cried Mr. Bhaer, managing to clasp his hands in spite of the umbrella and the bundles. "Jo, I haf nothing but much love to gif you; I came to see if you could care for it, and I waited to be sure that I was something more than a friend. Am I? Can you make a little place in your heart for old Fritz?" he added, all in one breath.

"Oh, yes!" said Jo; and he was quite satisfied, for she folded both hands over his arm, and looked up at him with an expression that plainly showed how happy she would be to walk through life beside him, even though she had no better shelter than the old umbrella, if he carried it.

Passers-by probably thought them a pair of harmless lunatics, for they entirely forgot to hail a 'bus, and strolled leisurely along, oblivious of deepening dusk and fog. Little they cared what anybody thought, for they were enjoying the happy hour that seldom comes but once in any life, the magical moment which bestows youth on the old, beauty on the plain, wealth on the poor, and gives human hearts a foretaste of heaven. The Professor looked as if he had conquered a kingdom, and the world had nothing more to offer him in the way of bliss; while Jo trudged beside him, wondering how she ever could have chosen any other lot. Of course. she was the first to speak—intelligibly, I mean, for the emotional remarks which followed her impetuous "Oh, yes!" were not of a coherent or reportable character.

"Friedrich, why didn't you——"

"Ah, heaven, she gifs me the name that no one speaks since Minna died!" cried the Professor, pausing in a puddle to regard her with grateful delight.

"I always call you so to myself—I forgot, but I won't, unless you like it."

"Like it? It is more sweet to me than I can tell. Say 'thou,' also, and I shall say your language is almost as beautiful as mine."

"Isn't 'thou' a little sentimental?" asked Jo, privately thinking it a lovely monosyllable.

"Sentimental? Yes. Thank Gott, we Germans believe in sentiment, and keep ourselves young mit it. Your English 'you' is so cold, say 'thou,' heart's dearest, it means so much to me," pleaded Mr. Bhaer, more like a romantic student than a grave professor.

"Well, then, why didn't thou tell me all this sooner?" asked Jo bashfully.

"Now I shall haf to show thee all my heart, and I so gladly will, because thou must take care of it hereafter

See, then, my Jo—ah, the dear, funny little name!—I had a wish to tell something the day I said good-bye, in New York; but I thought the handsome friend was betrothed to thee, and so I spoke not. Wouldst thou have said 'Yes,' then, if I *had* spoken?"

"I don't know; I'm afraid not, for I didn't have any heart just then."

"Prut! That I do not believe. It was asleep till the fairy prince came through the wood, and waked it up. Ah, well, 'Die erste Liebe ist die beste;' but that I should not expect."

"Yes, the first love *is* the best; so be contented, for I never had another. Teddy was only a boy, and soon got over his little fancy," said Jo, anxious to correct the Professor's mistake.

"What made you stay away so long?" she asked presently, finding it so pleasant to ask confidential questions and get delightful answers that she could not keep silent.

"It was not easy, but I could not find the heart to take you from that so happy home until I could haf a prospect of one to give you, after much time, perhaps, and hard work. How could I ask you to gif up so much for a poor old fellow, who has no fortune but a little learning?"

"I'm glad you *are* poor; I couldn't bear a rich husband," said Jo decidedly, adding. in a softer tone, "Don't fear poverty; I've known it long enough to lose my dread and be happy working for those I love; and don't call yourself old—forty is the prime of life. I couldn't help loving you if you were seventy!"

The Professor found that so touching that he would have been glad of his handkerchief, if he could have got at it; as he couldn't, Jo wiped his eyes for him, and said, laughing, as she took away a bundle or two—

"I may be strong-minded, but no one can say I'm out

of my sphere now, for woman's special mission is supposed to be drying tears and bearing burdens. I'm to carry my share. Friedrich, and help to earn the home. Make up your mind to that, or I'll never go," she added resolutely, as he tried to reclaim his load.

"We shall see. Haf you patience to wait a long time, Jo? I must go away and do my work alone. I must help my boys first, because, even for you, I may not break my word to Minna. Can you forgif that, and be happy while we hope and wait?"

"Yes, I know I can; for we love one another, and that makes all the rest easy to bear. I have my duty, also, and my work. I couldn't enjoy myself if I neglected them even for you so there's no need of hurry or impatience. You can do your part out West, I can do mine here, and both be happy hoping for the best, and leaving the future to be as God wills."

"Ah! Thou gifest me such hope and courage, and I haf nothing to gif back but a full heart and these empty hands," cried the Professor, quite overcome.

Jo never, never would learn to be proper; for when he said that as they stood upon the steps, she just put both hands into his, whispered tenderly, "Not empty now;" and, stooped down, kissed her Friedrich under the umbrella. It was dreadful. but she would have done it if the flock of draggle-tailed sparrows on the hedge had been human beings, for she was very far gone indeed, and quite regardless of everything but her own happiness. Though it came in such a very simple guise, that was the crowning moment of both their lives, when, turning from the night and storm and loneliness to the household light and warmth and peace waiting to receive them, with a glad "Welcome home!" Jo led her lover in, and shut the door.

CHAPTER TWENTY-THREE

HARVEST TIME

FOR a year Jo and her Professor worked and waited, hoped and loved, met occasionally, and wrote such voluminous letters that the rise in the price of paper was accounted for, Laurie said. The second year began rather soberly, for their prospects did not brighten, and Aunt March died suddenly. But when their first sorrow was over—for they loved the old lady in spite of her sharp tongue—they found they had cause for rejoicing, for she had left Plumfield to Jo, which made all sorts of joyful things possible.

"It's a fine old place, and will bring a handsome sum; for of course you intend to sell it." said Laurie, as they were all talking the matter over, some weeks later.

"No, I don't," was Jo's decided answer, as she petted the fat poodle, whom she had adopted, out of respect to his former mistress.

"You don't mean to live there?"

"Yes, I do."

"But, my dear girl, it's an immense house, and will take a power of money to keep it in order. The garden and orchard alone need two or three men, and farming isn't in Bhaer's line, I take it."

"He'll try his hand at it there, if I propose it."

"And you expect to live on the produce of the place? Well, that sounds paradisaical, but you'll find it desperate hard work."

"The crop we are going to raise is a profitable one;" and Jo laughed.

"Of what is this fine crop to consist, ma'am?"

"Boys. I want to open a school for little lads—a good, happy homelike school, with me to take care of them, and Fritz to teach them."

"There's a truly Joian plan for you! Isn't that just like her?" cried Laurie, appealing to the family, who looked as much surprised as he.

"I like it," said Mrs. March decidedly.

"So do I," added her husband, who welcomed the thought of a chance for trying the Socratic method of education on modern youth.

"It will be an immense care for Jo," said Meg, stroking the head of her one all-absorbing son.

"Jo can do it, and be happy in it. It's a splendid idea. Tell us all about it," cried Mr. Laurence, who had been longing to lend the lovers a hand, but knew that they would refuse his help.

"I knew you'd stand by me, sir. Amy does too—I see it in her eyes, though she prudently waits to turn it over in her mind before she speaks. Now, my dear people," continued Jo earnestly, "just understand that this isn't a new idea of mine, but a long-cherished plan. Before my Fritz came, I used to think how, when I'd made my fortune, and no one needed me at home, I'd hire a big house, and pick up some poor, forlorn little lads, who hadn't any mothers, and take care of them, and make life jolly for them before it was too late. I see so many going to ruin, for want of help at the right minute; I so love to do anything for them; I seem to feel their wants, and sympathise with their troubles, and, oh, I should *so* like to be a mother to them!"

Mrs. March held out her hand to Jo, who took it, smiling, with tears in her eyes, and went on in the old enthusiastic way, which they had not seen for a long while.

"I told my plan to Fritz once, and he said it was just what he would like, and agreed to try it when we got rich. Bless his dear heart, he's been doing it all his life —helping poor boys, I mean, not getting rich; that he'll never be; money doesn't stay in his pocket long enough to lay up any. But now, thanks to my good old aunt, who loved me better than I ever deserved *I'm* rich at least I feel so, and we can live at Plumfield perfectly well, if we have a flourishing school. It's just the place for boys, the house is big, and the furniture strong and plain. There's plenty of room for dozens inside, and splendid grounds outside. They could help in the garden and orchard: such work is healthy, isn't it, sir? Then Fritz can train and teach in his own way, and Father will help him. I can feed and nurse and pet and scold them; and Mother will be my stand-by. I've always longed for lots of boys, and never had enough; now I can fill the house full, and revel in the little dears to my heart's content. Think what luxury—Plumfield my own, and a wilderness of boys to enjoy it with me!"

It was a very astonishing year altogether, for things seemed to happen in an unusually rapid and delightful manner. Almost before she knew where she was, Jo found herself married and settled at Plumfield. Then a family of six or seven boys sprung up like mushrooms, and flourished surprisingly, poor boys as well as rich; for Mr. Laurence was continually finding some touching case of destitution, and begging the Bhaers to take pity on the child, and he would gladly pay a trifle for its support. In this way the sly old gentleman got round proud Jo, and furnished her with the style of boy in which she most delighted.

Of course it was uphill work at first, and Jo made queer mistakes; but the wise Professor steered her safely into calmer waters, and the most rampant ragamuffin was conquered in the end. How Jo did enjoy her "wilderness of boys," and how poor, dear Aunt March would have lamented had she been there to see the sacred precincts of prim, well-ordered Plumfield overrun with Toms, Dicks, and Harrys!

There was a sort of poetic justice about it, after all, for the old lady had been the terror of the boys for miles round; and now the exiles feasted freely on forbidden plums, kicked up the gravel with profane boots unreproved, and played cricket in the big field where the irritable "cow with a crumpled horn" used to invite rash youths to come and be tossed. It became a sort of boys' paradise, and Laurie suggested that it should be called the "Bhaer-garden," as a compliment to its master and appropriate to its inhabitants.

It never was a fashionable school, and the Professor did not lay up a fortune; but it *was* just what Jo intended it to be—"a happy, homelike place for boys, who needed teaching, care, and kindness."

Yes; Jo was a very happy woman there, in spite of hard work, much anxiety, and a perpetual racket. She enjoyed it heartily, and found the applause of her boys more satisfying than any praise of the world; for now she told no stories except to her flock of enthusiastic believers and admirers. As the years went on, two little lads of her own came to increase her happiness—Rob, named for Grandpa, and Teddy, a happy-go-lucky baby, who seemed to have inherited his papa's sunshiny temper as well as his mother's lively spirit. How they ever grew up alive in that whirlpool of boys was a mystery to their grandma and aunts; but they flourished like dandelions in spring, and their rough nurses loved and served them well.

There were a great many holidays at Plumfield, and one of the most delightful was the yearly apple-picking; for then the Marches, Laurences, Brookes, and Bhaers turned out in full force, and made a day of it. Five years after Jo's wedding, one of these fruitful festivals occurred—a mellow October day, when the air was full of an exhilarating freshness which made the spirits rise, and the blood dance healthily in the veins. The old orchard wore its holiday attire; golden-rod and asters fringed the mossy walls; grasshoppers skipped briskly in the sere grass, and crickets chirped like fairy pipers at a feast; squirrels were busy with their small harvesting; birds twittered their adieux from the alders in the lane; and every tree stood ready to send down its shower of red or yellow apples at the first shake. Everybody was there; everybody laughed and sang, climbed up and tumbled down; everybody declared that there never had been such a perfect day or such a jolly set to enjoy it; and every one gave themselves up to the simple pleasures of the hour as freely as if there were no such things as care or sorrow in the world.

Jo was in her element that day, and rushed about, with her gown pinned up, her hat anywhere but on her head, and her baby tucked under her arm, ready for any lively adventure which might turn up. Little Teddy bore a charmed life, for nothing ever happened to him, and Jo never felt any anxiety when he was whisked up into a tree by one lad, galloped off on the back of another, or supplied with sour russets by his indulgent papa, who laboured under the Germanic delusion that babies could digest anything, from pickled cabbage to buttons, nails, and their own small shoes. She knew that little Ted would turn up again in time, safe and rosy, dirty and serene, and she always received him back with a hearty welcome, for Jo loved her babies tenderly.

At four o'clock a lull took place, and baskets remained empty, while the apple-pickers rested, and compared rents and bruises. Then Jo and Meg, with a detachment of the bigger boys, set forth the supper on the grass, for an out-of-door tea was always the crowning joy of the day. The land literally flowed with milk and honey on such occasions, for the lads were not required to sit at table, but allowed to partake of refreshments as they liked—freedom being the sauce best beloved by the boyish soul. They availed themselves of the rare privilege to the fullest extent, for some tried the pleasing experiment of drinking milk while standing on their heads, others lent a charm to leap-frog by eating pie in the pauses of the game, cookies were sown broadcast over the field, and apple-turnovers roosted in the trees like a new style of bird. The little girls had a private tea-party, and Ted roved among the edibles at his own sweet will.

When no one could eat any more, the Professor proposed the first regular toast, which was always drunk at such times—"Aunt March, God bless her!" A toast heartily given by the good man, who never forgot how much he owed her, and quietly drunk by the boys, who had been taught to keep her memory green.

"Now, Grandma's sixtieth birthday! Long life to her, with three times three!"

After this, the boys dispersed for a final lark, leaving Mrs. March and her daughters under the festival tree.

"I don't think I ever ought to call myself 'Unlucky Jo' again, when my greatest wish has been so beautifully gratified," said Mrs. Bhaer, taking Teddy's little fist out of the milk-pitcher, in which he was rapturously churning.

"And yet your life is very different from the one you pictured so long ago. Do you remember our castles in the air?" asked Amy, smiling as she watched Laurie and John playing cricket with the boys.

"Dear fellows! It does my heart good to see them forget business, and frolic for a day," answered Jo, who now spoke in a maternal way of all mankind. "Yes, I remember; but the life I wanted then seems selfish, lonely, and cold to me now. I haven't given up the hope that I may write a good book yet, but I can wait, and I'm sure it will be all the better for such experiences and illustrations as these;" and Jo pointed from the lively lads in the distance to her father, leaning on the Professor's arm, as they walked to and fro in the sunshine, deep in one of the conversations which both enjoyed so much, and then to her mother, sitting enthroned among her daughters, with their children in her lap and at her feet, as if all found help and happiness in the face which never could grow old to them.

"My castle was the most nearly realised of all. I asked for splendid things, to be sure, but in my heart I knew I should be satisfied, if I had a little home, and John, and some dear children like these. I've got them all, thank God, and am the happiest woman in the world;" and Meg laid her hand on her tall boy's head, with a face full of tender and devout content.

"My castle is very different from what I planned, but I would not alter it, though, like Jo, I don't relinquish all my artistic hopes, or confine myself to helping others fulfil their dreams of beauty. I've begun to model a figure of baby, and Laurie says it is the best thing I've ever done. I think so myself, and mean to do it in marble, so that, whatever happens, I may at least keep the image of my little angel."

As Amy spoke, a great tear dropped on the golden hair of the sleeping child in her arms; for her one well-beloved daughter was a frail little creature and the dread of losing her was the shadow over Amy's sunshine. This cross was doing much for both father and mother, for one love and sorrow bound them closely together.

"She is growing better, I am sure of it, my dear. Don't despond, but hope and keep happy," said Mrs. March, as tender-hearted Daisy stooped from her knee, to lay her rosy cheek against her little cousin's pale one.

"I never ought to, while I have you to cheer me up, Marmee, and Laurie to take more than half of every burden," replied Amy warmly. "He never lets me see his anxiety, but is so sweet and patient with me, so devoted to Beth, and such a stay and comfort to me always, that I can't love him enough. So, in spite of my one cross, I can say with Meg, 'Thank God, I'm a happy woman'."

"There's no need for me to say it, for everyone can see that I'm far happier than I deserve," added Jo, glancing from her good husband to her chubby children, tumbling on the grass beside her. "Fritz is getting grey and stout; I'm growing as thin as a shadow, and am thirty. But in spite of these unromantic facts, I have nothing to complain of, and never was so jolly in my life. Excuse the remark, but living among boys, I can't help using their expressions now and then."

"Yes, Jo, I think your harvest will be a good one," began Mrs. March, frightening away a big black cricket that was staring Teddy out of countenance.

"Not half so good as yours, Mother. Here it is, and we never can thank you enough for the patient sowing and reaping you have done," cried Jo, with the loving impetuosity which she never could outgrow.

"I hope there will be more wheat and fewer tares every year," said Amy softly.

"A large sheaf, but I know there's room in your heart for it. Marmee dear," added Meg's tender voice.

Touched to the heart, Mrs. March could only stretch out her arms, as if to gather children and grandchildren to herself, and say, with face and voice full of motherly love, gratitude, and humility—

"O, my girls, however long you may live, I never can wish you a greater happiness than this!"

Love Is Not a Business Deal . . .

"You make it sound like you're marrying her for her money," she said.

"I am," Mason admitted with no sign of embarrassment. "Don't feel sorry for Caro. She knows exactly what she's getting into, and she's more than happy to trade a few million dollars of investment capital—which she'll get back many times over, by the way—for the Alexander name and address. In fact, I think she has it in her personal planner, under Goals. Caro and I see eye to eye on this. We'll do fine—*without* Mother's potions."

Raine glanced at his back with pity, then hustled to fall in beside him. A thousand responses ran through her brain, but she decided to keep them to herself. Nothing she could say would make any difference to a man who imagined you could base a marriage on anything other than love. And if he didn't believe in something as obvious as love, how was she ever going to get him to believe in the subtleties of *feng shui*?

Praise for *Razzle Dazzle:*

"A delightful, sexy story with enough humor and passion to keep even the most discerning reader satisfied . . . Hendrix is a bright new voice in contemporary romance. Reading should always be this much fun. *Razzle Dazzle* is a keeper."

—*Under the Covers*

Razzle Dazzle

LISA HENDRIX

JOVE BOOKS, NEW YORK

RAZZLE DAZZLE

A Jove Book / published by arrangement with the author

PRINTING HISTORY
Jove edition / September 1999

For information address: The Berkley Publishing Group, a division of Penguin Putnam Inc., 375 Hudson Street, New York, New York 10014.

The Penguin Putnam Inc. World Wide Web site address is http://www.penguinputnam.com

ISBN: 0-515-12612-8

A JOVE BOOK®
Jove Books are published by The Berkley Publishing Group, a division of Penguin Putnam Inc., 375 Hudson Street, New York, New York 10014.

PRINTED IN THE UNITED STATES OF AMERICA

10 9 8 7 6 5 4 3 2 1

To Cap'n Dave and the Mates
who kept the ship afloat.

Thanks, Crew

One

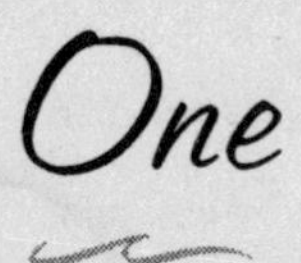

"I've never heard anything so ridiculous in my life." The beveled glass of the conservatory echoed with the ring of Mason's voice.

Titania Alexander, called Tish by friends and something rudely sexual by her few enemies, hadn't seen her son so irritated in years, not since she'd brought home her past lives counselor and the poor woman had tried to regress him during dinner.

Mason tossed down the last swallow of his cup of coffee and glanced back and forth between Tish and his sister, Miranda.

"Which of you came up with this idiotic plan?" he demanded, fixing Tish with a steely stare that had caused more than one accountant to slip into an unintelligible mumble. "Let me guess—you, Mother?"

"Really, Mason. There's no reason to make it sound like we intended something criminal." Tish stroked Magus, the delicate, white Persian cat who had curled up on her lap. The resulting purr immunized her against Mason's sarcasm. No wonder witches had always kept cats as familiars. "But yes, giving Caroline a love potion was my idea. We know how important this is to you."

"It's your own fault," Miranda chimed in from her seat at the far end of the couch. "If you didn't have such a disturbed aura, you wouldn't need a love potion to get Caro to marry you."

"Listen to yourself. Auras. Love potions. You sound like some Gypsy psychic con artist."

"*True* Gypsies make excellent psychics," said Tish. "However, we hardly qualify as Gypsies. Or as con artists."

"No, just witches."

"Yes, darling," she said patiently. "Miranda's right, though. With your negative vibrations, you need all the help you can get. Perhaps a ritual cleansing."

"Tish." Miranda brightened. "What a perfectly marvelous idea."

"Mother," Mason growled under his breath. "She's our mother, not your girlfriend."

Miranda ignored him and leaned forward, her bare toes curling on the antique Lavar rug in her excitement. "We can ask Raven to do it."

A snort of laughter escaped Mason. "Raven Brightwater. God, I wish I knew what she was smoking when she picked that name. Look, ladies, I don't have any control over you and your weirdness, unfortunately, but leave me out. And leave Caroline out. Our relationship is moving along just fine."

"But she said no," Tish pointed out.

"It's just a tactic. We're negotiating."

Miranda frowned. "You make it sound like a merger."

"More of a joint venture," said Mason. "Alexander Industries meets Wick Technologies."

"The whole thing is positively mercenary."

Mason met his sister's accusation without a trace of apology in his cool blue eyes. "It's also mutual. You can be certain Caroline plans to get exactly what *she* wants out of this partnership. Just as I do."

"That's a very callous attitude," said Tish.

"It's also a very realistic one, Mother, and one that served human society very well for thousands of years. I should think you'd appreciate it, what with your predilection for archaic practices."

Tish looked away and sighed. "I had hoped for something better for you."

"This is the best, for all of us." He set the juice glass on the Louis XIV table to his left. "Think how many crystals you'll be able to afford once the power cell gets to market."

"We don't do crystals anymore," Miranda said.

"Oh, that's right. Well, newts' ears and dogs' toes for the coven, then."

"That's '*eye* of newt and toe of *frog,*' " said Miranda, a grin tugging at the corners of her mouth despite her brother's efforts to bait her. "With a degree from Harvard, I should think you'd at least get your clichéd Shakespearean stereotypes correct."

"Whatever. As long as none of that brew ends up in Caroline's highball."

"Since you don't believe in the Craft anyway, what harm can a few herbs do?"

"The point is that *you* believe in it and, as a result, feel entitled to meddle." He turned back to his mother. "I want a promise. No interfering in my life. No spells, no incantations, and *no* love potions."

"But—"

"But nothing. I mean it, Mother. None. I don't know what you put in that"—he pointed toward the tiny blue bottle whose unfortunate discovery had led to this conversation—"but I took a sniff, and it smells pretty peculiar. I don't want you poisoning Caroline by mistake."

"Oh, don't be silly. We'd never—"

"Mother, I'm warning you."

"Oh, all right" Tish said, her shoulders sagging in defeat. "No potions or spells."

"No interference of *any* kind," repeated Mason.

"Of any kind. You have my word."

Mason's eyes narrowed suspiciously. "Do you have any fingers crossed?"

She held out her hands and waggled her fingers like a pianist loosening up, then touched the center of her chest. "No, but I will cross my heart if you'd like."

"That won't be necessary." He glanced at his watch and stood, and once again Tish thanked the gods that he'd inherited his father's commanding six feet instead of her own piddling five. "Now, I promised Caroline I'd show her the rose garden."

"It's terribly hot, darling. You should have some iced tea sent out for after you finish your walk."

"Good idea. But first . . ." He reached past her and grabbed the little blue bottle, and, before she could muster a protest, he dumped it in the potted palm and returned the empty vial to its spot. "Much better. No temptation. We'll see you later."

He headed out, his lips curved into a rather smug smile.

All that work for nothing. Tish stared after Mason as her daughter slid around to join her at the end of the couch. They'd timed everything so carefully, inviting Caroline to visit this particular weekend so that the elixir could be freshly prepared beneath a waxing moon, as close as possible to the summer solstice. It was simply too bad Mason couldn't see how their efforts would benefit them all. She sighed. "I worry about your brother sometimes."

"He's so damned *responsible,*" said Miranda, strangling a tapestry pillow that was apparently standing in for Mason.

"That *is* a good trait," Tish said in her son's defense. "If your father had exhibited a tad more of it, the company would be more sound and Mason wouldn't be in such a desperate position."

Malcolm had been a good man and an excellent husband and father, but he had lacked greatly as a businessman. Early on, he had become obsessed with developing a power cell that would change the world. He sunk all the company's cash—and most of his personal fortune—into worthless patents and borrowed more for R&D that led nowhere. When he died, Mason had been saddled with a company that could barely service its debts.

The truly sad thing was, Malcolm had had the patent for a great power cell all along, but hadn't recognized the possibilities. Mason had found the records in a file, but now he couldn't develop it either, because Alexander Industries had no cash flow. The company was slowly bleeding to death on out-of-date products and facilities more suited to the 1960s. They had enough to live on, thanks to some cleverly designed trusts, but Caroline Wickersham and her fortune were the company's only hope for new life.

"But does he have to carry the responsibility thing so far?" Miranda asked. "Here he is planning to get married and he doesn't even care that his wife-to-be isn't in love with him." She sighed. "But then, apparently he isn't in love with her, either. I mean, I knew he wasn't head over heels or anything, but I did think he was at least fond of Caro. Apparently he's reserving his affections for her bank account."

"I know, I know. But he's doing his best to take care of us all, darling, in what is a very bad situation. We should be grateful."

"I am. But it's so . . . unromantic."

"I'm afraid Elizabeth left him sour on romance." Tish didn't even like saying her former daughter-in-law's name.

"I suppose." Miranda reached for the empty bottle and sat staring at its cobalt glow. The silvery script on its side glistened in the sunlight that filled the conservatory: *For Love.* "I'm starting to think we made a mistake with this."

"I don't think so, dear. We followed the instructions in the Book of Shadows very carefully."

"No, not that. I mean, maybe we were wrong in assuming that only Caro needed a dose." Miranda paused for dramatic effect. "Methinks big brother could benefit as well."

Titania sat up a little straighter, contemplating the prospect of a true love match between Mason and Caroline Wickersham. *Perhaps.* Despite what Mason had said, Tish knew they shared some interests beyond the boardroom: Tennis. French food. The Arts Alliance.

Perhaps it could work. Perhaps they could have the best of both—a corporate combine that would keep the family fortunes intact and ensure Mason's happiness. After all, magick held the most power when it benefited the greatest number.

"I wish he hadn't made us promise not to interfere," Miranda said.

"Actually," Tish said carefully, "he only had *me* promise. I don't think you ever said a thing."

Miranda lifted her eyebrows. "I believe you're right. He must be slipping." She shot a wary glance toward the door where her brother had disappeared and held up the empty bottle. "You know, there's at least this much of the elixir left in the bowl from last night. I never dumped it out."

Tish toyed with a strand of her daughter's thick blonde hair for a long moment while she turned over the possibilities in her mind. *Perhaps.*

"I do want Mason to be happy," Miranda said softly.

Tish took a deep breath. "Then you should help him, my darling. So mote it be."

"So mote it be."

Yet another crisis averted at the Alexander Asylum for the Criminally Eccentric.

Mason stood on the terrace, blowing off the tension that had gathered in his shoulders over the past two hours, and considered his mother and his sister. The witches.

For Love. For the love of Pete was more like it. When was this going to stop?

Before witchcraft, there had been crystals and past lives, and a couple of years before that, they had been women who ran with wolves. Literally: they'd kept two on the property, until neighbors complained about the howling and the animal control people had stepped in. Three years before that, they had drummed. Constantly. The thought of it still made his head pound.

All in all, witchcraft had seemed pretty innocuous—until this morning.

Thank God he'd spotted Mother with that bottle before she'd had a chance to dump it into Caro's coffee. And then he'd had to sit there, with the bloody thing in his pocket all through breakfast, chatting with Caroline and waiting for a chance to confront his two personal sorceresses to see if they'd really been planning what he thought they had. Unfortunately, they had. As if things weren't bad enough.

"As if what weren't bad enough?" asked a carefully modulated voice.

Mason turned abruptly. "Caroline. I'm sorry, I didn't realize you were out here yet."

"Obviously." The musky notes of her signature perfume wafted around him as she stepped closer. "What's so awful that you're talking to yourself?"

"The weather," Mason improvised quickly. Why not? They were in the throes of an early heat wave, the temperature over eighty already this June morning. Seattle usually didn't get heat like this until August, if at all. "I heard a weather report while I was inside. It's supposed to get even hotter, if you can believe it."

"Good." She ran one red-lacquered fingertip down into the vee of his open shirt collar. "I like it hot."

Her brazen suggestiveness, so out of sync with the cool exterior she presented, would have excited Mason a lot more if he hadn't known it was a tease. She did it all the time, and not just to him. It was her way of testing men, to see if they were interested—and thus, interesting.

He started to prove his interest with a kiss, but she turned away. "Shall we go see the posies?"

"Let me make a call first." He reached for the phone that hung by the door and punched the buttons that would raise the kitchen staff. As he ordered iced tea for later, he observed the woman he intended to marry.

Caroline Wickersham was as polished and elegant as obscene amounts of new money could make a woman. From the tip of those perfectly manicured nails to the toe of her Italian shoes, she reeked of expensive afternoons with personal fashion consultants and long weekends in spas.

Her personality was just as polished: pure business over a well-hidden base of spoiled brat, the product of an upbringing that combined a practical mind and a superb education with the most outlandish catering a widowed and newly rich father could heap onto his only child. She was used to demanding and getting the best of everything, from ponies to sports cars to the top job in her daddy's biggest company.

Now all Mason had to do was finish convincing her that she wanted him. Or rather, that she wanted the house.

At something just under five acres, the Alexander estate, with its eighteen-room European-style manor house, was one of the largest in the Highlands, Seattle's most private of private enclaves. Residence in the Highlands was a highly guarded prize, not quite as hard to come by as it once was, but still granted only to those with the money and cachet to get past the membership committee.

Caroline wanted in, and she wanted in badly. She certainly had the money—in quantities that most of the inmates would envy. Unfortunately, cachet was lacking: not only were the Wickershams so nouveau that the ink on their calling cards was still wet, but her father had rolled over the chairman of the committee in the process of a corporate takeover, an unforgivable faux pas. If Caro was going to live in the Highlands, she was going to have to marry her way in. Mason intended to be the route to her fondest wish—in exchange for Wick Technologies' help in getting the power cell to market.

Things had progressed to a point; this weekend was designed as a teaser, a taste of the Highlands life to whet her appetite and get her to make that final decision. Mason had checked every detail, down to the orchids in her room. He was ready to woo and bribe and beg Caroline if necessary.

This had to work. He'd tried to get the money everywhere he could think of, from banks to private sources, but no one was willing to touch AI without collateral, and there simply was no more. If Mother and Miranda screwed this up with their damned silly witchcraft, he was going to string them up by their thumbs.

Hiding his desperation behind a smile, he led Caro toward the gardens. The first part of the path wound beneath firs and cedars older than the century, and after the blazing white of the terrace, the shade beneath them felt as cool as a mountain glen. They wandered for a while along the maze of paths, amid hostas and ferns and an array of shade-loving blossoms Mason couldn't name. Off toward the tennis court, a lawn mower roared monotonously.

"Your gardener works on Saturdays?" Caroline asked.

Mason glanced toward the sound. "Not usually, but he dropped a rock on his foot and we have some service coming in while he's off. They had to work us in."

"I met with my R&D people yesterday," she said as she ruffled the fronds of a sword fern. "They finished running the numbers on the power cell."

"And?"

She left the shade and strolled off across the lawn toward the white fretwork gazebo that sat in the middle of a huge wheel of rose beds. "If it does half of what they said, you're about to become more famous than the Energizer Bunny."

Mason followed, holding his tongue and waiting for her next gambit. She glanced over her shoulder and raised an eyebrow. "What? No sales pitch?"

"You've heard everything I have to say. You know we need Wick's help to make this go. And you know what Alexander Industries has to offer in return."

"What I'm more interested in right now," she said, turning so suddenly that he had to put his hands to her waist to keep from knocking her over, "is what *you* have to—What *is* that smell?"

Mason sniffed. There was definitely something rank in the air. "Manure?"

"Mason, dear, I've been around horses all my life. That is *not* manure."

"No, you're right. It must be something for the plants, though. Mother insists on organic amendments."

"It's awful."

He took her hand. "Come on. We'll go down to the terrace. The iced tea should be waiting." He waved toward the dining room window, where he could see his mother peeking around the curtains. She quickly stepped back into the shadows. Caro chuckled.

Unlike the stone terraces that abutted the house, the lower terrace, tucked away at the bottom of the property, was a sweep of perfectly manicured grass that overlooked Puget Sound and the Olympic Mountains beyond. A long, vine-covered arbor shaded the far end of the terrace, and in its cool shadow sat a table, its white linen cloth bright against the pattern of dark leaves and purple clematis blossoms. A crystal pitcher full of tea sparkled mysteriously in the dappled light.

"Privacy. Beautiful view. And no smell." Caroline moved into his arms and smiled up at him in a deliberately predatory way. "Now, what was that discussion we were having? Ah, yes. What you have to offer. Personally, that is."

They'd been playing this game for weeks, and suddenly Mason had had enough. With a growl of impatience, his lips came down on Caro's with bruising force.

A soft exhalation of surprise and excitement warmed his mouth, and Caroline curled her fingers into his collar and tugged him toward the arbor.

Mason felt a rush of triumph. So, she was interested in sex after all. He'd been wondering if marriage to Caro would be as icy as her appearance. Apparently not. He backed her against one of the wooden supports, sliding one leg between her knees. A soft moan was all the permission he needed to reach for the buttons on her blouse. Negotiations were definitely progressing.

"Ahem. Uh. Excuse me." An apologetic voice cut into the arousal that was beginning to fog Mason's brain. He looked up.

A girl was standing at the opposite end of the arbor. A very dirty girl, wearing shorts and a faded green shirt with a name over the pocket. "What the . . . ?"

Caro leaped aside like she'd been caught with the pool boy.

"I'm really sorry," said their visitor. "I didn't mean to disturb you, but I need to get through here to get out of your way."

"Who the devil are you?" demanded Mason.

The girl slipped off her leather work gloves and wiped one hand on her khaki shorts. "I'm with Johnson's. The landscape service."

"You won't be for long," Caroline said. "How dare you spy on us."

"Settle down, Caro," said Mason. "I'm sure she has some legitimate reason for being down here."

"Transplants," the girl said quickly. "And weeding. I was cleaning up the rock garden back there."

"And rolling through it, apparently," muttered Caro.

"You can finish later," Mason said, shooting Caro a warning look. "Next week."

"Yes, sir. I'll just get my things and get out of your way." She disappeared out the far end of the arbor and reappeared a moment later pushing a wheelbarrow piled high with seed flats, tools, and assorted jugs. The muscles in her well-tanned arms bulged as she steered the awkward load toward them.

The arbor was narrow, and with the table in the middle, she couldn't get through. She started to set the wheelbarrow down.

"Allow me," Mason said. He dragged the two chairs away and pulled the table to one side. The ice tinkled prettily against the sides of the crystal pitcher.

The girl flashed him a grateful look and started past the table, but the barrow hung up on something.

"Oh, hurry up," Caroline snapped.

"Yes, ma'am." The girl backed up a few inches and gave the wheelbarrow another shove just as Mason reached to move the table again.

His elbow bumped the end of a hoe handle. It was just enough to throw the whole pile off balance, and the wheelbarrow tilted crazily for an instant before she caught it. "Whew. That could have been a—"

One of the jugs sloshed once and tipped over. The top popped off as it hit the edge of the wheelbarrow, and a stream of filthy brown liquid shot out, drenching Caro from knee to toe.

"—disaster. Oh, geez."

A stench like the bottom of an old bait bucket rose around them. Mason took an involuntary step back.

"Oh. Oh, God." Gagging, Caro danced backward, as though she could escape the odor that engulfed her. A squishing sound revealed that some of the glop was in her shoe.

The girl grabbed for the jug and set it up before it could discharge the rest of its contents onto Caroline's shoes, then reached for a towel that hung from one handle of the wheelbarrow. She blotted frantically at the stain on Caro's pants, but the towel left as much dirt as it picked up.

"Get away from me." Caroline kicked at her, narrowly missing her shin. "Haven't you done enough?"

"I'm so sorry. Just let me wipe some of it—"

"Get away, you little bitch. You did that on purpose."

"She did no such thing," Mason said quickly and firmly. He pulled one of the linen napkins off the table. "It was my fault. Here, let me help."

Caroline snatched the cloth away and flung it at his head. "That won't do any good. It's ruined. The whole outfit's ruined. I've got to go change." She glared down at the girl. "I'll have your job for this," Caroline snarled at her, then stormed off toward the house.

The girl sighed and straightened up. "Gee. There goes the Maserati."

A smile tugged at the corner of Mason's mouth, and he turned to give her a closer look. She must be older than he'd thought. He doubted that an eighteen-year-old could display such nonchalance about getting fired.

"I must apologize for my friend. She's usually not so highstrung." He moved upwind a little as a fresh whiff enveloped them. He recognized it as the smell from the rose garden, magnified a thousand times. "What is that stuff, anyway?"

"Fish emulsion for the plants," she said as they stepped out from under the arbor. "You ought to smell the kind that's not deodorized."

"I think I'll pass."

"It goes away in a couple of hours. I'm really sorry, Mr. Alexander."

Twenty-three, Mason guessed as he got a good look at her in the sunlight. Maybe a couple of years older. "I'll take your word for it. You have an advantage. I don't know your name." He held his hand out.

"Raine. Raine Hobart." She started to shake his hand, then pulled back awkwardly. "I'm pretty grubby."

"It's my dirt. It won't hurt me." He kept his hand out until she took it. Her lightly callused palm felt lean and strong in his, almost masculine after Caroline's delicate grip. "I'll make sure you aren't fired, Miss Hobart."

"Thank you." The relief in her smile proved she wasn't as cavalier about her job as she let on. "Speaking of which, I'd better get back to work, or what you say won't make a bit of difference."

She started rearranging the contents of the wheelbarrow, bending over the tools in an unself-conscious way that gave Mason a ringside view of legs that were as remarkable for their healthy curves as for their grimy streaks. She carefully settled the half-empty jug of fish emulsion into a spot where it couldn't possibly spill again, then straightened and looked around.

"Is there something I can help you with?" he asked.

"There should be a hose bib around here somewhere." She held up a neon yellow sports bottle. "I need to fill this."

Mason glanced around, but couldn't spot the faucet either. "How about some iced tea instead?"

"Isn't your friend coming back?"

Mason thought of the look on Caro's face. "I doubt it. Allow me."

He took her bottle and braved the arbor, stepping carefully over the pool of fishy slime. Holding his breath, he quickly filled her bottle plus a glass for himself, and ducked back out into the fresh air.

"Thanks," she said as he handed her the sports bottle. She lifted it in a mock toast and took a workman's hearty swallow. "Are you sure you can talk your friend out of going to Mrs. Johnson? I didn't get the impression she's the type to forgive and forget, and I have rent due."

"Don't sell me short. I'm pretty persuasive."

"So I noticed," she murmured.

Mason shot her a sharp look, and she started laughing. She had a great laugh, low and rippling, the kind of laugh that could pull a person in, and despite the situation and the inappropriate comment, he let himself be drawn along. Gradually, they trailed off into chuckles, and then into an awkward silence as their eyes locked and held.

The color rose in her cheeks. She quickly swiped at her forehead with the back of her hand and took another sip at her glass. "Um, thanks for the tea. What kind is it? It's got an unusual taste."

"I don't know." He sipped at his glass. The aftertaste was familiar, but odd, like the flavor belonged to a smell he'd . . . Oh, no. They wouldn't. They hadn't. He took another sip and rolled it around on his tongue like a good brandy. As the cool liquid slipped down his throat, silvery letters formed in his mind's eye: *For Love*. He spluttered and nearly choked. "I'm going to kill them. I swear to God I'm going to kill them."

"Who?"

"My mother and sister. And not a court in the land will convict me."

"Isn't that a little drastic? I mean, it's just iced tea."

"It's not the tea that's the problem." Mason shook his head vigorously. "No. Those two—"

"Mason?" His mother's voice trickled down through the shrubbery from somewhere on the path. "Mason, are you still down there?"

He opened his mouth to answer, then paused and straightened a bit as an idea hit him. No. It was too outlandish. But then again . . . He turned back to Raine and looked her up and down. Young, unkempt, totally unsuitable.

"Perfect. Miss Hobart, you're about to fall in love with me."

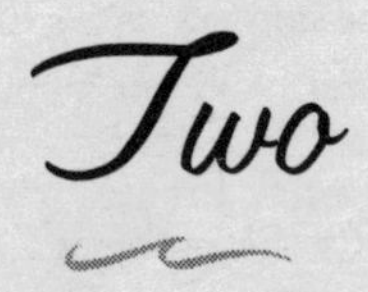

"Now there's a new approach," said Raine. She started to take another sip of tea.

"No!" Mason batted the sports bottle out of her hand. "Don't drink any more of that."

So, this was what it looked like when a rich man went crazy. And he was so gosh-awful handsome, too. What a shame. Raine sidled away a couple of steps.

"Mason?" called the voice again, slightly closer.

"Come here." He grabbed Raine's arm and dragged her into the cover of the arbor.

"Now hold on." She yanked free and drew one fist back instinctively, fight-or-flight hormones racing through her bloodstream.

"Whoa." Mason lifted his palms in surrender. His low voice was barely audible over the fitful breeze that riffled the vines. "My apologies, but I have an urgent need to teach my mother a lesson, and I need some help. Can you act?"

Humor him. She lowered her hand, but kept her fingers in a fist. "A little. I played Chava in my high school's production of *Fiddler on the Roof*."

"That'll do. Here. Hold this, but *don't* drink it." He spilled a little of his tea out on the grass and handed his glass to her, then hurriedly poured a second glass, filling it only halfway. "Pretend you've just this instant fallen in love with me."

"I don't know," Raine began. "This is pretty weird."

"Mason, darling?" The voice was almost to the terrace. "I hope we haven't come all this way for nothing."

"I know he's down here," said a second female.

"We don't have time to discuss it," Mason said urgently. "Just go along with me, and I'll explain everything later."

Raine hesitated.

"Please," he said. The corners of his mouth turned up a fraction, and tiny laugh lines appeared around his eyes, so that he looked less like a lunatic and more like a man about to pull off a great joke. "Be a sport. I'm persuasive, remember?"

You're a nut case, is what you are, she thought. Nonetheless, she found herself shrugging. "Oh, all right."

He took her free hand and lifted it chest high just as an older, silver-haired woman appeared on the terrace, followed by a lanky blonde female. The mother and sister in question, no doubt. She could see the family resemblance. They came toward the arbor.

"Oh, there you are," the woman said. "What on earth happened down here? Caroline came storming up to the house, filthy dirty and smelling like a cesspool."

Speaking of which, the arbor didn't smell so swift, either, now that the breeze had petered out again. Raine blinked hard twice.

"Look at me," Mason whispered. Raine obeyed, meeting his deep-set eyes just as an expression of total rapture spread over his face. A misplaced shiver lifted every little hair on her arm and tickled its way across her shoulders.

"What are you doing in there?" Mrs. Alexander demanded. She raised a hand to shield her eyes against the sun and peered into the shadows. "Oh. Oh, my."

"Just having some tea, Mother." His voice sounded vague and distracted. He lifted Raine's hand higher and brushed a kiss over her knuckles. Her knees wobbled a bit, and the ice in her glass—er, his glass—clinked slightly as she swayed. *Method acting,* she told herself.

"Oh, my heavens."

Mrs. Alexander tottered over to the terrace wall and sat down heavily.

"Tish?" The blonde woman hurried to her side.

Mason tore his eyes away from Raine—at least, that's how it felt on her side—although he kept his fingers firmly curled around hers. "Mother? Are you all right?"

"It'll be okay," the sister was saying. "We can—" She bit off her words as Mason approached them, dragging Raine along.

Mrs. Alexander smiled up at them, a bit wan. "Don't worry about me, darlings. I just got a little warm."

"You know how she hates the heat," said the sister.

"She's probably dehydrated," Raine said. "You should drink something cool." She held out her glass of tea.

She could have sworn Mrs. Alexander got even paler. "Oh, no. No, thank you. I simply need to sit a moment. Mason, why don't you introduce this . . . friend of yours?"

"It would be my pleasure. This"—Mason squeezed Raine's hand and gave her a smile so warm and intimate that she blushed like a teenager—"is Raine Hobart. Raine, this is my mother, Tish Alexander, and my sister, Miranda."

Raine nodded politely, unable to do more because of the iced tea in one hand and Mason's grip on the other. "It's very nice to meet you, ma'am."

Mrs. Alexander returned the nod.

Miranda just stared. "You're one of the grounds crew, aren't you?"

"Yes," Mason said, before Raine could answer. "Isn't it amazing that we've never met her before? She's been here at least three weeks, right under our noses." That warm smile again. Raine's heart did an inexplicable skip as she answered with an adoring smile of her own. Geez, if this were all real, she could fall for him big-time.

After all, he was her type: tall and lean, with the facial structure of a Viking and Nordic-blue eyes to match. He even had the chestnut hair she preferred on a blue-eyed man—blond over blue made a man look too surfer-dude, in her opinion, but a rich brown provided just the right contrast. He definitely had the right contrast.

Yep, it'd be really easy to fall for the kind of line Mason Alexander was obviously capable of dishing out. She wondered how long she'd be able to stand here and help him gaslight his mother without forgetting it was all an act.

Fortunately, she was saved from finding out by a squawk from the walkie-talkie that hung on her belt. "Hey, Raine!"

All three Alexanders looked at her expectantly.

"My crew boss," she explained. She extricated her right hand from Mason's grip and raised the walkie-talkie to her mouth. "Here, Craig."

"What's taking so long down there?"

"I was just heading up." Time to wind down this little floor show. She gave Mason an apologetic shrug as she slipped the walkie-talkie back into its holster. "I guess this is good-bye."

"Do you have to go?" Mason asked.

"Of course she does. Don't be an ass," Miranda said brusquely. She inserted herself between her brother and Raine and removed the glass of tea from Raine's hand. "She'll get fired. And besides, you need to see to Caroline."

"Caroline's perfectly capable of seeing to herself." He stepped around Miranda and trailed Raine as she retrieved her sports bottle. His voice was low and urgent, but loud enough to carry to his family. "I don't even know how to get hold of you."

Apparently he was going to drag this out to the end. Well, in for a dime, in for a dollar. Raine boosted the barrow and wheeled it off toward the foot of the path, meanwhile giving him the "I'm being torn away from my love" look that had won the audiences in *Fiddler*. Poor little Chava.

"I'm in the book," she breathed. "Or you can reach me through the service. Johnson's Landscaping."

"Johnson's," he repeated, as though committing the name to memory. "You'll hear from me. Soon."

Three long strides carried Mason to her side, and then he leaned over and kissed her. It was no little peck on the cheek, either, but a real, live, incredibly sexy, on-the-mouth kiss that could have curled Great-aunt Alice's toes, much less Raine's. The man should win an Oscar. She was vaguely aware of the gasps of the Alexander women, and of the tingle of her lips as he stepped back.

"I'll see you soon," he promised again, giving her a private wink that said he wouldn't. His mother looked like she wanted to cry.

Stunned into silence, Raine pulled herself together and started the wheelbarrow up the steep grade toward the main gardens. She was still in shock when Craig Stevens, her crew boss, appeared on the trail ahead of her. The awed look on his face told her that Tish and Miranda Alexander hadn't been the only audience for that little curtain-ringer.

"Holy Moley," he said with no preamble, his usually hearty

voice held to a low rumble so it wouldn't carry to the level below. ''What was that all about?''

Raine glanced over her shoulder, but the Alexander clan had disappeared behind the curtain of cedars. ''I don't know, Craig. I honestly don't know.''

That would teach them.

It was with a deep sense of satisfaction that Mason watched his bogus lady-love disappear up the path. For all her grime and earthiness, Raine Hobart had been both a sport and a believable actress—not to mention an excellent kisser—and if his mother and sister had any sense of shame, they would now confess their sins and apologize for inflicting their ridiculous potions on him and that innocent young woman.

Apparently they had none at all. His satisfaction evaporated on the sound of whispers from the peanut gallery. The words ''reverse'' and ''elixir'' particularly grabbed his attention.

Damn it all. They ought to be squirming with mortification, not plotting to work up some counterspell to try out. Well, if any man could make them squirm, he could.

He drained his tea glass.

When he turned to face his tormentors, their eyes were as round as barn owls'.

''Are you all right, darling?'' His mother's voice crackled with unnatural brightness.

''Maybe I should offer to help,'' he muttered, as though he hadn't heard her. ''I don't want Raine to hurt herself.''

''Oh, surely Miss Hobart is used to pushing her little cart up and down hills. She's a sturdy young thing. I, on the other hand, am your old mother. Come help me instead, darling.''

''Hmm? Oh, yes, of course.'' With a final, longing glance after Miss Hobart, Mason returned his glass to the table in the arbor, then went to his mother's side and offered his arm. Frail old mother, indeed. She swam a mile every day.

They made a solemn procession up the path, with Miranda in the lead and Mason and Tish trailing along behind. His mother dragged, providing time for Miss Hobart to vanish and for Mason to consider his next step.

He could always admit the hoax and demand promises for future good behavior, but he'd already seen just how far that sort of confrontation got him. What made it so bloody frustrating was that they thought they were doing him a favor.

What he needed was contrition, a complete change of heart. He wanted them out of the witch business altogether, particularly insofar as it concerned him. If they felt free to try to arrange his love life with their inane chants and potions, then there would be no limit to their interference. Someone really would end up poisoned. He had images of having to resort to the services of a food taster, like some paranoid medieval prince.

No. He needed to keep them on tenterhooks for a few days, believing that their first formula had been an unqualified success, but that all subsequent efforts to remove its effects were dismal failures. Sooner or later they would have to admit that trying to mess with the natural order was a huge mistake. At that point, of course, he'd tell them the whole thing was a hoax, but by then they'd be wiser little witches, much less likely to drop unknown herbs into people's glasses. The instinct that had led him to enlist Miss Hobart's aid had been right; he had to see this through.

The problem was Caro, of course. Somehow, he had to continue courting her while keeping his mother and Miranda convinced that he'd lost his heart to Miss Hobart. The weekend stretched before him like a marathon.

They reached the upper terrace and passed into the air-conditioned haven of the conservatory. Mason settled his mother on her favorite chair and phoned the kitchen for a pitcher of ice water.

"Well," said Miranda with false heartiness, "I imagine you're anxious to go smooth Caro's ruffled feathers."

"Not particularly," Mason said, enjoying the flustered look this statement brought to his sister's face. "But I suppose it's my duty as host. Excuse me."

The whispers began before the door swung shut behind him.

Caroline occupied a guest suite on the second floor, and Mason took his time on the stairs, debating how to handle her. Maybe he should just let her in on the game. After all, if anyone understood the power of manipulation, it was Caroline. On the other hand, he hated to reveal his family's screwball tendencies, at least until after a wedding ring sat securely on her finger.

Still undecided, he knocked on Caro's door. A maid opened

the door, then turned to announce him. "Mr. Alexander to see you, Miss."

"Tell him to come in," Caro called from somewhere inside.

The maid stood aside to let him pass, then picked up a tightly twisted trash bag and, holding it at arm's length, took her leave.

"Really, Mason, you took long enough. What on earth were you doing?"

Mason followed Caroline's irritated voice to the open bathroom door, where he spotted one bubble-spangled leg raised artistically above the edge of the tub. He elected to refuse the lure and took up a discreet position just outside, where the scent of Caro's wickedly expensive perfume engulfed him. There wasn't a dead fish on earth who could stand up to that much Boucheron.

"I had to explain to that poor young woman that you weren't really going to have her fired," he said.

"And why not? She ruined a brand new pair of Ferragamos." The water sloshed in the tub, and Caroline stood up, providing Mason with a superb, if brief, view of her smooth, creamy body.

"Loss of livelihood is hardly fair exchange for a pair of shoes," he said, ignoring his instinctive male reaction to the deliberate display. "Besides, it was my fault, and you know it. I bumped her tools and knocked her off balance."

"Very gallant of you, Mason, but she needs to be taught a lesson. She shouldn't have been spying on us in the first place."

"Good God, she was just work—" Mason stuttered to a stop as Caro emerged from the bathroom encased in nothing but two yards of Turkish terry.

Apparently his reaction pleased her, because she smiled a knowing smile and sighed. "Oh, I suppose I can afford to be magnanimous. I won't have her fired. Now, go away so I can dress."

He might have offered to stay and help if he'd had any hope it would go anywhere—and if an extended stay in her room wouldn't destroy the fiction he was presenting to his mother and Miranda. Instead, he pressed a relatively chaste kiss to Caro's mouth and excused himself.

So much for pulling her into his little play. On reflection, the idea of Caroline Wickersham willingly pretending "her" man had fallen for any other woman, much less for the groundskeeper who had just doused her with fish slime, almost made Mason laugh aloud.

No. He was definitely on his own with this one.

• • •

"We shouldn't have left them alone."

On Sunday evening, Tish held back the edge of the damask drapery just enough to see Mason and Caroline on the terrace below. Behind their silhouettes, the sunset painted a glorious scene of purple mountains against a rose and gold sky, and left their shadows stretched across the stone paving. But there was something distinctly wrong.

"Look at them," Tish said. "They could be talking stock prices, for all the romance between them. All weekend I've been expecting him to jump up and announce to Caroline that he's taking up lawn mowing as a profession. How could we bungle things so dreadfully?"

Miranda looked up from the thick, leather-bound book on her lap. It was their Book of Shadows, their personal record of the Craft meticulously hand-copied from various teachers' volumes.

"I could just kick myself," said Miranda. "I should have stayed down there until I saw Mason and Caroline drink that tea."

"It's just as much my fault as yours, darling, but now is not the time for self-recrimination." Tish let the drapery fall back into place and joined her daughter on the settee. She patted Miranda's hand, as much to draw comfort as to offer it. On the table, a cone of spicy incense burned in an enameled bowl, its smoke curling around them like a blanket. "Our task now is to set things back on their proper course, and as quickly as possible."

"It won't be that quick." Miranda flipped back to a page that she had marked with a length of purple ribbon. "According to this, a love spell can only be reversed on a waning moon, and the turning works best at the dark of the moon."

"But that's over two weeks away," wailed Tish. "We can't let this go on that long."

"I don't think we have a choice."

"There must be some other way to neutralize the elixir."

Miranda shook her head. "I've read every spell and ritual even remotely concerned with turning back a spell. There's nothing else, unless Raven has an idea."

"Do you really want to trot this little fiasco out in front of our high priestess?" Tish asked.

"She wouldn't laugh, if that's what you're afraid of."

"No," Tish said. "She'd just sigh with that way of hers, but

I'd die from the embarrassment anyway. Besides, I copied most of that section from her Book; if she had something useful, it would be there."

"We could try creating our own counterspell," Miranda suggested. "Raven said we're ready."

"To write a ceremonial chant, darling, not leap into free-form spell-casting."

"But what if the Threefold Law takes effect before we can act?" asked Miranda.

The very thought made Tish ill. One of the basic tenets of the Craft, the Threefold Law held that whatever a witch sowed would come back three times over. Accidental or not, they had sown disaster. Unless they set things right again, they were bound to reap disaster in return.

Tish took a deep breath. *Time to be sensible.* "No. We're dealing with powerful forces. We might make things worse by venturing into uncharted territory. We're going to have to muddle along until the moon is with us. Two weeks. Oh, my."

Miranda sighed. "The only saving grace in all this is that Caro will be gone until after the Fourth."

Tish perked up. "She will? I didn't know that."

"Weren't you paying attention at lunch? She's going to the Far East. She ran on about it for a good five minutes."

"I had things on my mind," Tish reminded her daughter.

"Anyway, there's some sort of conference in Tokyo, and then she's going to Singapore for a few days."

Tish blinked. "Well, then, there we are. If Mason does insist on seeing that young woman, all we have to do is keep them out of the public eye. Then the moon will change, and we can reverse the spell and send Miss Hobart on her way. And, of course, make certain that Caro and Mason get a fresh batch of the elixir. No one will be the wiser. Now, darling, go over the counterspell, so we can make certain we have what we need."

"A new-cut wand of willow." Miranda peered down at the book, her finger tracing over the words. "A white-handled knife. An arrow of wood. A fire. . . ."

Two weeks, Tish thought, staring at the glowing tip of the incense while her daughter read the ritual. Two weeks to repair the damage done in a single morning, or the Alexander fortunes could drift away just like the sweet smoke that surrounded them.

''Where's her head?'' asked Raine, staring down as Arne poured crimson liquid over the chalky form sprawled at his feet.

''Fell out of the truck. I figured it didn't matter.''

Raine shrugged. ''A body is a body.'' She squatted down and safety-pinned a label to the stained T-shirt that covered the mannequin's plaster breasts. ''City People's Mercantile. That's the last one.''

She straightened and licked corn-syrup blood off her fingers as she surveyed the rooftop. A twelve-foot facade, looking like a cross between the Berlin Wall and a hyper-modern low-rise office building, ran across the top of the abandoned warehouse, effectively cutting off the view of the Ship Canal beyond. Twenty-three dead bodies lay scattered before the wall, most hanging off the roof to one degree or another. Each was tagged with the name of a neighborhood business. Yellow police tape marked the ''crime scene.'' Above it all, an eight-by-twenty-foot banner, roped to utility poles, blared the reasons why MMT Properties shouldn't erect their monstrosity of a building on this site.

Guerrilla art.

Six months ago, MMT had abruptly announced development of its property in Fremont, a vibrant, avant-garde neighborhood just north of Seattle's Queen Anne Hill. The old two-story building sat well below street level, so its roof barely showed above the concrete guard wall on Thirty-fourth. Its replacement, a monolith of concrete and glass labeled Canal Place, would tower a full three stories above street level. That the proposed building would cut Fremont's business district off from its waterfront was bad enough, but the project presented bigger problems than a blocked view.

According to Raine's studies of *feng shui*, the ancient Chinese art of earth-divining, the MMT building would disrupt two of the three critical lines of *ch'i*, or energy, that ran through the area. Allowed to go up as designed, with all its daggerlike angles and reflective facades, the building would literally kill Fremont, draining it of vital energy like a vampire.

She'd tried to tell them, she really had. Written letters to MMT and to the newspapers that were never answered or printed. Made phone calls no one returned. Attended zoning board meetings where her comments were cut short. No one had been interested in hearing how the building would slice the heart right out of Fremont—at least, no one with clout.

But a few people *had* heard and, with no particular effort or intention on Raine's part, had coalesced into a free-form citizens group, elected her Fearless Leader, and launched an offensive based on an old Seattle tradition of mixing hit-and-run art installations with politics. The whole operation, now called FUSE—Fremonters United to Secure Energy—had developed a life of its own.

Which was how Raine found herself trespassing on the roof of a vacant building at four-thirty on Monday morning, engaging in guerrilla art.

"Righteous," said Arne, twisting the cap back onto the jug of blood-red Karo. "A perfect symbol of how big business oppresses the people."

"It's supposed to—Oh, never mind."

Arne didn't care, anyway. He never cared much about the movements he joined—he just liked to protest. But as Raine had just pointed out, a body was a body, and they'd needed as many bodies as possible to set this whole panorama up in under fifteen minutes. He'd been amazingly useful, too, shinnying up those telephone poles to string the banner. He'd probably learned that climbing trees for antilogging protests, but she didn't even want to guess where he'd learned to pick the padlocks on the gate so he could get up on the roof and pull the ladder bridges across from street level.

Raine checked her watch, then raised one hand over her head and snapped her fingers. "Wrap it up, people. We don't want to get caught on-site."

As if to reinforce her words, a siren wailed somewhere on Queen Anne Hill. The troupe swarmed back across the ladders and dispersed like dandelion seeds on a stiff breeze. Within sixty seconds, Raine stood alone on the sidewalk with her best friend, Zoe Levine. And good old Arne.

"Looks great, kiddo," said Zoe, grabbing Raine's arm. "What are we waiting for?"

"I'm not afraid of the pigs," said Arne, hoisting his syrup jug into the air in defiance. "Let's face them head on."

"Get a life," Zoe snapped. "Come on, Raine. It's starting to get light. Bail's expensive."

"That's an ambulance, and it's headed for Ballard," Raine said, laughing, but she let Zoe drag her across up the block toward the parking lot anyway.

Arne tagged along. "Hey, uh, I was wondering if you could give me a ride over to the U-District?"

Zoe frowned, but Raine nodded. "Sure. No problem."

They climbed into Raine's faded green pickup, and as they headed toward the University of Washington, Zoe fished her cell phone out of her bag and punched in a number. "Okay, Freddy," she said when someone answered on the other end. "Call in the dogs."

She laughed and flipped the phone shut. "The hounds of the media will be on their way shortly."

"I hope so," said Raine.

"Are you kidding? With the press release I wrote? It helps to have some background in PR."

"Cool," said Arne. "The ability to manipulate public opinion is vital to any revolution."

"And it's incredibly easy," Zoe said, suddenly more tolerant of Arne. She started explaining marketing psychology to him.

Amazing, considering Zoe had only temped for that PR outfit for three weeks. Raine bit her tongue and tuned them out, focusing instead on the traffic, already starting to pick up as trucks began their delivery routes.

The first rays of light reflected off the glass of the buildings at the University Med Center, off to the right. In a few minutes, the sun would be high enough for the photographers to get some shots of their installation that would look great in the evening paper. If they showed up. If they bothered to shoot any pictures. If what they shot made the paper. If they even got there before some good citizen notified MMT.

Privately, she'd lay ten-to-one odds that the whole project was down by seven-thirty.

What she was really hoping for was that whatever press coverage they got would flush out the actual owners of MMT Properties. In all her efforts to get some response from MMT, the one certain thing she'd learned was that its owners were very private people, who buried their identities under several layers of corporate flimflam. It was going to take a little poking around in public records to find out who they were, and she just hadn't had time. Maybe one of Fred's hot-shot media connections would do the legwork for them.

She realized that Zoe and Arne were staring at her, and she tossed them a shrug.

"It'll be okay," said Zoe sympathetically.

"Yeah, sure." Raine stepped down on the clutch, shifted down into second, and made the turn onto Forty-fifth. "Everything will be just peachy."

"Don't drop that thing on me."

"Not a chance, Rainey."

Later that same afternoon, Raine flopped belly down in the dirt at the foot of a huge lilac bush and stuck her head and shoulders into the gaping hole beneath the plant. The lilac had been dug out and levered up part of the way with shovels and two-by-fours, but now it was stuck, and Craig wanted her to crawl in and see why. That was the problem with being the skinniest person on the crew—it automatically made her the mole.

She felt around blindly until her fingers hit something solid. "It's a rock, all right," she announced. She felt around a bit more. "A big one, too. The roots are all bound around it." She reached for her pruning shears.

Raine could hardly blame the lilac for curling its toes around the nearest handy object. Over fifty years old and as big as a small house, it probably felt it had the right to stay where it was. Unfortunately, the new owner of its domain didn't agree and had decreed that it should move to the rear of the property. Even worse, said owner insisted that the lilac had to move right now, heat wave or no, and so, heavily pruned and bundled in twine, it was moving. The poor thing would be lucky to get through the summer alive.

She opened the shears and reached in to snip at the thick, corded roots. Within moments the bush popped free. Raine scrambled backward to safety while the more muscle-bound members of the landscape crew wrangled the plant onto a cart.

As the poor lilac trundled off toward the backyard, she stood up and dusted at her shorts. It was a lost cause. Grit was ground in the entire length of her body, clothes, skin, hair, and all.

"Nice look," Craig said, brushing a clump of dirt off her nose. "I'm sure he'll be thrilled."

"He who?"

Grinning like an obnoxious big brother, Craig put his hands on her shoulders and spun her around. At the foot of the drive, next to a very large, gray Rolls Royce, stood Mason Alexander.

Raine stared, her face frozen in a half smile. Maybe having a lilac dropped on her head wouldn't have been such a bad thing after all.

"He must have really enjoyed that kiss," Craig whispered in her ear. Aloud he added, "Go ahead and call it a day, Raine. We're going to knock off anyway, as soon as we get that bush watered in."

"I'm going to get you," said Raine through unmoving lips.

Craig just chuckled and walked off.

Nothing like having friends. Raine forced the rest of that smile onto her lips, and walked down the drive. Was it her imagination, or had it suddenly gotten hotter? "Mr. Alexander. Good afternoon."

"Miss Hobart." His glance flickered down the length of her and back up, and she could see that he was fighting back either a smile or a shudder. She must be a real sight.

"I was wrestling a lilac," she said, immediately hating the defensive tone in her voice.

"I assume you won."

"Barely. I hope you didn't come out here to tell me you couldn't talk your lady friend out of getting me fired."

"No." He lost the battle with the smile, but she didn't mind. "She calmed down remarkably well after a bath."

"Thanks. I owe you."

"Actually, I owe you—an explanation for what happened on the terrace the other day."

What happened on the terrace. Just the recollection of those final thirty seconds curled her toes all over again, and facing the man responsible didn't do a thing to straighten them. "It's really not necessary."

"Yes, it is. I hoped you might accept a ride home. We could talk on the way."

"I live in Fremont," she said. "It's out of your way, and besides, my truck's back at the nursery. I should just ride with the crew."

"I'll take you to the nursery then. Please, Miss Hobart."

Raine could think of several reasons why she shouldn't get into a car with Mason Alexander, from the amount of grit in her hair to her conviction that he was as certifiable as he was sexy, but none of them stood up to pure curiosity. Besides, a chance to ride in a chauffeured Rolls didn't come her way every day.

"Okay." she said. "On one condition. Call me Raine. I've always thought 'Miss Hobart' made me sound like the commercial dishwasher queen."

He gave her a blank look, and it occurred to her that this might be the first time she'd ever gotten into a car with a man who had never worked a single day in food service.

"Raine it is," he said after a moment. "Provided that you call me Mason."

"All right." She couldn't quite bring herself to that, so she avoided his name altogether. "Hang on while I get my gear out of the crew truck."

A few minutes later, when she'd settled into buff leather seats so soft they almost swallowed her and the car had rolled away from the curb, Raine realized that this was a bad idea. Not only did the immaculate interior make her feel like a chimney sweep, but she was apparently being kidnapped.

"We're going the wrong way," she said.

"I told Paul to take a couple of turns around the Arboretum on the way." Mason smiled at Raine's raised eyebrow. "It's going to be a long explanation."

That turned out to be a flagrant understatement, and not only was his tale long, it was bizarre. Raine grew more bemused by the minute. Witches. Love potions. Forget the Best Actor award; this guy should be writing pulp fiction.

"So, there we were," he wound up, "with a pitcher full of God-knows-what and my mother coming, and—"

"Are they really witches?" Raine interrupted.

"Of course not," he snapped.

"Ah." She'd obviously hit a nerve. "I take it you don't believe in their, um, abilities."

He drilled her with a glare. "Are you in love with me?"

"Uh . . . no," Raine said. After all, lust didn't equal love, a lesson she'd learned the hard way.

"Precisely. The only ability my mother and sister have demonstrated is an uncanny knack for creating maximum trouble with minimum forethought."

Raine shook her head. "I'm sorry, but I don't understand why you're so upset. So they put a few herbs in the tea. Big deal. It didn't do any harm."

"The point is that I had specifically told them *not* to use their so-called potion. They had promised they wouldn't, and yet less than an hour later, one or both of them had spiked the iced tea. I was, and still am, justifiably furious."

"And so you thought you'd teach them a lesson by kissing the gardener." She pretended to notice something out the window and muttered to herself, "Gee, it's a good thing I wasn't someone appropriate."

"You were simply the person at hand." It was his turn to sound defensive.

"How flattering. That doesn't exactly dig you out, you know." Raine laughed as a tinge of red crept above his collar. "So, what did your mother say when you told her the truth about our little performance?"

Mason rubbed his thumb over an invisible smudge on the burr oak trim. "I haven't."

"What?"

"I haven't," he repeated, more firmly. "And I don't intend to, until I accomplish my purpose. That's the other part of why I'm here. I want to hire you, Miss Hobart."

"Hire me?"

"To continue the charade we started on Saturday. I want to teach my mother and sister a very clear lesson."

"Lesson?" Raine knew she sounded thick, but she felt thick, too. The whole situation was just too weird.

"Our 'little performance,' as you put it, was only partly successful,'' said Mason. ''Mother and Miranda apparently believe that their potion worked, but now they feel obliged to counteract it with yet another of their concoctions, so that they can try again with Caroline and me. In other words, they still feel entitled to run roughshod over my personal life and my express wishes. I want to make certain their efforts to reverse their so-called spell fail miserably, but I'll need your presence to do that. I will pay you five thousand dollars to help me continue a convincing romance.''

Geez, that cleared the mind real quick, Raine thought. Five thousand dollars. Shoot, she'd do it for free, just to have the chance to kiss him again—which was exactly the reason she should throw herself out of the car right now. Not being into bodily harm, however, she grabbed at the first excuse that popped to mind. ''I'm sure your girlfriend will just love that.''

''Caroline is on her way to Tokyo.'' Mason checked his watch. ''As of five minutes ago, in fact. She'll be gone until the sixth.''

''And what happens when she comes back and finds out you've been romancing the gardener for over two weeks? No thanks.'' She shuddered. ''Just the idea of having her find out I've been playing cozy with her boyfriend, even if it was all pretend . . . Geez.''

''That prospect doesn't appeal to me, either,'' said Mason firmly. ''I assure you, I have thought of little else for two days, and I think I've considered every aspect. We will play this very close to the vest. Since the idea is to aggravate my mother and sister, we will spend most of our time at the house. Dinner. Bridge. Perhaps some tennis. You do play, don't you?''

''Not very well.''

''You'll improve,'' Mason said, as though he would personally see that she did. ''If we do go out, we'll choose places where I'm not likely to be recognized. Caroline will never know a thing.''

''Still . . .''

''Five thousand dollars,'' he repeated smoothly. ''Plus I can offer you other help in the future: introductions, referrals, perhaps a job reference down the road. Whatever you need. There are advantages to knowing someone with my connections.''

Raine almost said no. Almost, until Mason leaned toward her, and the faintest whiff of some unknown and particularly masculine cologne threw her right back into the middle of that kiss once again. Funny, she hadn't even noticed the scent at the time, but now she recognized the spicy undertones immediately, and with the power that smells have, they triggered delicious memory in every part of her body.

"This is very important to me," said Mason. "And I promise, once Caroline returns, your involvement ends, whether Mother and Miranda have sworn off witchcraft or not.

"Please, Raine," he urged. "Just two weeks."

Two weeks—maybe a few more of those kisses—and she'd have five thousand dollars. Raine thought about the nasty fight she'd just started with MMT Properties. What if they took FUSE to court?

Well, if those briefcase-toting weenies insisted on turning FUSE's perfectly legal protest into a vendetta, then she was going to fight back. Surely five thousand dollars would attract a hungry young lawyer with an interest in preserving their First Amendment rights.

Besides, the Universe clearly intended for her to have the money, Raine rationalized, otherwise someone like Mason Alexander wouldn't have come along to offer it. And as for her physical reaction to him, well, she was a reasonable woman. She could keep her perspective for a couple of weeks.

She realized she was frowning, and that her prospective employer was watching her with a look of patient amusement.

"All right," she said. "You win. When do we start?"

Mason smiled with the confidence of a man who was used to winning. "Tonight."

"Okay."

His gaze flickered down to her grimy knees and back. "We don't dress formally for dinner, but if you need something appropriate, I have accounts at several stores."

"I do own a *few* things besides shorts," Raine said tartly, even as she mentally ran through her closet with a growing sense of panic.

The car swung into the drive at Johnson's Landscape and cruised slowly toward the rear of the compound, the barely audible crunch of gravel sounding out of place inside the elegant automobile.

"There's my pickup." Raine pointed at the battered chunk of metal that was her baby and workhorse. Mason signaled his driver, who pulled in alongside the truck while Raine fished a notebook and pen out of her backpack and scribbled down her address and some rough directions. "I'll run ahead and you can pick me up in, say, an hour?"

Mason accepted the directions, but countered, "Forty-five minutes. Mother likes to have drinks on the terrace before dinner."

"Ah. A proper stage for my entrance."

Mason nodded. "Do you mind?"

"You're the director of this play," she said just as the door swung open. Mason lifted a warning finger to his lips, then stepped out of the car and reached back to offer her his hand.

The late afternoon heat seemed more intense after the cool haven of the air-conditioned car. Raine raised a hand against the slanting sunlight and gave Mason a lingering look—strictly for the benefit of his driver. "I'll see you in a little while, then."

"I can't wait," said Mason.

The driver lifted one eyebrow.

Eight minutes later, Raine set the hand brake with a tug and ripped her keys out of the ignition. The truck door, gate, and front door banged shut one after another as she rushed into the tiny guest house she rented.

As she tossed her pack on the table, she grimaced at the huge pile of unfolded laundry that occupied one end of the couch. Great. She'd have to be even quicker, so she could cut him off out front.

By the time she hit the bathroom, she'd stripped to her underwear. She turned the shower on full force, and while she waited for the hot water, she reached for the fastening on her bra.

A glimpse of her image in the mirror over the sink stopped her dead. Sun-parched blonde hair sticking out every which way, peeling nose, smudged cheek. No wonder women in six-hundred-dollar shoes got men like Mason Alexander: they never had to suffer the heavy hand of Mother Nature. It was amazing the poor guy hadn't run the other direction.

Or maybe, despite his protests, that was exactly the look he wanted in order to shock his mother.

Well, she'd be damned if she'd play scullery maid to his lord of the manor. She finished stripping and stepped under the scalding water.

Mr. Alexander had a surprise coming.

• • •

Mason occupied most of the forty-five minutes with a few phone calls, including one to the kitchen staff to warn them of a guest for dinner—a guest who was *not* to be mentioned to his mother and sister. While he worked, Paul located the address Raine had written down and maneuvered the car into a tight parking space behind her truck.

By the time Mason finished his last call, there were still five minutes to spare, so he settled back with that morning's *Wall Street Journal*. He found it impossible to read, however. He kept glancing up toward the stairs where he expected Raine to appear; he hadn't felt such a sense of anticipation in years.

No, not anticipation, he corrected himself, curiosity. Curiosity about how his protégée might dress. He probably should have insisted on taking her shopping. For all he knew, her clothes were as brash as her sense of humor, and while his mother and Miranda certainly believed their potion had made him fall in love with the first female who came along, they might not continue to do so if that female was too bizarre.

God, what was he doing? What if this girl was a complete social misfit, or a charming psychopath?

A moment of panic loomed, then faded as he dismissed the idea. He was a good judge of people. Raine Hobart was fine. This was just the jitters. Anticipation.

He made another abortive stab at the *Journal*'s Center Column, then gave it up and laid the paper aside. He checked his watch. Another minute or two. It never paid to rush a lady, but he popped the door open anyway. Paul jumped out and hustled around the car.

Mason waved him off. "I just wanted some fresh air."

Kids had started to gather, as they always did when a big car pulled into a working class neighborhood, and a couple of them started arguing over whether "that guy" was a movie star or a drug dealer. Mason shook his head and told them, "Neither. Manufacturing, mostly."

"See. I toldja," a third kid said. He slugged one of the other boys on the arm, but before he could hit the second one, he stopped and pointed. "Wow. Lookit Raine."

Mason turned. Look at Raine, indeed.

He never would have believed forty-five minutes and a shower could wreak such change on a woman. Gone was the grubby, unisex Johnson's uniform, replaced by a sleek, hot pink dress with a square-cut neckline that showed just enough cleavage to make a man want a better look. She had managed to wrestle her flyaway hair into some sort of twist at the nape of her neck, and although her arms and shoulders showed the uneven reddish tan of someone who worked long hours in the sun, she'd toned down the freckles across her nose with a layer of powder. For jewelry, she wore only gold hoop earrings and, except for the fact they were a little too big and her lipstick too neon, she looked terrific.

Of course, in his book, those legs more than made up for the lipstick. He'd already known they were good, but in strappy black heels and nylons, they advanced to outstanding, and her dress was the perfect length to show them to advantage without showing too much. Or at least, it would be if she weren't standing at the top of the stairs. Ungentlemanly or not, he couldn't keep his eyes off the point where the straight line of her hem bisected the curve of her inner thigh.

A sigh at his side reminded Mason that he wasn't the only man appreciating the geometry lesson.

Paul caught his glance and wiped the grin off his face, but as he stepped sharply back to the door, he murmured, "I believe it was worth the wait, sir." Mason agreed.

He met Raine at the bottom of the stairs and offered her a hand into the car.

She smelled faintly of lemons and peppermint, he realized as he slipped in beside her, and even at this distance he had no complaints about her appearance beyond the lipstick. She was actually prettier than he'd thought. Those cheekbones must have been hiding under a layer of dirt.

"Well, do I pass muster?" she asked.

Mason realized he was staring, and that the car had already pulled away from the curb. "Most definitely."

"Good. While I was in the shower, I realized that we need to clear up a couple of points."

Just the words "while I was in the shower" triggered a whole set of images Mason had no business considering. He forced his mind back to the issue at hand and checked to make certain the intercom to the driver's compartment was off. He trusted Paul, but only within reason. "Go ahead."

"First, just what do you expect for your five thousand dollars?"

"A convincing performance whenever anyone from my household is present or may be watching."

"Watching. You mean spying?"

"I wouldn't put it beyond possibility. Mother especially. She has a habit of peering out windows."

"Like Mrs. Perlmutter," said Raine. She added by way of explanation, "She owns the house I rent. Do you suppose it has something to do with hitting menopause? Peeping, I mean."

"I'm sure I don't know," said Mason, barely hanging on to a straight face. "You said you had a couple of points."

"Oh, yeah. The big one." She met his eyes with a level gaze. "Five thousand dollars doesn't get you sex."

"I didn't think it did." He bit back a laugh. "Is there anything else?"

She pursed her lips as though considering another question, but shook her head. "I think that covers the important items. So, you play tennis. How good are you?"

They spent the rest of the trip in the kind of trivial conversation that usually passed between people just getting acquainted, and, as they talked, Mason's concerns about social ineptitude and psychiatric history faded. Raine was casual and a bit impertinent, but bright and essentially well mannered. Before it seemed possible, the car slowed to pass through the guarded gate that marked the edge of the Highlands.

A mile later, the car swung into the long drive that led down to the house. Raine grew uncharacteristically silent, and the closer they got to the carriageway, the tighter her lips pressed together.

When the car stopped, Mason took her hand. She glanced up with a start. "What?"

"Try to be honest."

"You can't be serious."

"What I mean is, don't add any frills to our story. I tracked you down at work and asked you to dinner."

"Right. And I adore you."

He smiled. "And you adore me. As I do you." He lifted her hand to his lips and gave her a good luck kiss just as Paul opened the car door.

"I'll drive Miss Hobart home myself," Mason said as he got out. He enjoyed the flicker of surprise that crossed Paul's face.

"Pull the Jaguar around, and then you can have the rest of the evening free."

"Yes, sir." As he got back in the car and pulled away, Mason escorted Raine to the front door.

"Here we go," she murmured. He reached for the knob.

The view from the front entry stopped Raine dead in her tracks, as it did to almost everyone who walked in the door. The tall, arched window on the opposite wall looked out over a panorama of Puget Sound and the Olympic Mountains. Framed by the curved staircases to either side and the crystal chandelier overhead, it had the effect of a huge, ever-changing painting.

"Wow," she said. She walked in a few steps, her heels clicking on the sawn oak floors. "You could just walk straight through and out." There was something in her voice that said she didn't think that was such a good thing.

Distracted by her restrained reaction, Mason set his briefcase just inside the cloakroom, then pushed open the double paneled doors to the dining room. "Through here. Mother tends to use the covered part of the terrace when it's hot."

He noted with satisfaction that the drapes on the French doors had been pulled against the afternoon light, as he'd expected. They would have the element of surprise.

Raine dragged to a stop again, this time staring at a painting on the far wall. "Ohmigosh. That's a Monet."

"You have a good eye," he said, following her across the room.

"I spend a lot of time in museums. Look at the depth of the water under the bridge. Amazing. I can't believe you get to live with this."

He stood patiently while she peered at the painting, a look of rapture on her face. She reached out, and for a moment he thought he was going to have to warn her not to touch it, but she straightened and lowered her hand.

"I'm sorry," she said. "I'm acting like a bumpkin."

"Actually, it's rather refreshing to see things through your eyes. We get a little jaded."

"That's sweet, even if it's just manners. I'll try to behave better, now that I'm over the shock." She quickly patted her hair and pressed her lips together to smooth her lipstick. "Let's do it."

"Nervous?" he asked as they crossed to the doors.

She nodded. "I've worked around these houses a few times, but I've never been inside one, much less socialized with the family."

"Just be yourself, and you'll do fine." Mason leaned close and whispered confidentially, "Think of it as one of your museums, with some very peculiar live displays."

Her marvelous laugh drained away the last of his worries. She was perfect. This was going to work.

He gripped her hand, swept aside the drapes, and pushed open the door. "Good evening, Mother. Look who—"

"Mason, darling, look who—"

They both halted in midsentence. His mother's mouth rounded into a surprised "Oh," while Mason's clamped into a thin line, and they stood there in the most awkward kind of silence. Mason thought dully that someone ought to do something.

His mother recovered first, thank God. "Age before beauty, darling. Look who I shanghaied outside the club."

Mason used those few seconds to pull himself together, so he was able to step forward with a welcoming smile.

"Angus. Good to see you," he said as he shook hands. He turned to Raine. "Miss Raine Hobart, I'd like to present Mr. Angus Wickersham. Caroline's father."

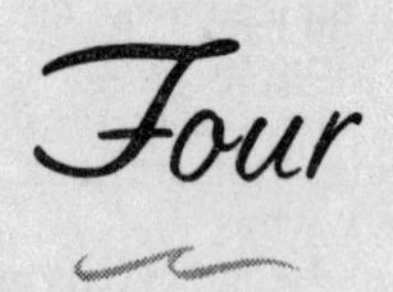

Four

Caroline's father.

The words seeped into Raine's brain with the approximate speed of a feather sinking in molasses. By the time she had absorbed their meaning and their consequences for her legal defense fund, three people were staring at her. Mason's eyes, in particular, practically willed her to save his rich behind.

Frankly, at that moment she was more disposed to rescue Angus Wickersham from the embarrassment of standing there with his hand out in space.

So she smiled and took his hand. "I'm so sorry. I'm standing here like an idiot. You just remind me so much of my uncle Dan." A minor fib, but she'd always wanted an uncle Dan.

"A favorite uncle, I hope." Wickersham said.

"Very much so. He used to pull quarters out of my ears," Raine embroidered. Mr. Wickersham grinned in delight.

Mason cleared his throat. "Mother, you remember Miss Hobart."

"Of course, darling. Hello, Miss Hobart. It's so nice to see you again."

"Mrs. Alexander."

They all looked at each other, trying to think of what to do next.

"So, you know my daughter," Mr. Wickersham said, breaking

the awkward silence. ''Raine Hobart. I don't recall Caroline mentioning your name.''

Mrs. A. blanched. Mason glowered. Raine's urge to roar with laughter conflicted with a more reasonable instinct to duck back through the French doors and hotfoot it toward her own slightly less bizarre neighborhood.

''Oh, I doubt she would have,'' Raine said cheerily, indulging in a microsecond of pleasure at the way Mason's eyebrows pinched together. ''We only met a few days ago. Just sort of . . . ran into each other. She left quite an impression.''

''That's my Caroline,'' Wickersham said with undisguised parental pride. ''Very impressive, and a hell of a businesswoman, to boot.''

''Her father's daughter, I'm sure,'' said Tish Alexander. ''Mason, darling, you haven't offered Miss Hobart a drink.''

''I'm fine, thank you,'' said Raine. ''I don't need anything.''

''Nonsense,'' Tish said. ''It's as hot as blazes out here. You need a sparkling water, at least, and we'll be happy to get it for you—won't we, Mason?''

''Where's Lawrence?'' asked Mason.

''It's Monday,'' Tish answered, as though that were explanation enough. She stepped in beside her son and curled her fingers over his arm, and even from where Raine stood, she could see the older woman's nails digging into Mason's sleeve. ''And Williams is helping with some crisis in the kitchen, so we'll have to make do on our own. Angus, let me freshen your drink.''

''Sure enough. Thank you.'' Wickersham passed his squat glass to Tish, who took it with a smile then practically dragged her son toward the service cart that stood a short distance away.

''Looks like a powwow,'' Wickersham observed as Mason and his mother put their heads together over the ice bucket. They could see Tish's agitation.

''Mmm,'' said Raine in her most noncommittal way.

She drifted away from the pair out of politeness, even though their words were muted by the chamber music that wafted out of some invisible speaker. Angus followed along, and they stopped at the edge of the shadow formed by the overhang, neither of them willing to brave the blaze of sun off the limestone terrace.

''So,'' said Angus, turning to her with a direct gaze that contradicted his casual tone. ''How is it you know Mason?''

Suspicious old coot. Raine smiled. So much for Mason's advice to stick to the truth.

"What on earth were you thinking?" Tish hissed as soon as they were safely out of earshot. "The very idea of dragging that girl home. And with Caroline's *father* here."

Mason might have laughed if so much of his future hadn't been riding on Raine Hobart's sunburnt shoulders. Leaving her and Angus alone was risky, but there had been no way to shake his mother loose without being obvious.

Of course, his mother could help handle Angus, but only if he confessed the whole charade. And even if he were so inclined, he could hardly launch into said confession with Angus thirty feet away—not when there would undoubtedly be a scene, complete with tears and accusations and inevitable mentions of witchcraft. Best to play things out a while longer, until they had more privacy. Maybe he could tell her after dinner. If they got through dinner.

He started sorting through the bottles on the service cart. "I didn't realize you were expecting Angus."

"I wasn't," said his mother. She set the tumbler on the silver tray with a thunk. "He drinks bourbon and branch water. I told you, I bumped into him at the club."

Mason raised an eyebrow. "I didn't know he was a member."

"He's not. He was playing golf with Buddy Faraday. I think they had a bet."

"I didn't see his car out front."

"There was some sort of problem with the air conditioner. His driver took it down by the garage to see if he could sort it out. Anyway, darling, you're avoiding the issue. Why is she here?"

"To have dinner," he said. He curled his fingers over the handle of the ice bucket. "I ran into her and thought—"

"Ran into her? You mean you spotted her riding her lawn mower down the median strip?"

"Meow."

Splotches of red appeared in his mother's cheeks. "You're right. That was catty, and I apologize. I have nothing against Miss Hobart or her occupation, but you have to admit, she doesn't move in the same circles as we do, darling. You didn't run into her, you hunted her down." She picked up the silver ice tongs and stood expectantly, waiting for Mason to lift the lid to the ice bucket.

"All right, I did." Mason ignored her and kept his hand on the lid. "I wanted to see her again."

"You're taking a terrible chance." She didn't bother to ask *why* he had chased Raine down, he noticed.

He shifted as though uneasy. "I know. But I feel the oddest compulsion. I'm drawn to her."

"You can't possibly—" She stopped and sighed, and a "that will go away soon" look passed across her face, which irritated Mason no end. The hell with confessing after dinner. If Raine could hold up her part of the act, he was going to carry this thing through.

"Oh, never mind," said Tish. "Let's just get the drinks and get back over there before she says something you'll regret. Do you think you can remember how to make me a vodka gimlet?"

Mason could and did, and soon had the drinks ready, including a plain tonic water for himself. What he really wanted was a good, stiff scotch, but he had a feeling he'd need a clear head to get through the evening.

That feeling was confirmed when he turned and saw Raine and Angus. She had her hand on his arm and was leaning toward him in a conspiratorial way. She had clearly just told him some secret. Angus nodded and patted her hand.

"I think I'm getting an ulcer," muttered Tish. Mason silently agreed.

As they approached the chummy duo, he met Raine's eyes over Angus's shoulder. Mason raised one eyebrow in question and was met with a cheery but uninformative smile.

Angus turned. "Ah, the drinks have returned, bearing our hosts."

Tish tittered, a girlish sound unlike anything Mason had ever heard outside a boarding school. It must be the stress, he decided, because it certainly wasn't the humor.

"At last," said Tish as she swept up beside Angus in a swirl of tangerine silk. She held out his glass. "Bourbon and branch."

"Thank you, ma'am."

Mason passed Raine her drink. Their fingers brushed, and the slice of lime balanced on the edge wobbled dangerously.

"Whoa," said Mason, steadying her hand. She wasn't as cool as she looked, which left him perversely pleased. "Got it?"

She gave him a significant look. ''All under control.''

With a slight nod of understanding, Mason turned to Angus. ''So, I hear you whipped Buddy Faraday.''

''Hardly.'' Wickersham chuckled. ''The little SOB ran me into the ground, as usual. You and I ought to play sometime.''

''He cheats, you know,'' said a voice from the doorway. They all turned. Miranda strolled out onto the terrace, yards of lavender gauze wafting around her. ''Ask him about the time he greased the handle of my putter.''

''That was fifteen years ago,'' Mason said, laughing. ''And you never proved it was me.''

''Hello, darling,'' said Tish. ''I thought you were going to read until dinner.''

''I was, but things sounded much too interesting to ignore. Good evening, Angus.'' Miranda shook Wickersham's hand, then extended her hand to Raine. ''And Miss Hobart. What a surprise.''

She didn't appear surprised at all, a fact that made all the muscles in Mason's shoulders lock up. He'd learned long ago not to underestimate his sister, and nothing in the way she looked from him to Raine and back suggested that he should start now.

''Let's all move under the tree, shall we? There's more breeze out there.'' Tish led the way across the terrace to a table and chairs that sat in the shadow of an umbrella-shaped sophora tree. Far below, a cargo ship stacked high with red and green shipping containers trailed a wide wake the length of Elliott Bay, like an underline accenting the jagged profile of the mountains beyond.

With a little judicious traffic directing, Mason was able to isolate Raine between his mother and himself, with Miranda on his left where he could keep an eye on her. He left Angus to his mother.

As he settled back in his chair, a flutter of motion on the house caught his eye. He glanced up. A second-floor window stood open, and the faint breeze had pulled one corner of the sheer curtain out to ripple against the terra-cotta stucco of the house.

A deep lavender curtain. He glanced to his sister and to the sorceress robes she affected in her current favorite color, deep lavender.

If Miranda had been reading in her room, in her usual chair, she'd been right beside that window. He mentally traced a line down the wall, right to where Raine and Angus had been standing.

Mason's gut knotted. He remembered just how well voices could carry from under the loggia to the second floor under certain conditions—he'd spent hours listening in on his parents' cocktail parties from that very window. No wonder Miranda claimed things had sounded too interesting to stay upstairs. What the devil had Raine said to Angus?

He had to wait to find out. Wait through drinks and a second round, wait through a dinner served alfresco that seemed to drag eternally, and wait a decent interval afterward while everyone sat watching the sunset and conversing about utterly trivial topics.

And all the while, he felt like he was juggling three very slippery balls, one of which he couldn't see.

He almost caught a glimpse of it when Raine excused herself for a moment. Mason found himself alone with Angus—his mother and sister had their heads together over by a potted star jasmine, discussing heaven knew what.

"I think Miss Hobart is a fine choice," Angus said under his breath. "She's already got a good grasp of your mother's personality. And I like her preliminary concepts."

"Thanks. It's nice to have a second opinion," said Mason, without a clue to what Angus was talking about. Concepts? He squelched an overwhelming urge to run into the house after Raine. Breaking into the powder room just wouldn't be good form.

A few minutes later, when Raine returned, his mother steered her into a conversation with Angus and Miranda, then quietly motioned Mason aside.

"You've got to get her out of here," she whispered. "Angus is bound to notice sooner or later."

"Notice what?" Mason asked. He thought Raine had been the model of decorum.

"The looks. Crush is written all over her."

"Is it?" He glanced toward Raine, curious.

Tish sighed. "And you're no better. Please send her home. For my sake, if not your own."

"All right, Mother. Shortly."

She returned to the others, but Mason lingered for a moment, watching and savoring the sense of triumph. He hoped he would get to enjoy it for a while.

Angus was in the middle of a story about a mutual acquaintance, the women clustered around him in a bouquet of calypso colors. Mason realized that Caroline's tasteful neutrals usually faded next to his mother's and Miranda's more outrageous hues. Raine's hot pink, on the other hand, made a perfect high note.

It also made her cheeks glow in the light of the torchieres, and when she looked toward him, he suddenly realized what had his mother so worried: she looked like a woman in love. He met Raine's incandescent smile with a grin, wondering if she'd been this good in that high school play she'd mentioned. His mother was right; he needed to get her out of the house before Angus picked up on her act.

Apparently Raine sensed the same danger, because when conversation lagged, she seized the opportunity. "I'm sorry to beg off so early, but I have an early appointment tomorrow. I really need to get going."

"Of course," said Mason, rising. "I've been inconsiderate, keeping you so late." He nodded to Angus and his mother. "If you'll excuse us."

"This was a lovely evening, Mrs. Alexander," said Raine. "Thank you so much for having me."

"It was a delight, Miss Hobart."

Good-byes were said all around, and within a few minutes Mason had Raine secure in the confines of his Jaguar and they were heading up the drive.

"You," he said.

She grimaced. "I'm sorry. He caught me so off guard."

"You were great. What are you talking about?"

"Mr. Wickersham. I was?"

"You were." He whipped the car onto Olympic Drive. "Why are you apologizing?"

"You said to stick to the truth, but he was so suspicious, and—"

"Suspicious how?"

"Asking questions. Looking at me like I was stealing his daughter's boyfriend—which I *am* supposed to be doing, you know. Anyway, when I mentioned I was doing some work on your garden, he misinterpreted and decided I was your landscape designer. I just went along with it and told him you had hired me to design some new perennial beds for your mother."

"So that's what he meant." Mason chuckled, and when Raine

looked quizzical, he explained about Angus's comments on her behalf. "I just hope he doesn't mention anything to Mother."

"He won't," said Raine. "At least, not if he can keep a secret. I told him the new gardens were a surprise, and that you had asked me to dinner so I could get a feel for your mother's personality and tastes without her knowing what I was up to."

"He bought that?"

"It sucked him right in," she said, sounding somewhat amazed herself. "You know, one of my psych professors used to say that there was nothing like a conspiracy to bind total strangers."

"Wise professor."

"He hit a few things right." She paused while they cleared the security gate at the Highlands entrance, then added, "And it probably didn't hurt that I flirted a little, too."

"With Angus? You're kidding."

"I figured it would throw him off the track."

"Apparently it did."

She shrugged. "There are occasional advantages to being blonde and twenty-four."

"Not to mention having legs like Cyd Charisse."

She tugged her skirt down a fraction of an inch and avoided his eyes, and Mason guessed that if the light were better, he'd see a blush.

"So," she said. "I guess things worked out."

"On that front, but I'm afraid we may have another problem." He told her about Miranda's open window, and the possibility that his sister had overheard her conversation with Angus.

"Uh-oh." She sighed. "Well, that was a short run. Sorry."

"There's nothing to be sorry about. And the 'run,' as you say, is not over."

She turned to look at him, her brows high over disbelieving eyes. "You still want to go through with this?"

"Absolutely. My mother believes we're under the influence of their potion," he went on. "And she and Miranda are both certainly aware that you know about Caroline after that little incident with the fertilizer. Even if Miranda overheard every word you said to Angus, she and Mother may convince each other that you were just trying to protect me from embarrassment in front of Angus.

"In fact," he continued, inspired, "we can work on convincing them of that ourselves, tomorrow night. We can play a couple of sets of tennis, and then join them for dinner afterward. Are you up for it?''

''Of course.'' The streetlights flickered past outside, making pale green sparks in her eyes. She was quiet for several blocks, then asked, ''What if your sister isn't convinced about us? Do you think she would, say, come nosing around my neighborhood?''

Mason hadn't considered that. ''I'm not sure. Anything's possible with Miranda. Why?''

''Mrs. Perlmutter,'' she said. ''She's as big a gossip as she is a snoop. We'd probably better go through all the boyfriend-girlfriend stuff when you drop me off.''

''I think I can manage.''

''I'm sure you can.'' Her mouth curved into that wry grin he was learning to expect. ''What should I wear?''

It took him a minute to figure out that the topic had switched back to the next evening's activities. ''Anything comfortable. We'll play at the house, not the club. But do bring a change of clothes for dinner.''

''Oh,'' she said doubtfully. ''Okay.''

They rounded the final corner, and Mason wheeled the car into the still-empty spot behind her truck. He helped Raine out, then escorted her up the steep, crumbling, concrete stairs.

The side gate creaked when he pushed it open, and within seconds a narrow beam of light sliced across the walk as a drape was pulled aside.

''Mrs. Perlmutter,'' whispered Raine. ''Right on cue. Oh, shoot. I forgot to leave the porch light on. Watch your step.''

She led him past the window into the dark backyard, through a garden full of odd shapes and earthy smells, and toward a tiny cottage attached to the garage at the rear of the property. Her keys jingled as she stopped on the narrow stoop and pulled open the screen door. ''This is it. Home Sweet Home.''

Mason held the screen while she opened her door and felt around inside for a switch. The light inside flared into yellow brilliance, and Mason got a quick impression of pale blue walls before she yanked the door shut.

''It's kind of a mess,'' she said apologetically. ''I guess this is good night.''

"Um-hmm." Very deliberately, he put his hands on Raine's waist and backed her against the door frame.

"What are you doing?" she asked.

"Boyfriend stuff. Per your instructions." He leaned close. The screen door banged gently against his shoulder and hip. "We can't disappoint Mrs. Perlmutter. Put your arms around my neck."

Her lips parted, and he quickly covered her mouth, catching the first words of her protest and turning them into a sigh of pleasure. She moved in his hands, and her arms slipped obediently around his neck.

He dragged the kiss out, spending the long moment enjoying the feel of a strong, young, female body in his arms. When he finally broke the kiss, Raine sighed, a faint sound that made him want to do something reckless, and he had to concentrate a moment before he remembered his purpose and stepped back. Needing something to do with his hands, he reached into his inside jacket packet and pulled out a black leather wallet, from which he extracted a business card.

"Here's my office number. If something comes up, call me." Mason pressed the card into her hand. "Otherwise, I'll pick you up here at five-thirty tomorrow. You do have a racket?"

"Old Faithful." The huskiness in Raine's voice raised his pulse by a good ten beats per minute. "I think Reagan was still president the last time it had new strings. Don't expect a lot."

"After this evening? Raine Hobart, I expect miracles from you."

Mason turned and strode away before she could muster an answer, waving to the invisible Mrs. Perlmutter as he passed her window on the way back to the car.

"I don't talk about my employers," said Paul Chang firmly.

"I should hope not," said Miranda. She looked her brother's driver straight in the eye with what she hoped was her most guileless expression. "But I'm not asking about Mason; I'm asking about Miss Hobart."

Paul shook his head and used the turkey feather duster to knock a few specks off the right front fender of the Rolls. "Nice try, miss. You wouldn't want me telling Mr. Alexander about *your* dates, would you?"

"He wouldn't ask," Miranda said, but the lift she detected at the corner of Paul's mouth made her ask, "Would he? Has he?"

"Not recently."

"I haven't *had* a date recently. That rat. What did you tell him?"

"Nothing." Paul hung the duster back on its hook and reached for a roll of paper towels and a spray bottle full of glass cleaner that sat on the shelf above. "Which is precisely what I'm going to tell you."

He sprayed the front window as Miranda considered her next tack and watched him work.

It was a pleasant sight. Paul had changed out of his uniform and into a pair of jeans and a navy and teal Seattle Mariners T-shirt. She'd noticed his great shoulders long ago, but it was the jeans that held her attention tonight: they fit like a second skin. She leaned back against the wall and watched the muscles in his butt and thighs ripple as he worked over the car; by the time he finished the glass and moved on to the chrome, she was entranced.

She sighed, then reddened as Paul glanced over his shoulder and raised one black eyebrow. She covered her reaction quickly, saying, "I don't understand why you're being so uncooperative."

"Call it job security."

"Mason would never fire you. You're the only driver we've ever had who could keep that bloody Jaguar of his running. Besides, he won't be mad once he figures out that I'm just looking out for his welfare."

Paul chuckled. "He used the same line once."

The rat. She really was going to have to set big brother straight once this was all over. "All I want is to know how involved he is with Miss Hobart."

Paul gave the taillight a flourish and stood up. He cocked his head to one side, listening. "Ask him yourself. He's home."

The distinctive purr of the Jag's big engine shook the air, and an instant later the garage door opener powered up. Miranda's eyes widened. "Oh, crap. Where can I hide?"

Grinning, Paul pulled open the nearest door, and Miranda ducked blindly inside. The lightless space smelled of grease and solvents. Great. A cleaning closet. Well, snoopers couldn't be choosers. She listened as the Jag's engine roared closer. It rumbled to a stop, and a car door opened and closed.

"Good evening, sir," said Paul. "How is she running?"

"The dashboard lights started acting up on the way home," Mason said, so close that Miranda involuntarily stepped backward—right into a damp mop. She bit back an exclamation of disgust.

"What was that?" asked Mason.

"Probably the cat, sir. I tossed some catnip on the floor upstairs a little earlier. What exactly happened?"

To Miranda's relief, Mason let himself be distracted and, after a brief explanation of the problem, told Paul good night and left the garage. As much as she wanted to escape the soggy cotton strands wrapped around her ankle, she stayed put, waiting for Paul to call all clear.

He took his own sweet time, and when he did finally pull the door open he was grinning. "Here, kitty, kitty."

"Quit enjoying this so much." She pushed past him.

"You have to admit, miss, it's funny."

"I don't either. Now, back to business."

"Exactly. I have a short circuit to find." He stepped to the outside door. "And you need to sneak back inside without getting caught."

She trailed after him. "Be reasonable, Paul."

"I am. I'm not going to tell your brother that you're enlisting the staff to spy on him." He pushed the door open. The motion sensor lights that lined the drive blazed to life. "Good night."

"Oh, all right. I guess I can recognize a stone wall when I run into one." She stopped in the middle of the doorway. "Maybe you could just tell me if he kisses her the next time they're together?"

"I'll bet you don't have your keys," he said, ignoring her.

"Of course I do." She touched her pocket, but it was empty, and she flushed. "I must have left them on the hall table."

Paul shook his head. "I'd offer to let you in, but you obviously don't want to be seen with me. I'd suggest the service entrance. Williams will still be awake."

"You are just no fun at all."

"I'm the chauffeur. I'm paid to be competent, dependable, and discreet, not 'fun.' "

"Come on, Paul, it's—"

"Good *night,* Miss Alexander."

With a sigh of disgust, Miranda slipped out the door and ran toward the house, tripping security lights all the way. As she waited for Williams to answer the service bell, a smile turned up the corners of her mouth.

She always had enjoyed a challenge. Paul would make a lovely one.

''Noon,'' said Zoe the next morning when Raine picked up the phone.

''Noon to you, too,'' said Raine. She yawned and peered at the clock on the dresser. ''Actually, it's five-thirty in the morning. What are you talking about?''

''The *P-I* says they didn't take the wall down until noon.''

Raine was suddenly wide awake. ''We made the paper?''

''Hell-o-o. We made *both* papers, plus KIRO picked us up on the eleven o'clock news. Where were you while we were getting famous?''

''I had sort of a last-minute date. I was barely even home.'' Geez, there was still laundry on the couch waiting to be folded.

''Well, you've got to see this. It's so cool. They quoted the press release and everything. Meet me down at the diner in half an hour.''

''Fifteen minutes. I've got to be at work by seven.''

''Oh, gack. Okay, but don't expect me to look very good. 'Bye.''

The phone went dead, and Raine dropped it back on the cradle and headed for the bathroom. So much for folding laundry.

Despite Zoe's protests, every hair was in place when Raine slid into the green leatherette booth across from her exactly seventeen minutes later. She had the morning *Post-Intelligencer* spread across the table, and she started reading out loud before Raine even got settled.

" 'The Berlin Wall appeared Monday morning on the Fremont waterfront,' " Zoe read. " 'This time it was a model built on a rooftop, but if a local citizens group is to be believed, a structure with the same chilling effect as the real wall is about to be built on the site by MMT Properties. According to Fremonters United to Secure Energy (FUSE), the group claiming responsibility for the wall, analysis of the proposed Canal Place development using ancient Chinese techniques indicates that the building will disturb the energy lines of the earth and may cause economic and cultural harm to the Fremont neighborhood.' Then there's a bunch of stuff about Fremont and MMT and all the history of the site and all that. And the *Times* was just as good. They even did a sidebar about *feng shui.*" She pronounced it "fing shooey," instead of "fung shway," but Raine had long since given up on correcting her.

"Let me see."

Zoe handed across the previous evening's *Seattle Times*, carefully folded to the right page.

Raine read the paper with growing disbelief. "I don't believe it. One pile of scrap plywood and a few cracked store dummies and we're suddenly legitimate. We should have done this a year ago."

"FUSE wasn't around a year ago."

"*I* was," said Raine.

Just then the waitress came over, pad in hand, and squinted at them through a heavy coating of gothic white makeup and black eyeliner. "Let me guess. The usual number four and large OJ for Blondie, here, and two over easy with hashbrowns and black coffee for Betty Boop. Like I need to ask."

"I'll have coffee instead of juice today," said Raine. "High octane."

"Wow. Massive change. I'm not sure I can handle it." The waitress slouched off.

"We've got to find a new place to eat cheap," Zoe said.

"She's not any worse than she was three months ago."

"She's not any better, either." Zoe drummed her red fingernails on the Formica tabletop and looked Raine up and down with the assessing eye of a yenta. "So. Out late, major caffeine fix. Who is he and where did you meet him?"

"Don't get all excited. It's that guy I told you about from Saturday."

"The rich one who kissed you because you slimed his girlfriend?"

"That's not why he kissed me," said Raine, laughing. "But, yeah, that's the guy."

"You went out with Mr. Moneybags and you tell me not to get excited?"

"We didn't really go out. It was more like business."

"Is he commissioning a piece for his garden, or what?"

"No."

The waitress came back with two stained crockery mugs and the coffeepot, and Raine took advantage of the interruption to think about how she wanted to put this. She hadn't really considered what her arrangement with Mason sounded like until it came time to say it aloud.

The waitress poured the coffee and moved on, leaving Zoe staring at Raine expectantly. "So? What gives?"

"He, uh, hired me to date him for a couple of weeks."

Zoe's jaw dropped. "There's got to be a better way to pad your bank account."

"I doubt it," said Raine, thinking for the thousandth time of Mason's obligatory but nonetheless sexy good-night kiss. There couldn't be a better way to earn money.

"Whatever it is, we'll fix it," Zoe was saying. "You don't have to do this. My old man's always good for a couple of bucks. I can call him tonight and—"

Laughing, Raine waved her to a stop. "It's not like that. Really."

Zoe wrapped her fingers around her mug and raised one eyebrow. "No *Pretty Woman*?"

"Kind of the reverse, actually," Raine said, grinning. "Kissing is permitted, sex isn't."

Her friend's shoulders relaxed. "Then why is he paying you? I don't mean it that way, but is the guy a total nerd, or what?"

"Hardly."

"Well?"

Raine hesitated. She'd love to tell Zoe everything, but she had a sense Mason didn't want his family business trotted out in public. "He just still wants to yank his mother's chain. Apparently they have some kind of joke going back and forth and he's willing to spend some bucks to keep it going—you know rich people.''

''I wish,'' said Zoe with sincerity. ''This all sounds pretty weird. Why're you going along with it?''

''Because he's paying me five *thousand* dollars.'' She paused to let Zoe absorb the figure. ''We're going to need it, you know. I figure MMT's lawyers are already working on something to make us go away.''

Zoe sighed. ''If we had any brains, we'd go away by ourselves. We're nuts, you know, taking on a big real estate developer and a bunch of lawyers.''

''We can't just sit back and let them kill Fremont without a fight. I can't, anyway.''

''I know, sweety. And that's why I'm behind you—even if I don't understand how the lay of the land can affect whether business is good or bad.''

''If you'd read that book I gave you . . .''

''I know, I know. I'll get to it. Some day.'' Zoe sipped at her coffee.

The waitress brought their plates, the cheap white platters piled high with the food that made breakfast at the diner worthwhile no matter who Karl hired to wait tables.

Zoe poked at her eggs and dipped a corner of her toast in the yolk. ''So, where did you go last night?''

''His house.''

''Well, that's pretty cheesy.''

Raine chuckled at her friend's analysis. ''He couldn't very well aggravate his mother unless we were right there with her.''

''Maybe. But he could have at least taken you to Canlis before he dragged you home to harass Mama.''

''It wouldn't have been as effective,'' Raine said, recalling Mrs. Alexander's pained expression as the butler or houseboy or whatever he'd been had served the tomato aspic.

She speared a triangle of pancake. ''You should see that place, Zoe. Servants. Quarter-sawn oak floors. Marble fireplaces. White peonies and pink roses all over the house, in these incredible crystal vases. Oriental rugs so old they're almost threadbare, but the work's incredible. It reminded me of some gorgeous old English country house, where they bought the very best but have held on to it for generations. You could open an antiques store with the dining room furniture alone. And the art—I had my nose this far from a real Monet. I could have counted the hair marks in the brush strokes.''

''Wow.'' Zoe sighed and leaned back in the booth, her eyes focused on some private vision. ''Can I date Moneybags when you're done with him?''

''Stop calling him Moneybags. His name's Mason. Mason Alexander.''

''I don't care if his name's Donald Tr—'' Zoe sat bolt upright, her round eyes wide. ''Mason Alexander. You're dating an *Alexander*?''

''Yeah.'' She really did look like Betty Boop when she did that with her eyes, Raine thought. ''What about it?''

Zoe scrabbled through the newspapers she'd laid aside. ''Where is it, where is it. Ah.'' She yanked one sheet of the newspaper out and quickly folded it down to a quarter page. ''I forgot to read this part to you before. You know how you were hoping the reporters would find out who really owns MMT. Well, they did. 'The Canal Place project is being developed by MMT Properties, a development firm quietly owned by Seattle manufacturing giant Alexander Enterprises.' ''

This was not the time for a headache, Raine thought numbly as a sharp pain stabbed just above her left eye. She stared at Zoe.

''Rainey?''

''It can't be,'' muttered Raine.

''Maybe not,'' said Zoe sympathetically. ''I mean, Alexander is a fairly common name.''

The clatter of dishes being cleared from the booth behind her shook Raine out of her fog.

''Let me see that.'' She snatched the paper away from Zoe and scanned down the column until his name jumped out at her. Surely not.

She grabbed at her backpack and dug her black nylon wallet out of the bottom. She'd just stuck his card in last night without looking at it. Fishing deftly into the bill pocket, she retrieved Mason's gray business card.

The elegant raised lettering confirmed the worst: *Mason Alexander, President and CEO, Alexander Enterprises, Inc.*

Raine handed the card to Zoe, who responded with an eloquent, ''Son of a bitch.''

''It's a good thing he gave me his number,'' Raine muttered to herself. She checked the coin purse in her wallet, but it only contained three pennies and a nickel. "Can I borrow a quarter?"

"What for?"

"We're supposed to go out again tonight. I've got to cancel. I can't fraternize with . . . with the enemy."

Zoe nodded. She pulled her tote onto her lap and started rooting around for her wallet, but froze with her arm buried up to her elbow. "You can't cancel."

"I suppose you're right. I should tell him to his face."

"No, no, no. You shouldn't tell him at all."

"You're right. He probably already knows."

"I hadn't thought of that." Zoe's face fell, and she extricated her arm from the bag. She sat glumly for a moment, then perked up. "What if he doesn't? Your name wasn't in the paper anyplace. They just referred to FUSE."

"Then *I* have to tell him, so give me the quarter."

"No, you don't. Just keep your mouth shut and go out with him. You said it yourself, we need money. He's got it."

"But it's *his* building we're protesting."

"So what? That's completely separate from what he asked you to do. Besides, it's justice. After all, he's the one siccing attorneys on us."

"He hasn't yet."

"You know he will. And then we'll need some of our own, and it will only be fair to pay them with *his* money."

There was some twisted logic to Zoe's suggestion, but Raine resisted. "It just doesn't seem right."

"Right, schmight. From where I sit, you can't afford to worry about the moral niceties." Zoe leaned across the table, her arms straddling her plate. "Besides, you've got the perfect opportunity to save Fremont."

"What?"

"Teach Moneybags all about *feng shui*. Convert him."

Mason slid the stack of papers into his top right-hand drawer, then punched the intercom button on his phone. "Send them in, Chris."

"Yes, sir."

Scott Johnson, chief of Operations at MMT, walked in flanked by Jake Kreutzmiller, senior partner at the legal firm that represented Alexander Industries, and Ben Pratt, head of Community Relations. They wore the wary look of men on trial.

Mason tossed a section of the morning paper down in the center of his desk and tapped the photo of graffiti-covered plywood which was featured midpage.

"What the devil's going on in Fremont, and why did I have to read about it in the *P-I*?"

They all looked at each other and came to some sort of silent decision on who was the fall guy: Johnson spoke up. "Because it wasn't worth bothering you. We've got it under control."

"The front page of the Local section looks like pretty lousy control." Mason nailed Johnson with a steely stare. "You told me things were clear. You told me all the citizens groups had been placated."

"We thought they had."

Pratt jumped in. "FUSE is a new group. We've only had one prior communication with them, although arguments similar to theirs were raised at some of the meetings last year. Anyway, I doubt we'll hear from them again."

"I wouldn't lay odds on it," Kreutzmiller said. "They have a cause. God save us from citizens with causes."

"I don't know much about this *feng shui* myself," Johnson began, "but I understand it has a lot of standing in the Far East. Large corporations often hire—"

"It's just more New Age crap," snarled Mason, cutting him off. "I have demolition crews standing by for those final permits, and I am *not* stopping that building, no matter how many lunatics cast the *I Ching* or hang banners on light poles. Therefore the question becomes, What are you gentlemen doing about it?"

"I'll file for a restraining order this afternoon," said Kreutzmiller.

"Don't," said Pratt. "That will play right into their hands. We'll look like Goliath trampling David's First Amendment rights, and public opinion could swing fast and hard and come right down on their side."

"But we'll also send a clear message," Kreutzmiller said. "They're too late. They had their chance to give public testimony, and now they need to stay off the property and out of the way."

"At least give it a few days," Pratt argued. "The press interest will die down. And they may just go away on their own. Frankly, some of these New Age trends have the life expectancy of a gnat—even in Fremont."

Mason and Kreutzmiller exchanged significant looks. The attorney knew just how long some New Age trends lasted: he'd had to deal with the legal consequences of urban wolf ownership.

"Ben's got a point," said Mason. He turned to Kreutzmiller, who didn't look at all happy. "Okay, Jake. Get the paperwork ready, but hold off filing until we see how this plays out."

"All right. But you need to step up security on the site. Fences were breached. There are liability issues here." Kreutzmiller swung into full lawyer mode. "You can't have people climbing around there in the middle of the night. That building is old. What if one of them falls through the roof?"

Mason grimaced. "God, I hate tort law. Some idiot gets hurt trespassing, and I get to support him the rest of his life." He drummed his fingers on the lacquered ebony desktop. "All right, security. Maybe getting arrested will discourage them."

"I don't know, Mason," said Pratt. "Groups like this enjoy martyrdom. Arrests seem to invigorate them."

"Only when they look good on camera," said Kreutzmiller. "That's the great thing about security guards: no one wants to admit they were busted by some overweight guy in a rented uniform."

Mason laughed and looked to his PR man. "Meantime, Ben, what are you doing other than shooting down the legal options?"

"Well, you can look for another article about the economic and social benefits of the project in the *P-I*—Thursday, I believe." Pratt opened the folio he was carrying and flipped a couple of pages. "MMT is now an official sponsor of the Fremont Almost Free Outdoor Cinema—we're making it truly free for the month of July—and, ah, now that Alexander Industries is out of the closet on this, it opens a couple of windows. Human Resources just conveniently discovered they have room for a few more kids in the summer internship program—priority to go to Fremont residents, of course. And then there's the Wilmott Foundation dinner dance on Saturday. We can use it as a—"

"Scratch that one. Miss Wickersham's out of town and I have other plans," Mason said. "The rest of it sounds good, though. No aggressive action at this point, but we'll nail them if they try anything else. Scott, you see to security."

"Right away."

Kreutzmiller shrugged and reached for his briefcase. "It's your call. But I think I'll have my people look into who these

FUSE folks are. Maybe we can figure out how likely they are to go away on their own. Or even come up with something that will encourage them to disappear."

Mason rose and shook all three men's hands. "All right. Stay on top of this, and I want to see anything you turn up *before* you take any action. Ben's right, it'd be too easy to come off looking like the Gestapo."

As soon as the door closed behind them, his phone buzzed. He hit the speaker button. "What is it?"

"Miss Wickersham on line three, sir."

"Thank you."

Mason picked up the receiver. "Caroline. How was the flight?"

"How are they ever? I made the mistake of watching some inane movie about a shipwreck. It put me right to sleep."

"And now there you are in Tokyo, wide awake at"—Mason glanced at his watch and made a quick calculation—"three A.M. You're going to have a long day."

"Too bad you're not here to keep me awake between meetings."

The calculated suggestiveness of the invitation raised no interest at all in Mason, but he gave the expected response. "Me, too. Maybe next time."

"One can hope. So, did you spend your evening pining away for me?"

"No." He could almost hear her back stiffen before he added, "Actually, I had dinner with your father. He and Mother ran into each other and she brought him home."

"Lovely. Daddy's been after me to get all of us together for dinner, and the two clans really should get better acquainted, considering. Well, I know you're in the middle of your day, so I'll get off the line. Don't forget, I'm at the Okura through Sunday."

"I have the number right here."

"Say hello to your mother and tell her again that I had a wonderful weekend. I'm bringing her some tea from those gardens in Kyoto she mentioned. You know the ones."

"Uji Gardens. The *Gyokuro* 'Jewel Dew.' She'll love it."

"That's it." A moment of silence told Mason she was writing the name down. "Well, I'd better try to sleep before this first meeting, at least. 'Bye, darling."

''Good-bye.''

Mason hung up, wondering if the whole call had been about getting the name of the tea, or if Caroline had had some other agenda. Her comment about the two clans getting together ''considering'' was as close as she'd come so far to admitting they would get married. Maybe absence did make the heart grow fonder.

Wait, this was Caroline Wickersham, not a mortal human. He shook off that particular flight of fancy and punched an extension on his phone. ''Chris. Where are those reports from the product team?''

Convert him.

It had sounded relatively simple over breakfast when Zoe had suggested the idea as a solution to all their problems. Now it didn't seem simple at all, especially not with a tennis ball rocketing toward her at a hundred miles an hour.

Raine charged across the court and missed yet another backhand. Convert him, indeed. She'd just like to convert a serve.

She struggled valiantly, but Mason trounced her 6-1, 6-2, and if it hadn't been so blasted hot, he probably wouldn't even have broken a sweat.

''I warned you,'' she said, meeting him at the net.

''You're just out of practice.'' He handed her a towel, then glanced at his watch as he mopped his own neck and forehead. ''You've got a lot of power in your serve.''

''Yeah. Now, if I could keep it in bounds occasionally.''

''There is that,'' he said, and she didn't even resent the amusement in his voice. ''We have just time for a shower and a couple of drinks before dinner. Are you up for tonight's dog and pony show?''

''Absolutely, O Love-of-My-Life.'' She gave him her patented besotted smile and got an appreciative chuckle in return. ''I imagine there will be a lot more opportunity to display our supposed affection this evening, without good old Angus around to chaperone.''

''I'm counting on it,'' he said as they gathered their gear and started toward the house. ''I think Miranda was out in the garage last night when I got home, grilling Paul.''

''Really?''

''He was acting oddly. He told me that the cat was making

the noises I heard, but Magus turned out to be in the house, shredding one of Mother's plants. And I heard Miranda sneak in shortly after."

"Uh-oh."

He spun his racket end over end, like a gunfighter twirling a six-gun, and caught it without breaking stride. "I doubt he told her anything. He's never given me much satisfaction when I've asked about Miranda's men."

"You spy on your sister?"

"Don't look so appalled," said Mason. "Miranda's judgment in men is about as sound as her judgment in philosophy. She has already been married to one fortune hunter who cost us a pretty penny to dispose of. Someone has to protect her from herself."

"She's probably using the same justification to spy on you," said Raine.

He laughed and spun the racket again. "You're not getting much of a fortune."

"That, Mr. Alexander, depends on where you're standing when you count the money."

"Point taken."

"Can I ask you something?" She interpreted his slight nod as a yes. "How did this whole thing get started? You told me what your mother and Miranda did, but you never really explained why they thought you needed a love potion in the first place. It seemed to me that you and Caroline were doing just fine on your own."

"What you saw was sex, not love. They're not the same."

"They should be." She meant it, too, and not just because her mother had tried to raise her that way. She'd strayed away from those ideals for a time, and the lessons had been hard on her heart. Now she was like a reformed smoker, Zoe said, always ready to help others see the error of their ways. "You can't separate them without losing part of your soul."

Mason raised one eyebrow. "For someone so young, you're amazingly old-fashioned."

"Love isn't old-fashioned. It's the foundation of human life."

"That's a nice thought, but in the real world, love's bottom line doesn't always live up to its prospectus. And love is certainly not the only—or best—basis for marriage."

"Marriage is not a business deal."

"In this case, it is."

"You make it sound like you're marrying her for her money."

"I am," he admitted with no sign of embarrassment.

"Why? You're rich."

He stopped in the middle of the path, and for a minute she thought he was going to tell her to mind her own business. Then he shrugged.

"Actually, I'm broke."

"I know what broke looks like," she said, scanning pointedly around the estate. "This isn't it."

"There are several kinds of broke. My kind might be different from what you're used to, but I assure you, it costs me just as much sleep. I need a capital infusion, and Caroline has the capital.

"Oh, there's that appalled look again," he said, grinning. "Don't feel sorry for Caro. She knows exactly what she's getting into, and she's more than happy to trade a few million dollars of investment capital—which she'll get back many times over, by the way—for the Alexander name and address. In fact, I think she has it in her personal planner, under Goals. Caro and I see eye to eye on this. We'll do fine—*without* Mother's potions." He turned toward the house.

Raine glanced at his back with pity, then hustled to fall in beside him. A thousand responses ran through her brain, but she decided to keep them to herself. Nothing she could say would make any difference to a man who imagined you could base a marriage on anything other than love. And if he didn't believe in something as obvious as love, how was she ever going to get him to believe in the subtleties of *feng shui*?

If he weren't paying her, she'd head straight for the front gate, abandoning him as a lost cause.

But he was paying, so she'd stay and play out his game.

And as if to remind her that it really was a game to him, as they neared the house Mason shifted his gear all to one hand and reached out to Raine. "In case anybody's watching."

Always conscious of the show. With a sigh, she put her hand in his and plastered a smile across her lips.

He showed her to a second-floor guest room where she could shower and change—a suite, actually, which was roughly twice as large as her whole house and which made her want to move in for the duration. She sat on the foot of the king-sized bed and bounced a couple of times, then sighed. Her back could stand a few nights on a mattress like that.

Ah, well. Like the man said, time for the dog and pony show, complete with an attempt to introduce Mr. Love-Has-a-Bottom-Line to the basics of Chinese geomancy. Raine kicked off her tennis shoes and headed for the shower.

"I grew up in northern Minnesota," Raine said in answer to one of Miranda's questions. "Bemidji, 'The Home of Paul Bunyan.' "

Tish pulled off a tiny piece of her dinner roll and buttered it. "I've always thought Minnesota sounded so cold."

"It is. That's why I didn't go back after I graduated from McKenna."

"McKenna?" repeated Mason, unable to hide his surprise. "As in Claremont? You're kidding."

Raine could barely repress a chuckle. She loved dropping the name of her alma mater into conversation like that: it so defied people's expectations. It was by far the best use she'd ever gotten from her degree. She looked at Mason with all innocence. "Actually, no. I have the little piece of paper and everything."

He looked flustered. "I'm sorry. I just—"

"What on earth is a Claremont grad doing mowing lawns for a living?" Miranda blurted.

"Miranda," said Tish sharply. "And you, too, Mason. I'm sorry, Miss Hobart, I thought I had raised my children better."

"Oh, it's all right," Raine said. "I get that reaction a lot. Especially from my parents." She stopped to blot a bit of vinaigrette away from the corner of her mouth, leaving a tiny smudge of plum lipstick on the linen napkin. "And to answer your question, Miranda, I worked in L.A. for a while after I graduated, but I discovered I really wasn't cut out for the corporate world. Too much kissing up, too much hype." *Especially from one particular young executive.* "I don't know why I ever thought head-hunting was my forte. Anyway, one weekend, I came up this way to visit a friend and I just fell in love with Seattle. I never went back."

"It's so difficult to find one's feet in a new city," said Tish. "Surely you'll find a permanent job soon."

"This is my permanent job. I've been with Johnson's for

nearly three years. I like the seasonal work because it gives me plenty of time for my other work."

"Oh? I didn't realize you had your own business," said Miranda.

"I have two, actually," said Raine. Okay, here was her opening. She'd have to choose her words carefully, or his mind was likely to snap shut. "For one, I help people arrange their homes and gardens—and businesses—to make them more pleasant and productive."

"Oh, are you one of those people who go in and organize closets and drawers?" asked Tish.

"No," said Raine. A quick smile of amusement curved her lips, and she relaxed a bit, though she kept a watch on Mason out of the corner of her eye. "I like to think of myself as more of an . . . energy consultant. I use an Eastern approach to analyze how *ch'i*, or energy, ebbs and flows in a given space. Then I can help the residents compensate for any problems by correcting the placement of furniture and adjusting for poor architectural features. I've had some amazing results, even with things like health problems."

As she spoke, the lines of Mason's jaw drew tighter and tighter. Carefully chosen words or not, this wasn't sitting well with Mason. Where did all those prejudices of his come from?

"You know, Miranda and I do the same thing, in a way," said Tish. "We're witches."

Mason smacked his water glass down so hard that the table shook. "Not at dinner, please."

"Oh, don't mind him," Tish said lightly, waving one beringed hand toward her eldest. "Mason doesn't like to admit to even the merest possibility that there are energies he doesn't understand. I don't know how I raised such a closed-minded son."

"I'm not closed-minded," Mason said, barely maintaining a civil tone of voice. Above his brilliant white shirt collar, his face darkened to match his crimson tie. "In fact, I'm quite open to rational discourse. If you can ever produce any hard evidence of any of this"—he caught himself and modified whatever he'd been going to say—"*stuff* working, I will be happy to discuss it with you. In the meantime, I'd appreciate a change of subject."

Tish and Miranda looked at each other and shrugged in an unconcerned way, but Raine felt the anger radiating off Mason.

Then, like a drop of water flashing to steam in a hot skillet, it was gone. The color faded from his face. Wearing a look of chagrin, Mason reached out and gently covered her hand with his. "I'm sorry, sweetheart. This is an ongoing issue with my mother and me. I'm afraid it brings on strong emotions."

Still the game. Reminding herself that, as far as his family was concerned, she had no idea what was really going on, Raine pulled herself back into character.

"I understand," she said, turning her hand to curl her fingers into his. Still, she couldn't resist a delicate jab. "My mother always says strong emotions are the sign of a *loving* family." She presented him with a beatific smile that brought a slight tightening of his fingers around hers. He wasn't going to concede the point.

The butler came in just then, and small talk reigned at the Alexander table for as long as it took him to clear the salad plates and serve the braised lamb and French green beans.

As soon as he disappeared, Miranda jumped back in. "You mentioned you have a couple of businesses. What else do you do?"

Raine smiled pleasantly, despite her feeling that dinner was turning into a cross-examination. "I spend most of the winter in my landlady's garage with a cutting torch and a welder."

"Are you a plumber, dear?" asked Mrs. Alexander.

"A sculptor, of sorts. I make garden art. You know, one-of-a-kind birdbaths and weather vanes, fountains, odd little figures to plant among the flowers, an occasional trellis, that sort of thing. I build them in the winter when Johnson's is slow, and then in the summer, I haul everything to the garden stores and the street markets. In fact, I'll have a stall at the Redmond farmers' market on Saturday and another at the Fremont market on Sunday."

"I'm looking for an unusual focal point for the rose garden," said Miranda. "Maybe I'll come see what you have."

Mason raised one eyebrow. "I thought you didn't like crowds."

"I'll go early." said Miranda, avoiding her brother's doubting gaze. "You're certainly a busy woman, Miss Hobart. Landscaping. Sculpting. Sorting out energy flows. Do you have any other talents we should know about?"

"That pretty well sums it up," Raine said. "At least for now. Who knows what I'll be doing next year."

Mason glanced at her, his eyes narrowed as though he disapproved of something she'd just said.

"For that matter, who knows what I'll be doing next month," Raine continued, ignoring him. It was time to earn her money for the evening. "I mean, a week ago I never would have imagined that Mason and I . . ." She let her statement trail off in apparent embarrassment.

Fortunately, Mason picked up his cue. The disapproval in his eyes changed to a glitter of warmth, undershot with mischief. He reached for her hand and pulled it to his mouth so he could press a kiss into the tender skin of her palm, hesitating there just long enough to swirl a hot, private circle with the tip of his tongue. "I'm so glad you came into my life."

A shiver of erotic pleasure ran up Raine's arm. For a man who didn't believe in love, Mason was sure good at faking it.

She'd have to keep that in mind.

It was a good thing this was just a temporary relationship, Mason reflected as he smiled into Raine's eyes. All he needed was one more female in his life who was "into" something new every year. And did she really believe that nonsense about energy flows?

Surely not. Of course, who knew what flaky theories those McKenna people were promoting these days.

Claremont McKenna. Who would have guessed?

Mason had assumed, when Raine had mentioned a psychology professor, that she'd been studying at some vocational school or junior college, or perhaps at best at a small state school. He certainly hadn't expected her to claim a degree from a private school as fine—and as notoriously expensive—as Claremont McKenna.

Of course, there had been her reaction to the Monet.

Maybe she was from a better background than he thought. Perhaps she was broke because she'd been cut off by her parents when she didn't meet their expectations. She had mentioned her parents didn't approve of her doing yard work.

And certainly her lack of direction was motive enough for any parent to cut her off.

Who knows what I'll be doing next year, she'd said. Mason cringed inwardly. Give him Caroline and her five-year plans any day.

The rest of the evening progressed pleasantly enough, however, and tweaking his mother and sister wasn't the half of it. There was a lot to be said for lovemaking, in the innocent, old-fashioned sense of the term: the looks, the familiar touches, the gentle words with private meanings. Mason had never been one for public displays of affection, but he quickly fell into the rhythm with Raine, tracing circles on her palm as they discussed the new Symphony Hall, or brushing a wisp of hair from her temple as he listened to her advise his mother on the best way to coax more blooms from a clematis. By the time they moved out to the terrace for marionberry sorbet, Raine's cheeks wore a heated flush like a wash of the berry juice and Mason's own nerve endings buzzed crazily. He hadn't been so excited by next to nothing since his days at Lakeside Prep.

He was still buzzing when Paul pulled the car into an empty spot down the block from Raine's house.

Time to give Paul a little show, just in case Miranda visited the garage again. Appreciating the excuse, Mason shifted so he was sitting closer to Raine.

''What?'' she asked.

The car rocked gently as Paul got out. Mason slipped his arm around Raine and pulled her into his arms.

''Oh,'' she said. She looked up at him with a good imitation of breathless expectancy just as Paul pulled the door open, then she subtly adjusted the hem of her dress, as though it had been pushed a little higher by a roving hand.

Mason was astonished. Lord, even *he* believed they'd been up to something. Perhaps they should have been.

They sat there for a moment, like any couple who had been interrupted in a moment of near intimacy, and then Mason pulled himself together and climbed out of the car. Ignoring Paul's practiced disinterest, he helped Raine out, retrieved the bag with her tennis clothes, then escorted her to her door.

Again, he held the screen door while she unlocked the door and flipped on the lights. And again, she pulled the door mostly shut before he could see anything inside.

''I haven't had a chance to pick up,'' she explained. ''I, um, guess it's time to give Mrs. P. her show.''

He nodded, and lowered his head to kiss her. There was a moment's stiffness, an instant of hesitation, and then her lips went all soft and welcoming. Mason pulled her into his arms.

He'd been waiting all evening for this, like a high school kid on a date, anticipation building with each touch and promising look. He teased her mouth open with the tip of his tongue, kissing her until her arms tightened around his back. It was so heady that he clung to her much longer than necessary for any but the most convincing performance, and when she finally stepped back, breaking his hold, they both glanced away in embarrassment.

"So," Mason began, but his voice was husky and he had to clear his throat and try again. "So. Do you have any preferences for tomorrow evening?"

She brushed a sweat-damp wisp of hair off her forehead. "Rumor on the grounds crew has it that you have a really wild pool."

"We do. Would you like to try it out?"

"Absolutely. It's supposed to get up over ninety tomorrow. I'd spend the whole day at the beach, if I could, but a swim after work is the next best thing."

"Then that's settled. Swimming for two, followed by a dinner theater performance of the Alexander-Hobart Repertory Company."

"All right. My suit and I will be ready. 'Bye."

"Good night." He bent for one more quick kiss, handed over her bag, then headed for the car, pursued by images of Raine in a swimsuit. He'd bet it wasn't one of those butt-covering, Esther Williams sarong things like Caroline wore, either.

Whoa. Time to stop comparing Raine to Caroline, Mason told himself sternly. It wasn't fair to either of them, particularly not to Raine, who was only occupying his thoughts so completely because of the nature of their arrangement.

Then again, there wasn't anything wrong with appreciating a nubile young woman in a bikini.

Raine in a bikini. He smiled. Now there was a thought to warm the cockles of a man's heart. As he reached the car, Paul gave him an odd look, and Mason realized he was whistling "The Girl from Ipanema." His smile broadened, and he breathed the last word of the line, "*Aaah.* Paul, I am a very lucky man."

"Yes, sir, you are. Home?"

"Home."

It had all been for Mrs. Perlmutter, Raine reminded herself as she locked the door. It meant nothing, especially not to her employer, and it was foolish to enjoy it so much. Further self-chastisement was cut short by the shrill ring of the phone.

"It's me," said Zoe when Raine picked up. "How did it go? Did you convert him?"

"Sure. Easy as pie," said Raine. She opened the fridge and pulled out a pitcher of orange juice. Shoot, almost empty. She put it back to save it for morning, and reached for the jug of ice water instead. "He's eating out of my hand. He just rolled right over and let me scratch his stomach like a big ol' hound dog."

"That bad, huh?"

Raine snorte "Let's just say *feng shui* is a sore point right now and I didn't even say the words. The only thing that saved me was his mother raising a subject that made him even madder."

"Like?"

"Like that's none of your business."

The line hissed over Zoe's momentary silence. "Hey. Maybe you could rearrange a room in his house, so he could see how it works."

"Oh, that would go over well. 'Good evening, Mrs. Alexander. Miranda. Excuse me, Mason, could you move that couch over by the wall, please?' Besides, I would have to do all of the calculations to get things right. I don't even know their birthdays, much less when the house was constructed."

"It was just an idea," Zoe said. "We'll think of something."

"Here's another fine mess you've gotten us into."

The old Laurel and Hardy line ran through Tish's mind as she lifted the edge of the draperies and stared out over the drive. A fine mess, indeed.

She was still standing there when the car finally wove its way down through the trees and still there when Mason's lean figure stepped out and strode up to the front door. Behind her, the bedroom door opened and closed, and footsteps padded across the floor. Tish released the drapes and turned.

"I see our wandering boy is home," Miranda said, dropping onto one of the tufted silk chairs beside the window. "I was starting to wonder if he'd decided to stay at her house tonight."

"I thought you told me you didn't believe they were really under the influence of the potion."

"Well, I thought there was something fishy, but after tonight, I'm not sure. I'm not even sure it matters anymore. People who look at each other like that generally wind up naked and horizontal sooner or later.''

Tish sighed. Her own thoughts had been running along the same lines. ''You don't suppose they have already . . .''

Miranda shook her head. ''Not unless Mason has the sexual habits of a weasel.''

''Miranda! Don't be crude.''

''What I mean is, they haven't really had enough time alone to do a good job of it. Unless they're up to something in the car.''

''Oh, surely not. Your brother has too much self-control to indulge in that sort of thing.''

''Ordinarily, yes.''

''He is behaving strangely, even allowing for the potion,'' Tish said. ''I can't remember the last time I saw him fawning over a woman like that.''

''And he barely even twitched when she brought up *feng shui*,'' said Miranda.

''Is that what she was talking about?'' asked Tish. ''She danced around it so, I wasn't certain.''

''She does seem to have a pretty good grasp of Mason's touchy spots already, doesn't she? Like a woman in love.'' Miranda ran her fingernail along the rose piping that trimmed the chair. ''You know, Kit Lester had some fellow in to do their place on Camano Island last spring. He switched all their furniture around and hung a chime and a mirror or two. Their decorator would die if he saw it, but she swears the whole house feels lighter and more positive. And she hasn't had a migraine up there since. She says she used to get them practically every time they went up for a weekend.''

''Really?'' asked Tish. ''Maybe we should ask Miss Hobart to look at the library. I've never been comfortable in there.''

''Really? I always thought it was just me.''

They got off onto a discussion of the library's possible energy faults, and it was several minutes before they got back to the subject of Mason and Raine.

''Well, the point I was making,'' Miranda said, ''was that he barely reacted to what she said. He's always on us like a tiger on a mouse when we mention anything the least bit off the beaten path.''

''He certainly pounced when I brought up the Craft.'' Tish

sighed. "This whole thing is just too confounding. Let's have some tea."

Without waiting for a response from Miranda, she crossed to the corner where an electric teakettle steamed quietly on a cart. She selected a small, silver container from among the half dozen on the tray, measured out a generous portion of Keemun tea into her favorite Spode teapot, and poured the hot water over the leaves.

"Small rituals are so calming," she said, half to herself, as she slipped the cozy over the pot. "I think that's part of what attracts me to the Craft—the ritual."

"Mmm," said Miranda, lost in thought.

Tish knew Miranda was being flip when she'd raised the specter of Mason being sexually involved with Raine Hobart, but now that she thought about it, it concerned Tish. Talk about disaster three times over—if their love potion led Mason to Raine's bed, disaster wouldn't be the word for it.

The tea brewing, Tish went to her dressing table and took the pins out of her hair. Brushing out her hair every evening was one of her small rituals, too, and the familiar motion soothed her as it always did. By the time she was done, the tea had finished steeping. She poured two cups and carried them to the window to join her daughter.

As Tish sipped her tea, Miranda simply stared at the reflections bouncing off the brown liquid.

"Saltpeter," she said aloud.

Tish nearly dropped her cup. "Absolutely not. I forbid it."

"I don't mean saltpeter literally," said Miranda, "although the idea has a certain appeal, considering some of the stunts Mason has pulled on me in the past. However, I bet Raven knows an herb or something that would take the spunk out of him."

"No," repeated Tish.

"We need to buy ourselves some time."

"Not by readjusting Mason's sex drive."

Miranda eyeballed her mother over the top edge of the cup as she took a sip of tea. "Haven't we already done that?"

"We have affected his heart, his emotions. Not his libido. And may I point out that we haven't done a very good job of that." Tish set her cup down on the side table. "Great Lord of the Night, if we ruined Mason's sex life, he'd never forgive us."

"If Caroline finds out he's bopping the gardener, *she'll* ruin his sex life. And then she'll start taking apart Alexander Industries."

"Your language is appalling."

"I'm right, though."

"Possibly," Tish admitted. "Caroline does not strike me as the type to forgive and forget. Nonetheless, your brother's 'spunk' will stay as it is, and that's a direct order from your mother. We will stick to our plan and wait until the dark of the moon, when we can properly reverse the spell."

"If the spell really did work, by the dark of the moon Mason may be enrolled in pruning classes."

"Then he'll prune for a few days. He'll lose interest once we set things right." Tish reached across and patted Miranda's bony knee. "Patience, my darling. Patience."

After a long day of accountants and engineering reports, Mason was more than ready for that bikini, and the tie-dyed T-shirt Raine wore as a cover-up when she came out of the guest room gave every indication he was going to get his wish, recalling as it did sun-drenched California beaches and volleyball games. As they walked to the elevator that ran from the second floor down to the pool level, he caught an encouraging glimpse of Lycra-clad bottom beneath the hem of the T-shirt. There were definitely times when it was good to be a man.

"Whoa," said Raine as the elevator doors opened onto the pool. "I had no clue."

Mason knew exactly what she meant. From outside, the pool area looked no bigger than the west terrace that formed its roof, but thanks to the slope of the property, it actually extended back under the house as a sort of subbasement. It made for a deceptively large space. Also, a few years before his father had died, the ceiling had been painted with a trompe l'oeil fantasy of clouds and flying birds. Combined with a greenhouse's worth of tropical plants and the huge bank of west-facing windows, the effect was of a huge oasis with a mountain view.

Raine let her fingers wander through the lush foliage, pausing to stroke the waxy leaves of a ti plant. "I bet your mother loves this place. It's a lot like her."

"Strange, but spectacular?"

Raine chuckled. "Those aren't quite the words I would have

picked, but yes, something like that." She glanced toward the pool. "Shall we?"

"Ladies first."

She peeled out of the shirt in one smooth move, destroying Mason's fantasy. Not a bikini, a turquoise tank suit.

But one with a low-cut back and high-cut legs. And very thin, very clingy material, Mason observed as she walked to the deep end of the pool and took a stance at the edge. It would do.

She dived cleanly and bobbed to the surface partway across the pool, then rolled into a lazy backstroke. "Are you coming in, or are you just going to stare?"

"Just sizing up the competition."

"I should have known you'd want to race," she said, sounding slightly perturbed.

"We don't have to."

"No, no. Let's get your competitive streak satisfied, and then we can just splash around. Do you mind if I at least warm up a little first?"

"Of course not." Mason didn't bother denying the competitive streak. He tossed his cotton robe on a chair and dove in, coming up where he thought Raine would be. She had vanished, and it took him a moment to spot the flash of turquoise beneath the water. She surfaced at the far length of the pool. Mason swam to join her, and they did a couple of easy laps, matching each other stroke for stroke. She was a strong swimmer, but Mason felt confident. He wasn't even pushing.

"I'm ready," Mason said. "How about you?"

Raine wore a relaxed smile as she pulled herself up on the edge of the pool. "Diving start, or in the water?"

"Diving. Two lengths."

"Aw, come on. Let's do it right. Four, just like real swimmers."

"All right. Four." He hoisted himself out of the water and they took positions next to each other on the tiled edge. "On three."

Raine settled into her stance. "One . . . two . . ." Her thighs tightened. God, she had beautiful legs. Strong legs. And her shoulders . . . Mason had a sudden feeling he'd made a mistake. "Three."

She rocketed out over the water, landing a good five feet beyond him, and it was downhill from there on out. He swam like a barracuda was after him, but even if that had been enough, and it wasn't, she'd have beat him on the turns alone. By the second lap, she was sailing past him in the opposite direction at about midpool. Sheer stubbornness drove him to finish, but she was sitting on the end of the pool, wearing a smug smile and squeezing water out of the end of her braid, when he wallowed up to the wall.

He took a gulp of air and raked his hair out of his eyes. "You set me up."

"Yes, sir." Laughter bubbled out of her. "I sure did."

The burn in his arms finally subsided enough that he could boost himself out of the pool. He flopped backward on the concrete beside Raine, breathing hard. "Excuse me, Miss Hobart, but I do believe you neglected to mention you swam competitively."

She just grinned and shrugged. "How else do you think I could afford McKenna?"

"Full ride?"

"No, but enough that I could make ends meet. Or at least get them to wave at each other over a distance. I'm still paying off student loans, though."

Mason levered himself up on his elbows. "What other surprises do you have up your sleeve?"

Laughing, Raine held out her bare arms. "Not so much as a cufflink. I didn't crush your masculine ego or anything, did I?"

"No. Miranda got me over that when we were young." He grinned. "She's going to be sorry she missed this."

"We could always invite her down and do it again," Raine offered cheerily.

"I don't think so." He pushed up, so he was sitting beside her with a perfect view of her legs dangling into the pool and an adequate view of the top curve of her breasts above her suit. He was just thinking he could probably sit there quite content for the rest of his life when she suddenly slid off the edge.

Her hands moved in slow, lazy eights as she treaded water at his feet. "Let's do a few more laps. This space has wonderful, open energy flows. I feel fantastic."

Open energy flows? Mason opened his mouth to point out how ridiculous that sounded, but she looked so relaxed, bobbing there in the water like some modern-day mermaid, that he decided it wasn't worth the argument. He dove in cleanly beside her, and they did a dozen easy laps before climbing out of the pool and heading upstairs to change.

Dinner was a repeat of the night before, with Miranda grilling an ever more bemused Raine, and Mason running a counteroffensive of blatant seduction to throw his sister off. It had the same result, too, leaving him in that state of pointless excitement to which frustrated young boys refer by a colorful name.

The enforced proximity of the car and the need to keep up appearances for Paul did nothing to help, and by the time they got to Raine's door, his best intentions were barely holding on by a thread. As she unlocked the door, he stepped close, so that when she turned she was practically in his arms.

She licked her lips nervously. "I didn't see Mrs. Perlmutter. She must have fallen asleep in front of the news."

"Good for the news."

She came into his arms like she belonged there, face tilted up, a soft smile on her half-open lips. He lowered his head, and suddenly it didn't matter that none of it was real. It was as though he'd been holding his breath all evening, waiting for this, and her kiss had finally allowed him to fill his lungs with purest oxygen. She groaned softly, and when he raised his head to catch the sound better, he discovered he could see the foot of her bed through the cracked door, beyond the living room. The image of Raine amid those tousled white sheets created a dangerous ripple of arousal down his spine and into his groin. So tempting.

And such a bad idea.

It took an effort to grip her arms and set her away, even more effort to step back and find his voice. "I enjoyed our swim tonight. Would you like to do it again tomorrow?"

"No." She glanced around in confusion, as though she wasn't sure where she was, then straightened and pulled herself together. "That is, could we just skip one night?"

He swept away the feeling of rejection that tried to attach to her words. This wasn't real, after all.

"I'd rather not. Mother and Miranda aren't showing much sign of movement yet. We have less than two weeks now."

"I know, but I really need some time to take care of life." She turned away, staring into the blackness of the alley beyond. "You can go out every night, all night, and your servants keep the home fires burning."

"Servants," he repeated, amused. "We call them staff now."

''Well, whatever they are, I don't have them,'' she snapped. ''It's just me, and I haven't had ten free minutes awake since Sunday. It's nearly midnight and I have to be at work at seven. There's a four-day-old pile of clothes on the couch waiting to be folded, I'm running out of stuff for lunch, and my poor cat thinks he's been abandoned.'' She spoke faster and faster, getting more agitated with each word. ''We won't even talk about the dust. It's either give me a free night or watch me fall asleep in the soup, because I'm going to have to stay up all night just to keep even.''

''Okay, okay,'' Mason held up his hands in surrender. ''You have an amazing knack for making a man feel guilty over the circumstances of his birth. I'm sorry. I've been so focused on my side of this that I haven't taken your life into consideration. You can have the night off. Or I have a better idea. I'll come over here. Being alone will make Mother and Miranda assume the worst, and I can help you catch up on your housework.''

She eyed him doubtfully. ''Somehow, I have trouble picturing you chasing dust bunnies.''

''It's like fox hunting, right?''

She stared for a moment, then broke into a laugh. ''All right, all right. You can't help it if you're a rich kid. But you're not exactly the prototype for Mr. Domestic, you know.''

''You wound me. My apartments have always been as neat as the proverbial pin.'' He conveniently omitted mention of the thrice-weekly maid service he always arranged. ''However, my thoughts *were* running more toward cooking you dinner while you wield the mop. I know how to grill a mean pork chop.''

''I don't have a grill. Or pork chops.''

''Broiler?''

''Sure.''

''Then we're set. I'll take you to the store first. You need to buy bologna and bread anyway, you said.''

That doubtful look again.

''I'll even carry the bags,'' he offered.

She eyed him with skepticism, then sighed. ''Oh, all right. How can I resist my own personal millionaire bag boy.''

''Five-thirty, then.''

''Six,'' she countered. ''I at least need time after work to make a list and get my undies off the couch.''

''Six, then. And now, I'd better let you turn in.'' He dropped one last kiss on her cheek. It was all he dared, with the word *undies* bouncing around in his skull. He stepped off the porch before he used up his daily allotment of chivalry. "Good night, Raine."

"Good night."

Did she wear cotton or lace? he wondered as he picked his way back through the fantastic shadows of the dark garden. Caroline could take lessons from this girl on how to drive a man to distraction—except on Caro it would be so deliberate. Raine simply said what was on her mind, and let other people take it where they would.

And tonight, he would take it straight home to a cold shower.

Raine stood on the porch until the bass rumble of the Rolls Royce engine faded, leaving only the faint drone of Mrs. Perlmutter's television and the whine of traffic on the Aurora Bridge to disturb the night. Why on earth had she agreed to spend an evening alone with that man, when he could so easily make her forget this whole thing was a sham? Because forget she did, for those few moments every time his mouth was on hers.

Before she could come up with an answer, the phone rang. Raine hurried inside and answered.

"Any more progress tonight?"

"Geez, Zoe, do you have a guard on my house, or what?" Raine dragged the phone back so she could lock the door. "I wasn't even inside yet."

"I don't need a guard," said Zoe cheerily. "I'm psychic."

"Since when? Let me guess: you must have started a new job at one of those 900 numbers."

"Nope. I'm transcribing notes for this physics professor up at the UW. Something about quantum mechanics and how when you do something to a subatomic particle in one place, it affects a particle in another place even though they aren't in contact. I don't understand the math at all, but the rest is really cool. Anyway, it must have joggled me or something when you opened the door."

"I'm not a subatomic particle," said Raine. She got out a can of cat food and the can opener.

"You know what I mean. Anyway, so have you gotten Moneybags to open his mind yet?"

"No. Although he managed to keep from exploding tonight

when I said 'energy flow,' so maybe he's desensitizing.''

''Ooh. This is going to work, Rainey. I can *see* it.''

''Zoe, I love you dearly, but you get flakier every day.'' It wasn't that Raine didn't believe that a few rare people were psychic—just that Zoe wasn't one of them.

''I'm telling you, it's real. Physics proves it.''

''Does your vision happen to include *when* this plan will work? Because at this rate I'll be lucky to explain *ch'i* to him before his tenants move into the building.''

''It won't take that long,'' Zoe said. ''You just have to persist. What's your next window of opportunity?''

''He's coming over tomorrow night.'' Raine regretted the words the instant they left her mouth.

''To your place?'' Zoe perked up. ''Cool. I can just sort of casually show up and we'll double-team him.''

''No.''

''But we could do—''

''No, Zoe.''

''But—''

''Zoe Rachel Levine, I swear, if I see so much as one of your false eyelashes outside my house tomorrow, I'll shoot you.''

''Oh, all right.'' Her pout was apparent, even by phone. ''I promise I won't come over. But you are going to keep working on him, right?''

More like he's working on me, Raine thought. She set the cat food on the porch for Bugsy and relocked the door. ''I really ought to tell him who I am. He's going to figure it out anyway; it's just a matter of time.''

''Come on, Rainey. Hang in there for Fremont.''

''Yeah, right.'' Well, if he was coming over, she wouldn't so much as let him touch her. That'd make it easier to stay rational. And she was going to have to hide her *feng shui* books in the closet—

''Rainey?''

''Sure, Zoe. For Fremont.''

Miranda relaxed when Mason once more opted to sleep in his own bed, but when she woke early the next morning, she decided that a face-to-face conversation might be in order—just to see where things stood. Toward that end, she decided to join him for breakfast—a sacrifice, considering that anything more than juice before ten A.M. struck her as repulsive. Mason, on the other hand, had always been a breakfast eater, and he sat across from Miranda in the octagonal breakfast room making her slightly nauseous with the amount of muesli, cantaloupe, and lean ham he was consuming.

"Are you going to be needing the car this afternoon?" Miranda asked. Five vehicles sat in the carriage house, but "the car" always meant the one with the driver. "Mother volunteered me for that affair for the hospital. The benefactors' tea. If I show up driving myself, they may lose hope that we'll ever donate again."

Mason glanced up from the yellow pad on which he was scribbling between bites. "No. Go ahead. In fact, that reminds me—I meant to tell Mother I won't be here for dinner. I guess I'll leave a note." He flipped to a fresh sheet of paper and continued writing.

"Going out somewhere?" she asked casually, hoping the answer was no. They didn't need any of Caroline's friends to spot Mason squiring the gardener around town.

"Actually, I'm cooking for Raine," Mason said. "I thought it would make a nice break from Dinner-as-Inquisition."

Miranda huffed a bit. "I was just trying to get to know her."

"Like the Special Prosecutor trying to get to know the President."

"Sorry," said Miranda. "I didn't know you were trying to keep her a mystery."

"I'm not, but neither do I need a complete dossier on her in the first forty-eight hours. We all have plenty of time to get to know her."

The matter-of-fact confidence in his voice rocked Miranda. He sounded an awfully lot like a man planning a long-term relationship.

"So, you're going to spend the evening at her house?"

His pen stopped midword and a slow smile spread across his lips. "Mmm-mmm." He started writing again. The smile stayed.

Why did he look so dreamy at the thought? The most obvious answer nearly put the finishing touch on Miranda's nausea. He wouldn't. He couldn't. She had to stop him.

She concentrated on keeping her voice casual. "Where does Raine live, anyway?"

"Fremont."

"I should have guessed. Very Bohemian." She needed more information than that, but the moment was lost as Mason finished scribbling on his pad.

He tore off the sheet and pushed it to the center of the table, then tossed his napkin down next to his plate. "I have a meeting in thirty minutes. If I'm going to drive myself, I'd better have Paul bring the Jaguar around." He stepped around the table to kiss Miranda on the cheek, then headed for the door. "I'll see you tomorrow. Have a nice time at the tea—and don't make any promises we won't be able to keep."

"Don't worry," said Miranda, trying to ignore how ominous that sounded. One of the things Mason had mentioned recently was how good it would be to have the family finances solid enough to bring their contributions back up to the levels that had once sent Seattle charities into spasms of gratitude. If he thought they might not be able to donate to the hospital anytime soon, then maybe the spell really had worked and he was planning to tell Caroline and her money to take a hike.

Oh, lord. This was so confusing.

But there was something she could do, patience be damned. As soon as she was sure Mason had gone, she hurried to the phone table in the hall and pulled out the White Pages. *Hobart. Hobart.* She riffled through the book until she found the right page, then ran a finger down the columns. *Hobart.* Oh, great. Half of them just initials, and not a single *R.* in the lot. She ripped the page out of the book.

"Miranda, please. The rest of us might like to use that."

She looked up to see her mother frowning at her. "Oh, good, you're out of the pool. Come here." She grabbed her mother's hand and dragged her back into the breakfast room and closed the door. "I just found out Mason is going to spend the night at Raine's house."

Tish sagged into a chair. "Good heavens. He told you that?"

"No. But he's cooking her dinner, and you and I both know what's going to happen afterwards. Or at least what would happen if I didn't have a way to keep their feet on the floor."

"One which involves shredding the phone book?"

Miranda glanced at the piece of paper in her hand. "Sorry. I just needed Raine's address. I've decided I'm going to chaperone them—from a distance."

"Chaperone from a distance?" Tish raised an eyebrow. "You mean *spy,* don't you?"

"Absolutely. It's perfect. I can keep an eye on them and create diversions as necessary, and at the same time, maybe I can figure out how much of this is our spell and how much is plain hormones."

Tish sighed. "Isn't there some other way?"

"Of course, but not as good as this. Now, all we have to do is figure out which of these listings is Raine." She laid the phone listings on the table. "There are three in or near Fremont: *A.B.*, *John*, and *L.M.* Frankly, I'm rooting for a husband named John. Love potion or not, Mason would never sleep with another man's wife, not after what Elizabeth did to him."

"That would be in our favor," said Tish. "But I think it's more likely to be *L.*, for Lorraine."

Miranda frowned. "I hadn't thought of that. You're probably right."

"But it's still just a guess."

"Well, there's someone who can tell us for certain."

"You can't very well ask Mason."

"Not Mason. Paul."

Her mother's eyebrows went up. "I suppose he does know, but it's really quite inappropriate to involve him."

Not as inappropriate as hiding in his supply closet, Miranda thought. She just smiled at her mother. "It's a simple question. Of course, if you don't think I should go to him, I can just run all over town tonight trying to figure out which house is hers."

Tish sighed. "You're right. It's the only logical thing to do. Just please be subtle, darling."

"Me? I'm the soul of discretion."

Fortunately, Miranda had plenty of time to consider just how to live up to her mother's request for subtlety, particularly during the hospital tea. After the obligatory chitchat and sucking up, the hospital representatives focused their attentions on people who'd indicated they were likely to make significant donations in the next couple of years—which left Miranda blessedly out of the mix. Free of the need to be graciously modest, Miranda enjoyed her cakes and crustless sandwiches and ruminated.

When she finally slipped out, she saw Paul reading one of the thick books he always carried, but by the time she reached the car, he had jumped out and opened the door for her.

He looked altogether too traditional standing there in his black uniform, Miranda reflected, like the sort of driver who never talked about his employer. The man in the T-shirt and jeans had been much more approachable. She stepped past him into the car, the memory of those jeans turning up the corners of her mouth. Definitely more approachable.

Paul shut the door behind her and went around to his side, and a moment later they pulled away from the curb. As they made the right onto the street, Miranda stared at the back of Paul's head through the open partition. He wore his hair a little long, and the thick, black strands brushing the top of his collar shone like the male version of one of those television ads for tropical-scented shampoo. Blue highlights beckoned, and she could easily imagine the silky weight of his hair between her fingers—not that she'd ever have occasion to feel it.

"Do you want something, Miss Alexander?"

She blinked and met his eyes in the rearview mirror. She hoped he couldn't see the color in her cheeks. "We're not far from Fremont, are we?"

"About ten minutes."

"I heard about a new esoterica shop. I'd like to see what they have." She didn't really care about the shop, but it was a good excuse to get a look at Raine's neighborhood.

Paul hit the turn indicator. "Yes, miss."

A few minutes later they passed the sign proclaiming Fremont as Center of the Universe and crossed the old drawbridge that spanned the Ship Canal. Miranda peered out the window, hoping that Fremont still lived up to its official motto, "Freedom to be Peculiar."

Thank the Goddess, it did. The aluminum commuters of the "Waiting for the Interurban" statue were decked in grass hula skirts and cardboard guitars. Funky secondhand shops and used book stores of all ilk lined the streets, patronized by a wide range of people, many of whom wore what could only be described as costumes, complete with parti-colored hair, tattoos, and multiple body piercings. Miranda spotted the rocket towering over Ah Nuts and leaned back, pleased. The Republic of Fremont was intact, keeping all the crazies neatly occupied in one corner of the city. The less imaginative denizens of Seattle were safe. Miranda might not be a citizen of the Republic, but she liked knowing it was there, guarding the fringes against creeping mediocrity.

She directed Paul to the shop, just down the street from the statue of Lenin, and popped inside for a few minutes while he circled the block. The store was a disappointment even though she hadn't been expecting much, but she bought a small vial of scented salve, just for appearances.

Back in the car, she responded to Paul's "Where next, miss?" by naming the Canal Place site. "I'm curious what the fuss is about."

Paul nodded and turned back toward the Ship Canal. A few minutes later, he pulled in next to an ancient wooden building surrounded by chain link construction fencing.

The site was nothing spectacular. It had been Alexander property since before the turn of the century, when Miranda's great-grandfather had run a lumber mill on the site. The mill had closed seventy years ago, to be replaced by an assortment of light industrial buildings. Those businesses had run their course and Alexander Industries had moved on to other interests, involving other properties. The last remaining building, an old warehouse and loading dock, had sat vacant for years. It wasn't exactly a blight on the neighborhood, but it didn't contribute anything, either.

"Why don't they want a new building here?" she muttered to herself.

Paul glanced over his shoulder, as though to see if she really wanted an answer. When Miranda nodded, he explained. "Most of the neighborhood is resigned to the inevitable, but a few people are convinced the Canal Place building will disturb the energy that makes Fremont unique. Cause a blight, of sorts."

"I know that's the argument. But I've seen the designs. It's not *that* ugly." She looked out the window. "Certainly not as ugly as that thing."

"It isn't a matter of being ugly. The building is reflective and full of sharp edges that could disrupt the flow of *ch'i*. Energy."

"*Feng shui* again," she muttered. "You're Chinese. Do you know anything about that stuff?"

"I've had some experience with it, yes."

"Do you believe in it?"

"It's been used successfully in China for thousands of years," Paul said without committing himself. "But *feng shui* aside, the design for Canal Place simply doesn't fit into Fremont. It belongs someplace over on the Eastside, in one of those office parks near Microsoft."

"You think the project's a mistake, then?"

"I think it could be done better."

"Did you tell Mason?"

"I'm Mr. Alexander's driver, not his real estate advisor."

"You told *me.*"

"You asked."

Traffic ground to a halt on Fremont Avenue, and Paul and Miranda both stopped talking to watch the Fremont Bridge rise for a tall ketch on its way into Lake Union. As the bridge started back down, Miranda said, "Raine Hobart lives someplace around here, doesn't she?"

She spoke in an offhand manner, and Paul answered just as offhandedly. "Up on Dayton, near Fortieth."

She saw when it hit him what he'd done, but it didn't matter. She had the bit of information she needed. Raine was "L.M." Or maybe—Miranda crossed her fingers—she was "L.M.'s" wife. One could hope.

Shaking his head, Paul turned around and rested his arm over the back of the seat. "You're very good. I take it Mr. Alexander wouldn't tell you."

"Tell me what? Raine's address? I didn't even ask him. Being in the neighborhood just made me curious."

"Right."

That single syllable contained enough doubt for a whole debate team to work with, but Miranda waved it off. "I've seen enough here; let's go. Oh, and when we get home, I'd like you to bring my car around, please. I have an appointment this evening."

"Are you sure you don't want me to take you on a tour first? Case Miss Hobart's house, snoop around a little?" Paul's brown eyes twinkled with mischief. "There's that spy outlet over on Greenwood. We could swing by and pick up some surveillance equipment."

Smart ass, Miranda thought. And as much as she would like him to show her exactly where Raine's house was, she just smiled sweetly. "Oh, no. I already have all the bugs I need back at the house. I just need to get into my black clothes and smudge my face first."

Chuckling, Paul turned back to the steering wheel. "I'll assume you're kidding, miss."

"Of course I am. Come on, Paul, I'm not that bad." Maybe not, but she had a feeling her competent, dependable, discreet driver wouldn't be so amused if he knew what she actually *was* planning for the evening.

Mason took the steps in front of Mrs. Perlmutter's house two at a time. As the side gate squealed open, the avocado green draperies parted and the tip of a nose appeared. Mason dipped his head and called out, "Good evening."

The drapes flicked shut. Shaking his head, he rounded the corner into the backyard.

So that's what all those odd shapes in the dark were—Raine's art. Various creations in copper, aluminum, and steel nestled among the plants of a cottage garden run amok. Mason passed a hammered birdbath with a dozen cartoon cats dancing in silhouette around its base. A few feet away, next to a leggy rosemary plant, stood a pile of mixed metal curlicues, somehow welded together to look like a waterfall frozen in midair. A stack of what looked like straw hats woven from copper balanced precariously amid a riot of pink cosmos, and assorted other half-finished constructions stood scattered through the flower beds. Some of the pieces wore thick coats of rust or of powdery oxidation, as though they'd been sitting outside for months; others reflected sun from highly polished surfaces that were barely touched with tarnish.

Mason paused by a slender statue, the only clearly human figure in the lot. She was a fully wrought Chinese maiden, about three feet tall, who held a globe in her outstretched hands. Her robes swirled around her feet like a cloud of butterflies shaped from brass strips—no, what were those things? Tossing his suit jacket over his shoulder, he squatted to get a better look.

"Not quite as impressive as the Monet in the dining room."

Mason looked up to see Raine standing in her doorway. She wore a pair of baggy khaki shorts and a Hawaiian shirt, and she held a rainbow of folded T-shirts in her arms. "More so," he said. "I inherited the Monet, I didn't paint it. Are these Chinese characters in her robe?"

Raine nodded. " 'Harmony' and 'Balance'—two qualities I'm always working to achieve. Not too successfully, I might add."

"Don't underestimate yourself." Mason stood up and stepped to the edge of the porch, so he was looking up into her smiling face. Her wet hair hung in a braid down her neck, and her freckles and sunburnt nose were bare of makeup.

"You look like summer epitomized," he said. "Gidget Goes to Malibu."

"Gee, thanks, Moondoggie. I'm surprised you ever heard of Gidget movies. I thought Sandra Dee was too déclassé for your breed."

"My secret passion. I had a belated case of chicken pox when I was fourteen, and the only thing on television besides soap operas was a Gidget film festival. I got hooked."

"All those bikinis appealed to your pubescent fantasies, eh?"

"That, and they aggravated Mother no end. What more could a boy want?" He loosened his tie and worked the top shirt button free. "I had no idea all your work was out here. You've never let me get back this far during daylight hours."

"I had to cut you off before you saw the mess in my living room." Her gaze flickered out over the garden. "Besides, these are my duds. My failed experiments. Mrs. P. steals them from the junk pile."

Mason gestured toward the maiden. "She's no dud."

Raine smiled, almost shyly. "No, not her, thank you. Come on in. I was just finishing up the laundry. I'll put these away, and we can hit the store."

She disappeared inside with her T-shirts, and Mason drifted in after her, the screen door banging shut behind him. From the bedroom came the sound of dresser drawers opening and closing. He caught a glimpse of folded clothes on the foot of the bed—which she'd made, to his simultaneous relief and disappointment—and shifted slightly to get a better view, but she'd already put her undies away. Damn. He felt like a middle-schooler who had just discovered that the janitor had plugged the peephole into the girls' locker room.

"I'll just be a minute," Raine called.

"Take your time."

He stopped playing lingerie fetishist and looked around Raine's living-room-cum-kitchen. Her decor was eclectic, to put it mildly: pillows covered in French country prints buried an early-Goodwill couch; cheap Mexican pottery stair-stepped up a heavy Japanese tansu; a round, red-lacquered Chinese mirror hung over a rococo side table; and carved Indonesian bookends held up the volumes on an antique cherry bookshelf. Colored bottles and potted plants and blue and white crockery filled the windowsills and lined the kitchen counters. And everything sat against walls painted like a Greek cantina, in pale shades of blue with bright white trim.

The effect was that of a serendipitous flea market. Somehow it worked. And somehow, it was pure Raine.

She reappeared at the door to her bedroom, a canvas bag over her shoulder and a half-sheet of white paper in her hand. "I'm ready. This should be a gas. I bet they don't get many Rolls Royces at Larry's."

"Sorry. Miranda needed Paul this afternoon for some charity thing. Will the Jaguar do?"

She sighed and lifted the back of her hand to her forehead like the heroine of a melodrama. "I guess it will have to. At least I get a driver. To the store, James."

"Yes, miss." He opened the door with a flourish worthy of the cheesiest Hollywood chauffeur. "Whatever you say, miss."

She directed him to the Larry's Red Apple, just up the road in Ballard, and Mason pushed the cart while Raine picked her groceries. Fortunately, her shopping technique was nothing like her method of decorating. She went from item to item on her list like Patton marching through Italy—no muss, no fuss, no prisoners. Mason, on the other hand, felt like a dawdler because he took the time to pick out the plumpest chops and curliest endive. Crusty sourdough rolls, some saffron, a bottle of twenty-year-old balsamic vinegar, and a pint of the best vanilla ice cream in the store completed his list. Raine claimed to have rice and chicken broth at home, as well as the other minor ingredients he needed. And as much as he'd like to introduce her to a truly fine bottle of Cabernet, he decided to pass. The way his mind was running already, he did not need to deal with inhibitions lowered by alcohol.

At the checkout stand, Raine declined the store sack and had the clerk pack her purchases into her canvas bag—bags, actually, since she had another one stuffed inside the first.

"Very ecological," said Mason. He turned back to the cashier. "I'm unenlightened. I'll take plastic."

Transaction complete, Mason grabbed all three bags and headed for the door. As the blast of hot air hit them, Raine leaned close and muttered sotto voce, "I do it for the nickel."

"Do what?" he asked, silently chiding the portion of his mind that read unwarranted sex into her comment. If he didn't stop it, he'd drive himself crazy before the salad.

"Drag these bags along. They give you a nickel credit when you bring your own sack."

"Oh." *See,* he told his libido. "I didn't know that."

They reached the car and Mason deposited the bags in the trunk while Raine watched.

"So how long has it been since you were in a grocery story?" she asked.

Mason laughed and shut the lid. "A couple of years. Is it that obvious?"

"You're just sort of . . . overly deliberate. Most of us who have to do this all the time are less enthralled with the process. Are you sure you remember how to cook? I'm pretty hungry."

"Positive. It's like riding a bicycle." He held the door open for her. "You look doubtful again."

She raised one eyebrow. "I was just thinking I should have picked up a frozen pizza as insurance."

Her doubts proved to be unfounded. Not only did Mason remember how to cook, he moved around her tiny kitchen with such panache that Raine found herself stopping in the middle of sweeping to watch him whisk the vinaigrette.

"You were the Galloping Gourmet in a different life, right?"

"Not I." He gave the dressing another flick and set it aside. "It's all show. This is the only meal I can cook. Other than an omelet, of course."

"Dinner and breakfast. Good combination."

"I've always found it useful."

Raine spotted a dust bunny under the table and dove after it with a sense of relief. Bending over provided a good excuse for her face to be so red.

While the rice was simmering, she managed to dust, scrub the bathroom, and water the plants. By the time she finished, the scent of saffron and herbs was already starting to beat out the smell of disinfectant.

"How much more time do I have?" she asked.

"The chops are ready to go." He lifted the lid for a quick peek at the rice. "Say, fifteen minutes."

"Good. I can wash out a dress."

She retrieved her dress and ducked into the bathroom. "I hope you liked this pink one. You're going to be seeing it again. Probably several times."

"Fine. It looks well on you."

When she came out, the table was set and Mason was laying a sprig of fresh rosemary across the top of the chops.

"You've been outside."

"Requisitioning garnish. I found that in the garden, too." He pointed toward the back of the couch, where a tortoiseshell cat lazed in a late sunbeam, eyes half-closed. "Or maybe it found me."

"Hi, Bugsy. You always show up in time for food, don't you?" She gave the cat a quick scratch behind the ears, and was thanked with a thunderous purr.

"What's that you called him, her, er, it?"

"It, formerly him. His name's Bugsy."

"As in Malone?"

"Yep. He's my psychotic Mafia kitty. He has some very nasty habits, like sneaking up behind people and jumping on their backs. Especially people sitting in *that* chair."

Mason, who had been about to set a plate down in front of a colorfully painted ladder-back chair, switched directions. He glared at the cat. "I don't suppose we could throw him back outside."

"Depends on how much you like the skin on your arm. That's his other bad habit. He pretty much comes and goes on his own terms."

"You know, it's hot in here from the broiler, and we don't want to disturb old Bugsy's nap."

"Oh, it's okay. I'll sit there and he usually leaves the other chair alone."

"Why don't we eat outside anyway."

"Chicken," she said, laughing. "Just for that, I'm going to make you sit on the splintery part of the step."

Oh, good lord. They were coming outside.

Heart pounding, Miranda crouched down low behind the ivy-smothered picket fence that ran along the alley behind Raine's house.

This was really too much. First, she'd had to park the Explorer three blocks away behind a Dumpster to make sure Mason didn't spot it—the Goddess only knew whether it would still be there when she got back—and then sneak down back alleys. Then Mason and Raine hadn't been at the house when she'd finally figured out which one it was, which had left Miranda panicked until she'd heard the Jaguar roar up out front. Then Mason had decided to go herb picking just as she'd been trying to find a spot where she could see into the house better.

And now this. If Mason caught her spying, she'd have to move to Antarctica to escape his temper.

But at least she might be able to hear them now, once her heart stopped pounding so loudly. Miranda crawled to her right a couple of feet, to where a rangy buddleia provided some cover, then cautiously poked her head up.

She had a perfect view of her brother between the long purple flower spikes. He was sitting on the wooden porch step and, by shifting slightly, Miranda could see Raine perched next to him. They were talking about a cat, of all things. Maybe the love potion really had worked. Miranda settled back to listen.

Unfortunately, her makeshift blind was just a few feet from a pair of trash cans, complete with ripe aromas and swarming yellow jackets. Miranda loathed yellow jackets, but she couldn't go anywhere so long as her quarry was outside. Despite a temperature that still hovered well above eighty, she quietly pulled on the jacket she'd brought for later, snugged the collar tight to keep any bugs from flying down her back, and prayed that the clouds she had seen over the mountains moved in before she succumbed to heat prostration.

She lurked behind the buddleia while Mason and Raine ate their dinner and chatted about everything from art to baseball.

with the mop handle and, laughing, he lifted one foot at a time for her to mop under him.

The air of domestic bliss made Miranda want to storm the front door and yank her brother out by the short hairs. This was *not* the Mason she knew. It had to be the potion, that was the only explanation.

And yet, so far, she hadn't seen any signs of passion between him and Raine—not even a kiss, and certainly not the blatant seduction that had been going on at the house the evening before. Very interesting. She leaned against the fence and settled in for the long haul.

Raine let the cat out and turned down the stereo, then she and Mason settled down at the table with big glasses of iced tea and a backgammon board between them. "Now this is a summer evening: nice and long, all the work done, good music, plenty of iced tea."

"And no audience."

"True. Thank you for letting me get caught up, by the way. I don't feel nearly so stressed out. Even Bugsy looks happier."

"How can you tell?"

"He smiled at me." She shook her head at the way he rolled his eyes. "Oh, come on, surely you've seen Magus smile."

"Not since Mother decided he was her 'familiar.' I don't think she's noticed that he runs for cover every time she and Miranda pull out their cauldron and wands." He handed her the white pieces and took the black for himself. "There have been a couple of times when I've been tempted to crawl under the bed and join him."

"You really don't like their involvement in Wicca, do you?"

"No," he said flatly.

"Why?"

"I don't enjoy being a guinea pig for their toxic brews."

Raine finished laying out her pieces on the board. "I get the impression it's more than that."

His eyes narrowed and he stared at her a long moment, then took a draught from his glass. "I suppose it is. I get so tired of dealing with the nonsense and the way they drag each other from one dippy philosophy to another. If they'd just settle on one thing—anything—I could learn to tolerate it, but I never know from one day to the next whether I'll be assaulted with tantric chants or gurus in purple robes or primal howls or . . . love potions."

"They're searchers," she said softly. "That's not such a bad thing. We're all searching for something."

He raked his hair back, and she could see the stress lines around his eyes. "Well, while they're scouting the universe for karmic bliss, I'm out in the real world, doing real work and trying to keep Alexander Industries afloat."

By marrying Caroline Wickersham, she supposed, but she kept her mouth shut. It wasn't her business. She picked up the dice and rolled for starting position. "Six and five. Beat that, Alexander."

Nightfall finally brought the clouds and cooler temperatures the weatherman had promised. In fact, in a period of about twenty minutes it got downright chilly, and a distant flash of lightning in the east announced the end of the dry spell, at least over in Kirkland. The sweat that had soaked her blouse earlier now evaporated in the breeze that had kicked up, leaving Miranda chilled and miserable.

For two hours, the most action she saw was dice passing back and forth across the table. From what she could tell, Mason was trouncing Raine, but that was to be expected—his cutthroat instincts would hardly go dull just because he had the hots for his opposition. The two of them laughed a lot, and Miranda thought she heard her own name several times, but the sound was muffled, and she couldn't be sure.

She concentrated so hard on reading their lips that her first clue that she had company again was a flashlight beam playing across the fence in front of her. Damn those kids. She took a deep breath and prepared herself to come up with an elaboration on the stink bomb story.

"Turn around slowly, ma'am. Hands out where I can see them."

Oh, shit. Holding her hands well out from her sides and smiling sweetly, Miranda turned around. "Is there something wrong, Officer?"

"Why don't you tell me? I have reports that you've been hanging around back here all evening."

"I'm just looking for my cat."

"Since six-thirty?"

"Oh, I haven't been here that long. But I have come through several times. Whoever called in probably saw me at different times and assumed I had been here all along. I'm sorry if I scared anyone."

"Your cat, huh? What kind of cat?"

What had that animal of Raine's looked like? "A tortoiseshell. Very sweet. He's been missing for a couple of days, and some boys told me they'd seen him around here. I thought I heard him in this yard." She glanced away into the dark, as though still hunting her cat, and concentrated on the image of the cat, willing it to appear. "Here, Archibald. Here, kitty, kitty." *Please.*

A soft meow answered her.

Wow. Maybe she was starting to commune with animals. Trembling with excitement, Miranda called softly again, "Here, Archie. Come on, baby."

Obeying her summons, the cat leapt lightly to the top of the fence, then jumped down and came over to weave around Miranda's legs. She bent down and scooped him up, hugging him close in gratitude. "There you are, baby. You naughty kitty." She gave the officer a "told you so" look. "I just knew this was the right place. May I go now?"

The policeman flicked the flashlight off. "Okay, lady. Just don't hang around in dark alleys anymore. It's not safe."

"No, sir. I mean, yes, sir. I won't. Good night." Clutching the cat, who rumbled like a dump truck, Miranda obediently strolled off down the alley. Behind her, the officer's radio crackled to life. She heard him answer, then counted off his footsteps as he dashed toward the other end of the alley.

Instead of going straight back, however, Miranda turned left when she reached the street and simply walked around the block. The farther she went, however, the less the cat's rumbling sounded like a purr and the more it sounded like a growl, but she hung onto Puss as an alibi in case the officer hadn't gone after all.

She was almost halfway around when dear, sweet Archie, or whatever his name was, decided he'd had enough of being hauled around by a stranger. With one last warning yowl, he launched himself toward the nearest parked car, taking a good portion of Miranda's wrist with him when she made the mistake of trying to hang on too long.

"Ow! You stupid—"

The cat hopped back down from the car and rubbed against her leg again. Sucking on her wounded wrist, Miranda glared down.

"What do you think I am? An idiot?" she demanded in a whisper. "Get lost." She put her foot under the cat's belly and gently lifted him aside. In yet another personality swing, the demon made a brief, valiant attempt to debone her toe through her shoe, then dashed off.

"Ppht," she hissed after him. Thank the Goddess for sturdy English walking shoes. She'd have to write the makers a testimonial: "How Your Shoes Saved Me from a Mad Cat." Maybe they'd pay her and the evening wouldn't be a total loss. She headed back toward her post.

"Is your alley always so busy?" Mason asked. He scooped the dice up off the green felt of the backgammon board and rattled them loosely in his fist. "That's the second time tonight I've heard voices."

"Oh, there's always someone back there. A lot of people keep their trash cans in the alley, plus some of the neighborhood boys like to play ninja after dark," said Raine. "I've gotten to where I just tune it out."

"I don't think it's kids. At least not this last time." He shook his hand again and tossed the dice down on the board, and a slight, satisfied smile curved his mouth as he started moving the pieces. "Double sixes. That's the game." As he cleared the last of his men off the board, the smile faded. "I keep thinking one of those voices sounded like Miranda."

"My, aren't we paranoid?" Actually, Raine had been thinking it sounded like Zoe, but she wasn't about to open that can of worms. If Zoe had been dumb enough to show up when she'd been told not to, she could just sit out there in the dark. "What would your sister be doing in my alley, anyway?"

"I don't know. Maybe going through your trash looking for fingernail clippings for her next spell."

"You're kidding."

"I wish I were." He stood up. "Do you have a flashlight?"

Raine got up and crossed to the junk drawer, where, with Mason lurking over her shoulder so closely it made all the hairs on her neck go on nuzzle alert, she rooted around until she found a red plastic flashlight. She handed it to him. "I'm telling you, it's just kids. You're going to be really embarrassed, busting Petey Matthiesen for riding his bike after hours. Serious stuff."

He stopped halfway to the door. "You know, you're probably right. I'm just not used to having strangers wander past my windows."

"I guess not." She took the flashlight away from him and plunked it down on the counter. "I'm sure nobody wanders in the Highlands, strangers or not. It's just not done."

"You know, you're very class-conscious. If I made as many cracks about class as you do, you'd call me a snob."

She looked offended, then realization crossed her face. "I am, aren't I? If you'd asked me last week, I would have told you I wasn't."

"Is spending time with me so unpleasant?"

"No." *Hardly.* She sat down at the table and started twiddling her tea glass. The half-melted ice cubes swirled. "But it's different. More different than I would have guessed. It's more than just the money and the things you own. It's how you all relate to the world. Take neighbors, for instance. Has anyone *ever* knocked on your door just to say hello?"

"God, no."

"We do it all the time in this neighborhood. It keeps us in touch with what's going on."

"We gossip, too. We just do it over champagne and caviar instead of coffee and donuts." He sat down across from Raine and leaned back, a crooked smile lifting one corner of his mouth. "And, naturally, we use lots of big words."

"You're making fun of me."

He shook his head. "Not you, just your stereotypes. It so happens that we're very good friends with our neighbors. We have dinner together often, and we usually run into each other at the club a couple of times a week. The forum is different, Raine, not the structure. You're getting a very warped view because of the circumstances. My life usually doesn't consist of parading women in front of my mother and sister for nefarious purposes. For instance, if I were really romancing you, I'd—"

Some object hit the front door with the force of a cannonball. Mason was on his feet and to the door before Raine had a chance to spill her tea. He started laughing.

"What?" She joined him at the front door, swiping her hands on her shorts.

Bugsy was hanging there on the screen doing his best terrified kitty imitation, his claws curled into the mesh. Raine pushed the door open, cat and all, and carefully unhooked him from the sagging screen.

"What's the matter, kiddo? Is Zenyar loose again? Zenyar's the German Shepherd down the street," she explained to Mason as she carried Bugsy inside. "He's a good people dog, but he thinks cats are chew toys on the hoof."

"Is that what happened here?" Mason reached out and scratched Bugsy behind his left ear, the one with the torn tip and a long, jagged scar that made it look like the ruffled petal of a Rembrandt tulip.

"I think so."

Bugsy wrapped his front paws around Mason's wrist and leaned into his palm. The weight dragged Mason's knuckles across Raine's breast.

It was an accident, but the unexpected contact broke the physical barrier carefully maintained all evening. Raine stood there, breath frozen, uncertain. If Mason had jerked his hand away in embarrassment, she might have known what to do, how to joke it off and make them both comfortable, but he didn't. He just let Bugsy hang on to his hand, not scratching him anymore, but not pulling away, either, his fingers just millimeters from her suddenly aching nipple. If she moved a little, either direction, she could signal what she wanted, but she wasn't sure she knew what she wanted, and so there they stood.

Finally, Mason took a breath, and that let her breathe, and she moved just enough to take them out of the danger zone. There. They'd pretend it hadn't happened, that was it.

Bugsy released Mason, rolled in Raine's arms, and oozed to the floor with a muffled thud, leaving nothing between her and Mason.

"Where were we?" he asked. "Before your cat decided to come in for a landing."

"You were telling me . . ." It took a moment for her mind to rewind that far. She felt herself color, knew they were treading dangerous ground, but went on anyway. ". . . what you would do if you were really romancing me."

"Ah, yes." He lifted a hand to push a strand of hair off her cheek. A soft huskiness lowered his voice. "If I were romancing you, I would take you dancing until midnight, and into the mountains at dawn. We'd sample wines and go sailing and sit front row at concerts. I'd make reservations at an inn I know up in the San Juans where they have bicycles and an endless beach and a Scotch salmon that could make the angels cry. I'd find some way to show you off to every person I know and still keep you utterly to myself.'' He stepped in, closing those last few inches, and whispered into her ear, ''And I'd do my damnedest to keep that blush on your cheeks.''

He kissed her, and this time it wasn't the kind of kiss meant to end an evening, but the sort that starts a night, full of passion and promise and erotic suggestion. Under the heat of it, common sense burned away like dry grass, and when his fingers brushed her breast again, she lifted into his touch. Their groans mingled in a mist of warm breath.

''It's a good thing you aren't really romancing me.''

''Isn't it?'' he breathed. His lips covered hers again, then moved to the tender skin at the base of her jaw. ''You always smell of lemons.'' His fingers slipped tentatively beneath the bottom edge of her shirt and trailed a shiver up her spine. ''How do you manage that?''

Miranda stared at the couple inside, twined together in an embrace that gave every indication it would be moving to the bedroom.

Five hours of nothing, and the first time she turns her back, this. Damn it, Mason. Well, she had to stop them, and now.

She whipped out her cell phone, flipped it open, and punched in Mason's number. A moment later a canned male voice told her that the cellular phone she was calling was not answering at this time, and to try her call later. Mason never turned his phone off. Never. She'd been counting on that. She slapped her phone shut with a frustrated smack and jammed it back in her purse.

So now what? By the time Mason turned his phone back on, she could be on the way to becoming an aunt.

She couldn't very well just knock on the door and tell him to come to his senses. Well, she could, but she didn't really want to explain to Mason how she happened to be in the neighborhood.

Distraction. Maybe a rock against the side of the house.

She picked up a pebble and tossed it.

It hit the window. Glass shattered, and she got a quick image of Mason sheltering Raine with his body, and then instinct took over and she was running down the alley as though her life depended on it.

Knowing her brother, it just might.

"Are you all right?" Mason demanded.

"Fine."

He grabbed the flashlight and hit the door at full stride. "Stay inside."

"Paranoid and sexist," muttered Raine behind him. He heard her following him, but kept going.

Clearing the fence like a steeplechaser, he made a quick check both directions that showed the alley empty. He ran to the near end, but the street was empty, too, and when he turned back, Raine was pelting down the alley in the opposite direction. She, too, found no one. They met back by her gate.

"Kids," said Raine.

"Miranda," said Mason. He started poking around and flashing the light into corners, but could find no evidence to support his theory. As the beam swept past Raine, he had to grin. "A baseball bat?"

She hefted the aluminum bat like a club. "Me Oonga. Kill enemy. Okay, so I'm paranoid, too, in my own way. Come on. Whoever it was is long gone."

Mason held the gate for her and latched it behind them, and they walked to the porch. Raine stopped outside the window. "Geez." She used her bat to pop loose a long knife of glass that dangled from the frame. It crashed down and shattered, to be lost among the thousand other shards that covered the table and floor beyond.

Mason swore softly and put his hand on her shoulder. "I'm sorry. I didn't think she'd go this far over a kiss."

Raine got very still under his hand, and when she spoke, her voice was artificially bright. "Well, it flushed her out, anyway. We must have looked pretty convincing from out in the alley."

There was a moment between heartbeats when Mason wanted to tell her that he had been kissing her because he wanted to, because he wanted *her,* but reason won out. If he hadn't been thinking of aggravating Miranda, he should have been. That's what this was about—setting his sister and mother straight, not seducing Raine. Let her believe it had been part of the act; it was safer for both of them.

He was saved from saying anything at all by a thin, reedy voice from the main house. "Are you all right, dear?"

"We're fine, Mrs. Perlmutter," Raine called toward the back door, where someone lurked behind the crack of an opening. "Some kid broke my window, that's all."

"Shall I call the police?"

"Not until after I kill her," muttered Mason.

"Hush." Raine nudged his arm. "No, ma'am. We've got it under control."

"I'm not sure the insurance will pay if we don't report it."

"Don't worry about that, ma'am," said Mason. "It's indirectly my fault. I'll see that it's fixed immediately."

"That's very responsible, young man. He's a good boy, Raine."

"Yes, he is. Thanks for checking on me, Mrs. P.," said Raine. "You go on back to bed."

"Oh, I wasn't in bed, I was just getting ready to watch Jay. He's got that boy I like from *Indiana Jones*. Harrison Ford."

"Well, you don't want to miss him. Good night."

"Good night, dear." The door shut, and the light went out.

"Bless her heart," said Raine. "You know she had to be scared, but she still checked on me. That's what I meant about neighbors."

"You're very fortunate." He wanted to say more, but didn't know what would have any meaning. "Let's get this taken care of."

"There's a half-sheet of plywood in the garage," said Raine. "Let me grab a hammer, and we can nail it up."

"Not necessary."

"I'm not going to sleep with an open window, even if I do have a bat."

"You'll have new glass in an hour."

Raine snorted. "Yeah, right. It's after eleven."

Mason held open the screen door. "Just give me your phone book and watch how we do it in the big leagues."

She dropped the bat into the umbrella stand by the door, then pulled the Seattle White Pages out of a drawer and handed it to him. A few minutes later he had his party on the line.

"Don. This is Mason Alexander. . . . Fine, thanks. Sorry to

disturb you at this hour, but I have a broken window that needs glass tonight.'' He described the window and gave Raine's address, then thanked Don and hung up. ''He'll have a man here in fifteen minutes.''

Raine blinked. ''You have your own all-night glazier?''

''I know where he hides the bodies,'' said Mason, trying to dismiss the desire he had to cancel the glass man and check Raine into a hotel with a king-sized bed and discreet room service. ''You sweep, I'll hold the dustpan.''

They carted three wastebaskets full of glass to the trash can, and Raine was dabbing up slivers with damp paper towels when the repairman arrived.

Mason shook his hand. ''Thanks for coming out. I didn't want to leave the lady here with an open window all night.''

''Hey, it's your dime.'' He pulled on a pair of heavy leather gloves and started working loose the last few shards that hung in the frame. He dropped one into the wastebasket with a crash. ''What happened?''

''Some kids threw a rock,'' said Raine. ''It wasn't very big.''

''Old glass. Not tempered. I bet it went like a bomb.'' He took out a knife and started stripping the crumbly old glazing compound. ''One good thing about these old single-pane double-hungs, there's not much to the repairs. Give me half an hour or so.''

Mason drew Raine aside. ''Will you be all right here? I'd like to get home before Miranda has time to cover her tracks.''

She nodded. ''I'm fine. Go ahead. And thanks for dinner, by the way.''

''You're welcome.'' He started to kiss her, hesitated, then settled for a nice, safe kiss on the cheek. ''Good night.''

''Good night, Mason.''

He started for the car, frowning. It was the most formal goodbye they'd had since the day they met. He found that he didn't like it at all.

Miranda punched the button for the garage as she rounded the house and ran the car underneath the opening door before it was up all the way. She immediately hit the button again twice, so the door stopped and started back down, and was out of the car before it closed.

"Paul," she called. "Paul!"

Footsteps pounded down the stairs from the living quarters above the garage, and Paul rocketed through the door. "What?" He skidded to a stop, staring. "What happened? Are you all right? You're hurt."

"No, I'm not. What are you talking about?"

"There's blood on your hand." As he spoke, he went to the cabinet over the sink in the corner and pulled down a first aid kit. He rifled through it quickly, setting items on the counter next to the sink. "And you're a mess. Come here."

Miranda glanced down. The damned cat scratches had been oozing, and several thin streaks of red trickled down her wrist. "It's just a scratch."

"Let's clean it up," Paul said.

"There are more important things right now," she argued, but she went to the sink anyway and stuck her hand under the faucet. A glance in the mirror showed her that Paul was right: she was a mess. Her hair was full of leaves, her blouse looked like she'd worn it into a sauna, and she had a smudge of something nasty-looking across her cheek. She yanked a paper towel off the holder to her left and wiped her face, then patted the blood off the three angry claw marks on her wrist. "If my brother asks, could you tell him that I came home, oh, three or four hours ago?"

Paul straightened and his eyes narrowed to black slits of disapproval. "Does this have something to do with Miss Hobart?"

She considered reminding him who worked for whom, but this wasn't the time to get high-handed. Besides, technically, he worked for Mason. "It's not really—"

He slammed the lid of the first aid kit shut, cutting her off. "You went to her house, didn't you?"

Miranda squirmed. "Yes, but—"

"You abused the information you weaseled out of me, and you got caught."

"No. Well, not quite."

He gave the cap on a bottle of hydrogen peroxide a vicious twist. His eyes blazed at her. "I thought you were joking this afternoon. If I'd had any idea you were actually going to her house—"

God, he was mad. This was hopeless. She shook her head. "Forget it. I'll take my chances with Mason."

"They're better with me," he said flatly. "Give me your hand." His fingers bit into her palm as he dumped peroxide over her wrist.

"Ouch!" She jerked, but he held tight.

"Stand still before you splash this on your clothes and ruin them." He spilled a little more peroxide over the scratches, and when the foaming slowed, he used a fresh paper towel to blot her wrist dry, squeezed on a line of antibiotic cream from a tube, and ripped open an extra-wide bandage. "What exactly did you do?"

"Mostly I just stood in the alley, watching them."

"You spent the night in an alley? My God. What if you'd run into some pervert?"

"There weren't any perverts," Miranda assured him. "Just me and a policeman."

"Wonderful." He stuck the bandage over her wound and tossed the wrapper into the can under the sink.

"I didn't get arrested or anything." She explained about the cop and the cat and walking around the block. "When I got back,

Mason and Raine were—how shall I put it?—on the verge.''

Paul stepped back, and she could actually see his mind solidify. ''I don't need to hear this.''

However, now that she'd begun her confession, Miranda felt compelled to finish. The words tumbled out quickly, right through the part about the broken window and running down the alley with Mason in hot pursuit. ''And now he's probably going to be here any second, and if he figures out it was me, I'm a dead duck.''

''Figures out? He didn't actually see you?''

She shook her head. ''I don't think so. *Please,* Paul. I'm not suited for life on the run.''

He pushed the first aid kit back onto the shelf and shut the door, then leaned on the counter with both hands, his back to her. Her stomach roiled with tension, until finally he shook his head and turned around. ''I don't believe I'm saying this, but yes, I will cover for you. I'll tell Mr. Alexander that you went out early in the evening, but that you came home sometime around—let's see, three hours would make it about eight-thirty. The rest of the lie is yours to create.'' He glanced at her bandaged arm. ''However, may I suggest that you wear long sleeves tomorrow?''

''What, this? Magus scratched me,'' Miranda said lightly, waving off his concern. Her smile faded. ''I've got to talk to Mother.''

''She went out. Don't tell me she's in on this insanity, as well. What is going on? Why are you so obsessed with Mr. Alexander's—''

''This will have to wait.'' Miranda cut him off. ''Mason will be here any second. Thanks, Paul. You're a gem.'' She ducked out the side door, and three minutes later she'd washed her face, de-leafed her hair, slipped into pajamas, and was reading in bed, as though she'd spent a long, quiet evening at home.

What to do with Miranda.

The thought plagued Mason all the way home. For all his talk about bodily harm, he loved his sister and wouldn't harm a hair on her ditzy head. To be honest, there really wasn't much he could do while still maintaining the fiction that he was in love with Raine and pretending he had no idea why Miranda would care one way or the other. However, he wanted to warn her off.

This was no mere flakiness or peccadillo, after all, but outright vandalism. He doubted Miranda had meant to break the window, but Raine could have been hurt anyway.

The first step, of course, would be to confirm that it really had been Miranda, easy enough considering that Paul always knew who was out in which vehicle. And anyway, the exhaust manifold on Miranda's car would still be hot. All he had to do was lift the hood and he'd have some hard evidence that she'd just gotten home.

His cockiness vanished as he approached the carriage house. The garage doors stood wide open, the Explorer was running with the hood up, and Paul was behind the wheel. So much for a simple hand to the engine.

Paul shut off the engine and stood up as Mason got out of the car. "Good evening, sir."

"Paul." Mason circled so he could look under the hood. "Is something wrong?"

"No. Just the weekly maintenance." Paul reached for the oil dipstick and wiped it on a cloth he pulled from his back pocket.

"Awfully late hours for maintenance work."

"I would have gotten to it when Miss Alexander first came home, but I was fighting my way through a monograph on Sino-Japanese relations and didn't want to stop."

"How's your dissertation going?"

"Fine, sir. Another six months or so."

"Good. What time did my sister get in?" Mason tried to make the question casual, but it sounded nosy, even to his ears.

Paul glanced at his watch. "Oh, eight or eight-thirty, I'd say."

"Mmm." Damn, it hadn't been her. Or perhaps that was good—it would mean it was just kids after all. "Well, good. I'd hate to think Miranda was making you work this late."

"Oh, no, sir. Entirely my choice. I needed to relax before bed. Let my brain decompress." He checked the oil level and slipped the stick back into place. "If you're in for the evening, I'll see to your car tonight, too."

"That will be fine."

"Usual time in the morning, sir?"

"Yes. Good night."

Mason strolled toward the house, suffering from a certain degree of disappointment.

He'd always gotten a certain thrill from uncovering Miranda's stunts when they were kids, one which hadn't diminished much over the years, even when he'd moved back into the house after Elizabeth had left him. As far as he was concerned, snickering at Miranda and his mother and their New Age experiments fell under the same heading as holding his sister in thrall for a month after he'd discovered her substituting Mogen David for Dad's best Cabernet: juvenile, but entertaining. Tonight might be different in some aspects, but it had brought out many of the same instincts.

He let himself in through the side door and took the stairs to the main floor, where his suite took up the far end of the library wing. He was just stripping out of his shirt when he heard a car pull up out front. Curiosity got the best of him, and although he hated to join his mother and Mrs. Perlmutter in their annoying habit, he went to the window.

A black stretch Cadillac sat before the front door, engine idling, the driver standing by the near-side passenger door, from which Angus Wickersham emerged. Mason's ruminations on what Angus Wickersham would be doing visiting at midnight were cut short when Angus reached into the car and helped out a lady.

Good God. Angus and Mother. Out together. Mason dropped the drape like a hot coal. That's what he got for spying. Angus and Mother. Good God.

Tish hummed some light Viennese waltz as she climbed the stairs—one of those Strauss tunes, she never could sort out the titles. It suited her mood, though she couldn't articulate why.

A band of lavender light underlined Miranda's door, and Tish knocked lightly.

"Come."

"It's just me, darling," Tish said, poking her head through the door. "You look disappointed. Were you expecting someone else?"

"I thought it would be Mason. He came home a few minutes ago. Close the door and come sit down." Miranda patted the side of her bed, slipped a marker into her book, and scooted over a few inches to make room.

Tish kissed Miranda on the cheek before she settled on the edge of the bed. "What happened to your hand?"

"The official story is that I was playing with Magus and he got carried away."

"And the real story?"

"Raine's cat has bipolar disease. It's nothing." She quickly ran through the evening's events for her mother.

"You broke her window?" Tish exclaimed.

"Shhh." Miranda held a finger to her lips. "He could be listening, you know."

"Mason is not the sort to lurk about eavesdropping, unlike you. I knew this was a terrible idea. He's going to absolutely explode when he finds out."

"He won't. He didn't see me, and I've arranged for Paul to cover and say I was here most of the evening."

"Paul? Miranda, you cannot draw him into our private affairs."

"We don't have any choice. He's already in. He's agreed to say that I got home at eight-thirty or so."

"Why?"

"Because that puts me in well before the window got broken."

"No, I mean why would Paul agree to cover for you? He's Mason's driver. Mason will very likely fire him if he finds out. So why would he help you?"

"I don't know." Miranda shrugged. "Because I'm cute?"

"You're being flippant. This is something you should think about. There might be hidden costs to his cooperation." Frowning, Tish drummed her fingers on her knee. "The Goddess knows I like Paul, but he must have some motive to risk his job."

"He certainly didn't ask for anything." Miranda stared at her lap and fiddled with the ribbon bookmark. "At any rate, my story is that I got a massage and went for a little walk in the Arboretum, then got home sometime between eight and eight-thirty. I've been reading ever since. Fortunately, no one besides Paul saw me come in, so they won't have any idea what time I got home. And of course, you won't be able to say one way or the other, since you were out." She perked up. "Speaking of which, where were you?"

"Peeg Flaherty called and said they needed a fourth for bridge. I had Paul drive me over, but then it turned out I was partnered with Angus Wickersham, and he offered to bring me home so Paul didn't have to stay."

"Which turns out to be a good thing for me. So, you ran into Angus again. This is becoming a regular occurrence."

"I know. I wish I'd never promised Mason I'd stop driving. It leaves me at the mercy of others."

"Be grateful it was Angus instead of that son of Peeg's. He wrapped his car around a tree last week."

"Actually, I think Angus did it mostly to finagle his way into an invitation to join us Saturday night."

"For the Wilmott Foundation dance? I didn't think he did those charity things. It's usually Caro who shows up to get her picture taken."

"I know, but with Caro out of town, I think he feels obligated. The Wilmott Foundation is one of Wick's pet corporate projects, you know. He dropped so many hints, I wound up asking him. Do you mind?"

"Of course not. The more the merrier."

Tish plucked a single, pale hair off Miranda's pajama sleeve and let it float to the floor. "Do you think Mason will mind if I take a couple of spins around the dance floor with his future father-in-law?"

"I don't see why. He's not planning to go . . ."

They looked at each other in sudden, awful comprehension.

"Oh, Great Lord of the Night," said Tish.

Miranda groaned. "That means he's going to have another whole evening alone, unsupervised—with *her.*"

It occurred to Mason, in the middle of the long, restless night that followed his discovery of his mother's outing with Angus, that he and Raine hadn't made arrangements for their next rendezvous. The end of last evening had just gotten too complicated. Distracting. So the next morning, as soon as he thought she'd be up, he dialed her number.

"*What,* Zoe?"

He laughed. "You sound cranky. I'm glad I'm not Zoe, whoever she is."

"Mason." Her voice softened immediately, a fact that sent a surge of warmth through Mason's veins. "I'm sorry. Zoe's a very good friend, but she woke me up at five o'clock this morning to ask my opinion about what to wear to work to impress a physics professor. I thought she was calling back. So, what happened with Miranda?''

As quickly as that, she was cheery again. Mason smiled. There was no chance Caroline would be that good-natured if she'd been phoned twice before seven A.M.

''Nothing. Paul was working on her car when I got home, and he claimed she'd been back for several hours. Unless she got him to roll over, she couldn't have broken your window.''

''Roll over. You mean lie for her? Would he do that?''

''I hope not. I'd have to fire him.''

''Oh, Mason, no.'' Concern tightened her voice. ''Don't let this thing get out of hand. You can't fire people over something that isn't even real.''

''This 'thing,' real or not, is not the issue. At times, I do serious business in that car. I need a driver I can trust absolutely, even when it involves my own family.''

There was a long, disapproving silence over the line, and then she sighed. ''I'm sorry. I have no business critiquing your personnel policies. He just seems so polished and efficient.''

''He is. I'd hate to lose him, especially over something my mother and sister should have stayed out of to begin with.'' Mason carried the cordless phone into his closet and selected a fresh white shirt, heavy starch. ''But that's not why I called. We neglected to make arrangements for the next couple of days. What are you doing Saturday?''

''I have a booth at the Redmond farmers' market all day, remember? I can't skip it. I already missed last week.''

''I meant the evening,'' he said.

''I'm all yours, boss.''

''There's a charity dinner dance I'd like to take you to.''

''I thought you said we had to stay out of the public eye.''

''I did, but I've reconsidered. We have to crank up the pressure on Mother and Miranda.''

''But at a society function?''

''I had been planning to skip this thing and spend the evening alone with you,'' he said. ''However, that doesn't seem to have gotten us anywhere, so I reconsidered and concluded that this dance is a perfect opportunity. Picture you and me doing the tango out in public. Mother and Miranda will be in knots so tight, it will take a Boy Scout to untie them.''

''Me, too,'' muttered Raine. ''I don't tango. Look, you don't want to trot me out in front of all your friends. All *Caroline's* friends.''

''None of them will be there. Laura Cobb is getting married and that whole bunch will be at her reception. I did a little calling around to check. Besides, the Wilmott Foundation dances usually attract an older crowd anyway. You and I will cause a stir, no question, but I doubt it gets back to Caro very quickly. Not before I have a chance to explain, at least.''

''What about her father? He's older. Won't he be there?''

Mason dismissed the thought with a flick of his hand. ''I can't remember the last time I saw Angus at one of these affairs. What do you say?''

''Oh, Mason. This isn't my kind of event. I'll probably embarrass you, ruin your reputation, screw things up with Caroline, *and* make your mother hate us both, all at the same time.''

''No, you won't. You're one of those rare people with natural social grace.''

''Thank you, but whatever grace I have came from sitting through my mom's Ladies' Guild luncheons back in Bemidji—the most *un*natural social situation you can imagine. Anyway, it doesn't matter. Nobody's going to notice my manners or lack of them when I show up in my standby pink dress. It's the best I've got, and even *I* know people don't wear hot pink minidresses to charity benefits.''

''Maybe they should,'' said Mason. He cut in over her groan of frustration. ''Don't worry. I'll take you shopping tonight, and by the time we're done, you'll look like you've been running with the Highlands pack your whole life.''

''Do I have any choice at all?''

''Not really, no. And I'd like you to plan on staying here at the house afterward.''

''My first impression was right,'' said Raine. ''You're a lunatic.''

''I come by it legitimately,'' he said. ''Look at my family. Raine, staying here makes perfect sense. You'll have a good time, and it will really crank up the heat on my moonstruck relatives. So how about it?''

''Oooh, all right. It's your furnace. Look, I've got to get ready for work.''

''All right. We'll work out the details tonight. I'll see you at the usual time.''

• • •

"You're early," Raine called out in response to the knock at the door that evening. "Hang on a minute." She finished the last course of a French braid and secured it with a covered elastic, then quickly put on her lipstick. Grabbing for her favorite tortoiseshell barrette, she bumped the bathroom door open with her hip and headed for the front door. "Hi."

Her smile faded as she saw Mason's driver standing on the porch, his cap tucked under his arm. "Paul. Hello." Flushing, she turned under the end of her braid, pushed the barrette into place, and slipped into the shoes she had set by the door earlier. "Where's Mason?"

Paul held out a small, perfect bouquet of bright pink baby roses. "Mr. Alexander sends his apologies, but he has been tied up at the office by business."

Raine accepted the flowers with a smile: they matched her dress within a shade or two. "Thank you. Tell him he certainly knows how to stand a girl up with style."

Paul smiled, too. "Actually, you haven't quite been stood up. Mr. Alexander will explain, himself. He's on the phone in the car."

"I thought you said he was at the office."

"Let me rephrase that. He *is* at the office, but he has phoned the car and is waiting to speak to you. Whenever you're ready."

"I'm ready now, I guess," Raine said, a bit disconcerted. As Paul opened the screen door, she reached for her purse and a lightweight cardigan for later, since it had clouded over again this afternoon. A quick flip of the door lock and they were on their way.

At the front curb, Paul held the door open and helped her into the car, then leaned in, lifted a handset from a recess on the console, and handed it to her. "Just press the red button."

She waited until he shut the door before she touched the button. "Mason?"

"Good evening." Mason's voice sounded warm over the cellular hiss. "I'm sorry, but I'm not going to be able to make it tonight. Our Everett production line went down in the middle of a critical run. I shot most of the afternoon up there, and now I have to spend my evening soothing an anxious client."

"All that just to get out of shopping."

He laughed. "Let me assure you, I would much rather shop

with you and any ten of your friends than deal with this."

"That bad, eh?"

"Worse."

"You have my sympathy. I guess that means tomorrow night is off, then." She couldn't keep the hopeful sound out of her voice.

"No. I'll have this under control within a few hours. Besides, I'm looking forward to tomorrow," he added in a tone that sent a tremor of anticipation up the back of Raine's neck.

"But we're back to the problem of me not having anything to wear," she said.

"Not at all. I made a few calls. The store is expecting you. There will be someone available to help you choose an appropriate gown and whatever else you need."

"That's not necessary."

"They also have instructions to help you pick out a couple of new outfits to get you through next week," he went on, ignoring her. "I do like that pink dress, but I can't expect you to live in it."

"I don't mind. It's just a few more days, and it doesn't make sense for you to spend that much money just to—"

"The arrangements are already made."

"But—"

"No arguments," he said in a tone that would brook none, then added more gently, "This is my treat, Raine. I can't be there, but at least let me have a little fun with it."

"I'm sorry. Of course. It's going to be wonderful."

"That's better. Paul knows where to take you and he'll give you any help you need; however, please keep in mind that Miranda will probably grill him later. Don't give him anything worth passing on, in case he's tempted."

Raine frowned at the back of the seat as it came back to her that there was nothing personal to Mason's generosity; it was all just part of the scam. "Don't worry. I won't carry tales out of school."

"If I really was worried about either of you, I wouldn't let you go off alone together. Now, I have that client waiting in reception, so I'll call you tomorrow morning to arrange to pick you up."

"Make it early. I'm usually out of the house by six on market days."

"Early it is. And have fun tonight, Raine."

"I will. Good night."

"Good night. Would you have Paul pick up the phone, please."

Raine glanced at the intercom, but couldn't figure out the controls quickly enough, so she knocked on the partition glass and signaled to Paul to pick up. When he nodded, she hung up and leaned back. A moment later, the car pulled away from the curb.

She tapped again and the partition went down with an electronic whine. "Yes, miss?"

"Would it violate some unwritten rule of chauffeurdom if you helped me pick out a dress for the Wilmott Foundation dance?"

"No. But you'll have help there at the store."

"I'd rather have you."

"I'm not what you would call fashion conscious."

"But you've at least seen what Miranda and Mrs. Alexander wear to these things. I have no idea. I'd really appreciate it if you'd come in and give me some advice. Please, Paul."

"All right, miss."

At the small but well-stocked boutique Mason had chosen, she tried to follow his advice to have fun, a feat that would have been easier if she hadn't kept remembering Zoe's comments about *Pretty Woman.* With sales clerks fawning and Paul loitering in the background, the whole scene took on tones of a cheap remake, starring Raine as the gold-digging prostitute.

What made it more uncomfortable was that the clerks were clearly thinking along the same lines, bringing out sexy little numbers that revealed more skin than they covered. She wanted to shout at them, "I'm not his sex toy," but it would have blown her cover with Paul and the clerks wouldn't have believed her anyway. Instead, she tried hard to project blushing future fiancée instead of brassy hooker and steered them toward more sedate choices until they got the message.

She finally found a gown that both felt comfortable and made Paul smile and nod, and quickly had them set it aside before the four-figure price tag could trigger an attack of the Minnesota Frugals. A matching pair of overpriced shoes and a tiny evening bag were produced by another saleswoman, and suitable undergarments by a third.

The process repeated itself for the everyday clothes Mason had specified, until Raine crossed her fingers in front of her face as though she were warding off a vampire and called, ''Enough.''

Everything was soon bagged and placed in Paul's capable hands; by the time they finished loading him down, he looked like a Sherpa.

''That represents my clothing budget for at least five years,'' Raine muttered as they walked out into the cool late evening. ''Maybe ten.''

''If Mr. Alexander weren't prepared to spend that kind of money, he wouldn't have chosen this store.''

''Does this a lot, does he?''

Paul stopped dead beside the rear bumper and shot her a critical look. ''Never.''

Oops. In an effort to recover, Raine turned on a pleased, shy smile and examined the tips of her shoes as though they carried the image of her beloved. ''That's sort of nice to hear, actually.'' And actually, it was.

Paul seemed satisfied. After he loaded the packages into the trunk, he came around to open the door for her.

''Thank you for your help in there,'' said Raine. ''You made a wonderful stand-in for Mason.''

''You're welcome, but the evening isn't quite over.''

''What could he possibly—''

''Dinner, of course.'' He motioned her into the car. ''Mr. Alexander had reservations for the two of you at the Hunt Club. The table is still available, but if you'd like to go somewhere else, I'm at your disposal.''

''The Hunt Club, alone?'' She visualized herself sitting, either solo or with Mason's driver, amid the couples at what was reputedly Seattle's most romantic restaurant. ''I don't think so. I'm in more of a hamburger mood. I need a chunk of meat to balance all that saccharine those clerks were dishing out.''

The corners of Paul's mouth curved upward. ''How about Zesto's, over in Ballard?''

''Perfect. And Paul?''

''Yes, miss?''

''I'm buying.''

''I understand, miss.''

The Frugals set in around the time Paul finally got her home, and by the time Raine's alarm went off Saturday morning they were in full uproar.

It all had to go back.

There was no getting around it. Raine stood in the golden glow of early morning, staring at the clothes that hung on the back of the bedroom door. They were beautiful, particularly the evening gown with its silk chiffon in layers of muted pinks and peaches, but she couldn't accept a gift of this magnitude from Mason. Maybe Brynn would be willing to watch the stall for a couple of hours while she took it all back and went shopping for something else to wear tonight . . . but even as that idea formed, Raine rejected it. She'd never find anything suitable that she could afford in one afternoon.

She fingered the hem of the gown thoughtfully. Maybe if she were very careful and didn't sweat all evening, Mason could return it Monday morning along with the other things. And as for the remaining evenings at the Alexander house, well, she'd borrow something from Zoe if she had to—with all the black Zoe wore, surely she'd have something dressy-looking that would fit.

Or if Mason really wanted to freak out his mother, she could go shop at one of the used clothing stores down on the Avenue.

Something with a 1950s cowboy motif would probably do the trick. Yee, haw.

She showered and dressed quickly and swung into the kitchen to heat some water for tea and smear some cream cheese on a bagel. Holding half the bagel between her teeth, she stuck a picnic jug under the faucet to fill and pulled her little gray cash box out from behind the roasting pan on the bottom shelf. She opened it, only to groan at the sight of the paltry stack of ones. She should have cashed a check on the way home from work last night. Spending every evening with Mason was sure screwing up her routine.

It was screwing up more than that, she thought. She turned the tap off.

She was finding it harder and harder to keep the perspective she'd promised herself she would. This was a job, an arranged relationship with no basis in reality; Mason certainly saw it as nothing more. Yet every time he touched her, even for the most innocuous reason, every nerve in her body fired at once. Shoot, every time she so much as thought of him, she got the kind of all-encompassing spinal meltdown usually associated with a high school crush. It was as stupid as a crush, too—a purely sexual reaction, two bodies that found each other attractive, and oh, lordy, did hers ever find his attractive. She'd even dreamed he was in her bed last night, the second amazing, fiery night of dreams in a row, and it had left her aching with want, even now. A sudden wash of heat made her fan her face with a sweepstakes envelope from Friday's mail.

The teakettle began burbling, and she took it off the burner before it could work up a full whistle. She dropped a bag of green tea into her biggest mug and started pouring the water just as someone knocked on the front door.

She looked out the window, expecting to see Zoe's face, but Mason's blue eyes greeted her instead. Desire fluttered low in her belly. Hands suddenly shaking, she set the kettle back on the stove, then went to the door and pulled it open too quickly. "What are you doing here?"

"You are just charming in the morning, aren't you? '*What now,* Zoe?' " He imitated her. " 'What are *you* doing here?' "

"Both legitimate questions," she said. "And when you're done making fun of me, you can come on in and answer the second one."

Maybe it was the reddish sky behind him, but he looked even more like a Viking than usual, and she had a sudden sense that plunder was imminent. Already primed by the recollection of her nighttime fantasies, her lips tingled in anticipation of a good-morning kiss.

But he walked past her, smelling of soap and whatever that cologne was he favored, and her disappointment was unaccountably sharp.

''I interrupted your breakfast,'' he said. ''I'm sorry. I wasn't sure what time to come.''

''Come for what?''

''To help you get to market,'' he said, as though she should have been expecting him. He peeled off his blue blazer and tossed it over the back of a kitchen chair, and, with the jacket gone, it dawned on Raine that he was wearing a yellow T-shirt and jeans. They didn't look anything like the sort of T-shirts and jeans she and her friends owned, but they certainly weren't a Brooks Brothers suit, either.

''Wow. You're serious.''

He raised an eyebrow. ''Of course I'm serious. Haven't Mother and Miranda convinced you that I'm way too serious about everything?''

''They're working against personal experience.'' She turned back to her breakfast. ''Would you like a bagel or some tea or something?''

''No, thanks. I stopped at Starbucks on the way over.'' He started to pull out a chair, then stopped and looked around. ''Where's your attack cat?''

''He took off first thing. The chair's a safe zone.''

''Good.'' He sat on the rainbow-painted chair and leaned back, settling into the space as though he belonged there every day. ''So, what's involved this morning?''

''Mostly grunt work,'' she said as she carried her meal over to join him. ''Everything's already packed up, so it's just a matter of loading it into my truck and hauling it over to the market. I share a stall with a friend who sells flowers. We make sort of a garden setting with my art and her flowers.''

Mason nodded. ''That sounds like a good marketing strategy.''

''Mostly it's a way to share costs,'' she admitted. ''Plus we sometimes can take days off without losing our spots. Like last

Saturday. If it hadn't been for Brynn, I wouldn't have been in your arbor to be recruited.''

''I'll have to thank her,'' he said, in a tone that made the breath catch in Raine's throat.

She had to think to exhale. ''Speaking of thanks, I owe you some. The shopping trip last night was pretty spectacular.''

''Paul said you found a dress.''

She nodded. ''It's gorgeous, but it's also way too expensive. And the other things. . . . I understand why you felt a need to outfit me—heaven knows I don't have many decent clothes—but I realized when I looked at it all this morning that I can't keep it. I can't keep any of it.''

''Nonsense.''

''Mason, it's just too much.''

''By whose standards?''

''Mine.''

''Then raise your standards.'' He leaned forward and took her free hand between his. ''You're a beautiful woman who deserves to wear beautiful clothes. It so happens that I have both an excuse to buy them for you and the means to pay for them.''

''No, you don't. You told me yourself that you're broke. Those clothes are expensive. You could be putting the money into your company.''

Mason laughed. ''I could buy you a gown like that every day for the next year and it wouldn't touch the kind of money I need to turn Alexander Industries around.''

''But it all adds up. The clothes, the cars, Paul's salary. That house, for heaven's sake. It must cost a fortune to keep up. Can't you—''

''The cars are all over ten years old, and I keep Paul because Mother doesn't see well anymore and it keeps her off the roads. The house was paid for a couple of generations ago and it's in trust, as are funds for the upkeep and the staff. My grandfather—Mother's father—was smart enough to set that up when he realized my father was no businessman. He also set up personal trusts for Miranda and me, which is a good thing, considering I gave up my corporate salary three years ago. We tried breaking the trusts to get to the principal, but Gramps was a smart old bird with smarter lawyers. I'm afraid we're condemned to this lifestyle at least until I'm fifty.''

"I don't get it. If you can live off the trusts, then why are you so worried about the company?"

"First, because thanks to inflation, the distributions are just big enough to keep us in pocket change—rather splendid pocket change from your viewpoint, I know, but we have certain obligations and expenses necessary to keep our standing so I can have access to the people I need to keep AI on its feet. And secondly, I want to pass something on to my daughter other than a feeling of entitlement, which is all she's likely to get from her mother."

"You have a daughter?"

"I do." He turned and fished around in the breast pocket of the jacket draped over the back of the chair. He pulled out a wallet and flipped it open in front of Raine. "Samantha. She's eleven. She lives back in Boston with my ex-wife."

Raine liked the face that looked out of the photo, full of mischief and resembling a small, black-haired version of Miranda. She closed the wallet.

"She's cute. I, on the other hand, feel like an idiot."

"Why? Because you tried to help?" He took her hand again.

"I'm sure you didn't want to sit here and justify your life to me."

"No. But it's not so terrible to remind myself what I'm doing, either. I just have one favor to ask."

"What?"

"You probably know more about my finances now than anybody outside my accountant."

"I was brought up not to discuss family finances outside the family, though I guess you'd never know it from the way I act around you. I promise I won't tell anyone."

"Good, I didn't think you would." As he talked, his fingers traced unconsciously over the back of her hand and along her wrist, playing complete havoc with her thought processes.

"But about that dress." She stared at the invisible lines he drew on her skin and it was all she could do to get back on topic. "Back in Bemidji they have names for women who accept expensive gifts from men."

His fingers tightened around hers. "None of which apply to you. Damn it, I know this relationship between us is odd—"

"To say the least."

"—but you have nothing to be ashamed of other than getting

sucked into my bizarre family life.'' His eyes darkened for a moment, and then he released her hand and shook off the mood. ''And that's all we're going to say about my family or your clothes. I'm keeping one, you're keeping the other, and we're both stuck. Now, finish your breakfast and show me what to start loading.''

An argument sprang to Raine's tongue, but the determined way Mason's jaw underlined his smile made her clamp her lips. She already recognized his no-nonsense look. Conceding defeat—and not altogether unhappily, if she were honest with herself—she popped the last of the bagel into her mouth, rinsed it down with tea, and stood up.

''Do you at least want to see what you bought?''

He shook his head. ''Surprise me this evening.''

She looked at him, then sighed. ''Fine. We've kind of gotten behind, here, anyway. Let's get to work.''

She led him outside and around the end of the house to the garage that formed the other half of the building. Fitting the key into the padlock, she fiddled it open, then hoisted the door on its creaky track. Sunlight filtered through the whirling dust motes to reveal metal figures in all shapes and sizes, most crated or in boxes. ''You asked for it.''

Mason drifted in, examining the few freestanding pieces with the careful eye of a museum patron. He stopped in front of a big piece covered with a drop cloth. He reached for a corner of the cloth.

''Don't,'' said Raine.

''Ah. A mystery. You pique my interest.''

''A work in progress. I'm trying something new. I don't want anybody to see it until I get it right.''

''All right.''

He moved on to her workbench, with its anvil and racks of hammers and various cutting tools, and touched her welding mask and gloves, which lay on one end of the bench. ''Intellectually, I knew you needed all this to turn out those pieces in the garden, but face to face, it's pretty intimidating gear.''

''Not very delicate and ladylike, that's for sure.''

He turned. His eyes gleamed like blue diamonds from the depths of the garage. ''A *lady* is a woman who can make the people around her feel comfortable, in any situation from a back street bar to the Queen's tea. I've watched you for a week, and you're very much a lady, Raine Hobart. Now, should I load all of this?"

She stood there feeling amazingly awkward and unladylike, her heart thudding, and it took her several beats to sort out the proper answer.

"Thank you. And no, not everything. Just those." She indicated two big boxes that held an assortment of pieces. "And these four little ones, plus that big trellis and the birdbath in that crate. Drag them out in the alley while I pull around. And don't hurt your back," she added, grinning, as she headed for her truck. "I don't carry workers' comp."

By the time she got back, he had everything out and the garage locked tight. Together they loaded the truck, packing pieces into the bed puzzle-style so they wouldn't shift. They tied down the bigger pieces.

"Great," said Raine. "I'll meet you down at the market."

Mason shook his head. "I'm riding with you. Just let me grab my jacket, and I'm yours for the day." He laughed at the surprise on her face. "I told you I was serious."

He got his jacket and the jug of water while Raine shoved a stack of cheap plastic drinking glasses into her backpack and grabbed the cash box. A few minutes later they were heading toward the highway.

The Redmond farmers' market wasn't much compared to the Sunday market in Fremont, but the bustle of vendors setting up their stalls still made for a traffic jam in the parking lot. Raine steered slowly through the mess until she found her path blocked by a truck loaded with cantaloupes and sweet corn which had stalled in an unfortunate spot.

"You picked a bad day to volunteer. We're going to have to haul," she said, but Mason was already climbing out of the truck.

She met him by the back bumper, and he handed her one of the small boxes and grabbed the crate with the birdbath. His muscles bulged as he hoisted it off the tailgate. "Lead on."

The stall was unmanned, but Brynn had already set up her block-and-board shelving and arranged her flowers in their tall, galvanized, French flower buckets. With the white canopy overhead, it always reminded Raine of a rainbow trapped between a cloud and a lake.

Raine and Mason had just deposited their second load when Brynn appeared with an armload of cellophane, bouquet paper, and ribbon. "God, what a mess. Somebody should call a mechanic for that guy. He broke down last week, too. Hi." She stopped and grinned at Mason. "Who's the hunky muscle?"

"Mason Alexander," he said. "And thank you. No one's called me hunky in years."

"He volunteered to help out today," added Raine.

"Sucker," said Brynn.

"Oh, *that's* nice," said Raine. "Mason, this amazingly forward woman is Brynn Williams." The two shook hands, then Raine and Mason made several more trips. After they teamed up to haul the trellis, they got their personal gear and piled it under one of the makeshift benches that held Brynn's flowers.

Raine went to move the truck. When she got back, she found that Mason had broken open the boxes and was busy sticking dragonflies and ladybugs and frogs in amongst the flowers while Brynn carefully wove a strand of sweet peas into the trellis. The first cars were already pulling into the parking lot.

"Hey, Brynn, I didn't make it to the bank last night. Do you have some extra ones and fives to hold me until I take in some cash?"

"Sure, I think so." Brynn dug into the money apron she wore and came out with a wad of bills. They sorted out the money, and within minutes the early rush hit.

Mason kicked back in a corner, chatting with her and Brynn and customers, people watching, and making Raine's heart skip the occasional beat just by being himself.

This could be a long day.

Tish knocked on Mason's door at about ten that morning. She'd long since taken her swim and had breakfast, and had seen no sign of Mason. It wasn't unheard-of for him to sleep in so late, but it was certainly unusual, and if she hadn't watched him come in last night, she might believe he'd spent the night at Miss Hobart's, a thought that made her cringe.

There was no answer. She knocked again, waited, then pushed the heavy door open. His bed lay unmade, the ivory linen sheets rumpled and the pillows wadded up at the foot of the bed. She smiled. His pillows had always ended up at the wrong end of the bed when he was a boy, and the mother in her was glad that at least one thing hadn't changed, when so many others had. She pulled the door shut and went looking for her younger child, instead.

She found Miranda in the alcove adjoining their sanctuary room, unloading herbs from a flat, split-ash basket. Tish gave her a kiss on the cheek, then fingered the herbs, releasing their mingled scents. ''Angelica. Lemon balm. Lovage. Comfrey. Verbena. You've been busy this morning.''

''I cut a new willow wand, too. I think I'll use that piece of carnelian you gave me for the tip.''

Tish nodded her approval. ''Have you seen your brother this morning?''

''No. He must be sleeping in. He looked wrung out last night when he got home. That Zimmerman is such a bastard.''

Tish shushed her. ''Don Zimmerman kept us profitable for years when your father wasn't paying very careful attention to the business.''

''I know. But he sure takes advantage of it now. Every time there's a little bump in production, he puts the screws on for a better deal.''

''It's business, dear, not personal.'' Tish picked up a length of blue yarn and tied a bundle of sage together. ''At any rate, Mason's *not* sleeping in. I checked his room.''

They tied a few more bundles of herbs and hung them on the wooden pegs that lined the sides of the alcove, each hesitating to say what they both knew to be true.

''Maybe he just decided to go for a run,'' said Tish.

''Well, there's one way to find out.'' Miranda picked up the phone and punched two numbers. ''Paul, did my brother go out early this morning?'' Her face fell. ''Oh. Thank you.'' She hung up.

''Great. Paul says he left just after dawn, which probably means he's with *her* and that leaves them agitating each other all day and then spending the evening alone. I should have ignored you and bought that saltpeter.''

''Miranda. . . .''

''Well, it would have worked.''

Tish frowned, but understood her daughter was joking. ''Perhaps it's not so critical today, at least. Didn't Miss Hobart say she sold her artwork at some sort of market on Saturdays?''

''The Redmond farmers' market,'' said Miranda, cheering a

bit. "And I said I wanted to look at her work, too. I can pop out there and kill two birds with one stone."

Tish rearranged a bunch of lemon balm on its peg so it would dry more evenly. "I don't approve of your spying, but I really don't see any other way of keeping those two under supervision. Go with my blessing, but please, dear, no more rocks."

Miranda kissed her on the cheek and headed for the door. A quick stop by her room for a purse and a straw hat, and she was on her way.

When she left the house by the side door, she saw that all six garage doors were up, and four out of five cars sat in their bays, with a gap one from the left where Mason's Jaguar should be. There was no sign of Paul, which was probably just as well considering the way things had been left the last time she'd seen him. No use asking for trouble.

Moving as quietly as possible, Miranda slipped into the garage and opened the door to the Explorer. She tossed her purse onto the passenger seat and slid behind the wheel, pushed the key into the ignition, and turned it over.

Nothing. Barely a click. She moved the transmission into neutral and tried again. Nothing. Her first instinct was to call for Paul, but she bit her tongue. No point risking unpleasant questions over a stupid car. She'd just take her mother's old Lincoln. She crawled back out and went to the lock box on the wall where the extra keys were kept and punched in the code. The box popped open to reveal a bank of empty hooks.

Muttering, she went back to her car, popped the latch on the hood, and stood staring into the engine compartment, hoping some obviously disconnected wire or hose might catch her eye.

"Looking for this?"

She spun around to find Paul holding up an octopuslike collection of wires in black and red.

Ignoring the heat in her cheeks, she forced a smile. "I didn't know my car was out of commission."

"It isn't. At least, it wasn't until I disconnected your ignition system." He tossed the wires onto the workbench. "I've also got all the spare keys." He reached into his left-hand pocket and fished out a couple of key rings, which he dangled from one fingertip momentarily before sticking them back in his pocket. "We're going to talk."

"Very amusing, Paul. Now put my car back together."

"So you can chase down your brother again?"

She glared at him. "I have a hair appointment."

"Then I would guess you'll be late."

"Are you *trying* to get yourself fired?"

"I probably already have, thanks to you. I just want to know *why* before I have to start packing."

She waved off his fears. "Mason hasn't even brought it up. You must have been quite convincing. I'd have been out here to say thank you, but you've been gone so much, up in Everett and all."

"And you were sneaking out now because . . . ?"

"I wasn't sneaking," said Miranda.

"Yes, you were. I've been here six years and, to my knowledge, this is the first time you've ever opened the hood of your own car. You don't even gas the thing up."

"I'm trying to become more independent."

"You're trying to yank my chain, is what you're trying, but it's not working. I want to know why you're so knotted up about your brother's new girlfriend that you're willing to drag the help into it."

"Not the help. Just you," she said. "You know more about Mason than almost anybody. And you certainly know more about how he acts with Raine in private."

"I can hardly claim the same level of expertise that you can; I haven't spent any time in the alley."

Avoiding his eyes, she swept an invisible arc on the floor with the toe of her shoe.

He gave her a moment to respond, but when she didn't, he prodded. "From the questions you were asking earlier, I take it you think Mr. Alexander is leading Miss Hobart on for some reason."

She glanced up. "Not her. Mother and me."

Paul raised an eyebrow. "You think Mr. Alexander is dating Miss Hobart because of you and your mother?"

Miranda started to nod, then turned it into a shake of the head. Paul might be professionally tolerant of excursions to witchcraft shops for supplies, but she didn't know how he'd react to word that she'd been casting spells against his employer. It might not be pretty. She decided to skirt the truth. "It's really about Caroline Wickersham. Mason is supposed to marry her—although that's not official yet, so don't tell anyone."

Paul folded his arms across his chest and leaned back against the workbench and waited.

"Anyway, he knows that Mother and I are, um, highly vested in their marriage, and you know how he likes to jerk us around. Or me, at least." She looked to Paul for confirmation, but he just stared, unblinking. Miranda licked her lips and flashed another smile, this one weaker. "Well, I think that maybe he's trying to pull a fast one by dating Raine and pretending he's in love with her. And, naturally, I'm worried he's going to foul things up with Caroline over some dumb joke. Of course, if he's really serious about Raine, that would be different, but—"

"Would it be different?"

"Of course."

"Mmm," he said, with a clear lack of commitment. "So, what do you think now, after what you saw at her house?"

"I'm not sure. They certainly have some physical thing going, but I'm still not certain he's in love with her, and Tish and I just want to—What?" she asked as Paul's eyes narrowed and he shook his head.

"Oh, I was just thinking you Alexanders have got to be one of the weirder families that has never appeared on a television talk show." He reached for the bundle of wires and walked to the car. Leaning over the engine, he started plugging and arranging. " 'Today on "Jenny Jones"—Sisters Who Spy on Their Brothers, and the Mothers Who Encourage Them.' "

Miranda watched silently, conscious that she was lucky he'd bought her explanation, even if he didn't think much of it—and even more conscious of the way his T-shirt rode up when he stretched over the engine, revealing a two-inch stripe of smooth brown back just above his jeans. She was sorely tempted to run her fingers along the gap, just to see how his skin felt.

Her palms were starting to itch when he straightened and his shirt dropped back into place. He pulled a rag out of his back pocket, wiped his hands, and pulled the hood down. "You're set."

Without realizing it, she'd moved closer, so that when he turned, he was so close she could feel his breath on her cheek.

They both froze, inches apart.

His gaze swept her face and locked with hers. "Don't go."

"Why?" she breathed, caught in the moment, and in the exotic sexiness of his dark, almond eyes and his nutmeg skin. His lips drew into a thin line. He took a deep breath, and the raggedness of it made Miranda's own chest tighten.

"You can't win," he said. "If your brother really is pulling some sort of joke on you, you'll just play into his hands, and if he's not, you're interfering where it isn't your business. Either way, you'll come out looking like a fool."

She already felt like one. Paul had meant *Don't go after Mason,* not *Don't leave me.*

By the Goddess, if she'd taken to fantasizing about the family driver, then it had been way too long since she'd been with a man. She stepped back physically, but making the mental step was harder. "Thanks for the advice, but I have to get my hair done for tonight."

He nodded, and Miranda got into her car, backed out, and roared up the drive and onto Olympic Drive, but by the time she stopped at the security gate, she'd seen the truth in what Paul had said. Besides, Mason and Raine couldn't possibly get into any trouble at a farmers' market. Instead of heading east toward the highways and Redmond, she turned toward downtown and her favorite stylist. Surely Natalia would be able to work her in.

She was doing fine pretending, until she saw a billboard for teriyaki sauce, and the model's Oriental features reminded her of Paul and what an idiot she'd been. She felt like a prepubescent twit. Imagine thinking Paul and she had some sort of mutual attraction.

Imagine.

Oh, screw it. She'd just have to find someone to get her mind off of Paul. Tonight.

Brynn made the bulk of the sales, of course, people being more likely to buy a five-dollar bunch of flowers on impulse than a thirty-dollar copper dragonfly or a three-hundred-dollar birdbath, but Raine had her share of business, too, especially once the looky-loos replaced the folks out for dew-fresh produce. Bless impulse buyers with too much money on their hands, and there were certainly a lot of those in Redmond.

At noon, Raine and Brynn took advantage of the extra body and sent Mason out foraging for food while they dealt with another small rush. He came back from the nearby Town Center laden with Styrofoam containers of falafel and cucumber-yogurt salad, and big paper cups of minty iced tea. The traffic never really slowed, however, and they had to snatch bites in between wrapping bouquets and making change.

After the umpteenth interruption, Mason stood up. "You two eat before your food spoils. I can handle this." He stepped up to the front, nudging Raine aside as she finished wrapping a bouquet.

"Sounds good to me," said Brynn. She made change for the customer, a woman in pink cotton leggings and a baggy T-shirt, then untied her money apron and handed it to Mason. "Just make sure that if somebody buys one of Raine's pieces, you keep the money separate."

Mason tied on the short apron and turned to a couple who were hanging back, mumbling to each other.

"Which ones are your favorite?" he asked.

"Sweat peas," said the woman. She colored slightly when she met Mason's gaze. "I absolutely love them. I was just telling my husband how my grandmother used to have a whole fence of them."

Mason lured her into a discussion of which of Brynn's sweet peas looked most like Grandma's, and by the time he was done, she held two good-sized bunches of flowers and one of Raine's copper hummingbirds and was smiling.

"Ooh, he's good," mumbled Brynn around a mouthful of falafel as Mason collected the husband's hard-earned money. "I bet he could get a girl into all sorts of trouble if he wanted to."

"No doubt," said Raine, and her belly tightened at the thought of how sweet that trouble would be.

Enough. She stabbed a slice of tomato with her plastic fork.

Mason did fine until some clown decided he had to know Brynn's growing techniques before he could possibly buy any flowers, but by then Brynn had finished and was ready to take over again. Raine finished, too, and excused herself for a few minutes, and when she came back Mason was on his cell phone.

"Good," he said. "I'll see you shortly." He stuck the phone back in his jacket pocket.

"See who?" Raine asked.

He grinned. "You'll find out. You have some yogurt on your lip."

She swiped at her mouth, but Mason shook his head. "No. Hold still." He stepped close and reached to smudge it off with his thumb.

Senses overtuned, Raine jumped back at the electric contact. She hit one of the poles that held up the sun shade covering the stall. The canopy wobbled and collapsed. Raine ducked.

Mason grabbed for the frame as it crashed down just inches from her head. A customer squealed.

"Geez."

"Are you okay?" Brynn and Mason asked simultaneously.

"Fine. What the heck happened?"

Mason held the canopy high as he inspected the loose end of the pole. "It looks like the bolts weren't tightened properly. There's a nut missing."

"I'm going to run my husband up by the thumbs," said Brynn. "He was supposed to check that before he left."

"Let's fix it first, so you can devise your tortures without fear of bodily harm." Mason glanced around the stall and pointed. "That looks like the nut over there. Do you have a wrench?"

"Sure do," said Brynn. "Raine, check in my tool bucket while I get this woman her flowers."

Raine pulled the white plastic bucket out from under the table and found the wrench. When she looked up, Mason was standing there, holding up one corner of the canopy, like Atlas supporting the world, and she had to push aside the image of bulging thighs and loincloth conjured up by her overactive imagination. He was too lean to be Atlas, anyway, she told herself.

She dragged one of the chairs over and climbed up to thread the bolt back into place. The folding chair was wobbly on the uneven ground, and when she wobbled, too, Mason put a hand to her waist to steady her. The contact startled Raine, and she glanced down at him.

"You're certainly jumpy." He smiled up at her, and their eyes met and held, and it suddenly dawned on her how much she liked this strong, responsible, serious, funny man. How much she loved him.

She dropped the wrench.

Mason danced backward like a sand crab. The canopy swayed, but held, and Raine jumped off the chair. "Oh, geez. I'm sorry. Here, sit down."

"No, it's all right. You missed." The corners of his eyes crinkled with amusement. "But even if you hadn't, I still wouldn't send that dress back. It's going to take more than a broken toe to keep me from dancing with you." The crinkles faded. "What happened? Right before you dropped that thing, you looked like you'd seen a ghost."

She blinked and glanced away. "Don't be silly."

"Excuse me, Raine," said Brynn. "If you two are done trying to wound each other, this man wants to know if you have any other trellises."

Raine leapt to help. "Certainly. Let me show you some photos."

It took a good half hour for the man to look through her portfolio and decide he wanted the one in the stall after all, and the whole while, she could feel Mason's eyes on her back.

No. It wasn't so. It was just a passing, fanciful thought. Hormones. If nothing else, it was stupid, and she wasn't stupid when it came to men anymore. Been there, done that.

Just as she finished arranging to deliver the trellis, she caught a glimpse of a familiar face over an unfamiliar red T-shirt and chinos. "Paul?"

"Good afternoon, Miss Hobart. Mr. Alexander."

Mason came up behind Raine, resting his hands lightly on her shoulders. "Good. You're here." He introduced Paul to Brynn, then asked Raine for the keys to her truck and to her garage. "Paul's going to be filling in for you the rest of the afternoon, and he'll take everything home for you and unload it."

"I beg your pardon?"

"He wanted to kidnap you," said Brynn. "I told him it was okay if he got me some help. This guy looks like he'll do. God, where do you get off, having two gorgeous guys at your beck and call."

"Just lucky, I guess." Raine could barely think, with Mason's hands still on her shoulders.

"If you'll tell Paul where the truck is, we'll be on our way," said Mason.

"On our way where?" asked Raine.

"You have an appointment. Now, where did you park?"

"Over there," Raine said. She pointed to her truck, under a tree. Paul nodded and took her keys. "But you don't know how to—"

"Brynn will help him sort it out," said Mason firmly. He reached under the shelves for Raine's backpack and picnic jug, and turned to Paul. "Make sure you get back to the house in time to take Mother and Miranda to the Wilmott Ball."

"Yes, sir. The parking lot was full. You're up about a block on the west side of Leary. Have a good afternoon."

Mason took Raine's hand. "Let's go."

She followed. "Where are we going?"

"Right now, to your house to pack. All remaining questions will be answered at the appropriate time."

They found the Jaguar in a No Parking zone, but the police either hadn't gotten to it yet or had ignored the expensive car. Mason handed Raine the backpack, helped her in, then dropped the Thermos in the boot before he got in.

"Didn't you leave this thing parked in front of my house?" she asked.

"Paul shuttled over in his personal car and picked it up. No more questions. Just lean back and relax."

Once they got back to Fremont, she took only a few minutes to pack, tossing what she needed into a small soft-sided gym bag and popping the long store bag back over the gown before she handed it and one of the other dresses to Mason. "You're taller. Don't drag it."

Back in the car, he turned toward downtown, waiting until they were across the Fremont Bridge before he announced, "I'm taking you to a day spa that Miranda particularly likes. You'll get massaged with sea slime and whatever else they do in those places, and then someone will do your hair and makeup for you."

"You know, I manage that every day, all by myself."

"Don't get defensive," he said. "You do a fine job, but you'll be much more comfortable walking into that ballroom on my arm tonight knowing that no one but me can tell you run around dark alleys wielding a baseball bat."

"Mason . . ." She started to refuse, but he had that stubborn look again. And besides, he was right: it was going to be tough enough tonight to relax with his tony friends without worrying about whether she passed inspection in the powder room. "Thank you."

They cruised south along the edge of Lake Union and past the Space Needle. A few minutes later, Mason pulled in to the curb before a plain door with only a number marking it, wedged between upscale retail fronts. Instantly, a uniformed valet appeared to take the car, and Mason escorted Raine inside to a reception area so draped in heavy tapestry and thick rugs that all extraneous sound was absorbed. Fifth Avenue might be ten feet outside the door, Raine thought, but you'd never know it in here.

Mason introduced himself and Raine, and she was quickly whisked upstairs to a private room where she was told to strip and lie facedown on a table draped in surgical green sheets.

A "technician" with an unlikely Hungarian accent came in, introduced herself as Tova, and started kneading Raine's back, attempting to "loozen ze muscles." When she was satisfied, she ladled some warm mudlike substance over Raine.

"Sea slime," muttered Raine.

"Rare algae and precious minerals," countered Tova the Technician, pronouncing it "al-guh." "Eet will draw ze toxins."

Toxin remover or not, after the initial ugh factor, the mud proved to be very relaxing. Raine was doused neck to foot, then asked to roll over so the process could be repeated on the other side. The sheets were then pulled up around her, a heavy blanket laid on top, and a small, buckwheat pillow tucked under her neck.

"Eet is such a rush with you, mees," said Tova as she placed a cool, cucumber-scented cloth over Raine's eyes. "Ve have only a few 'ours instead of the ze whole day, so we do everyzing at once. Someone will come now to put a pack on your hair while ze algae verks. Such spleet ends. And ze sunburn. Eet is ter-r-r-ible."

She had no sooner left than another technician, this one apparently French, came in and applied a facial treatment that smelled like strawberries. The hair specialist arrived close on her heels, worked something slightly slimier than the mud into the offending hair, and replaced the pillow. The door clicked shut behind the two as they left Raine alone to compost for half an hour.

And to think, unfortunately, something she had successfully avoided for the past hour or so.

She tried not to. She hummed show tunes. She composed a mental grocery list. She tried to nap. She just plain refused to deal with it.

But Mason's face swam in front of her closed eyes. The merest thought of his kisses sent such a rush of heat through her blood that the seaweed pack felt cool in comparison. And there was no way she could fall asleep when she knew for a fact that she'd just dream of him, over her, his hands wandering freely.

Worse, much worse, she kept thinking of his smile, the way

he threw his head back when he laughed, how he looked with his hands in a sink full of dishes, pink roses, a sweaty yellow T-shirt, the amusement in his eyes as the spa staff had led her off.

Oh, geez. She had it bad.

And so, slightly more than twenty minutes into her thirty-minute encasement in mud, Raine admitted to herself that somehow, against all rhyme or reason, against all the promises she'd made herself, against any shred of logic, it was true:

In precisely one week, she had fallen in love with Mason Alexander.

Nervous about sitting down in a two-thousand-dollar dress—silly, when she'd have to fold herself into thirds to get into Mason's Jaguar later—Raine paced back and forth, her insubstantial evening sandals whispering across the carpet. The guest suite where Mason had installed her was as silent as a library, but the underlying tension had every hair on her arms standing at alert.

Or maybe it was the turmoil inside her own heart.

Part of her—most of her, perhaps—wanted this evening, wanted the glitter, the game, the chance to dance with Mason, wanted a few kisses and a little more make-believe.

But the rest of her recognized the danger. Somewhere along the line, the difference between pretense and reality had blurred. She already felt as raw as a rug burn.

She had to face facts. It didn't matter that she loved Mason if he didn't feel the same. He didn't even believe in love. She had a job to do, five thousand dollars to earn, and a neighborhood to save.

She had to get herself under control.

She stopped in the center of the room and closed her eyes, allowing her head to loll forward. Her breath slipped into a measured rhythm, six in, hold four, six out, a pattern that came naturally after years of practice. Consciously moving through her body, she relaxed forehead, neck, arms, spine, and legs in turn, keeping just enough tension in her muscles to stay upright. She was on the edge of that place where she might recover a sense of perspective when a familiar, spicy scent wafted around her and stole every bit of peace away.

Surrendering, she let the smile form itself and raised her chin, defiant in defeat. "Mason."

She looked like a sunrise standing there, wisps of peach and rose floating about her shoulders and fading down to lavender gray around her feet, like early morning clouds. Beneath the transparency, a sliplike sheath of soft, shimmering gold skimmed her body and played tricks of light and shadow over her curves. A few rebellious strands of hair had come loose from the sleek chignon into which the spa had forced her hair, and they played around her temples and along her neck in a halo through which diamond ear studs sparked, like a pair of morning stars.

"I knew it," said Mason, "You're going to put every woman there to shame."

She met his gaze. "It's the dress."

"It's the woman in the dress. You're beautiful."

Her eyes narrowed slightly, as though his words pained her, but she dipped her head in acknowledgment. "Thank you. So are you. Men always look so good in tuxes."

"Dinner jackets," he corrected.

"Whatever you call them, you look like you were born to wear one."

"I think there are some old headwaiter genes in the family."

She considered. "More like Ivy League hunk."

"That's the second time I've been called a hunk today. It's going to my head. I came to see if you needed anything."

"Just some nerve."

In an ideal world, he'd kiss her now. He'd find a million excuses not to go to this party and just one excuse to unzip that long zipper he knew must run down her back. Instead he reached into his inside breast pocket.

"When Paul picked me up last night, I asked if you'd gotten everything you need. He indicated a certain lack in the jewelry department." He pulled out the thin, black satin box he'd picked up while she was at the spa. "This should handle it."

"Mason. You know I can't."

"Yes, you can." He opened the box and pulled the slim diamond bracelet free of the pins that held it, then tossed the box onto the bed and crossed to Raine.

She glared at him, ready to scold.

"It won't work," he said, reaching for her hand. "Remember, I get to have fun with this." He draped the bracelet over her wrist and pulled the ends together to fasten them.

"It goes back Monday," she said stubbornly.

"I bought it on sale. No returns."

"Baloney."

"True, but I warned the man about you. He won't take it back, no matter what you say. Besides, every woman needs one good diamond bracelet, or so my mother tells me."

"I don't have anyplace to wear it after tonight."

"You can weld in it. The stones will catch the light from your torch." He stood back. "Paul was right. A necklace would have been too much."

"You're stubborn."

"So are you. We're a matched pair," he said, and it was true enough. In many ways, Raine was a better fit than Caroline. Then again, so had Elizabeth been, for all the good such romantic nonsense had done. "Are you ready, or would you like to have a drink first?"

She drew in a deep breath, then blew it off as though she were preparing for the start of a race. "I think I'd rather just take the plunge."

"All right, then. Shall we?"

She retrieved her beaded evening bag from where it lay on the foot of the bed and took his offered arm, and they were on their way.

The cream and gold Spanish Ballroom of the Four Seasons Olympic Hotel looked like it was ready for a presidential dinner. The display of polished crystal and sterling spread over sparkling white tablecloths was as conservative as they came: no colorful linens or outrageous themes for the Wilmott Foundation. Not even something as well-suited to summer as a garden party. The Wilmotts shunned gimmicks, relying instead on tradition combined with simple but well-presented food and a great band to keep patrons and their donations coming back.

In the same spirit of tradition, Tish led the way toward their table. Her entrance wasn't quite as much fun as it used to be. In the old days, not so long ago, they used to sponsor a whole table and drag along a half dozen friends, so that entering the ballroom was like a royal procession. It had been the one time of the year she'd allowed herself that ostentation, leaving it up to others the rest of the time.

But with the company's trials had come a certain amount of cutting back, and the past few years they'd bought only their own places, relying on friends to join them of their own accord and at their own expense. Most did, and they still had their usual table near the Wilmotts, so tradition still held as she led the way in this evening.

Friends greeted them as they crossed the room, and along the way Angus and Miranda got pulled into conversations with one of the Wilmott heirs and an old boyfriend, respectively, so that Tish arrived at the table by herself. Wes Gorsheim leapt up to give her a kiss and help with her chair, and within moments Tish was playing catch-up with Wes's wife, Betty, and the two other women who were at the table, both old acquaintances.

Tish had just discovered that Betty was now a grandmother, for goodness' sake, when Miranda roared up.

"Tish. we've got to talk."

"Darling, you remember Betty and Wes. Betty was just telling me—"

"Nice to see you," said Miranda brusquely. "Mother, now." She took Tish's arm with bony fingers and tugged. "Excuse us, Betty."

"I'm sorry. I'll be right back." Tish allowed Miranda to drag her over to a noisy no-man's-land between the bandstand and the doors to the kitchen.

She frowned at her daughter. "I presume this is important enough to justify your rudeness."

"You tell me. Mason's here. With Raine."

"What?"

"I just saw them. They're right outside, on the landing."

"Oh, great Goddess. Not again. What does he think he's doing?"

"We've got to get them out of here before Angus spots them."

"I can't imagine how," said Tish. "Mason has developed an extraordinary blind spot where Miss Hobart is concerned. If he brought her here in the first place, he's past caring about consequences. He's out of his mind. And here we were afraid of what they might be doing *alone* this evening."

"Then what are we going to do? There won't even be enough places at the table. Angus and Raine are both supposed to be in Caro's seat."

Tish squinted around the ballroom.

"Damn it, I hate getting old." She fished in her evening bag for her glasses. "Where is Angus?"

"He's still over by the hors d'oeuvres with Bucky Wilmott." Miranda pointed.

Glasses in place, Tish spotted him. His companion appeared to be working an invisible crank. "Bucky's telling him a fishing story. He's good for a couple of minutes. What about Mason?"

"He's talking to Walt Rasmussen. There. Just outside the door, by Laurel and John Hirshberger."

Laurel Hirshberger got her hair color from the same bottle as Lucille Ball, so she made an easy-to-spot reference point. Tish quickly located Mason in the same group, next to a blonde she didn't recogni—"Is that Miss Hobart? She looks lovely."

"She's prettier than Caro," Miranda agreed. "Which should just about put the nails in the coffin as far as Angus is concerned. Oh, no, they're drifting in here."

"Stop them," ordered Tish. "Lure Mason and Miss Hobart off to the side. Shove them in a corner or something, anything, just so I have a chance to get Angus out the door."

"How?"

"I have no idea."

"Tish—"

But she was already making a beeline for the hors d'oeuvre table.

"Great seeing you, John. Laurel." Mason shook hands with the former and kissed the latter on the cheek, while Raine said her more formal good-byes. As the Hirshbergers wandered off, he turned to Miranda. "Why are you bobbing around like a mongoose?"

"Am I?" She laughed nervously. "I'm just trying to see who's here."

"Speaking of which, where's Mother?"

"Around someplace," said Miranda, her eyes flashing over

the crowd yet again. "I'm not sure. Let's sit down over here or something."

"That's not our table, Miranda." Mason did some cursory surveillance of his own and was pleased to note that he'd been right. Caroline's crowd was notably absent. There were a few people that knew them both, but no one who particularly had Caro's ear or who would trot off to the nearest phone to report his indiscretions. This could actually turn out to be fun.

"Oops, watch out." Miranda grabbed Mason's and Raine's arms and tugged them two steps in her direction, nearly making both of them stumble.

Mason glanced over his shoulder and saw nothing that warranted such concern. "What the blazes are you doing?"

"There was a waiter with a tray coming our direction, but he turned right. Sorry." She bobbed again. "So, what are you doing here? I thought you weren't coming."

"The tickets were already paid for, and I realized this would make a great way to introduce Raine to a few of our friends." He gave Raine's hand an obvious squeeze. "Sort of a coming-out party."

Miranda rolled her eyes, but refrained from comment, and before Mason had time to tweak her again, a short, balding man in a badly cut jacket waylaid them. For the life of him, Mason couldn't remember the fellow's name, though the opposite clearly wasn't true. After a few minutes, Mason started drifting toward their table, hoping the man would take a hint.

Tish reached Angus just as Bucky shook his hand and walked off smiling as though he'd personally reeled in Moby Dick. She slipped her arm into Angus's, not even trying to hide the tension in her face.

"Is there something wrong, Titania?"

"I've come down with the most abominable headache, just in the last few minutes." She squinted past Angus's shoulder, trying to decide whether he'd be able to see Mason, and decided to turn him a few degrees to the left, just to be safe.

"Let me have one of these boys bring you some aspirin," offered Angus, gesturing toward a waiter.

"I'd rather not. I try not to take too many drugs. I think I just need a walk. Would you mind taking me out for a few minutes?"

"Of course not." He handed his glass to the man behind the

table and pressed Tish's hand into the crook of his arm. "Do you have a wrap?"

"No, no. I didn't bring one." And even if she had, she'd bloody well freeze before she'd let him hang around while she got it. "So, which fishing story was Bucky telling you—giant Alaska salmon or marlin?"

"Marlin. How did you know?"

"I could see him casting from the other side of the room. Do you fish?"

He did, and he was happy to talk about it, as all fishermen are. She kept him going all the way out the door, hanging on his every word so that his eyes never left her adoring face—which flirtation just proved to what extremes Mason was driving her. The gauntlet took them within a dozen feet of Raine and Mason; as they passed, Miranda's eyes bulged most unattractively, but Tish was too preoccupied with the acid burn in her stomach to bother with so much as a warning shake of the head. And all the while, Angus kept talking and so did Mason, blithely unaware of the near disaster.

She decided it might be wise to breathe again when she and Angus reached the bottom of the grand staircase. *Safe.* The relief must have showed on her face, because Angus commented how much better she looked.

"You know, I do feel a bit better already. I suspect it's the lighting in the ballroom. Now that I have these glasses, I occasionally react to artificial lighting, and I've never been able to determine what triggers it. It's annoying, but not deadly. I suppose I'll just have to go home tonight."

"It's a shame to waste the evening, when you're already out." Angus hooked a finger into the collar of his shirt and tugged. "You know, I'm not much for sitting through speeches anyway, and I already promised Bucky a hundred thousand, so he's had his pound of flesh. How about if I take you out? I can think of at least one place where the lighting won't bother you."

"Well . . ." She had no real interest in going out with Angus, but if she let him take her home right away, there was a chance that he'd turn around and come back here. Dinner would keep him occupied well away from the Four Seasons and let her control the situation a little more.

Besides, he'd just donated a hundred thousand dollars to Seattle's best program for underprivileged children—he deserved a night out. "That's a lovely idea, Angus."

"We'd better let Miranda know." He turned back toward the stairway.

"No!" she clutched at his arm. "I mean, there's no reason to go all the way back up. I can just leave a note for a bellman to deliver."

They stopped at the concierge desk, and Tish scrawled a brief message to Miranda, although with Angus lurking over her shoulder, she could hardly give explicit suggestions about how to handle Mason. She'd just have to trust her to keep him on a short leash.

She addressed the note to Miranda, and handed it and the pen back to the statuesque brunette behind the desk. "I have to leave unexpectedly. Can you see my daughter gets this in the next few minutes? She's at the Wilmott Foundation dinner."

Angus plunked a five-dollar bill on the marble counter and tapped it.

Tish groaned inwardly over the lack of finesse, but the concierge didn't seem to mind. She smiled and reached for the bill. "Of course, ma'am. And thank you, sir."

"All right, then." Tish turned to Angus. "I put myself in your capable hands."

"You won't regret it, dear lady. You have my word."

The dinner part of the evening was pretty much what Raine had expected, a very formal affair during which she finally had the opportunity to use all that maternal training on cutlery and etiquette. The table was filled with friends and business associates of the Alexanders, all curious about Caro's apparent replacement but much, much too polite to say anything over the salmon. If it hadn't been for the glaringly empty chair that should have held Tish Alexander, things would have been fine.

But the chair was empty, and the fact that Tish had been on the premises and had disappeared at about the same time Mason and Raine had arrived left a question hanging over the table—had she left because she disapproved of Raine? The arrival of a message from the missing lady along with the salad did nothing to address the implied criticism, especially when Miranda carefully folded it and stuffed it in her purse after she'd read it. Headache, indeed.

Mason went out of his way to be attentive, of course, and although he barely touched her, after the speeches when the crowd started breaking up into those who danced and those who hung around the edges and gossiped, Raine had a pretty good idea who was fodder for the latter.

Her suspicion was reinforced when all conversation crashed to a halt as she walked into the ladies' lounge with Miranda. It took everyone a good thirty seconds to recover—they must have been really dishing the dirt.

"So, Miranda," said a woman in a strapless, hussy-red dress who sashayed up when they paused at the mirror afterward to touch up their makeup. "Introduce me to Mason's new friend."

"Louise Demarco, Raine Hobart," said Miranda. The way she held her lipstick up gave the impression she might like to scribble on Louise's cheek. "Louise used to date Mason. It didn't work out, but hope springs eternal."

Louise's smile stiffened. "Oh, no, darling. I gave up on him when he started seeing Caro. They're just so perfect for each other. So . . . mutually mercenary. Well, Raine, is it? How do you know Mason?"

"She's a family friend," said Miranda quickly.

"Actually, Caro's the one who introduced me to the Alexanders," said Raine. She pulled her compact out of her bag and opened it. "I don't find her mercenary at all. Mason, either. I suppose I just don't have that sort of mind."

Someone snorted back a laugh at the far end of the marble vanity, and Louise turned to glare. Raine quickly touched the powder puff to her nose, slipped the compact back into her purse, and headed for the door before Louise could regroup. Miranda was right behind her.

"I'm sorry," said Raine when they'd made good their escape. "She was just—"

"—asking for it." A laugh burst from Miranda. "Caro introduced you. That's rich. How did you learn to handle people like Louise?"

Raine shrugged. "We have bitches in Bemidji, too."

"They *are* universal, I suppose. Anyway, well done, but let's get back to the table before this bitch recovers and comes a-hunting. I'm not so certain you could handle Louise if she gets a hair up her ass, but she won't go anywhere near Mason these days."

• • •

The table gradually emptied as couples got up to dance, and soon it was only Mason, Raine, and Miranda.

"My, isn't this exciting," said Miranda. She scanned the crowd and apparently spotted someone interesting, because she started to stand up.

Mason put his hand over her arm and held on firmly. She stared at him, then sagged back into her seat.

"You're not going anywhere until you tell me where Mother went."

"Mason, you don't want to get into this right now." She glanced at Raine.

"Did she leave because of me?" Raine asked.

"Sort of, but . . . Oh, hell. You're going to find out anyway. Angus was here. Mother hustled him out with the headache excuse."

"Oh, Christ." Mason leaned back, swiping one hand across his forehead as though that would take away the ache in his own brain.

Raine didn't miss a beat. "Oh, my. Thank goodness we didn't bump into him. Wouldn't it be terrible if he called Caroline before you had a chance to talk to her, Mason?" She leaned forward, as though to confide in Miranda. "A woman just shouldn't hear about a breakup from her father."

"Oh, great Goddess," said Miranda.

"It was very sweet of you to try to protect my feelings," Raine went on to Miranda. "But you really don't have to worry. I know Mason has certain obligations to Caroline. Neither one of us wants to hurt her unnecessarily."

She looked so much like a woman trying to be understanding in a difficult situation that Mason felt guilty. He leaned over and kissed her cheek.

"Oh, great Goddess," repeated Miranda, louder. "Not in public. I can't deal with this."

She shook her arm loose, stood up, and smoothed her dress over her hips. "You'll excuse me if I don't stay to watch this little extravaganza." She stalked off across the ballroom.

"Bull's-eye," said Mason, feeling like he'd narrowly avoided a train wreck, only to have the baggage car door pop open to spill a million dollars in loose change at his feet. "And you,

Raine Hobart, take the gold. How on earth do you keep so cool?''

Her gaze flickered down, toward her hands, folded in her lap. ''It's all part of the act.''

''I feel like celebrating. Come, dance with me.''

She squeezed her eyes shut, then opened them and flashed him a big smile. ''All right. As long as you remember that I'm strictly a two-step and jitterbug kind of girl. Very basic.''

''Deal.''

They weren't exactly Fred and Ginger, or even Fred and Cyd, but they found their rhythm by the middle of the second dance, an easy swing version of the old standard, ''Tangerine.''

''So, what do you think?'' asked Mason as they stepped through a simple turn. ''Of the party, I mean. Ignoring the by-play.''

''Well, it's not the Bemidji High gym,'' she said. ''But hang a few hundred yards of twisted crepe paper and we could pretend.''

''I bet you were the prom queen.''

''Hardly. I got stood up that night.''

''I'm sorry.''

''Oh, don't be. He was too full of himself to be worthwhile, and besides, I had a ball. My best friend, Mary Ellen Johannesen, didn't have a date either, so I ran out and rented a tux—excuse me, *dinner jacket*—and we walked into the gym arm in arm. I gave her a corsage and we danced and everything. Half of Bemidji probably still thinks I'm a lesbian. Especially since I live out here in Seattle. Liberals, you know.''

Mason laughed. ''So I'm dating a woman with a history.''

Her smile flickered. ''Developing more every minute.''

He led her through another spin just as Miranda danced by with Todd Dennison.

''You're frowning,'' said Raine as they came back together. ''What's wrong?''

''Nothing crucial. That fellow Miranda's with is an idiot,'' said Mason as the idiot in question slipped his arm around Miranda's waist. ''They dated for a while after her divorce, but he was always chasing after some other woman. She usually refers to him as Two-Timing Toddy.''

''Apparently she's changed her mind.''

''The question is, why?''

"I don't know. Maybe so you'll focus all your attention on her instead of me? That's what I'd do if I was trying to keep my big brother from romancing the wrong woman."

Mason watched as Miranda glanced sideways at him and self-consciously tucked her hair behind her ear. He chuckled. "Again I bow to your brilliance."

The number ended and the band moved into a slow ballad. Smiling, Mason pulled Raine close, close enough to remind himself how pleasant it was to hold her. They had barely taken a step when he felt a hand on his shoulder.

Todd Dennison stood there, grinning. "Hi, Mason. Just cutting in."

"I don't think so," said Mason. His gut rebelled at the idea of Raine in Todd's smarmy hands.

"Mason." Raine put her hand on his arm. "It's all right. There's lots of music left."

So he released her and stood off to one side, watching her dance and chat while he waited for the song to end.

It eventually did, and the band took a break, so he didn't have to arm wrestle Dennison for the right to take Raine back to the table. They sat through Wes's recounting of an avalanche in Gstaad, and got up as soon as the next set started.

The same thing happened again three times. They danced the fast dances, the swing numbers and upbeat pieces, but as soon as the band moved into something slow and romantic, someone showed up to cut in—a different guy each time, but all with something in common: each had previously dated Miranda.

"We're being set up," Raine said when she met him on the sidelines after the fourth cut.

"I know. I've been trying to spot her. I haven't seen her since she danced by with Todd."

Raine studied the room, too, with no more luck than Mason. "Maybe we can make an end run. If the band takes requests, we might get one slow dance in before she recruits her next flunky."

Grinning, he nodded. "I like the way your mind works. Excuse me for a moment."

After a brief conversation with the bandleader, he returned to Raine's side and tugged her onto the floor for the last few bars of "Paper Doll."

"Here we go."

Without a pause, the band slowed and segued into the Glenn Miller classic, "Moonlight Serenade."

"Oh," she breathed. "Good choice."

Impatient after an evening of waiting for this, he pulled her close, so that they had to move as one. A certain amount of danger lay in dancing that close. Danger that she'd notice how much he wanted her. Danger that other people would notice. But it was worth it, having her there in his arms for a few minutes. He whirled her across the floor.

Miranda's lips moved in a quiet chant of Separation while she watched her brother and his inamorata from the corner where she'd taken up vigil behind the sound equipment. They were on to her, that was certain. Mason had looked ready to send out the hounds to find her, and now he'd fouled up her schedule by paying off the bandleader.

"Where's Philip?" she muttered when she'd cycled through the chant three times.

"Probably in the head," said Todd. "He didn't expect to be on for another ten minutes at least." He watched with her. "They move pretty well together."

They did, but as Miranda watched, she realized there was more to it. There was something in the way Mason looked down at Raine, a tenderness, a sweetness that Miranda hadn't seen in her brother's eyes for years. He loved her, and, potion or not, that was a good thing for Mason. And the way Raine looked up at him. Miranda sighed.

They spun off across the floor to the building lushness of the saxes. *Lucky Raine,* thought Miranda. "Moonlight Serenade" was a great number. Sexy. Romantic as hell. Just the kind of thing she'd like to be dancing to, with the right man.

Unbidden, an image of black hair, dark almond eyes, and tight blue jeans swam into Miranda's mind.

Not a chance. Not only did Paul firmly believe in the sanctity of the chasm between garage and house, he thought she was a total flake, and there were times, like now, watching Mason with Raine, that she suspected he was right.

She really needed to get her mind off such an unproductive tack, and one possible means for that was standing at her side, part of the reason she'd nominated Todd to the board of Operation Cut-In-Cut-Out. Toddy was always good for a little good-natured debauchery.

Just then, Philip Watts made his way to Mason's side and tapped his shoulder. Mason whirled on him, and for half a second Miranda thought he was going to deck poor Philip. Then, to her relief, he stepped aside and stalked off the dance floor. His eyes raked the corners of the room, searching for the real source of his torment, and then, with a snarl of frustration, he disappeared into the crowd.

"Toddy," said Miranda, shrinking deeper into the shadows. "I don't think I'm going to be very welcome at home tonight."

His eyebrows went up in a familiar, lascivious way, and he edged closer, slipping one arm around her waist. "Maybe you should consider alternative lodgings."

"Why, Todd." She looked up at him as though she hadn't been planning it all afternoon. "What a good idea."

Philip spun Raine through a reverse turn and into a triple chasse. He was a better dancer than Mason, but, to Miranda's eye, he and Raine didn't look right together, and suddenly she knew that the game had gone far enough. She'd tell the rest of her commandos to back off. Let them dance.

The band swung softly through the last chorus of "Moonlight" and into the crescendo of runs that marked the end. At the final chord, Philip kissed Raine's hand, then, with his usual mix of charm and good sense, he escorted her back to her table and quickly vanished into the crowd before Mason reappeared.

When Mason finally did come back, though, he didn't sit down, but simply leaned over to whisper something into Raine's ear. She brightened, and then they were off, pausing barely long enough to say good night to the Gorsheims and Neustetters before they dashed for the door.

"Damn it," said Miranda. "They're bailing." She headed for the door, Todd at her heels.

"Miranda." Philip joined the pack halfway.

"Sorry, can't talk."

"You almost got my nose broken."

"I know, sweety, and it's such an expensive nose, too. I'm sorry. I'd buy you a drink as compensation, but I really have to run."

She darted around a knot of chatters gathered on the landing and ran down the stairs. A glare from the woman behind the concierge desk slowed her down through the lobby. She hit the door just in time to see the taillights of Mason's car disappear onto University.

Eleven

It was probably just as well that Paul had been promised to Mother and Miranda for the evening, thought Mason as he made the turn onto Sixth Avenue and headed out of downtown. He wasn't quite sure what he would do if he had to sit in the back-seat with Raine and had nothing to do with his hands.

Of course, if Miranda were around, he'd just wrap his fingers around her traitorous neck, but thanks to liberal tipping of valets, she wasn't. Besides, he didn't want her dead until he found out how she'd gotten so many men to give up dances with their dates just to keep him from dancing with Raine.

She'd done a good job of that, but if her goal had been to keep him from becoming aroused, she'd certainly blown it. Not being able to dance the slow dances, or rather, having just that brief moment of swaying with Raine so close he could feel her heart beat, had left him frustrated beyond words, literally aching to hold her. If he hadn't had the driving to hold his attention and the steering wheel and gear stick to occupy his hands, he would undoubtedly be getting himself slapped.

Or *would* she slap him?

He glanced at Raine. She was watching him, her lips in a soft curve of amusement or . . . "What?"

"That was a very James Bond moment," she said. "Double-oh-seven grabs the lady of the moment and dashes out of the

Grand Casino to escape the evil Blofeld, making his getaway in his classic Jaguar.''

Mason laughed. ''Bond drives an Aston Martin DB5, and I'm hardly Sean Connery.''

''No. More like Pierce Brosnan,'' she said. ''How did you manage to have the car waiting right in front of the door with the engine running?''

''I went downstairs while Phil Watts was commanding your attention.''

''Ah. And where are we going now that we've escaped?''

''Back to the house, unless you have something else in mind.''

She lifted one eyebrow. ''You did this whole Bond thing just to go home?''

''I was tired of not dancing with you. The mad dash was mostly to yank Miranda's chain.''

''Aren't you afraid Angus will be at the house?''

''I doubt Miranda or Mother will let that happen.''

She rolled down the window and closed her eyes, letting the breeze wash over her, ruffling her hair and billowing the chiffon of her dress so that shadows danced over the high, sweet curves of her breasts.

''It's been the most beautiful night, in spite of Miranda. Thank you.''

''You're welcome.'' The words were thick in his throat.

He had to remind himself to look at the road. Remind himself that he was only dating Raine to teach his mother and sister a lesson, and that she was only sitting beside him because he was paying her. Remind himself that five thousand dollars didn't buy him sex. Remind himself that he was going to marry Caroline Wickersham, a woman infinitely more suited to his world and his bank account.

Damn Miranda and her plotting, anyway, getting him into this position, into this state.

He spent the rest of the trip home contemplating his sister's perfidy, which was a damned sight more productive than lusting after a woman he couldn't have.

''Oh, shit.'' Miranda hiked her skirts, gathered the excess fabric over her arm, and sprinted for the gray hulk she knew was the Rolls.

She yanked the door open before Paul had time to react. ''I've got to catch up with Mason.'' She started to pull the door shut, but a foot got in the way. The foot was followed by Todd, who slid in beside her.

''Can't leave without me, sweets. You know how much I like a good chase.''

Paul raised an eyebrow.

There went the last of that daydream—like she had any business falling for her brother's driver anyway.

''It's okay, Paul. He's with me. Let's go.''

''No.''

''What do you mean, no?''

''I mean no, miss. I have answered your questions. I have given you information you shouldn't have. I have lied for you. But I draw the line at chasing your brother through the streets of Seattle just because you don't approve of his girlfriend.''

''Where do you get off talking to her that way?'' demanded Todd.

''Shut up, Todd.'' Miranda glared him into silence, then turned back to Paul. ''Angus Wickersham is probably at the house. If Mason walks in with Raine—''

''Then he'll have some explaining to do. Mr. Alexander is very articulate. I'm sure he can handle it.'' Paul pulled the keys out of the ignition and pushed his door open. ''I'm going to get a cup of coffee, after which I will be happy to drive you home.'' His gaze met hers, then flickered to Todd. ''Or wherever you want to go.''

The door slammed, leaving her and Todd alone in the silence of the big car.

''Arrrgh.'' Miranda screamed in frustration and embarrassment. Her cheeks burned as though Paul had slapped her, and she felt like a fool.

Todd put his arm around her shoulder and pulled her close. ''There, there. Whatever's wrong, old Toddy will fix it.'' He feathered a few kisses across her brow. ''I'll have the valet get my car.''

''It's too late,'' said Miranda. ''They'll be home before we even get started. Hand me the phone.''

She punched in her home number and fidgeted until her mother answered.

''Thank goodness you're there.'' A quick explanation earned Tish's promise that Angus would be gone before Mason got there. Miranda returned the phone to its cradle. Stupid. She should have just phoned in the first place, before she'd embarrassed herself so thoroughly.

"There," said Todd. "Now, whatever that was about, you've taken care of it. We'll get my car and go over to my place."

Miranda lifted an eyebrow. "*Your* place?"

"Sure. You know you don't want to go home to face Mason." He kissed her again, this time on the lips.

Todd always had been a good kisser—a good lover, in fact, part of the reason Miranda had put up with his philandering ways for much longer than she should have. She let herself dissolve into his arms.

Todd kissed his way down her neck and across her bare shoulder. "Love these strapless things," he murmured. His fingertips played across her breasts, just above the top of her gown.

This was it. This was what she needed, to get Paul off her mind.

Paul. Oh, damn, it was Paul she wanted, not this bozo. Todd not only wasn't second best, he wasn't even on the list. Talk about stupid.

She sat up and pushed Todd's hand away. "Sorry, Todd. This was a mistake."

"No, it wasn't, baby." He reached for her breasts again. "You know we're good together. You just need a reminder." His fingertips brushed over her nipples with practiced ease. A shiver ran up and down her spine, reflex to a familiar touch.

"You're good with everybody. That's the problem." She shifted away.

He followed, persistent. "Come on, Miranda. You've been giving me signals all evening. You said you needed a place to sleep. I'm all warmed up for this. You've got me hot and bothered." He grabbed her hand and pulled it to his crotch. He was hot and bothered, all right.

She yanked her hand away. "For God's sake, Todd. I changed my mind. Turn me loose and get out of the car."

"Give me five minutes to change your mind back again."

Things quickly degenerated into a wrestling match. Somehow he got a hand up under her skirt.

"Todd. Damn it." She planted both hands in the middle of his chest and shoved, just as his door popped open. Todd went over, then sailed out of the car backward, as though lifted by an invisible hand. All she could see was the bottom of his feet, flailing as he tried to get them planted on the ground.

"Let go, you son of a bitch."

There was the sound of a scuffle, and then the unpleasant smack of flesh against flesh.

Miranda pushed her skirt down and scrambled across the seat to stick her head out.

Paul had Todd by the collar and one arm, and was hauling him across the Grand Motor Entrance. Blood streamed from Todd's nose, spattering the polished granite with scarlet as five valets, the doorman, and two bellmen stood watching, unsure what to do.

Paul deposited him in front of the doorman, stood him on his feet, and dusted his lapels. Todd, ever the jerk, took one last swing. Paul blocked it and drove his fist into Todd's stomach, crumpling him like an old paper bag.

Paul straightened, adjusted his own jacket, and reached into his pocket. He pressed a bill into the doorman's hand, then turned smartly and marched back to Miranda.

"Are you all right?"

She nodded. She wanted to hug him. Even more, she wanted him to hug her, to tell her he didn't think she was the fool she knew she was. If she leaned forward, just an inch or two, he'd have to put his arms around her to steady her. It would be easy.

"You didn't get your coffee," she said instead. Her voice quavered on the edge of tears.

"Yes, I did." He reached over her head and took a squat, white paper cup off the top of the car where he'd apparently set it before saving her questionable virtue. "Here. You look like you could use it."

She nodded and took the cup.

Her knees started to shake, and she crumpled back on the seat with no grace at all, coffee sloshing onto the skirts that billowed around her. She wrapped her fingers around the cup, suddenly cold despite the warm night air.

Paul shrugged out of his jacket and leaned into the car to wrap it around her shoulders.

"I'll take you home now." Paul hit the lock on the door, shut it, then walked around the car.

As he got in, she heard Todd's voice, angry, complaining, coming through the open door, and another man, the doorman perhaps, trying to soothe him. Then Paul closed his door and it was just the two of them as he quietly drove her home.

Relief made Tish giddy as she watched the taillights of Angus's car disappear up the drive.

He'd been a bear to pry loose, his penchant for storytelling well lubricated by several glasses of bourbon and branch over the course of the evening. Not that the storytelling was bad. She'd enjoyed listening to him, right up to the point when he'd brought her home. Then she'd been so conscious of the need to get him out of the house before Mason came home, that anxiety had begun to outweigh the amusement factor of his stories.

Even so, she had let him tell a couple more about his days as a roustabout until Miranda's phone call had made chasing him off imperative. She'd finally pled a vicious return of her headache and shooed him out the door despite a tempting last-minute offer of a neck massage.

It would have been lovely, she was sure; Angus had such nice, strong-looking hands, big and square, like the rest of him. It had been a long time since anyone had given her a massage and not expected a tip.

She closed the front door and strolled back to the living room, and settled in to wait for Mason and Miss Hobart.

She didn't have to wait long. A puff of night air carried them in about ten minutes after Angus left, so close they might have passed his car on the way into the Highlands.

"Mother. How nice of you to wait up."

"I hadn't been planning to," she said as Mason came over and kissed her cheek. She marked the book she was reading with a ribbon and laid it aside. "You're very early. Was the party a bore?"

"Far from it." He winked at Raine, some secret between them.

"Good evening, Mrs. Alexander." She pretended to ignore him, though Tish noticed the flash of a smile.

"Miss Hobart. Is Miranda coming home, too?"

"I suspect she'll be along soon," said Mason. "If Todd didn't distract her."

"Todd. Todd Dennison? Oh, don't tell me."

"I'm afraid so."

"What could she be thinking?"

Mason shrugged and shook his head. "I'm not sure she is."

"It seems to be a common problem these days," said Tish, and pursed her lips when Mason glared her direction. "So, what do you two have planned for the rest of the evening?"

As if she had to ask. It was written all over them, in every self-aware move either of them made. Miss Hobart was particularly bad, standing there on the verge of a blush, looking up at him through her eyelashes, and apparently completely unaware of what she was doing, too.

Mason tugged his bow tie loose. "I don't know. Backgammon? Tennis?"

Raine pinked up a little more, still not quite a blush, just a glow. "Swimming?"

Another of their personal jokes. Tish cleared her throat. "I was just about to have some tea."

"I asked Lawrence to put a bottle of champagne on ice before he left for the evening," said Mason.

"I'd like that," said Raine.

Am I even part of this conversation? Tish wondered. "Is that a good idea? If Miranda doesn't get back with Paul, you'll have to drive Miss Hobart home."

"She's staying here. I had Lawrence see to the guest room."

"Really, Mason, you might have told me. Not that you're not welcome, dear," Tish added hastily. No reason to hurt the girl's feelings. "It's just a . . . surprise." And a god-awful temptation, both of them under the same roof.

"I'll get the champagne." The hard leather soles of Mason's dress shoes echoed across the oak floors as he headed for the kitchen.

As soon as the sound faded, Raine turned to Tish. "If it's not convenient for me to stay, I can—"

"No, no. It's fine, dear, truly. We have plenty of room, and house guests are in and out of here all the time. I just usually know about it first."

"I'm sure Mason meant to tell you. He was so busy with that problem in Everett yesterday, it must have gotten away from him."

"Yes. I'm sure that's it." So, he was talking to her about business, and she was apologizing for him to his mother. If the implications hadn't been so appalling, it might have been endearing.

Clearly too nervous to sit, Raine circled the room slowly, her gaze wandering from object to object as though she were viewing items in a shop. Tish half expected her to do something crass, like comment on their value, but she refrained. That showed some breeding, at least.

Truth be told, the girl wasn't as bad as Tish had first thought she'd be. She had a certain natural charm, and she really did polish up quite well. The dress Mason had bought her, for surely he had bought it, floated around her in a wash of watercolors that set off her skin and left her clear aqua eyes sparkling. She looked less like a beach baby and more like a well-heeled yachtswoman come to shore for the club dance.

"You really are quite lovely tonight," Tish said aloud. "I saw you across the room earlier and was quite taken with the transformation."

Raine smiled, if a bit warily. "Thank you. I'm sorry you couldn't stay. It really was a wonderful evening."

"Things don't always work out the way we've planned."

"They certainly don't," Raine said. Was that sadness in her voice?

Mason came back with the champagne, open, in one hand and three crystal flutes in the other, and conversation quickly shifted to gossip and a discussion of the evening's most delicious incidents. Tish missed having Miranda's analysis of the worst dresses, but she could catch up on that later. Her main goal now was to keep these two awake and apart until one gave up and went to bed—without the other.

Miss Hobart obliged first, excusing herself just after midnight.

"I'm tired, too," said Tish quickly, before Mason had time to react. "I'll just go up with you and make certain everything was taken care of in your room before I go to bed."

Mason glared at her, clearly disgruntled, but Tish was relying on his inability to announce his intention to take the woman to bed in front of his mother, and he lived up to her expectations.

After a moment, he simply walked over to Raine. "I'll see you in the morning."

"All right. Good night."

He kissed her, sweetly, the kind of kiss a man gives a woman when his mother is watching, but nonetheless, sparks flared between them so hot that Tish, for all her sixty-four years, colored and had to look away.

"Sweet dreams," he whispered.

"No question about that," Raine answered.

"Well, shall we? I'm sure you want to get to bed. You've had such a long day," said Tish. She led the way out into the foyer and up the stairs. Raine trailed behind, like tendrils of some clinging vine held her to Mason, but eventually she broke their grip and caught up with Tish.

Tish prattled nonsense as she checked the towels and paper goods and made sure a spare robe hung in the closet and that there were fresh flowers in the vase. There was no real reason she had to do this. The room was always changed out and re-stocked as soon as one guest left, and Lawrence always left things perfect for weekends, just in case, but it was force of habit. And she wanted to give Mason a few minutes to cool down and take himself off to bed.

"Do you need anything, dear?" Tish asked.

"Help with this zipper, if you wouldn't mind."

"Of course, dear." Tish undid the zipper, one of those fine, hidden things that would have been impossible without help. She wondered who had zipped it up, since Raine had clearly changed here sometime after Tish and Miranda had left. Perhaps all this foofaraw about keeping them apart was too little, too late. Had a maid straightened that bed?

No, of course not. If they'd stopped for sex, they wouldn't have gotten to the hotel that early. They would have walked in during the middle of dinner, with that bedroom look all over them and Angus sitting right there. Thank the Goddess they'd avoided that particular scene.

"There we go," she said.

"Thank you. You've been very kind." Raine held the front of her dress so it didn't gape. "Good night."

Modest, thought Tish. *That's nice.* "Good night."

She padded off to her room feeling very smug about everything except Miranda, who was apparently out with that appalling Todd Dennison again after all these months. She'd have to have a talk with her youngest. Or maybe once they straightened out this mess with Mason, they should cast a spell on Miranda's behalf. She needed a good man in her life.

Miranda sat in the car, staring at the front of the house while Paul waited patiently by the open door.

"Take me on around to the side," she said. As much as she loved her family, she didn't want to go in. She just didn't feel like dealing with them tonight, having to explain, having to talk at all.

"Is there something wrong, Miss Alexander?"

"No." She couldn't look him in the eye. "I just need some air before I go in."

"Yes, miss." He closed up the car, shutting the doors with barely a click, as though he understood she didn't want the people inside to know she was out here. He got back in, and a moment later the car rolled down the drive with a low rumble.

She got out just outside the carriage house, slipping from the car when Paul stopped to let the garage door finishing rising. Security lights came up in series as she walked around the end of the house, until she reached the box and could punch in the code that let her turn them off. The dim safety lights that glowed on the underside of the balustrade provided plenty of light for her to see her way across the creamy stone of the terrace.

She pulled off her shoes and padded barefoot across the stone to a shadowed place near the wall, under the sophora tree. The garden beyond the terrace was a dark mass of bushes and trees, lit here and there by paler blossoms. She sniffed the air, trying to catch a whiff of jasmine or rose, but instead smelled spice and leather and something vaguely male, and it was only then that she realized she still wore Paul's coat, and that it smelled like what she'd always thought of as the car but now realized was partly him. She squeezed her eyes tight and pulled the jacket closer, reveling in the warmth, physical and mental. It was probably as close as she'd get, after tonight.

Voices carried from inside: her mother, Mason, Raine, all smooth and untroubled. Miranda sat for a long, long time, half listening, until she saw Mason move past the open French doors, saw him kiss Raine, heard the good-nights all around. A few minutes later, the lights in the guest room came on, shining around the edge of the curtains, and Mason locked the French doors and turned off the lights in the living room. Moments later, a deep green glow from the end of the first floor told her that he'd put the lights on in his suite. The soft sounds of the stereo washed through the night, easy jazz tunes that were his favorite night music.

So, Tish had managed to herd them off to separate bedrooms.

Not that they'd necessarily stay there. With nothing better to do, Miranda decided to keep watch from her spot under the tree until all the children had settled down. Tish's lights came up and eventually went out, and, much later, Mason's windows darkened. Only Raine's lights stayed on.

A shadowy movement on the wall at the far end of the terrace caught her eye. She turned toward it, unafraid. After all, they were behind two fences; anyone walking the grounds at night had to belong here.

"Mason?"

"Paul, miss." He stood up and crossed to her, his shirt glowing an odd, greenish white from the safety lights. "I'm sorry if I disturbed you."

"Have you been sitting there all this time?" she asked.

"I wanted to make certain you were all right."

"I am. Really."

"Did he hurt you?"

"No. He was just getting fresh."

"That was way beyond fresh, approaching date rape."

"It wouldn't have gone that far. Todd's a little slow on the uptake, but he would have gotten the message about the time I popped him in the balls."

Paul's eyes narrowed. "You didn't seem so cocky right afterward." He grimaced. "Excuse me, that was a bad choice of words."

"It certainly was." The chuckle they shared was good. Miranda felt the weight lift a little. She took a deep breath, filling her lungs with night-scented air. "It's been a bad week. Todd was just the low point. Thank you for rescuing me, whether I needed it or not."

"My pleasure." His eyes twinkled in the moonlight.

"You enjoyed hitting him, didn't you?" she asked, incredulous.

"Most men would, under the circumstances."

"Did you hurt him?"

"I'm pretty sure I broke his nose."

"Lovely. He'll have to ask Philip for the name of his plastic surgeon." She stood up, wincing as the blood rushed to her nether extremities. "God, these chairs are hard without the cushions. I think my butt's embossed with little cast-iron leaf prints."

Paul cleared his throat and wiped a smile off his face with his hand. "May I see you to the door?"

This time she hadn't forgotten her key, and she opened the French doors to the living room. She shrugged out of his coat and held it out. "I guess you want this back."

His fingers brushed hers as he took the jacket, barely a touch, but enough to make Miranda catch her breath. The slight sound was harsh compared to the jazz still playing in the distance.

"Good night, Paul," she said quickly, to cover her reaction.

Paul's eyes grew strangely intense, even in the darkness, and she had the sudden, sweet impression he wasn't thinking competent and dependable anymore.

"Good night, Miranda."

She slipped inside and hurried to the security panel to type in the code before her sixty seconds was up. When she returned to look out the doors, Paul was gone. She was halfway upstairs before she realized that for the first time in six years, he'd called her Miranda.

If only Mason hadn't kissed her good night, Raine thought. She'd been doing fine until then, maintaining the distance she needed, until he'd leaned over to give her that kiss. It was the least blatantly sexy kiss they'd ever shared, and yet it had stirred something so deep inside her, created such a maelstrom, that her soul might never settle down.

The routine of getting ready for bed hadn't even touched the storm. Neither had a shower, or fifty pages from the wordy literary novel she'd found on the night table, or a half hour of pacing. And never mind meditating; she couldn't even begin to calm her thoughts enough for that, a failure that would disappoint Takana-*sensei* no end.

Maybe if she couldn't hear the music, Mason's music, drifting up from somewhere below, she could sleep. But she could hear it, and that meant he was awake, somewhere in that house, and knowing that made it impossible to disconnect from that one sweet kiss. She cranked her window wide open and pulled a chair over to where she could listen to the same music that soothed him, hoping it would do the same for her.

The CD ended and the silence stretched until she thought that maybe he'd finally gone to sleep and she'd be able to coax herself into some rest as well. But there the music came again, and this time it was the familiar strains of "Moonlight Serenade." Her heart skidded to a halt, then started again on the same rhythm as the string bass that kept the beat.

He was calling her, and she wanted to go.

It was crazy. It was absolutely insane, but even as she was telling herself that, she was stripping out of her pajamas and pulling on the gown, wrestling the zipper up as best she could.

The cotton panties she'd put on after her shower made an awkward lump under the silk. She stripped them off and glanced around for the tiny silk thong that went under the gown, but she couldn't remember where she'd dropped it and had no inclination to begin a search. *He'll never know,* she told herself, and smoothed the gown down over her bare hips.

She slipped out into the hall barefoot, not knowing where she was going, but following the sound like a moth following flame, utterly unable to resist. The music was softer, but still clear in the silence of the hallway. An open door beckoned and she went through it into another suite, this one all pink. The music seemed to come from one corner, where a thin glow came up from the floor. She followed the glow into a circular stone staircase that went downstairs. From there she followed it into a hall and out a door onto the terrace.

Mason stood there, still in his dinner jacket with his loose tie, framed by a pair of French doors that led into what must be his bedroom.

He smiled when he saw her.

"It occurred to me," he said, "that Bond would have found some way to finish that dance."

Raine started toward him.

"Just a minute." The hand he held up to stop her gripped the slim rectangle of a remote control. "We're going to do this right."

He pointed the remote toward a tiny red electronic eye deep inside his room and moved his thumb over the buttons. The stereo dropped silent in the middle of a phrase, and, without looking, he tossed the remote toward a wing chair sitting just inside the door. It hit the cushion with a soft thump.

"James would be proud," she said. His mouth toyed with the idea of a smile.

They stood there, waiting, until the song started over and the saxes glided into their sweet refrain. Mason held his arms out.

"Raine, may I please have this dance?"

His soft stress on the word *please* spoke of need, the kind never mentioned out loud in polite society nor in middle-class homes in Minnesota, but which she recognized because she felt it, too, raw and demanding and sweet and warm as summer, all at once. He needed her, and that fact melded with her own yearning to squeeze all the air out of her lungs.

She moved into his arms as though she belonged there, as though it were perfectly natural and proper to dance outside a man's bedroom in the middle of the night, wearing a dress that wasn't zipped all the way. But it didn't matter if it was proper or not, or even whether it was wise or not, because, right now, there wasn't anything else she could do that would let her breathe.

They swayed to the simple melody and rich chords, Mason's shoes scratching a beat on the stonework next to Raine's bare feet. As the harmonies built and he swirled her across the terrace to their rhythm, she closed her eyes, lost in the movement and the feel of his body guiding her. She didn't need anything else, no reference points except his touch and the song. They could have been whirling through the night sky, for all the connection she had to the earth or to anything but the music and Mason.

She thought she was going to die when they slowed and stopped, the last note hanging on the air. Her breath escaped in a moan of disappointment. "No."

Mason understood. He didn't want it to end either, and when Raine sagged against him, her forehead resting against his chest, he couldn't help but gather her closer. It was then that he found the open zipper.

Desire kicked him in the chest, knocking the breath out of him. The earlier fantasy, so carefully avoided, flooded back, as real as the woman in his arms. His fingers meandered down the gap, tracing skin cooled by the night air until he found the dangling tab. It wasn't open far.

He could zip it up like he should and be a gentleman, or he could do what he wanted to and zip it down. Down meant danger, a yard of bare back curving under his fingers. Down meant the night and the dance would go on.

"Raine?" The hollow agony in his voice spoke of how much he wanted the night to go on.

She looked up, and for just an instant he saw her eyes, glittering with surprise and moonlight and desire.

And then he was kissing her, and there were no more questions, just answers in the questing pressure of her lips and the arc of her body against his. With a groan of surrender, she lifted her hands to tangle them in his hair, and the sound only confirmed what he'd been trying to deny all evening. All week. He wanted her. Naked and in his bed. Now.

But he wanted it to last, too, so not the zipper. Not yet.

He forced himself to slow down, to let his hands drift away from that particular temptation.

It was better touching her through the silk anyway, enjoying the way the two layers slid over each other and over her skin, making every rise and dip of her body more seductive, as though he needed more seduction. He took his time tracing every curve, knowing he could go back to that zipper any time.

He particularly appreciated the way the silk made his hands slip over her bottom. Smooth. Round. With that incredible combination of softness and firmness that only a woman's ass could have. It took him a moment to notice that nothing, not even the slimmest bit of elastic, disturbed the flow of cloth beneath his hands.

Oh, God.

He traced a path back up her sides to cup her breasts. No, no trace of a bra either; her nipples swelled and hardened as he brushed his thumbs over the tips, only those two thin layers of silk covering them. He couldn't resist. He bent his head to sample one peak through the gown, molding a damp circle of cloth to its shape and drawing a gasp from her before he broke away to ask, even though he knew the answer might drive him over the edge, "Do you have anything on under this?"

Her breath escaped her in a ragged shudder. She shook her head. "I was in too much of a hurry."

Hurry. She had been in too much hurry to get to him, and the confession was like a release for both of them. Their hands were everywhere at once, his skating over the silk of her gown so quickly that sparks crackled between her skin and the cloth, and hers snatching at the gold studs that kept her from reaching bare skin.

He helped with that, shrugging out of his jacket and stripping his braces away to hang at his sides, but she ripped his shirttail out of his pants herself. The last studs dropped to the ground, ringing like tiny golden bells, as she yanked the shirt open and peeled it off his shoulders.

"Cuffs," he said against her mouth, and held up his hands, and she fumbled at his wrists with trembling fingers until he was able to shake the shirt free.

Finally. Raine splayed her hands over his chest, her palms burning from the heat that poured off him. The urgency that drove her melted into a need to see if she could do to him anything remotely like what he was doing to her. She found out quickly, running her hands over his chest and shoulders until she located all the places that sent tremors through him.

And then she went back, more slowly, to find them again with her mouth.

She did her worst: a soft kiss where his ribs rose over his heart, a gentle nip where his neck curved into his shoulder, a breath of warm air over the diamond of hair that covered his chest. Guided by his reactions, she kissed her way from point to point until she settled on the best, the flat coins of his nipples. With exquisite deliberation, she traced a circle around one, spiraling in until the center hardened and he groaned, and then she moved to the other one to do the same thing and force the same sound out of his throat.

All the while Mason kept his hands moving over her, tracing her curves, trying to distract her, but she was resolute, and he finally had to crush her against him to stop her from doing any more damage to his senses. He held her close, so she couldn't move, couldn't steal what last little bit of control he had. The tab on the zipper dangled against the back of his hand. *One good pull.*

Not quite yet.

He kissed her, and focused on the sensation of her nipples against him, pebbled and hard beneath the liquid fire of the silk. A streak of masochism made him lift her a few inches, just so he could let her slide down and feel the delicious agony of her nipples raking his chest.

Too much, it was too goddamn much. With a convulsion, he set her down and stepped back before he embarrassed himself.

"Ohhh." A tiny wail of disappointment issued from Raine. She stepped toward him.

"No, it's all right, sweetheart. I'm not stopping. I've just put something off too long. Stand still."

She obeyed, not understanding until Mason stepped behind her and she felt his hands at her zipper. He skimmed kisses over her shoulders in a line. His breath stirred the hairs on the back of her neck, sending a shudder down her back that he followed with more kisses, and she swayed with the effort of not turning to him. Her fingers curled until her nails bit into her palms.

He took the zipper down by millimeters, savoring every second that it took to reveal her back to the moonlight and his eyes. She had a beautiful back, muscled from her years of swimming and her work, but still with a feminine curve. In fact it was that curve that got him, those last eight inches that made the blood pound into his groin as the gown peeled away to expose the small of her back and the rise of her hips below.

Holding his breath, he dipped into the opening, let his fingertips dance over the shadowed skin to find the base of her spine. There was just enough play in the gown to slip one hand inside and fit it to the shape of her bottom. Heat rose off her, damp, scented with something indescribably female, and he took a deep breath. And lost it totally.

The groan that ripped from him was animal, crazy with need, and it loosed an answering craziness in Raine. She whirled to rise into his arms, pulling his head down, covering him with kisses. Her nails raked across his shoulders and down his arms, and in self-defense, he grabbed her wrists and held them as his lips ground down on hers. She wrestled free and reached for the waist of his trousers.

Somehow they made it into his bedroom before they lost all their clothes, and then Mason was over her, his weight carrying her down onto the bed, his lips and hands convincing her that his bed was where she belonged, whether it made sense or not. She loved him and she wanted him, and that was the only thought she could hold in her mind, and so she abandoned herself to the scent of him and the feel of his body, heavy against hers, and the sound of his voice murmuring his desire.

It was all Mason could do to remember to reach for one of the condoms in the drawer, and rolling off of Raine long enough to get the damned thing on almost cost him his sanity. She wasn't helping any, either, with the way she squirmed beside him, hands dancing over his skin, urging him to hurry, but he finally got it, and then he was back in her arms, moving with her, pressing her deep into the mattress. The vague knowledge that he should take his time, make it sweet, was lost in the overpowering fact of his need. He drove deep into her, laying claim to her in the most primal way.

A cry of pain and pleasure ripped from her throat. The word *virgin* flickered through Mason's brain, but before he could get his mind around it, she'd hooked her heels behind his thighs and pulled him deeper. The question vanished in the erotic grind of her hips against his, and within moments he was lost in her all over again.

Raine's release came hard and suddenly, without any warning. One second she was trying to drive Mason over the edge, and the next, she'd gone over it herself, the surprised victim of his fingers against her nipples. Her world centered on the shock waves rippling out through her being, and she barely heard his low exclamation of delight. As the tremors subsided, she felt the change in him, as his rhythm shifted and the tension increased in his body, and she had barely regained control of her arms to gather him close when he called out her name and convulsed deep within her.

"Oh, sweetheart. Sweet, beautiful Raine." He trailed kisses over her cheeks and eyes, and down her throat as he murmured her name. After a long time he shifted his weight off of her, but kept her in his arms. His kisses and sweet words slowly drugged her, until finally she surrendered to the darkness and the exhaustion of a long day, and sleep dragged her eyes shut. Her last conscious thought was of how much she loved this man, and what a huge mistake she'd just made.

The carpenters' pounding was annoyingly persistent, thought Tish as she fought her way up from sleep. She finally woke up enough to recall that they weren't doing any renovations these days, and that it must be someone at her door.

"Who is it?"

"Lawrence, madam. There's a telephone call for Mr. Alexander and I can't seem to rouse him. I thought perhaps you should take it."

Enough sleep still fogged her brain that she thought for a moment he meant Malcolm, but no, he meant Mason.

"Just a minute."

She quarreled briefly with a sheet that wanted to cling to her feet, but managed to get out of bed. Her robe was, as always, on the chair at her dressing table, and she slipped into it and raked a brush through her hair before she opened the door.

"Good morning, Lawrence. What do you mean you can't rouse Mason?"

"I tried his room several times. There was no answer. It's Mrs.—that is, Miss Lathrop. About Miss Samantha, she said."

"Thank you, Lawrence. I'll take it. What time is it?"

"A quarter past six, madam."

She went to the hall phone. She'd always refused to have one of the tedious things in the bedrooms, but Malcolm had insisted on this compromise. And of course, Mason had put one into his suite when he'd moved back in, along with a line for his computer.

She picked up the receiver. "Hello, Elizabeth. Is Samantha all right?"

"Oh, Tish. Hello. I was expecting Mason. I've been on hold forever."

There was no way Tish was going to apologize for taking a long time to get to the phone at this ungodly hour. "He seems to have gone missing, temporarily. He's probably in the pool or something. What about Samantha?"

"She's fine. You'll see for yourself in a little while."

"What do you mean?"

"I found out there's an auction in Milan that I *have* to go to. She'd be coming out there in a couple of weeks anyway, so I decided to let Mason have her ahead of time. I popped her on a plane early this morning."

"It still *is* early this morning." Tish stared out the window at the sky, flat gray and barely touched with light. "You can't mean you just put that child on a plane without talking to any of us first. What if none of us had been home?"

"I just found out last night late, and I had to get her and myself both packed. Besides, I know you aren't going too far these days, and Lawrence or Paul or somebody would have picked her up and kept her safe until you got home. Listen, I have to meet with the curator before my flight this afternoon, so I've got to go. Write this down." She rattled off the airline flight number and arrival time.

"For God's sake, Elizabeth. That's barely an hour from now."

"I know. Sorry. I had to pick up some paperwork on the way back from the airport and I didn't want to wake you up even earlier. These things come up. I'll fax you with my hotel and flights, and Sam knows my e-mail. Ta."

The line went dead.

"Bloody bitch," Tish said aloud before she hung up. That poor child, shipped off like an inconvenient kitten. Elizabeth was nothing if not consistent. She'd treated Mason the same way, taking a series of lovers and filing for divorce when the business had started making *him* inconvenient.

And speaking of Mason, where had he gotten off to?

"Lawrence!"

He appeared so quickly, Tish knew he'd been lingering just

around the corner, probably listening in. "Yes, madam."

"Check to see if Mason's in the pool or on the tennis court. And have someone see to Samantha's room. Her visit is starting a little early this year."

"I will take care of it myself." He looked delighted, and Tish knew she'd feel the same way as soon as she got over her irritation at Elizabeth and found Mason.

Miranda appeared in her door, bleary-eyed and sleep-rumpled. "What's going on?"

Tish summarized the conversation with Elizabeth. Before she finished, Miranda was headed toward the guest room.

"He's not in there," said Tish. "I made certain they went to bed separately."

"We'll see." Miranda knocked twice, then pushed the door open. "Cover up, I'm coming in."

Tish peered over her daughter's shoulder. The room was empty, the bathroom stood open and silent, and Miss Hobart's nightgown lay on the floor. "Well. At least the bed shows signs of having been slept in. Maybe they've gone for an early morning walk together. Lawrence will find them."

"At his pace, it will take all morning. I'll get dressed and make a quick run through the garden."

"All right, darling. I'll get dressed. If we can't find Mason within ten minutes, I'll go after Samantha myself. Have Paul bring the car around."

"It's Sunday, remember? He's off. If I don't find Mason, I'll just get the Explorer and we'll both go." Miranda leaned over and gave her mother a kiss. "See you on the terrace in ten minutes."

She dashed off, and Tish headed for her own room, where her first step was to put on a kettle of water for tea. She made short work of her morning beauty routine, then slipped into a comfortable gauze skirt and tunic in a raspberry shade that compensated for a lack of makeup. Out of consideration for the distances at airports, she picked out a pair of flat sandals. By then her kettle had started to steam, and she made her tea and carried it downstairs to wait for Miranda. Eight minutes had passed.

She strolled out on the terrace with her cup, enjoying the few moments of calm before the storm named Samantha arrived. Unless the child had changed since Easter, she rose with the robins, and there would be no such thing as a quiet cup of tea on the terrace or anywhere else until she left again—thank the Goddess. Sometimes this old barn was too quiet.

Far below, a freight train rumbled by on the Burlington Northern tracks that ran on the narrow band of land at the base of the cliff. You could only hear the trains when the air was right, but the sound always reminded her of a trip she'd taken with the children when they were small, through the Swiss Alps. She wandered closer to the edge.

A streak of brilliant white on the stones outside Mason's room caught the corner of her eye. She turned to look and noticed Mason's doors open.

Concerned, she took a closer look. His shirt. That was Mason's shirt. And that black was his jacket, lying underneath. And his tie, a few feet away. Here and there, gold studs sparkled in the early light.

She was drawn toward the open doors almost against her will. More clothes lay inside on the carpet: his trousers, her dress, someone's underwear—she couldn't bear to identify whose.

And there, on the bed, Mason and Miss Hobart.

They lay twined together, clinging to each other amid the rubble of the bedclothes like the survivors of some natural disaster.

She stood there, staring at them, not quite sure how to proceed. She must have stared long enough that it disturbed Mason. He stirred, passed a hand across his eyes, and lifted his head.

His eyes focused, and his mouth set. He reached to pull the coverlet over the sleeping woman beside him.

"For God's sake, Mother." His voice was a harsh, accusatory whisper. "Don't you have the decency to knock?"

Beside him, Raine shifted sleepily.

"The door was open," said Tish. "I assumed everyone was invited for a viewing. By the powers, Mason, do you have any idea what this will do to your prospects with Caroline?"

"My prospects, with Caroline or anyone else, are not up for discussion. What do you want?"

"Elizabeth called. She has to go to Europe, and, in her usual logic, she decided to send Samantha out early. Her plane will land at Sea-Tac in"—she glanced at her watch—"fifty-three minutes. I thought she deserved to have her father meet her, but seeing as you're indisposed, Miranda and I will go."

"She's my daughter. I'll go." He sat up, the linens barely covering his crotch. "Unless you want to see more of me than you have since I hit puberty, you might want to leave. Have Paul—''

''He's off today. Miranda is bringing her car around. You can drive that.'' She left, taking a moment to close the French doors behind her.

''Oh, geez,'' said Raine. She pulled the covers over her head.

Mason tugged the blanket away. ''You heard.''

''Oh, yeah.'' She turned away, unable to face him. ''You'd better go take a shower. You don't want to show up at the airport smelling like me.''

''I'm sorry.'' He leaned over and kissed her on the forehead. ''This wasn't how I pictured things.''

''I know.''

He headed for the bathroom.

Stupid. Stupid. Stupid.

As the shower pounded down in the adjoining bath, Raine sat on the bed and berated herself. How could she have lost such touch with reality that she let herself be drawn in by Mason and his plotting?

Five thousand dollars didn't get him sex. Shoot, she wasn't nearly that expensive: just a dinner dance and the right CD, and she made a perfect display for his mama. The dress had bumped the price up, but overall, he'd gotten a deal.

She had no delusions about her part: she'd been a demo for Tish, nothing more. In fact, she was surprised he hadn't arranged something for Miranda, too. Surely with such a graphic display of their handiwork run amok, he would have no trouble getting them to swear off witchcraft forever.

Now, if she could just find some way to swear off him.

The shower went silent, and seconds later Mason emerged, damp and gorgeous in his deviousness.

''Marine shower,'' he said, toweling his head. ''Sixty seconds or less. Of course, they don't have hair.'' He tossed the towel in the corner, then ripped off the one at his waist and tossed it, as well.

Raine sneaked a peek while he hit his dresser for some jockeys and a T-shirt. He was magnificent, and, for a fleeting instant, she wished that things were different, that he wasn't a scumbag who had just used her to teach his mother a lesson.

But he was, and she was the fool who had thought that somehow loving him would be enough. It was a naive fantasy. She knew that now, in the light of day. But last night, when he had kissed her and whispered desire into her ears, it hadn't seemed like a fantasy at all. He'd made it seem like a real possibility. She ought to know by now that men did whatever it took to get in a girl's pants. Why should Mason be any different?

He pulled on khakis and a navy polo shirt, slipped on a pair of loafers with no socks, and came to sit on the bed beside her. His fingers were warm on her back, not fevered like last night, and he silently stroked her shoulder. He dropped a quick kiss on her cheek.

"I wish I could spend the morning with you, but there's an eleven-year-old who's going to be in tears if no one shows up for her."

Raine felt tears prick at her own eyes, and just nodded. "Go on. I'll be fine."

He kissed her once more. "You're a sport. Go back to sleep and I'll be back in a little while so we can sort out the day."

Raine nodded, but as soon as he was gone, she gathered herself, stole a thick robe from his closet, and slipped back up the circular stairs to the guest room. It took her less than ten minutes to shower off his smell and throw the few things that were really hers into the gym bag she used as an overnighter, and then she ran back down the circular stairs and out the door. This time she headed for the carriage house.

The garage was empty when she got there, but she found a buzzer and pressed it, and Paul soon came trotting downstairs.

"Miss Hobart," he said, surprised. "May I help you with something?"

"Yes, please. I know you're off today and I hate to ask, but I really need to get home. Can you help?" She hoped her voice didn't sound as shaky to him as it felt to her.

He looked at her, long and hard, as though he could see what was bothering her, and then he folded the book he was carrying.

"Of course, miss. Give me a minute to get my license and the keys."

She was safe in the backseat of the Rolls Royce before the tears began to fall.

Thirteen

"Daddy!"

It was the best word in the world, and anyone doubting it needed only to look at the smile on Mason's face as Samantha rushed out of the jet way. She'd grown a good two inches since spring, he realized as he hugged her, so much that his arms went around her at a different angle. Such changes were the worst part of being a long-distance father, but there wasn't a damned thing he could do about it, so he squeezed her.

"I love you, squirt."

"Me, too, Daddy. Guess what? Libby Crawford and her parents were on the plane. She's from my school." She flipped her long black hair, like some half-size fashion model. "Her mom was born here, so they summer up in the San Juans, and they were just back East because her other grandmother was sick. Can we go up and spend a week with them while I'm here? Libby's mom gave me her cell phone number."

"We'll see."

The woman from the airline came up behind Sam, smiling. "I would take that as a positive I.D., but I'm afraid the company has stickier standards."

"We know the drill," said Mason. "We do this often."

Too often, and not often enough, he thought. Summers, Christmas, spring break, an occasional weekend when he could make it back to Boston. Still, since Sam would be starting boarding school in Connecticut this fall, he'd see her almost as many total days as Elizabeth did, just not as frequently. He pulled his wallet out of his jacket pocket and handed over his driver's license to the airline woman, then he and Sam followed her to the desk to sign off on all the paperwork.

"We won't have to do this baby stuff on the way back. I'll be twelve and they'll let me travel alone."

"Hey, that's right. I've got you for your birthday this year. This was all so abrupt, I hadn't sorted that out yet." He had a lot of things he hadn't sorted out, thanks to Elizabeth. "Your mother and I will have to consult about your traveling alone. I'm not quite sure we're ready."

"Da-a-addy."

"Already with the preteen whine? I don't mean you, I mean Mom and me. You know, your grandmother and aunt are going to love this birthday deal."

"Party?"

"I wouldn't be surprised. After all, twelve is an important birthday."

"Wow. One of Gran's famous parties just for me. I'll invite Libby, and Marnie Hirshberger, and . . ." She chewed on one corner of her mouth as she tried to figure out who she knew in town. "Can I ask adults?"

"You can ask whomever you'd like, but maybe you should wait for your grandmother to actually offer to have a party before you start mailing invitations."

They collected her luggage—too much and too light, as usual, Elizabeth's backhanded method of ensuring Sam came home with new school clothes filling up all the space—and headed for the car.

Sam chattered all the way home. Mason tried to keep up, but he lost track of the Madisons and Madelines and Ashleys and Brookes that his daughter rattled off while telling him about school and summer so far. He resorted to the sage parental nod and "Mmm," which allowed his mind to wander.

Naturally, it wandered to Raine. Mason's groin tightened as he thought of her, last seen looking tousled and sleepy and not-so-happy in his bed.

That last bothered him. A lot. Last night shouldn't have happened. He'd known better even as he'd hunted for a Glenn Miller CD in his mother's collection, but he'd justified it—it was just a dance, and she probably wouldn't come downstairs, anyway. And then she had and there had been that zipper. That damned, delightful zipper.

He shook off the mood. He'd straighten things out with Raine when he got home. Right now his daughter deserved his attention, even if he did have Maddy Hoffman and Maddy Livingston terminally confused.

Besides, she was watching him.

"What?" he asked.

"You weren't paying attention."

"I'm sorry, squirt. I didn't get much sleep last night, and it's hard to focus. What did I miss?"

"They were *what?*" Miranda gaped at her mother across the breakfast table. "You actually walked in on them?"

"They were asleep," Tish said. "But it was evident what had happened. There were clothes clear out on the terrace, for the Goddess' sake. Silly me, I thought actually getting them to bed separately was enough to ensure this didn't happen. I should have camped in front of her door."

"I doubt it would have done any good," said Miranda. She drummed her fingers on the table, her long nails clicking against the lacquered mahogany. "So, big brother stripped down with his girlfriend on the terrace in the middle of the night."

"Really, darling, you could take this more seriously."

"I'm taking it quite seriously. But you have to admit, this fling with Raine has loosened him up a bit."

"I don't think I can stand things any looser," said Tish with a sigh. "Speaking of which, if that abominable Todd Dennison is floating around upstairs, I want him gone before Samantha gets here."

"Todd? Why would he be here?"

"I heard that you were with him last night. The implication—"

"From Mason, naturally."

"Of course. The implication was that you might be rekindling things with Todd, and since you're here this morning I thought that perhaps you'd . . ."

"Brought him home? What a perfectly loathsome idea." Miranda's light tone disguised the revulsion she felt over last night's behavior—both Todd's and hers. The only one who had behaved with any class at all was Paul. ''I considered it, but Todd's still Todd, only more so. I have my sights set higher.''

''I'm glad to hear you say that,'' said Tish. ''You never were very sensible about him.''

''Well, I'm being sensible now.'' Which was why she decided to change the topic. ''What did you end up doing with Angus last night?''

''Oh, we went to dinner.''

Miranda rolled her eyes. ''How was it?''

''Most pleasant, as a matter of fact. Don't look so stunned.''

''Oh, come on, Tish. He's so . . . Texas.''

''I know, dear, but that's just surface. He's actually quite charming and interesting.''

''So, where did you go?''

''The oddest place down by Kent. Caveman Barbecue, I believe it was called. There were dozens of long tables outside, like some great huge picnic with strangers, and we ate ribs with our fingers. Very peculiar.''

''He took you to a rib joint in a Dior gown? Whatever possessed him?''

''It was the story I told him to get him out of the Four Seasons. I said the lights were giving me a headache, so he took me someplace with no artificial lights.'' Tish nibbled at her dry toast. ''Anyway, someone had told him about it, and he claimed he hadn't had good barbecue since he moved his offices to Seattle. As it turned out, the food was excellent, if a bit blue-collar.''

''Well, good.'' Miranda wasn't sure what else to say.

''You know, your father used to take me to strange little places like that before you children came along.'' Tish closed her eyes and saw Malcolm's face in her mind, so much like Mason's except never quite so intense, and sadness fluttered through her chest. ''Someone in the office would mention a place, or he'd overhear one of the workers at the plant talking about their favorite restaurant, and off we'd go. Sometimes it would be terrible, but other times we'd have the most divine meal.''

''It sounds so romantic,'' Miranda said. Her eyes widened. ''Are you and Angus . . . ?''

''Oh, no, darling.'' Tish got up abruptly to pour herself some more orange juice. ''We just had a nice leisurely dinner, stopped for dessert and drinks at the Sorrento, and then came home. We were having another drink when you called.''

Miranda thought she caught a wash of color in her mother's cheeks, but maybe it was a reflection from her pink dress. "Well, all right. So we're both being sensible, which is why I'm going to go upstairs, take an incredibly hot shower, and try to be fit for human company by the time Samantha gets here. I don't do as well on five hours of sleep as I used to."

The little house was too quiet and Raine too disgusted with herself to sleep, despite the exhaustion that made her bones ache. She couldn't just sit, either, so she changed into a clean pair of jeans and a T-shirt, grabbed a rain jacket, tossed a couple of boxes in the back of the truck, and headed downhill toward the Fremont Sunday market. The parking lot behind the Red Door bustled with vendors, mostly already set up. Raine found a temporary parking spot, got out, and grabbed a box.

She found Brynn and her flowers near the end of a row. As she dumped the box at the back of the stall, Brynn put her hands on her hips.

"I thought you weren't coming today."

"I wasn't," said Raine. She sounded more curt than she intended.

"So, it's like that."

"Like nothing. It's just a change in plans. Of course, if you don't want me here—"

"Nice try. I always sell more with your bugs flitting around in the flowers. And I know you wouldn't be here if you didn't want to be real bad."

"Fine, then. I'll go get the other box."

"Just two boxes today?"

"Yeah, I decided to come down at the last minute, so I just brought the little critters."

"That's okay. Mama Brynn's magic big toe and a good look at the sky says we're not going to have a ton of customers today."

"That doesn't surprise me. Be right back."

"I'll be here. And you'll have lots of time to tell me what has made you so sour on the world this morning."

Yeah, right.

Mason watched Samantha and her aunt Randi, as Miranda had been christened back in Sam's baby days. They were a pair, engrossed in talk of the great birthday extravaganza as soon as her grandmother had given official permission. Their scheming provided him with the perfect opportunity to take care of unfinished business. He motioned his mother aside.

"Where's Raine?"

"I don't know. I would assume she either went back to sleep or decided to wait for you someplace out of the public eye."

Mason eyed his mother. "Did you say something to her?"

"I haven't even seen her, darling, and if I had, I assure you, I wouldn't have said a word to hurt her. I may not approve, but I'm not deliberately cruel."

"Of course not. I should know better. She's probably still asleep in my room. Keep Samantha occupied for a little while, okay?"

"Whatever you say, darling. But please use sound judgment on this."

Mason took a deep breath and headed for his suite. It was a little too late for that.

She wasn't in bed, or in the shower, although her gown still lay in a rainbow puddle on the floor next to his dress pants. He scooped both up, and as he hung them in his closet, he noticed that his robe was gone.

Her room, of course. Carrying her dress on a hanger, he went up the back stairs and through the pink room to the guest room. A soft knock produced no answer. He pushed the door open.

She was gone. He could tell as soon as he glanced around the room, even before the diamond bracelet and earrings winked at him from the nightstand. He checked to see if her things were in the drawers or the closet. Her overnight bag was gone, as were her clothes, but she'd left behind the dresses he'd bought her, and on the floor of the closet lay a minuscule pair of silk panties that must have belonged under the gown, the ones she'd been in too big a hurry for last night.

Damn it.

He hung the gown in the closet and stepped out to the hall phone to dial the carriage house. Paul picked up after a few rings.

"Yes, sir," he answered in response to Mason's question. "Miss Hobart asked me to take her home, and I did so."

"Was she upset?"

"I think one could safely say that."

"Damn it."

"Is there a problem, sir?"

"Nothing for you to concern yourself about. Thank you for taking care of her, Paul. Sorry to disturb your day off."

"It's all right, sir."

Mason hung up and dialed Raine's number. The phone rang and rang.

Damn it. She wasn't answering.

She thought he'd done this on purpose, taken her to bed and used her to make the ultimate point to his mother and sister over that damned love potion. He knew that's what she thought, because it had occurred to him, after the fact, that his mother's arrival had been as fortuitous as it was embarrassing. He'd just been hoping Raine gave him more credit than that.

But why should she? He might not have set out to use her, but it had worked out that way.

Jackass.

He punched the wall.

"Hey, what are you doing here?"

Raine turned from a middle-aged gay couple she was helping to see Zoe standing at the side of the stall. "I'm just helping these folks out. Hang on a minute."

The pair had some money and an interest in something bigger than a copper dragonfly, so she dragged her portfolio over on the table. "Here are pictures of some of my larger pieces, but I do commission work, too. Look through here and see if there's anything you like, and if not we can work together to design what you want. I'll be right back."

"That could be a nice sale," said Zoe under her breath as Raine stepped over to the side. "Good thing. You look like hell."

"Thanks, Zo. Lovely to see you, too."

"Hey, if you can't get honesty from a friend, who can you get it from?"

"Who, indeed?"

"So, why *are* you here?" Zoe repeated. "I figured you'd be up at the Alexanders' until late."

"She's not answering those questions," said Brynn as she grabbed a sheet of florist paper and twisted it around a bouquet. "I've been listening to her sigh all day, but it's all I've gotten out of her."

"Let's just say I'm available evenings again and leave it at that."

Zoe studied her for a minute, then shrugged. "Okay. Well, then, want to come over and do laundry with me tonight?"

"Laundry. That's about my speed. Why not?"

"Okay, swing by after you get off. I'll do vegetable soup and some garlic bread."

"I'll bring a half gallon of butter-brickle."

"Nasty." Zoe waved good-bye and left Raine to her customers.

Unfortunately, the prediction of Brynn's big toe held—no sale. Raine moped through the rest of the drizzly day, then packed up her stuff and went home. The phone started ringing almost as soon as she walked in the door, but she didn't answer it. A quick check under the bed for stray socks, and she was back out the door with her dirty clothes and laundry soap in under two minutes. The phone was still ringing.

Good food, ice cream, and the numbing sound of laundry tumbling in a machine: it was a perfect evening from Raine's point of view. Zoe talked just enough to keep her from thinking, but refrained from asking the Big Question even though it must have been driving her nuts.

"I hadn't realized how much I missed doing laundry," Raine said as she dumped the last of four loads into her big wicker basket to haul home. "The little stuff is so satisfying. Tell Bob thanks again."

Zoe's laundry room was nominally for apartment residents only, but the manager, Bob, turned a blind eye in exchange for a dish of whatever the ice cream flavor of the night happened to be.

Zoe held the door open for her and they started for the parking lot. "Are you up to talking about FUSE real quick?"

"I guess. What's up?"

"A bunch of us ran into each other at the Dubliner last night. Fred and a couple of the others are wondering why we haven't done anything since the Wall. I told them you were working under deep cover."

"Oh, great, Zoe. Look, I didn't accomplish anything at all with Mason."

"All the more reason to get things going again, before we lose our momentum."

"But we don't have anything planned."

"Oh, that's easy. I'll just call everybody and tell them we need a really hot idea ASAP. They'll come through. Especially if I can tell them you'll make lasagna for whoever is brilliant."

"You should be Fearless Leader. I'm a loss these days."

"You're just temporarily off your mark. We can set a meeting for, say, Tuesday night?"

"Okay. No, wait. The neighborhood softball game is that night. Make it Wednesday."

"Wednesday's out for me," said Zoe. "Hey. What about Wednesday morning? We can meet for bagels. I bet John B. would open an hour early for us."

"Perfect. The final permits for Canal Place are going to come through any day now. If we're going to even bother at this point, it's going to have to be good, something that will get the neighborhood so riled up that the Alexanders and the planning board can't ignore it anymore."

"Even better than the Wall," agreed Zoe. "Look, this is a brilliant group—well, except Arne, maybe. They'll come through."

"I hope so." Raine thought of the monstrosity of a building and the man behind it, and her anger flared. "I want to stick it to him big time."

"So, just what did Moneybags do?" asked Zoe quietly.

"He set me up." She banged her fist into the side of the truck. "His mother walked in on us this morning."

"Walked in on . . . Ohmigod. You *slept* with him?"

"Do you have a bullhorn? We can announce it so everybody hears."

"Sorry." Zoe dropped her voice. "It's just hard to believe that Miss Love-and-Sex-Can't-Be-Separated slept with some guy just because he paid her five thousand . . . Ohmigod. You *wouldn't* do it because of the money. You're in love with him, aren't you?"

"Oh, Zoe." The anger burned off like a puff of hydrogen, leaving a hollow feeling, and Raine sagged against the side of her truck, the tears streaming, hot and salty, down her cheeks. "I don't understand it. There's no reason I should feel this way about him. He's not in love with me. We've just been pretending so well that, I don't know, I lost track or something. I wanted him so much. The incredibly stupid thing is, I still do, in spite of the way he used me."

"Oh, man. I understand." Zoe hugged her, patting her shoulder like a baby. "I was like that with Chris, remember? He was such a schmoo, and yet there I was, every time he called. It's like you're under a spell or something."

Raine looked up sharply. "What made you say that?"

"It's just a way to describe the feeling. Why, do you think somebody cast a spell on—"

"No. Don't be ridiculous. There's no such thing as a love spell." Raine swiped tears off her cheeks with the back of her hand and straightened up.

"I don't know about that. A lot of people believe in witchcraft and voodoo and all that stuff."

"No, Zoe. This is ridiculous. You were just making an analogy, like you said." She ripped open her truck door and pushed the basket of laundry inside, then gave Zoe a quick hug. "I'm not under a spell, and I've got to get home and get some sleep. I'll talk to you tomorrow or something."

She got in her truck, turned the key, and stomped the gas pedal. The old piece of junk roared to life, just like it had done for the past one hundred and sixty thousand miles, and she pushed it, whining, up the steep hills toward her house.

No. Not the love potion. That was just too farfetched. It couldn't be. Mason had sworn they weren't real witches.

But what if they were? What if their silly potion had actually worked?

She was so appalled by the possibility that she almost didn't spot the low-slung carriage of Mason's Jag before she made that last corner.

She stopped quickly, doused her lights, backed up, and eased on past the street at a dead crawl so the muffler—maybe—wouldn't give her away. She circled the block and found a parking space on Bowdoin, then dragged the basket out and used the tiny flashlight on her key chain to pick her way around the block and down the alley to slip into her house the back way.

For fear Mason would spot the house lights from the street, she brushed her teeth and washed her face in the pitch black of her windowless bathroom, then felt her way into the bedroom and made up the bed in the dark with the sheets she'd just washed. She stripped down to her T-shirt and panties. The sheets were cool and welcoming.

A few minutes later, as she lay there worrying over the love spell like a terrier at a rat, she heard footsteps on the stoop and a knock at the door. She lay in the dark, silent and unmoving, her heart pounding in her ears as though Mason were a burglar trying to break in, instead of the man she'd spent the night loving.

He knocked again, then spoke to Bugsy as she lay there, and the sound of his voice made the tears start streaming all over. After a time, she heard him again, first on the step, then moving away on the back walk. She lay there a long while, waiting, the words to a dumb old country-western song running through her head: *I have tears in my ears from lying on my back in bed, crying over you.*

He didn't come back, and eventually she got up and let Bugsy inside.

There was something going on.

Samantha wasn't sure what, but she intended to find out. She loved mysteries, and being a big fan of Harriet the Spy, she knew just how to go about solving them.

So, first thing Monday morning, when she wasn't so fuzzy-brained from the plane ride, she got a notebook from Aunt Randi, who was always good for things like really nice notebooks with stiff covers and graph-paper pages. Of course, if she'd been a truly great detective, she'd have remembered a notebook of her own, but hers didn't have graph paper, so this was better, anyway. Aunt Randi also had great pencils. They were made by some Indian tribe, and they came in a wooden box made like a little crate. They smelled of cedar and wrote really well. Sam got a couple of those, too.

Back in her room, she sharpened her pencils and curled up in the rocker to list out what she knew on the first page of her notebook: One, Dad was distracted and kept going off to try to make phone calls that never got answered. Two, Gran and Aunt Randi whispered to each other a lot and stopped talking whenever she came in the room. Three, Dad had gone off alone after she went to bed. Four, he didn't come back very soon, and Five, Aunt Randi kept staring out the windows toward the carriage house. Weird.

Sam contemplated the list with a critical eye. It didn't look like much, but in a house where nothing very exciting *ever* happened, it was a lot.

Sam smiled. Yep. There was definitely something going on. And she was the perfect person to find out what.

"He didn't look very happy this morning," said Tish to Miranda over coffee. "And, perversely, that makes me hopeful."

"There's obviously some strain between them."

"When she didn't come out yesterday, I thought it was embarrassment over me walking in on them, but then it turned out she was gone altogether and, frankly, I was relieved. It would have been too awkward with Sam here. She's much too young to see her father behaving like he has during the past week. And speaking of Samantha, is she planning to go into town with you?"

"Of course. She insisted on her first-day lunch with Daddy, even though Mason hadn't scheduled her in. She's picking out clothes as we speak." Miranda took a sip of coffee and set the cup down. "Did you see how tight-lipped Mason got when Raine wouldn't answer the phone yesterday?"

Tish nodded. "He looked even grimmer when he got home last night. I got the impression she refused to see him."

"It must have been a hell of a fight."

"I hope so," said Tish. "A real humdinger, as Angus would put it. A clean break would be so much tidier than a peaceful parting of ways, and that's what we might end up with from simply reversing the spell. That could easily leave some residual affections to cloud the waters. We don't want that."

"I suppose," said Miranda.

"We'll still reverse the spell next week, of course, even if they have broken up," Tish went on. "We are going to leave nothing to chance. In fact, if I could arrange it, Mason would never even think about Raine Hobart again once this is over."

"I wouldn't want to go that far."

"Miranda, I'm surprised at you. Are you somehow in sympathy with this relationship?"

"No, well, I don't know." She sighed. "She's very nice, you know, and a lot more pleasant to be around than Caroline."

"Yes, she is. But she is also poor, and while that doesn't make her less human, it does make her less than suitable for Mason under current circumstances." Tish poured herself another glass of orange juice. "It's a shame that we can't combine the best features of both: Miss Hobart's personality and Caroline's financial statement."

"You should have seen Mason and Raine dancing Saturday. There was something so different about him. It would be terribly sad for him not to remember he was ever in love with Raine."

Tish patted her hand. "Oh, darling, of course it would, if he never loved anyone else. But by the time we're done with him, he'll be as much in love with Caroline as he is with Miss Hobart. And he'll have the money we need, too. You'll see, he'll be ecstatic."

"But he's ecstatic now. Or at least he was until yesterday."

"But that's changed, and I suspect the reason is that this relationship was never meant to be in the first place. Those two have separate paths to walk, darling. We will do everything we can to ensure they walk them."

"Daddy?"

"Hmm, squirt?"

"Did I hear you go out last night after I was in bed?"

"Yes."

"Where did you go?"

Mason glanced over at his daughter, who had come to have lunch with him, an annual "first summer day with Dad" tradition. As a further part of the tradition, she had stayed to commandeer his big ebony desk for a few hours of "work." It was the first time he'd trusted her unsupervised at the desk, and she was busy sending e-mails and snooping through his drawers while he went over sales reports on the couch. Just now, Samantha had one index finger pointed at the reminder line on his appointment book.

"I'm the parent here," he said. "I'm supposed to ask *you* that kind of question."

"I know. I just thought maybe you went to see Caroline, but your calendar says that she's in Singapore."

"She's doing some business in the Far East," said Mason. "I guess this *is* the day she goes to Singapore." Strangely, he'd lost track of Caro's itinerary. He supposed he'd better try to touch bases with her at Raffles Hotel a little later, when it would be tomorrow morning there.

"Are you still seeing her?"

"Not while she's out of town."

"Da-a-addy. She travels a lot, doesn't she?"

"Quite a bit."

"As much as Mom?"

"Fewer trips, but usually longer ones."

"Mom's going to spend a whole month in Europe this time. That's pretty long. Who's J. Kraut—"

"Kreutzmiller. He's the corporate attorney. You met him last year, remember?"

She considered. "The man with the silver hair and the growly voice?"

"That's him."

"What are you going to see him about at four o'clock?"

"Some trouble we've been having on our new building at Canal Place. Are we playing Twenty Questions?"

"Of course not. If we were doing that, you'd have to answer yes or no." She flipped some more pages. "Who's R. Hobart?"

"A friend."

"A girlfriend?"

"Samantha. I'm trying to work."

"Well, this name's on practically every day last week. That looks pretty girlfriendy."

Mason flipped the report shut and threw it down on the table in front of him in surrender.

"All right. *R* stands for Raine, and yes, we've been seeing each other. She's a struggling artist who graduated from a very good school, and she's twenty-four years old with blonde hair and blue-green eyes. Anything else you'd like to know, Miss Investigator?"

"Twenty-four is pretty young for you."

"I know, but we thousand-year-old men like to run around with the young cuties every now and again."

Sam giggled, then sobered up. "Does that mean you aren't seeing Caroline anymore?"

"No, it doesn't. As I said, Caroline is out of town."

"Are you going to date both of them?"

"Samantha, this isn't appropriate conversation for us to be having."

"I'm just curious." She spun Mason's leather chair around twice. "When do I get to meet R. Hobart?"

"I'm not sure you do, squirt. She's mad at me right now."

"Then you should go see her and say you're sorry."

"It's a little more complicated than that."

"Tish says it's hardly ever more complicated."

"Please don't call your grandmother 'Tish.' It's disrespectful."

"But she told me to this morning at breakfast. And I think it would be more disrespectful not to mind her, since it's *her* name," she said with perfect eleven-year-old logic, then tossed her black ponytail to dismiss the subject.

"Sam," Mason warned.

"Hey, I forgot to e-mail Daria." She turned back to the computer, already on to other concerns.

Despite Sam's impertinence, her advice hung on his mind, and after Miranda came by to pick Sam up at half past three, Mason buzzed his assistant. "Cancel the rest of my appointments and put me through to Johnson's Landscaping."

"Are you sure, sir? I believe Mr. Kreutzmiller has the information you wanted regarding that citizens group in Fremont."

"FUSE." Mason turned it over in his mind. "That will hold. Reschedule him for later in the week."

"Yes, sir. I'll have Johnson's for you in just a moment."

Raine was steering a riding mower across a half acre of lawn when she spotted Mason's car pulling up at the curb. Fortunately, she'd already done the end of the lawn closest to the street and was working her way toward the house. She continued moving away, watching out of the corner of her eye as Paul got out and opened the rear door.

So, the scumbag was here to sweet-talk his way out of things. She resented him showing up at her job, trying to trap her like this. On the other hand, she felt fairly safe on the mower. The roar of the engine would keep her from hearing Mason if he called out, and she could just pretend she didn't see him. However, when he stepped out and the sun hit that trademark gray suit, the nice straight line she'd been tracking took a distinct bobble in the middle. She finished the row and made a tight turn to go back the other direction. That was better; she couldn't even see him.

But while she wasn't watching, he made an end run straight to Craig, who, not knowing any better, came over to flag Raine down. She pretended not to see him, too, until he walked right in front of the mower and her only choices were to acknowledge him or run him down. She knew what her choice would have been if Mason had tried that technique, but it was Craig, so, reluctantly, she shut the engine down.

"Your boyfriend wants to talk to you," said Craig.

"I don't have time. I still have to make the second pass. You know how Mr. Tiedeman likes his cross-hatching."

"Ooh." Craig flinched as though he were the one taking the hit. "Like that, is it?"

"Pretty much, yeah."

"Should I tell him you'll be putting in overtime?"

"Sure, as long as I don't really have to."

"Damn. Didn't fall for it."

"Thanks, boss."

She fired the tractor back up and finished the first pass on the yard, taking a minute to correct the bobble. By the time she checked the street, Mason was gone.

Craig avoided mentioning her problems on the ride back to Johnson's, and Raine didn't ask how Mason had taken being blown off. She was tense as they pulled into the yard, half expecting to see the Rolls sitting there, Mason ready to pounce, but only work trucks and the crew's personal vehicles filled the back lot.

Good. He'd gotten the message.

She drove home quickly, anxious to get her life back into its familiar groove. She'd have a shower, play with Bugsy a little, water the plants. Maybe she'd ask Zoe to go out for dinner. She could stand a little Greek food at Costas Opa, and they could splurge on a bottle of Roditis to forget the past week.

Just to be sure, she checked the streets around her house before she parked. There was no sign of the Rolls nor of any other Alexander car, so she pulled into her usual spot in front of the house and grabbed her gear. The mailbox was empty, drat. She trotted up the stair and through the gate.

And almost turned around.

He was sitting there, on her front step, with Bugsy swirling around his legs and leaving multicolored streamers of hair hanging off his gray linen pants.

"Just go away," she said.

"No."

"Oh, damn it, Mason. What's the matter, didn't you get enough for your money?"

He stood up and brushed at his pants. Clouds of cat hair whirled in the air and settled back on his shoes. "Do you really want to discuss this in the garden for all your neighbors to hear?"

"I don't want to discuss it at all." She stepped around him. "Buzz off."

He tried to hold the screen open for her while she unlocked the door, but she jerked it out of his hand. She tried to slam the door on him, but he stuck his foot in and followed her into the house anyway, uninvited.

"You must think I'm pretty low," he said.

"You've got it." She tossed her backpack on the kitchen counter and dropped her water bottle in the sink.

He leaned on the end of the counter, watching her rinse the bottle. "And it must be embarrassing for you, being such a sap to fall for the flimsy trick I played on you Saturday night."

"That's an understatement."

"Well, if it makes you feel better, I had to work pretty hard setting that up. Getting Miranda to have her friends cut in. Arranging all that stuff with Elizabeth to make some excuse to send Samantha out early and call at just the right time so my mother would walk in and see us. But the really hard part was getting you horny enough that you'd be sure to come downstairs half dressed so I could fuck you."

She slapped him. "You son of a bitch."

His eyes narrowed and his jaw went solid beneath the white imprint of her hand on his skin. "You don't like that word, do you? Good, because it has nothing to do with what happened between us."

"Gee, it sure felt like the right word."

"And for that, I'm sorry. I screwed up, and I'm sorry, and I don't know what else to say. I used very bad judgment—hell, I used no judgment at all—but I swear to you, what happened was *not* planned as some sick show for my mother."

"Then how do you know that's what I think it was?"

"Because, being the single-minded bastard that I usually am, I thought of it, too, after the fact, and when I did, I realized how bad it looked."

"Yeah, right, especially since *before the fact,* you had mentioned you wanted to turn the heat up on your mom and Miranda. Boy, I guess you managed that.''

''I wanted to turn up the heat, not scorch their eyeballs,'' said Mason. ''Having them think we were sleeping together would have been enough; they didn't need a demonstration. And if I *had* wanted them to catch us in bed together, all we had to do was fake the afterglow. Hell, you could have even left your clothes on. It would have been a damned sight easier to put together than that unfortunate set of coincidences Sunday morning.''

''Oh, yeah, and it was just coincidence that you left the doors open.''

''Were *you* thinking about doors?''

Her cheeks flamed. She turned away and started unloading her pack.

''Being a single-minded bastard,'' he continued, ''there was exactly one thing on my mind at the time.''

''Getting me to bed.''

''Absolutely. But sure as hell not because of my mother and sister.''

''Then why?''

''The same reason you came downstairs in the first place. Because I wanted you. Because we wanted each other.''

''All I wanted was to dance with you. I just wanted to finish that one dance.''

''So what happened?''

''You know what happened.''

''I'd like your take on it.''

''You seduced me.'' She grabbed the ice pack out of her lunch kit and tossed it in the freezer.

''I could make a case that you seduced me. That dress. The zipper. No panties. And after all, you came to my room.''

''To dance. That's all.''

He came around and trapped her in the corner between the counter and the fridge. ''I told myself the same thing, Raine, that I just wanted to finish the dance, that it would just be a few minutes of holding you, a harmless thrill. And then I had my arms around you and all bets were off.''

''And I'm supposed to believe all this?''

''No, but you're supposed to believe this.''

He slipped his hand behind her head and pulled her to him.

"Mason." She started to add "Don't," but it never came out.

His kiss was firm, but tender, as sweet as it had been in front of his mother Saturday night. It burned just as hot, too, ripping through the past two days of anger and hurt like fire through a haystack.

She didn't want a clean burn, she wanted to stay mad at him, so it would never happen again. She put up her hand to fend him off and felt the pounding of his heart under her palm, and remembered how his skin felt against hers. Her groan parted her lips, and he kissed her more deeply, his tongue sweeping into her mouth.

Her fingers curled into the front of his shirt, turning the push she had planned into a tug that drew him closer, and she raised on her toes to better return his probing kiss. His hand dropped away from her head just as she laced her fingers together behind his neck, but his lips demanded more.

He gave more, as well, leaving her mouth to sear kisses over her face and down her throat to find the place where the pulse beat in her throat. His tongue swirled over the spot, and she threw her head back and arched into him.

"See?" he said against her throat.

It was then she realized his hands weren't on her and hadn't been on her for a few minutes. She was backed against the cabinets, but his arms, to either side of her, shook with tension, and when she looked down at his hands, he was gripping the counter's edge with fingers bleached white from pressure.

She met his eyes, a question frozen on her lips.

"If I touch you right now, it will be just like Saturday night," he said carefully. "Except it will be here instead of in a bed, and we'll never get all of our clothes off. And you know it."

The center of her throbbed. It was exactly what she wanted and precisely what she didn't need. Making herself small, she covered her burning cheeks with her hands and tucked her elbows in close to her body so she didn't touch him by accident and set off a chain reaction neither one of them would be able to stop. She could feel the effort as he pulled himself together, and, after a moment, he stepped back.

The old pine flooring squeaked as he walked into the living room. His back to her, he adjusted his tie. "Again, I apologize. I don't know what comes over me."

" 'It's like you're under a spell,' " murmured Raine.

He shot a look over his shoulder. "What?"

"Something a girlfriend said about times when things get out of control, that it's like you're under a spell."

"Come on, Raine. You can't possibly think—"

"I don't know."

"Well, I do, and there are no such things, which is what we're in the midst of proving to my mother and sister. You'd better get showered and changed."

Raine's jaw dropped. "You expect me to go over there and face her?"

"You would if we really *were* under a spell."

"But—" What could she say to that argument?

"I can safely promise you that my mother will not say one word to indicate she ever saw a thing."

"But *I* know she did. Geez, Mason, what do you want from me?"

"The rest of our—The time we agreed on." He paused and cleared his throat. "I did some research. It seems that the witchy ilk consider the waning moon to be the best time for reversing spells. There's a new moon the first part of next week, so assuming Mother and Miranda are following the rules, they'll try something within the next few days. And they'll fail and have to come to me with a confession. Just a few more days, Raine. Please."

A few more days so he could trot back to Caroline with no worries. Raine suddenly realized there was a lump the size of a bowling ball sitting in the middle of her chest, right under her breastbone, and that it had been there for days.

But she wasn't about to tell Mason about it, and she wasn't about to tell him she couldn't continue with the charade, because if she did either one, she'd have to admit she'd fallen in love with him, and right now she couldn't imagine doing that. It would just be too mortifying. She tried a diversion.

"You don't want your daughter exposed to all this."

"She already knows about you—that we're dating, I mean."

"Knowing about it and seeing it are two different things. Kids don't like to see their parents drag in new people all the time."

"Three women in the past four years hardly amounts to all the time, and, besides, she's the one who asked if she'd get to meet you. Will you finish what we started?"

She'd love to—but that wasn't what he meant. This was so stupid. She'd just get hurt more.

But only for a few more days, and it would be a few more days with Mason. She would have all the hot, lonely nights after that to get over him and to kick herself for doing this.

"I guess so."

He nodded. "Good. Thank you, Raine. You won't regret it."

"I already do. What do I wear this time?"

"Sam and I often take a ride around the Highlands before dinner. We have a couple of extra bikes around. One should work for you."

"Shorts, then?"

"Fine. And a dress or something for dinner, of course. Speaking of which, the clothes you left behind are in the car. I'll walk over to where I left Paul and wait out of temptation's way. I can bring them back in, say, twenty minutes."

"All right," she said. And although the logical part of her brain was grateful for his restraint, there was one little piece of her that wished he'd strip down and shower with her. She was going to have to get that part under control.

'Cause it just wasn't going to happen.

Not noway, not nohow.

Fifteen

"Didn't we pass that tree ten minutes ago?" muttered Raine under her breath as she pedaled a mountain bike through what passed as Mason's neighborhood—not that you could see any neighbors.

The Highlands set was private in the extreme. Raine couldn't spot so much as a chimney top from the road, and although most of the driveways had gates or pillars to mark them, some blended so well into the native woods that they barely made a gap between the cedars and rhododendrons. And God forbid anyone should post an actual address. Privacy she understood, but this was ridiculous.

The guys on the landscape crew had told her that once, a few years back, a house in the Highlands had burned down because the fire fighters had gotten lost on the unmarked roads inside the gates. She could see how it could have happened. She'd had problems finding houses for landscape work. Even on a bicycle in the clear light of a summer evening, she had no idea where she was—on a rainy night, from a fire truck, it would be impossible.

She finally spotted a familiar-looking native stone pillar. "Now I know I've seen that before."

Samantha cruised up beside her on her bike. "Maybe. There are a couple sort of like that. Most of these roads hook together. I think we're going in a big circle."

"In other words, you don't know where we are, either."

"Not really. I know some of the roads, but I'm never at Gran's long enough to really figure them all out."

"Gran's? Wasn't—isn't this your house, too?"

"No. We had a condo by Lake Washington. Daddy moved back in here a while after he and Mom got divorced. I'm kind of glad. It's more fun than the condo."

Mason, who had been straining at the leash almost since they left the house, hit his brakes and let himself fall back beside them. "Are you two lazy or just out of shape?"

"Oh, my. He's taunting us," said Raine to Sam, without otherwise acknowledging Mason's presence. "Whatever shall we do?"

"Cream him!" Sam shouted. She hunkered down into racing position. "Ready-set-go!"

Mason shot off, and Sam straightened up and started laughing hysterically. Mason circled around to rejoin them. "That was the worst cheating I've ever seen. Don't you know you're supposed to win if you cheat?"

"Oh, great," said Raine. "You're telling your daughter to cheat."

"No. But if she's going to bother, she ought to do it right." He grinned at Sam, who stuck her tongue out at him. "Come on, squirt. I'll give you a five-second lead."

"I don't want to race, Daddy. Raine and I are talking."

"Uh-oh. I think I've just been told to take a hike." He grinned. "Tell you what, I want to work up a sweat, so while you two chat, I'm going to do some wind sprints. I'll ride ahead a little, then come back. Stay on this road so I don't lose you, okay?"

"Okay," said Raine. Wherever "this road" was.

He raced off up the road, pumping hard. Raine couldn't keep her eyes off his buns. She knew firsthand that they didn't just look rock hard.

"Where do you live?" asked Samantha, interrupting her thoughts at a fortunate moment.

"The world's smallest house." Raine described her place, then found herself answering more questions, about her work, her family, her education, even her art, which Mason had apparently mentioned to Sam. It was Miranda the Inquisitioner all over again, which wasn't surprising considering how much they looked alike, with their slim, straight lines and bony elbows. But at least Sam didn't leave the impression she was searching for an exploitable weakness. That made answering her much more pleasant than facing off with Miranda.

As they talked, Mason sprinted ahead and back several times, staying just close enough to make certain they didn't get lost. Then they got onto a long sweep of road and he took off and disappeared around a curve.

"I think I know where we are," said Sam. "See. There's the McMullens' drive. Our house is over there on the other road." She pointed off toward the right.

Raine dropped the pitch of her voice and put on a bad movie-gangster accent. "Sose, if we blow off your old man, can you get us back to duh joint?"

Samantha giggled and tried to do the same accent, but it just wasn't in the blood. "I think so."

"Den lets us looze duh dude."

They whipped around the next hairpin right while Mason was still out of sight. As they barreled down the slight hill, Raine started to recognize the territory. They were on Olympic Drive, and the house was just ahead on the left. Pedaling hard and laughing harder, they zipped through the gate and down the drive.

They braked to a stop in front of the lions that guarded the entry and leaned their bikes against the beasts' front claws.

"I'm dying of thirst," said Sam. "Let's go around to the terrace."

"I think maybe we'd better wait for your father, in case we need to go on a rescue mission. He may wander around forever looking for us, like the *Flying Dutchman*."

"The who?"

"The *Flying Dutchman*. It's a ghost ship that wanders the seas looking for its crew."

"Wow. Do you believe in ghosts?"

"I believe in the possibility," Raine said carefully. This was Mason's daughter, after all. "I've never seen one myself, though."

"Daddy says there are no such things as ghosts and witches and stuff. That's why he gets so upset at Gran and Aunt Randi sometimes. Oops." Her eyes widened and she smacked her hand over her mouth. "He doesn't like me to talk about it. It's kind of a family secret."

"It's okay. I already know they're witches, although I'm still not clear why your dad thinks that's so terrible."

"Me, either," said Sam, starting toward the door. "I'll go get us something to drink from the cook."

From the cook, thought Raine. That pretty well summarized the difference between Sam's childhood and her own.

Mason finally showed up about fifteen minutes later. By then, Sam had liberated three bottles of mineral water from the kitchen, and she and Raine were putting on a show of extravagant boredom on the front steps.

"Some people are so slow," said Sam to the sky.

"That's twice you've jerked me around in one ride," said Mason. He leaned his bike against the side of one of the lions, then came to sit by Raine. Sam passed him a bottle of water.

"I rode all the way around the loop looking for you two before I figured out I'd been jettisoned." He took a long draw at the bottle, then wiped his mouth on the back of his hand. "I think one of you is a bad influence on the other, but I can't figure out which one is which."

"That's because neither one of us is as bad as you, Daddy, so it's hard for you to compare good to good."

He reached across Raine to aim a playful swat at Samantha.

He had worked up the sweat he'd wanted, and as he leaned over Raine, his natural aroma was pleasantly sharp and male. One whiff carried her right back to the last place she had been so close to him: in his room, in his bed.

Abruptly, her body went into full recall. Every inch of her was suddenly flushed and ready for sex.

The banter between Mason and his daughter was lost as Raine struggled to rid herself of the sensations, a task that would have been easier if he weren't right there. It wasn't until he stood up and suggested they change for dinner that she was able to shake them off and bring herself fully back to the present. Even so, her skin felt hot and sensitive.

Her second shower in slightly over an hour fixed that. She tweaked the water spigot to cooler and cooler until she was on the verge of hypothermia, then hurriedly dried off and pulled on the aquamarine linen suit that was the sharpest of the outfits she'd picked out on Mason's tab. She figured she might as well give the man his money's worth.

That was good. Thinking about the money gave her the right

perspective. Between that and the cold shower, she regained a bit of self-control. She did a quick job of her makeup, added some lipstick, and headed downstairs.

Mason was waiting in the foyer, and when she appeared, he nodded in approval.

"You look very cool and fresh." He reached for her hand, frowning when he touched her fingers. "And it's not just a fashion statement. You're freezing. Are you all right?"

"I was warm from the ride," she said. "I just took a cool shower."

He curled his fingers more tightly around hers. "I've been doing that a lot recently, too. Smile. We're on."

•

This was not good.

Tish sipped at her glass of white wine and watched her son pull out a chair for his girlfriend. It was the first time she'd permitted herself to think of Raine Hobart by that term, but something in her had finally admitted it was accurate, at least for the time being.

The fight, or whatever it had been, apparently hadn't lasted. They were back on speaking terms. For that matter, they were back on courting terms. And in front of Samantha, too.

Not that they weren't being more circumspect than usual, but really, they did not need one more witness to potentially carry the story back to Caroline, especially not a witness as naively talkative as Samantha.

However, short of sending the child to bed without her supper, there wasn't much to be done to remove her from the scene. Tish concluded she'd have to have a talk with Sam later and explain things.

Samantha was chattering a mile a minute, and as she talked, she poked at something that Raine had laid out on the table.

"Gran," called Samantha. "Can you do this?"

Tish strolled over to the table, where there lay twelve paper matches arranged in a grid of four equal squares.

Tish exclaimed in delight. "A brain teaser. I used to love this sort of thing as a child. What are we supposed to do?"

Raine looked up. "Turn these four squares into three squares. But you can only move three matches to do it."

"That doesn't look too difficult."

Tish stared at the pattern, mentally shifting matchsticks. It took her a few moments, but then she saw it.

"Here. One, two, three." She made the three squares.

"Ooh," said Raine. "How about this one?"

She tore another four matches out of the pack, for sixteen, then arranged them in five squares in a sort of jagged vertical line, so that two squares were next to each other.

"Now, move just two matches to get four squares of equal size."

Staring didn't work this time; Tish started pushing them around on the table.

"By the Powers, I don't see a solution at all. Miranda, Mason come help us."

With the two of them joining the group, the Alexander competitive streak kicked in. Pretty soon, the whole family was poking at the matchsticks as though solving the silly puzzle would reveal the mysteries of the universe. And of course, they squabbled good-naturedly over the rights to try, too, just as they had when Miranda and Mason were young and would come home with these sorts of challenges for each other. Tish loved it.

She even enjoyed the way Raine watched the whole thing with a look of bemusement for a good fifteen minutes before she said, "Gee, you people are stubborn, aren't you?"

"Mason is," said Miranda. "I just act that way in self-defense."

"Okay, we give up," announced Sam. She waved off her father and aunt, who were still fussing, and set the matches back in their original form. "I don't think you can do it, either, Raine."

"I'm entertaining wagers," said Raine.

"I'll bet you—"

Mason clamped his hand down on his daughter's shoulder. When she looked up, he shook his head. "Sucker bet, squirt. She knows she can solve it or she wouldn't have started this in the first place."

"Geez. How's a girl supposed to earn her pocket change with you around enlightening the marks?" Grinning, Raine held her hand over the figure. "Okay. Watch. One, two."

Where there had been five squares, there were now four.

"Wow. Show me again," said Sam. Raine put everything back and did it again.

"Very clever, Miss Hobart," said Tish. "Did you come up with that yourself?"

"No, but thanks for the faith in my intelligence. Mason was on the right track when he warned Samantha. This is an old bar bet. A lot of this stuff went around Claremont while I was there."

"Do some more," said Samantha.

"I only have a few," Raine said. "Swim team limited the amount of time I could spend, ahem, broadening my education. However, if your dad has ten pennies in those pockets of his, I can do one."

He didn't, Tish knew. Mason seldom carried very much cash and never let change accumulate. However, at Miranda's suggestion, Raine substituted candies out of the bowl that had been set out for Samantha's benefit. She soon had them involved in another puzzle—planting ten trees in five rows of four each.

Tish remembered this one from her own school days, so she stood back and let the others have the fun, taking advantage of the break to cross to the service cart to refill her glass.

Miranda noticed and came to join her, and together they watched.

"Raine really is quite good with Sam," Miranda observed quietly. "Much more at ease than Caro was at Easter."

"She would make an excellent nanny, I'm sure."

"Probably. But I wouldn't be surprised if Mason's thinking more along the lines of stepmother."

Tish turned to frown at her daughter. "Are you trying to upset me, darling?"

"No. But look at him."

Mason was leaning over the table, working on the puzzle.

Tish raised an eyebrow. "So?"

"Put your glasses on," said Miranda.

Tish retrieved the glasses from where they hung on a chain around her neck and slipped them on. It didn't take long to spot it once she saw Mason's face clearly: he was watching Raine and Samantha with a look of utter, absorbed fascination, the way men often look at the mothers of their children.

Or the potential mothers.

"Oh, my," said Tish. "This is not good. This is not good at all."

It got even worse as the evening progressed.

First, there was dinner. Not only did both Samantha and Mason fawn over Miss Hobart all throughout, but afterward, when the topic of the next evening's activities came up, Mason agreed he and Sam would join her at some sort of neighborhood baseball game.

Inappropriate, thought Tish. Totally inappropriate.

And then there was the discussion that occurred while tucking Samantha into bed. She was too old to be tucked in, according to her, but it was one of the perquisites of having her in the house, and both Mason and Tish had agreed they would take turns until she raised such a fuss they had to give it up.

However, she almost wished she'd skipped tonight when Sam started raving about Miss Hobart.

She was pretty. She was fun. She rode bikes really well. She knew all those funny puzzles. She made Daddy laugh and could play pretty good tricks on him, too.

And the crowning blow: "Do you think Daddy's going to marry her?"

"Oh, my, I hope not," said Tish.

Sam's eyebrows went up. "Don't you like her?"

The question caught Tish off guard. She had been so preoccupied with how Mason felt about Miss Hobart that she hadn't considered her own feelings.

Actually, she did rather like the girl. While unpolished and apt to shock every now and again, she was usually pleasant to have around. And as Miranda had pointed out, she did bring out a softer side of Mason that was very nice to see again after so many years. But that wasn't what she wanted to tell Samantha.

"I haven't known her long enough to like her or dislike her, and neither has your father." Tish folded back the bedspread and smoothed it across the foot of the bed. "To be honest, Samantha, I think he'd be better off marrying Caroline. They have much more in common. Miss Hobart is young and pretty and your father enjoys spending time with her right now, but I don't think she's really right for him. Samantha, you do know that you should never discuss one of your father's girlfriends with another."

"Why not?" Sam hopped up on the bed.

"Well, think about it, darling. If you were Miss Hobart, would you want to hear about what your father did with Caroline?"

"No."

"And if you were Caroline and went off on a trip, would you

be happy if you found out your boyfriend had been seeing someone else while you were gone, even if it wasn't serious?''

''Probably not,'' said Sam, frowning. ''But won't Daddy tell her anyway? I mean, he shouldn't lie about something like that.''

Tish pulled up the blankets and tucked them around Samantha. ''I'm sure your father will discuss whatever he needs to with each of them, but it's not your business to bring it up. You can be discreet, can't you? That means keeping private matters private.''

''I'll try.'' She turned her pillow over a couple of times until she got it the way she wanted it, then flopped down. ''But, Gran?''

''Yes, darling?''

''I don't like Caroline as much as I do Raine.''

''She's not as comfortable with children as Miss Hobart is,'' admitted Tish. ''But that will improve as she gets used to you. And she is *much* better for your father and will make him happier in the long run, which is what is important for us to keep in mind. Now, good night, darling. I'll see you in the morning.''

''Good night, Gran. I love you.''

Tish bent and kissed her cool forehead. ''I love you, too, my darling.''

Which was why she was going to have a talk with Mason as soon as she got him alone.

The interior of the Jaguar crackled with electricity on the way back to Raine's house that night, and it had nothing to do with quirky British automotive wiring.

Mason knew most of the charge was rippling off him. He wanted Raine, there was no way around it. Despite all his resolutions, his promises, his good intentions, he wanted her.

It was pure physical desire, made more intense by the knowledge of what it was like to be buried in her sweet warmth. He wanted that again, over and over.

Not just sex. Sex with *Raine*.

What's more, he was relatively certain he could have it. With just a little effort and sweet talk on his part, he could have her back in his bed. He could experience the delight of pinning her beneath him, of taking her, and of taking her over the edge.

The problem was, when he was done, she'd hate him, which was more than adequate reason for him to keep his pants zipped and his hands to himself. He didn't want her to hate him.

So he concentrated on the road and drove her home like a gentleman, and, like a gentleman, he carried the bag with her biking clothes and walked her to her door.

"See, that wasn't so bad." Was he talking to her or to himself? He wasn't certain.

"No," she said softly. "Samantha is a super kid. I had a good time tonight."

"I think that's the first time you've said that since we started seeing each other."

"Is it?" She thought a moment. "No. I clearly remember telling you that I'd had a wonderful time the night of the Wilmott Foundation dance."

"You're right, you did. But I assumed that it had been canceled out by what happened afterward."

Raine turned away and stuck the key in the lock. A turn and a slight push opened it, sending a puff of warm air swirling past them. "It's not that it was bad, you know. In fact, it was pretty . . . breathtaking."

"Breathtaking," repeated Mason. He liked the sound of that.

"Mm-mmm." She nodded slowly, then looked up and met his eyes. "And breathtakingly wrong. For both of us."

There was no argument to be made on that point, so Mason just stood there with her bag, wishing he hadn't been the one to put that pinched look at the corners of her eyes.

"The game is at six tomorrow," she said. "We have to start early because of the kids."

"Samantha and I will be here by five-thirty."

She nodded. "Okay. Good night."

"Good night." And then he had to make the choice: kiss her as usual, or play it safe and just go home.

He'd never been one to play it safe.

He bent his head, and barely touched his lips to Raine's. She didn't bolt inside, so he tried again, lingering a bit longer this time to savor the sparks that jumped the gap between their bodies.

When he reminded himself to pull away, the corners of her eyes had miraculously softened and the ghost of a smile curved her lips.

"You're right," she said, her voice soft surrender. "It's not so bad."

She took the bag out of his hand and stepped inside. The door closed quietly in his face.

Mason walked back to the car a satisfied man. Sexually frustrated, but satisfied, nonetheless.

That satisfaction quickly evaporated when he got home and found his mother installed in the living room with her petit point. She had that look, the one he equated with being scolded when he was eight, and with receiving the "I'm so disappointed in you" speech in college.

He crossed straight through to the library and the wet bar, where he girded himself with a glass of scotch, reminded himself that he was under the influence of a love potion, then came back and plopped down on the couch directly across from her.

"What?" he asked.

Tish pushed the needle into the canvas and pulled the silk thread through with a thin, zipping sound. "I didn't say anything."

"Don't play coy, Mother. You're about to burst. What is it?"

"You exaggerate," said Tish. She took another tiny stitch. "I was just thinking about this evening. Samantha was quite taken with Miss Hobart."

Just as he'd thought. "Good. It was mutual. Raine likes her very much."

"And you're pleased about that?"

"Of course." He took a sip of the scotch.

"Do you really plan to take Samantha to that baseball game tomorrow night?"

"It's softball, and I do."

"Do you think it's wise?"

"To play softball? Well, Mother, I know it's not polo or archery, but I'll bet Sam will survive the experience."

"You are being deliberately obtuse." Tish stabbed the needle into the canvas and tossed the piece aside. "I'm not talking about the game. I'm talking about continuing to expose your daughter to this temporary infatuation of yours."

Mason stared at her. "Temporary?"

"It's not fair to let her start building a relationship on such a flimsy foundation. She's had too many people come and go in her life."

"Not because of *my* choices."

"I realize perfectly well it's Elizabeth who's done that to her, dragging all those men in and out of the house, but that's precisely my point. You have always been the stable one, and Samantha counts on you for that. And now for you to introduce Miss Hobart into her life when you know very well she will be gone as soon as Caroline gets back. . ."

"She will?"

"Of course she will. Mason, you haven't any choice. Our financial situation has only gotten worse in the past week, what with the Everett line going down. You've told me yourself that Wickersham money is our last, best hope at turning Alexander Industries around. You've been working toward marriage to Caroline for months. You cannot just toss all that away over a fling."

"You're right, of course, Mother. Not over a fling."

"Thank goodness," she said.

She wasn't paying attention to him at all, Mason decided.

"You must see how unfair it would be to let Samantha start thinking of Miss Hobart as a potential parent when it's just not going to happen."

"You seem very sure of that. Don't be."

She blinked twice, startled. "Mason . . ."

"First, with all respect, I'm the one who decides to whom my daughter is exposed, not you. Raine is quite probably the best example of a *rational* woman my daughter has met in the past several years. Second, her name *is* Raine, and it's time you started calling her that, because, third, it's not a fling, it's very serious."

"You only think so because—" She stopped herself.

"Because what?" Mason held his breath for the impending confession.

"Because your hormones are involved. You've confused sex with love."

Mason snorted, partly in amusement, partly in disappointment. "I stopped making that mistake years ago, Mother. Elizabeth trained it right out of me."

He set his glass aside. The heavy crystal clunked against the solid mahogany of the side table. "I assure you, the only confusion I have right now concerns how quickly it's possible to plan a wedding."

"A wedding. By all the Powers, Mason, you've only known her a week!"

"Ten days." He went in for the kill. "But it doesn't matter.

I knew from the minute I saw Raine that I wanted her in my life forever.''

''Oh, good Goddess.'' Tish jumped up as though he'd poured hot coffee in her lap. ''Mason, darling, please tell me you haven't asked her yet.''

''Not yet. But I plan—''

''Don't. Please. Just hold off a few days. Give yourself some time to think it through.''

More likely for her and Miranda to work their counterspell. ''I have thought it through.''

''Then hold off for my sake. Promise me. Just sit on it, and if you're still intent on this by next week, I will personally plan the wedding. One week.''

He looked at her, wondering if he and Raine could actually survive another entire week of this.

He nodded. ''Okay, Mother. One week. But I warn you, that will give you that much less time to plan the wedding, because I'll wait to ask her, but I'm not going to wait to marry her.''

''Thank you, darling.'' She practically ran out the door, her heels clicking across the oak floor in the foyer as she headed for the scrolled staircase. ''Good night.''

There was a half finger of scotch left in the glass, and as soon as Tish was safely upstairs, Mason lifted the glass in a toast.

''To family, in all their glorious weirdness.'' He tossed back that last swallow and got up to check doors and set the alarm system.

It had been a good evening. Raine had forgiven him and, if he wasn't mistaken, Mother and Miranda were making plans this very minute to reverse the spell.

Just let them try.

Miranda stood at her bedroom window, staring out toward the carriage house, trying to think of some excuse to go out there. She'd been trying for two days.

The lights were on in Paul's quarters, so she knew he was in, probably working on his dissertation. Maybe she could find a book in the library to take out there under the pretense of offering it for his use.

Maybe. If she knew what his topic was. Unfortunately, she didn't, and if there was any better indication of how self-centered she'd been the past six years, she wasn't sure what it could be.

"Give it up, Miranda," she said aloud. "You blew it long before Toddy jumped in the car."

A staccato knock rattled the door and Tish sailed in before she had time to answer.

"Tish!"

"I'm sorry, darling, but this is an emergency." She pushed the door shut and flipped the lock. "We've got to reverse the potion."

"I know, but—"

"No, I mean tonight. We have to do the counterspell tonight. He just told me he intends to marry her."

"Oh." Miranda collapsed on the end of her bed, her head suddenly pounding. "When?"

"Right away. I got him to promise to wait a week before he asked her, but I don't trust him under the influence of that potion. It seems to be affecting him much more powerfully than I would have expected."

"The Book said the spell was unpredictable and powerful," Miranda reminded her.

"I know, darling, but this is ridiculous. We're going to have to find a tidier love spell to use in the future. In the meantime, we must reverse this one tonight."

Miranda pushed her hands into her hair and tugged, to distract herself from the throbbing in her brain. "But the moon's not right. It may not work."

"Then we'll repeat it tomorrow and the night after and the night after that, until it does work. But we must at least try before this becomes a total disaster. Where is the Book of Shadows?"

"In the sanctuary. Everything we need is there."

"Then get your robes, darling. It's only an hour until midnight."

She sailed back out of the room. Miranda just stood there, staring after her, wishing she had a way out.

She wasn't ready to do this, to take away the happiness she'd seen in Mason's eyes. Not without figuring out a few things first.

However, with Mason ready to take the irretrievable step of marriage, there wasn't time for analysis. She had to assume that she and Tish had been right from the outset, that Mason and Caroline belonged together, as Mason intended, and that the love potion had to be neutralized.

She went to the closet for her robe.

Forty-five minutes later, head still whirling, she joined her mother in the glen beyond the rose garden to cast the circle. The tools they used were simple: a wand to draw the circle, sea salt to cleanse it, and candles for each element of the compass.

They went around the circle clockwise, carving out a sacred space from the mundane world and summoning the elemental presence for each corner, beginning in the East with a white candle for Air, then continuing with orange for Fire and the South, blue for Water and the West, and green for the Earth and the North.

Finally they came together in the center to light the fire in the iron brazier, invoking the Goddess of Love to give their circle power and protection. Tish dropped herbs onto the flames to enhance their purpose: rue, to open one's eyes to mistakes, and lavender to rid one of old ideas. The air grew heavy with the perfume of the herbs and the cedary smell of the smoke.

Tish laid out the objects of the spell on a flat stone. Beside them, she opened the Book of Shadows to the page marked by a ribbon.

"It's time."

A shiver of trepidation ran down Miranda's spine as Tish began to read the words:

"Aphrodite, hear our plight . . ."

Miranda listened, trying to focus on the rightness of what they were doing for Mason and having very little luck.

". . . Love was never theirs to share."

Her voice ringing with certainty, Tish named Raine and Mason and called on the Goddess to negate the misbegotten love between them. As she wound up the incantation, she lifted a wooden arrow from the flat stone.

"Cupid's arrow on its flight
Has by our fault gone astray.
Now we set our error right,
To try again another day."

On these words, Tish broke the arrow and tossed the pieces in the fire. Sparks flew skyward to dance with the tiny insects drawn in by the light.

"Miranda?"

Miranda looked up, startled and guilty.

"The bottle," prompted Tish.

The blue bottle lay on the stone, a large cobble beside it. Moving mechanically, Miranda lifted the cobble and broke the bottle into a myriad of pieces.

> "I break this bottle as a token
> Of the magick to be broken
> Bottle shattered, arrow burned.
> Goddess, let this spell be turned."

They repeated the last lines three times while Tish dug a small hole with a trowel. When she finished, Miranda swept the pieces of the bottle into the hole and they buried them.

"It is finished," intoned Tish. "So mote it be."

"So mote it be."

They thanked the Goddess and released the circle from the center out, extinguishing the candles in the reverse order, finishing with the traditional witches' farewell, "Merry meet and merry part, and merry meet again."

When it was done and the only light was from the fire, Tish sighed.

"I can feel a difference already. Aren't you glad we did this?"

Miranda couldn't find an honest answer. "You look tired. Go on to bed, I'll stay with the fire until it's out."

"Are you sure, darling?"

Miranda nodded.

When her mother had gone, she loaded everything into the big garden trug they used to carry things, then sat and watched the fire burn down.

Poor Mason. If this worked, his feelings for Raine were burning out the same way right now. Whether that love had been destined or not, that was a sad thing.

When the last embers barely showed red, she poured the jug of water they always brought for such things over the ashes and stirred the sludge with a stick.

There was a flashlight in the trug, and although she could see just fine to work in the dark, she took it out to make one final check to see if she'd missed anything. As the beam played past the flat stone, it caught a glint of blue in the grass. Miranda bent and picked it up.

It was a piece of the bottle which she'd somehow missed burying with the others.

On it were two words in silver. *For Love.*

Sixteen

''What on earth is the matter with Samantha?'' asked Tish as she sat down at lunch on Tuesday. ''I told her we were having *salade Niçoise* and she said she'd rather starve.''

''I thought that was her favorite,'' said Miranda.

''It was, last year.'' Tish unfolded her napkin and pulled it across her lap. ''She must be turning into a teenager. Fickle creatures. You were abominable. Actually, you still are, on occasion.''

''Oh, good. It's part of my plan to stay youthful.''

''For example, now,'' said Tish.

Lawrence came in with the tray and began serving. He came to the third plate and hesitated.

''Shall I call Miss Samantha?''

''No. She's made up her mind not to come down,'' said Tish. ''Tell Cook if she tries to cadge food later, she's not to have any. If she can't join the rest of us, she'll do without until dinner.''

''Yes, madam.''

He poured the iced tea, then withdrew.

''She didn't seem very happy this morning, either,'' said Miranda. ''I asked if she'd like to play tennis or swim and she said she'd rather read.''

''I wonder if she isn't getting homesick,'' mused Tish.

''That's not like Samantha.''

"I know, but she's not usually packed off so suddenly, either. She probably had plans with friends or some such and is feeling put out that we're not eleven."

"It would be helpful if Elizabeth would call her." Miranda cut a wedge of hard-boiled egg and stabbed it, visualizing her former sister-in-law in the rubbery white.

"Yes, it would, but I hope I don't have to speak with her again. I'm not sure I could be civil, after the way she handled this." Tish took a sip of tea. "I'll call up Kate McMullen and see if Adeline can find a break between all those music lessons. Samantha was asking about her yesterday. Having a playmate might snap her out of this funk."

"I thought they were planning to go to France for the summer."

"Only for August. And it's Switzerland."

They traded opinions about the McMullens' trip and ate their salads, then Paul came with the car and Tish headed off for a massage.

"If you hear any good news about Mason and Miss Hobart, let me know right away."

Miranda nodded, but she doubted it would happen, considering the broken bit of bottle currently residing in the back of her jewelry case. Combined with the fact that she hadn't stayed focused in the circle, the implications for the previous night's work were significant. The counterspell was incomplete. It would probably never take.

They'd be redoing the work tonight, of course—though with variations in the incantation and with different and less charged tokens—but in the meantime Mason would likely stay in love with Raine. Somehow, that didn't seem so bad to Miranda, which was the real reason she hadn't told her mother about the bottle.

She had some correspondence to take care of for the family office, so she settled in at the desk in the conservatory and went about her business. At about three o'clock, she tried again to get her niece to come down for a bike ride or a swim. The effort got a resounding "No," which made it very clear that whatever was bothering Samantha, it was somehow Miranda's fault.

Miranda went back to her letters.

Samantha stayed in her room all afternoon.

• • •

"Hey, battah, battah, battah."

The razzing from the outfield picked up as Mason took his stance for his second pitch.

The ball whizzed by, high and inside. "Strike two."

Mason stepped back while the catcher returned the ball, then went through the ritual of pounding the plate and settling back in. He may not have played much softball in his life, but he knew how he was supposed to look doing it.

And appearance counted for everything at the Dayton Street Independence Day Invitational Softball Game.

That's what the crudely painted banner on the backstop called it, even though Independence Day was a week away. According to Raine, the game had fallen victim to scheduling problems during its first year, and now the early date was part of the tradition.

So was creative interpretation of the rules, if the last ten minutes had been any indication. A base runner in a tight purple T-shirt cut halfway down to her navel had led off by strolling from first to second while the pitcher was talking to the umpire. The umpire called it a steal and gave the pitcher a drubbing for trying to throw out a lady. Shortly after that, the catcher and the umpire had traded positions out of boredom, and called an out in the process, just on principle.

Of course, the rest of the neighbors might be perfectly nice, quiet, rule-abiding folks, but Mason couldn't tell over the noise from Raine and Sam, center- and right-field, respectively, and the source of the catcalls. He knew which one was worse this time, and he was embarrassed to admit she shared his last name.

The pitcher wound up and threw hard. Mason got nothing but air.

"Strike three. You're out."

The right-fielder hooted. "Daddy's out. Daddy's out." She danced around the baseline.

The worst of it was, Sam got a good clean single when she came up at the bottom of the inning, thanks to a giveaway pitch.

Her partner in crime managed to pull a double out of a fielder error in the second. Could he help it if the sun got in his eye?

"Daddy, you dropped the ball."

"Shut up, squirt."

But he who laughed last, laughed most obnoxiously. In the fifth inning Mason connected with a ground-rule double, and in the ninth, he popped a two-run homer. The west side of the street beat the east side by three, and Mason got to lord it over the women, which he did with much delight.

"But we played better," said Raine. "You all just got lucky because Evie had that shirt on. Every call went in her favor. Shoot, all she had to do was bend over a little and somebody handed her home plate."

"You sound jealous."

"Me? Jealous? Hah!" She laughed, then lowered her voice. "But only because it's all plastic. Two years ago she was as flat as Sam."

"What happens next?" asked Sam. "Is there food or something?"

"Well, when the game falls on weekends, there's a potluck picnic and we hang out for hours. But for the weeknight games, we usually do pizza. Are you up for it?"

"I'm starved," said Sam. "I didn't get lunch."

Frowning, Mason calculated the diameter of his daughter's bony arms. He'd have to have a talk with Mother and Miranda. They needed to ensure that Sam ate.

She made up for the skipped meal at the pizza parlor, a noisy place with enough pinball machines and video games for a stand-alone arcade. When Sam had inhaled four pieces of Luau Special, double pineapple, and finally looked happy, Raine snagged Petey Matthiesen as he went by.

"Hey, bucko, Samantha here hasn't had a chance to play many video games. I think they don't have them where she lives. Show her the ropes, okay?" She handed Sam a ten-dollar bill. "Get yourselves a roll of quarters and make sure you blow it all."

"Wow. Really? Can I, Daddy?" Sam disappeared without waiting for an answer.

"Oh, hush," Raine said, flapping a hand in Mason's face as he started to call her back. "Don't think of it as slumming, think of it as class cross-pollination. Cultural enrichment."

"It's not that and you know it." Mason said. "It's the content of the games. I don't want my daughter kicking holes in people's chests, even electronically."

"This place doesn't have that kind of stuff. It's too gross to encourage eating, even in fourteen-year-old boys. She might blast a few starships, but there will be very little blood and she'll be saving Earth or the Federation or something."

"How uplifting," he said dryly. "However, my other objection is that they're such a mindless waste of time."

"So is golf." Raine shifted and leaned forward on her elbows. "Actually, I think video games are pretty cool that way. Not only are they fun, but to do well, you have to be truly in the moment, doing what you're doing, with no ego in the way. It's very Zen. Mind-lessness. No Mind."

"No Mind. Now that would explain a lot about my sister and mother. Zen was what, six years ago? No, seven. It's been downhill ever since."

"So Zen's on your list of flaky philosophies, too? Boy, are you limiting the possibilities."

"No, I'm not. Rational thought opens up the whole world to possibilities. Rational thought brought us everything our lives depend on, from telephones to, I don't know, earthquake-resistant buildings. Even those video games are a result of rational thought."

"But combined with wild creativity." Raine's eyes were bright, and she was obviously warming to the debate. "I know a guy who develops computer games and, by your standards, he's the biggest flake in town. He meditates and he wears crystals and sorcerer's runes, and most of the time he wanders around with his face painted half blue, like Braveheart, because that's how he comes up with most of the outrageous images for his games. See, he writes warrior-quest games, and he claims dressing the part gives him the ideas."

"But it doesn't," said Mason. "The ideas, or the potential for them, are already in his head. He's just convinced himself that he needs certain crutches to get to them. People do not have to immerse themselves in weirdness or turn their lives into a parade in order to be happy and successful. Your friend could do the same thing without making a spectacle of himself."

Raine drew back and looked him up and down. "Oh, I get it. It's the spectacle, isn't it? You're afraid your mom and Miranda are going to make spectacles of themselves and embarrass you in public."

"They already have, thank you, and yes, I resent it. I resent having to explain to people that, no, they're not insane, they're just witches. I resent not knowing who or what's going to turn up at dinner—or in my iced tea—from night to night. And I particularly resent having to spend the time cleaning up their messes.''

''Life is messy sometimes.'' She stared at the table, spinning a napkin under her finger. ''I may be out of line here, but can I assume that Samantha's mother made a spectacle of herself in some way?''

''You can. However, she made the biggest spectacle out of me, with the lovers she needed to 'find her bliss.' '' He wasn't sure why he was telling her this, but there it was. ''You were wondering why I don't like searchers. I guess Elizabeth's at least part of your answer.''

''I'm sorry.''

Somewhere in the background, Samantha squealed with delight.

''I'd better go check on her,'' Mason said. He started to get up, but Raine put her hand over his.

''Elizabeth was wrong. You can't ever find your bliss by hurting someone else.''

''I've seen no evidence you can ever find it at all. You just get through life doing the best you can.'' He turned his hand to curl his fingers into hers. ''Let's go see what Sam's up to.''

They found her chasing aliens, and thrilled about it because she had gotten onto the high scores list on her second try.

''Beginner's luck,'' grumbled Petey, who was hanging on the edge of her machine.

''Hey, she had the best teacher,'' said Raine. ''Now, if I'd been showing her how, she'd probably still be on level one.''

''Yeah,'' said Petey, visibly cheering. ''You suck at this one.''

''Big time.''

They watched Sam for a few minutes, until she accused them of ruining her concentration.

''Come on, big guy,'' said Raine. ''It's time you tried one of these yourself.''

She led Mason over to the counter, where he bought a roll of quarters and handed her half.

''Here, this one's beginner speed.'' She fed a couple of quarters into a game where the goal was to guide a bouncy little character in armor through several levels of adventure, then stood back and let Mason take the controls.

He was a total loss. The buttons seemed to have little to do with the character's motion. When he'd blown a couple of dollars without even getting the little guy past the first level, Raine finally stepped in front of him and put her hands over his on the controls.

"Your money won't last long that way. Let me show you until you get the feel. See, here you go. Through the portal, past the dragon—you have to whack him a couple of times, but no blood, see?—and over this bridge to grab the magic sword."

Raine made it seem easy, bouncing the little guy on the screen through his life.

And why not? She appeared to move through her own life in much the same way, taking what came, rolling with the punches, enjoying the adventure. He, on the other hand, was more like the dragon guarding the bridge, hackles up, just waiting for someone to come along and try to steal his sword.

Life lessons in video games.

Not to mention in front of video games. Raine was right there in his arms, backed against his chest, not noticing what it was doing to him. He tightened his arms just a fraction to pull her closer.

She stilled, and the little guy fell off the bridge with a resounding electronic splash.

"We have at least forty chaperones," he murmured against her hair. "Nothing's going to happen. Let's enjoy it while we can."

"That's not very rational."

"I know. But it's Zen. Being in the moment. And I promise, I'll keep learning."

He did, too, especially once she snuggled back against him and relaxed. He learned he really hadn't enjoyed the past couple of days, not smelling lemons and mint.

Over at her machine, where it was Petey's turn, Samantha watched her father and Raine cuddle and added one more fact to her list. She didn't even need to write it down. On top of what she'd seen last night in the garden, she was starting to get a pretty good idea of what was going on.

Now she just needed to figure out what it meant.

"Daddy, why didn't you kiss Raine good night?"

"Excuse me?"

"Why didn't you kiss her good night?" Sam repeated. "You both looked like you wanted to smooch."

"Samantha . . ."

"I would have closed my eyes. You could have even stuck your tongue in her mouth, like they do in the movies."

"Samantha!" In his shock, Mason almost put the Explorer into the back of a little green Subaru.

In the interest of safety, he hit the right turn indicator and pulled into the first drive he came to, the parking lot of some restaurant on Aurora Avenue. He shut off the engine and set the brake, then swiveled to get a better look at his daughter in the backseat. "What's going on?"

"Nothing."

"Try again."

She twisted the hem of her T-shirt. "I'm trying to figure something out."

Oh, please, not yet. He hesitated, then asked, "About men and women?"

She looked confused, then amused. "You mean sex?"

He nodded.

"No. Mom already talked to me about that and bought me some books. Plus we do it in school."

"You *what?*"

"Study about sex in school. How babies get made and, you know, menstrual periods and all that."

"Oh. Um, good." He wondered if puberty was any easier to deal with for fathers who were around their girls all the time. "So, what exactly are you trying to figure out?"

"About you and Raine and Caroline."

"I thought we cleared that up."

She shook her head. "Not really. You just blew me off."

Mason turned his laugh into a cough. "I'm sorry."

"Apology accepted," she said primly, and he coughed again.

"Why are you so curious about my girlfriends?" asked Mason.

She looked at her knees. "I figure one of them is going to be my stepmom soon."

"We're quite a ways from that."

"We who?" she asked. "You and Raine, or you and Caroline?"

Mason knew he was treading a thin line. His mother had been right in one regard: it wasn't fair to let Sam form an attachment to Raine and then announce it was really Caro who would be her stepmother. On the other hand, his lovely little eleven-year-old had the tenacity of her aunt and the volubility of a talk show host, a deadly combination for any secret. He really didn't want her blurting out that Daddy really intended to marry Caro after all, not when he was so close to getting Mother and Miranda where he wanted them.

So to buy time, instead of telling her, he asked her, "What do you think?"

"I think you're in love with Raine but there's some reason that you and Gran and Aunt Randi think you should be in love with Caro."

Maybe she understood more than he thought. "What makes you say that?"

"Because first off, you kept trying to call Raine on Sunday, and you were really upset when she didn't answer."

"How do you know I was trying to call Raine and not Caroline? Or someone totally different?"

She looked at him as if he were an idiot and didn't even bother to dignify the question with an answer.

"Okay," he admitted. "I'll give you that one. So why else?"

"Because you two look like you want to touch each other all the time, but you don't. But it's not like you and Caroline don't touch each other, because you two look like you don't want to anyway, and it's okay."

"I'm trying to keep up, kiddo, but you lost me there someplace."

"You and Caroline look like you don't touch because you don't especially want to. Or maybe like it's okay if you do, but it's just as okay if you don't." She talked slowly and clearly for the benefit of the dense adult in the front seat. "You and Raine look like you *do* want to touch, but it's like there's this big piece of glass and you're on one side and she's on the other, so you can't."

"Samantha, people don't have to touch simply because the urge strikes." Considering his reaction to Raine, his personal hypocrisy astounded him, but it was important Sam hear this. She sure wasn't going to get it from Elizabeth. "Sometimes it's just not appropriate for two people to be physically affectionate, even if they like each other."

"Isn't it appropriate for Raine and you?"

"I have a different relationship with her than I do with Caroline," he said, sidestepping again.

"Because of Gran and Aunt Randi?"

"Why do you keep making them a part of this?"

"Because they were out in the garden last night, trying to make you fall out of love with Raine."

Mason's hands curled into fists. So they'd done it. They'd tried to reverse the potion. He'd suspected as much—hell, he'd done everything he could to force them into it—but the news that they were actually so arrogant as to try to continue to manipulate his life, without regard for him or Raine, still sent his blood pressure climbing through the roof.

Damn them. What business was it of theirs whether he was in love with Raine Hobart or Caro or the goddamn Duchess of York.

He wanted to take them apart, and when the time came he would, but right now Samantha was sitting there, waiting for him to sort this out for her.

First things first, though. "What were you doing out in the garden at midnight, Samantha?"

"I heard them chanting, so I sneaked out. I wanted to see what witches do."

"Sneaking out of the house by yourself is dangerous. I'm not happy, but we'll deal with that later. What exactly did you see?"

"Nothing gross. They don't kill chickens or anything. They just said some poem to Mighty Aphrodite and broke a little blue bottle and an arrow and buried them. It was all kind of silly anyway. All those weird chants and herbs and 'so mote it be's,' whatever that means. They're stupid."

Mason felt himself relax a bit. As similar as Sam was to her aunt, he'd been afraid she'd buy into witchcraft, but he was pleased to learn that at least one Alexander female had some common sense.

"You're right," he agreed. "It is kind of silly. But I don't want to hear you call your grandmother and your aunt stupid. You still have to respect them."

"But they said you shouldn't be in love with Raine and they were trying to make you stop. It made me *so* mad!" she blurted.

"It makes me mad, too, squirt." That, at least, he could be completely honest about.

"I didn't even talk to them today," she said. "It's not fair for them to try to say who you should love. You ought to just go ahead and marry Raine, just to show them."

"But I'm—" *not in love with her,* he intended to say, but his throat tightened around the words. "I'm working things out."

"*Are* you going to marry her?" she asked.

"You like Raine, don't you, Samantha."

She chewed on her bottom lip as she thought. "I think she'd be okay as a stepmom."

"She probably would be," he agreed. "But so would Caroline. You know, Sam, when you run a large company and have a family and thousands of employees that rely on you, you have to take those responsibilities into consideration. I have decisions to make, a lot of things to weigh to figure out what's in the best interests of you, and the family, and the company, in that order."

"You think about that stuff all the time, don't you?" Sam cranked the window down a few inches. "Mom doesn't worry about responsibilities so much. She just has fun."

There was an understatement. Mason kept his mouth shut.

Sam sighed. "I think I'll be somewhere in between when I grow up."

He thought of next week, when Caro would be back and he'd have to say good-bye to Raine forever.

"That's probably not a bad idea, squirt."

"God, I love the smell of bagels," said Zoe to the world at large. "If I could afford to come down here every morning, I'd have to start wearing pants with elastic waists."

Raine knew exactly what she meant. They were standing on the sidewalk in front of the bagel shop at five-thirty on Wednesday morning, waiting for the doors to open. The yeasty aroma of baking bagels wafted around them, as sweetly seductive as the smell of poppies.

But despite the temptations awaiting her stomach, Raine's mind was only marginally interested in food. Sleep ranked higher, as in the sleep she hadn't gotten last night, thinking about what Mason had revealed during the great video game debate. He just might have handed her the key to getting his attention.

She was still turning over the possibilities and the options as the other FUSE members trickled up from various directions. Traffic was starting to pick up, both on the roads and on the water, and the air vibrated with the rumble of heavy trucks and marine engines. A few blocks away, the klaxon sounded as the Fremont Bridge prepared to rise.

Zoe nudged her arm. ''Looks like almost everyone's here. If John B. won't open three minutes early, maybe we should start the meeting out here on the walk without him.''

Raine looked around. ''Where are Arne and Fred?''

''I don't know,'' said Zoe. ''They both said they'd come. Let's go ahead and I'll fill them in later. Who has an idea worth some lasagna?''

''A big, old-fashioned protest march,'' said Pauly. ''We could shut down the bridge.''

Zoe sneered. ''Oh, that would make us popular.''

''What about painting the whole lot black, warehouse and all, like the blight it will be? We could find one of those big spray trucks and do it in under thirty minutes, I think.''

Raine closed her eyes and listened as her crew swapped ideas and shot each other down. They had some great ideas. Some of them were feasible, and a couple might even be legal.

John B. showed up at the door, and FUSE members poured inside. The next few minutes were lost to shouted orders and the general hubbub of getting twelve people organized at tables designed for only four.

When everyone was busy smearing cream cheese on warm bagels, Raine stood up.

''Okay, troops. I'm really proud of you. These are all great ideas. But I've rethought our strategy, and, well''—she took a deep breath—''I've decided we shouldn't stage another raid.''

''What?'' The tables exploded with argument, and it took Raine several minutes to wave everyone quiet.

''I don't get it.''

''We just started getting some press.''

''I know,'' she said. ''But I don't think it's going to get us very far. At least not as far as we could get other ways.''

''Rainey.'' Zoe looked worried.

''Geez, Zoe. Not *that* way.''

''What way?'' demanded Theresa.

Raine pushed her hair back out of her face and ignored her. ''Okay, the thing is, I've gotten to know Mason Alexander over the past week. For those of you who missed the line in the paper, Alexander Industries is the owner of MMT.''

"Aah." The restaurant resounded with the clatter of conclusions being leapt to.

"So you're selling out on us," accused Pauly.

"Caving about the building," added Mark.

"No," she said firmly. "Canal Place is as much of a hazard to Fremont as ever, and I'm going to do everything I can to stop it. But I had a discussion with Mason—"

"Mason? That sounds pretty friendly."

"Don't be nasty, Mark," said Zoe.

"I talked to Mason last night," repeated Raine. "He said some things that led me to think that making a big scene is probably not the way to get through to him. He doesn't like spectacles, as he puts it. The Wall was okay. It got us some attention, but Mason is going to close right off if we embarrass him and his family any more. I think if I present the whole case to him in a calm, logical way, he might just consider what we have to say."

"You tried talking for a year already."

"Sort of." She nodded and took a sip of her mocha. "I sent out letters and talked to people until I was blue in the face, but I don't think any of it ever got to Mason. At least not directly, and certainly not the way I can explain it to him in person. I can ease him into it."

"Wait a second," said Zoe. "I thought you were trying to ease him into it all week. Wasn't that part of why you went out with him?"

"You mean you knew she was consorting with the enemy?"

"Shut up, Marcus." Zoe didn't even bother to look at the heckler. "You told me you couldn't even talk about *feng shui* without him going ballistic."

"I didn't do a very good job," Raine said. "I tried to slide it in a few times, but the timing was all off and his family was there, and it just . . . well, let's just say it didn't work. But if I sit down with him now, alone, with all the charts and maps and calculations, and present it like a business report—"

"Hey, where's our Fearless Lasagna Lady?" Arne burst through the door carrying a stack of bright yellow paper. He walked straight to Raine and gave her a squeeze. "Hope you've got the fixings, because I have won the prize."

"Sit down, Arne," said Zoe. "There's not going to be any prize."

"Huh? You promised. And I did the work already, so I want my prize."

"Raine is going to try talking one more time."

"She may be talking, but my feet done did the walking. Well, mine and my buddies. Check these out."

Arne set the stack on a table and pulled off the top sheet, which began unfolding accordion-style. With Pauly's help, he held up a six-foot strip of paper upon which foot-high black caps screamed, "GOING OUT OF BUSINESS!"

It took Raine several seconds to notice the much smaller, fainter line above that read, "If Canal Place comes in, we may be . . ." A few more seconds passed before she spotted the tiny line at the bottom encouraging readers to "Light the FUSE."

"Wow," said Zoe. "That cuts right to the heart of it, doesn't it?"

No kidding. Raine wished they'd thought of that a week ago. With a few modifications, it would have been better than the Wall.

Several of the gang stood up and reached across tables to shake Arne's hand. "Masterpiece, man."

"Just picture those all over Fremont," said Theresa. "People would be ready to storm the barricades."

"Man, you don't have to picture them," said Arne, his chest swelling with pride. "Just walk outside and take a look."

"What?" asked Raine.

The tables emptied.

Zoe grabbed Raine's hand. "Come on."

They pushed their way to the knot in front of the door. Raine groaned. Every storefront on the street had a sign, except the bagel shop. From a distance of more than forty feet or so, she couldn't make out the top line at all, and the signs appeared to trumpet "GOING OUT OF BUSINESS."

Raine's stomach slid sideways. "Arne, what did you do?"

"Cool, huh?" said Arne. "The whole block took me under five minutes. Slap on some paste, stick it up."

"Arne, you boob," said Zoe. "You were just supposed to come up with an idea."

"Yeah, but I knew it was right, so I figured, why waste time? We ran a couple hundred copies and this is all that's left. We've got them up everywhere."

Raine looked at the stack in his hand. Allowing for six or

eight sheets of paper per banner, he had maybe twenty banners left.

"Please don't tell me you put up almost two hundred of those things."

"Sure. My buddies helped. It didn't take long."

"Where are they? What businesses did you do?"

"Man, everywhere and everything. We even got a few up on the Adobe building without their security people noticing."

Raine took a deep breath and tried to stay calm.

"Arne?" she said sweetly. "Did you bother to, oh, I don't know, *ask* any of the business owners before you put them up?"

"Nah. They were all closed by the time I thought of it last night. But it's cool. I stuck a note under the doors to explain it. You might get a few calls, but—"

"*I* might?"

"Hey, all I've got is the phone at the bar. They can't call there."

"So you put *my* phone number on these notes."

Arne looked confused, like he wasn't quite sure why her voice had gotten so murderously low. "And your name, natch."

"Oh, God." Raine looked skyward. "Give me the forbearance not to kill him." She looked back to Arne and the others. "They've got to come down. Now. Every one of them." She ran to the nearest shop and ripped the sign down.

Everybody stood there, watching her.

"Come on, people," she shouted. "Get 'em down."

"But they look pretty good, Rainey," said Zoe. "And it's all done already. I know it's not what you think is best, but can't we just—"

"Zoe! *He didn't get permission,*" she said clearly as she marched back to the group. "These store owners are going to show up and find Going Out of Business signs on their windows. They're going to be pissed. Half of them are going to sue. And thanks to Arne, they're going to know exactly who to come after." She tapped her chest. "Right here. And we won't even talk about the fact that 'Light the FUSE' might be interpreted as incitement to arson and bombing."

"Holy shit," said Pauly. Zoe and several others groaned.

"Who-o-a," said Arne, finally getting it. "Sorry. Like, skip the lasagna."

''Come on,'' said Mark. ''We've got to get Raine out of this. Terri and I will take Fremont Avenue.''

''I'll get Thirty-fourth,'' said Pauly.

Galvanized, the group split into pairs and dashed off in different directions. All except Arne, who stood there, cogitating.

''Get a move on, Granola Boy,'' said Zoe.

He blew out a breath. ''I was just thinking. You probably want the big banner down, too, huh?''

Raine closed her eyes, counted to five, and opened them. ''What big banner?''

''On the building. My buddies are down there now putting it up. And Fred's supposed to be down there with all the news types by now.''

''Fred? He was in on this?''

''I just told him to get everybody there by six.''

''Come on, Zoe.''

They ran the two blocks to Thirty-fourth, but even before they got there, they could see a huge, triangular banner fluttering over the old building. It was suspended about thirty feet up, between two huge silver weather balloons that were being let out on ropes.

''Is that a sail?'' asked Zoe.

''Yeah. One of my friends owns a sail loft,'' said Arne. ''He gave me a dead sail and I got a sign-painter friend of mine to stay up all night enlarging one of Fred's cartoons.''

Fred was an aspiring political cartoonist, waiting to make his name. This might be his day.

The sail displayed a huge human heart in garish red and black paint. A knife was raised above it and, below, the words read ''Alexander Industries and MMT. Carving the heart out of Fremont.''

But the real piece of work, the one that might make Fred's reputation and ruin Raine's, was the figure holding the knife: a huge and exceptionally well-drawn caricature of Mason Alexander.

Seventeen

Victory Security Services Officer Roger Sproat sat at the stoplight tapping impatiently on his steering wheel. He was supposed to make a run past that old warehouse in Fremont every thirty minutes, but he was running late, the result of a quick stop at Donut Delite that had turned into twenty minutes of flirtation with Carmen the filling girl. He wasn't too concerned—he could always pass the delay off as a dead battery or traffic—but the Fremont stop was the last of the night, and he wanted to get home to Nadine.

It was still early, but the sun was climbing over the mountains and as he crossed the Fremont Bridge, a silvery glint of light off to the left caught his eye. He stared, slack-jawed, at a pair of what looked like weather balloons rising over what he calculated was the old warehouse. Then at the end of the bridge, he started spotting the signs: huge, yellow suckers that said the whole freakin' town was Going Out of Business.

A ripple of excitement ran down Sproat's spine. His boss at VSS had said to watch out for some wackos that had a vendetta against the owners of the warehouse—like wackos would stick out in Fremont. If it was them and he got the bust, maybe he could get that raise Nadine had been bugging him about. He cruised past the signs up to Fremont Place, hung a left, and drove out Thirty-sixth a few blocks, then turned back toward the warehouse, ready for bear.

It was the wackos, all right, and they were definitely on the warehouse roof. He spotted them and their freakin' weather balloons and what looked like a painted boat sail as soon as he made the corner. There were also a bunch of cars and a couple of TV trucks parked on Thirty-fourth Street above the warehouse. Some guy was already snapping photos with a still camera while the TV people got their gear ready.

He had to hand it to the wackos: they knew how to attract attention, but why the hell did they have to do it on his shift? He was going to have to do some fancy dancing to explain how they'd gotten all this done between rounds, but he could handle it.

But he'd never explain it if these clowns got away. He got on the radio to HQ right away to run down the situation and ask for backup.

"Your supervisor is rolling. ETA twelve minutes," said the dispatcher. "And city officers will be right behind him."

"Copy. Have 'em bring a truck. There's a herd of 'em," said Sproat as he watched three more—a guy with long frizzy hair, a pretty blonde, and a curvy little brunette—run across the street. The blonde and her friend started waving off the reporters, while the long hair climbed up on the railing and stepped out into space.

"Jesus! Oh. Hey, they've got a plank or something running out to the roof. Tell the city boys to hurry before one of them kills himself."

Engine idling, he sat back to wait for the cops to show. About then, the trio on the roof started hauling on the ropes that held the balloons and sign.

Hey. Wait a minute. They were taking it all down. Out of the corner of his eye, he noticed a couple of other people ripping down the yellow posters up the street.

With visions of that extra twenty-five a week going down the tubes, Sproat hit the button for his lights and siren and gunned the car down the street. He whipped in next to a TV truck and, hand on gun, hopped out of the car and hustled over toward the railing. "Hold it right there, all of you."

"Cops," shouted someone. The guys on the roof turned loose the balloon ropes and dove for a trapdoor that one of them yanked open. As they dropped out of sight, Sproat looked at the plank that ran out to the roof and cursed. *No way* was he going out there. Up the street, the poster rippers vanished between buildings. The streets echoed with running feet and revving engines. Below, the security fence rattled. Sproat glanced over the retaining wall just in time to see the guys from the roof climb the fence to make their getaway.

Shit. Where were the cops and his backup?

Sproat was left with only the blonde and her wide-eyed friend. Technically, they hadn't even been on the site, but they were better than nothing. "You're under arrest, ladies. You oughta get braver friends."

As he spoke, a truck from KOMO roared up and a girl with a camera piled out and started filming.

"Oh, geez," said the blonde. She looked like she was going to either start bawling or lose her breakfast or both. And then, right in front of him, she snapped out of it. She brushed the tears out of her eyes and faced the little mob of reporters.

"If you all are ready, I'd like to make a statement before the police arrive."

"Rainey, keep your mouth shut," whispered the brunette. "We weren't doing anything they can charge us with. We're just innocent bystanders."

"You stand by. Our options are shot. I've got to salvage what I can out of this mess."

The photographer waved and a reporter crawled out from behind the wheel of a car across the street, looking like she'd slept in her clothes. She dodged a couple of cars to cross over with her skinny reporter's notebook, and pulled a black pen out from behind her ear. "Shoot."

"Speaking of shoot," the blonde said, "after I'm done, please make sure you all get some good tight shots of the Going Out of Business signs we put up." The photographers nodded.

The blonde smoothed her hair and adjusted her clothes, then stood up straight and faced the cameras like she was some D.C. politician at a press conference.

"My name is Raine Hobart," she said clearly. "I'm the leader of FUSE, the group responsible for this action, as well as for last week's construction of the mock Berlin Wall on the same site. We are here to make a statement against the design of the proposed Canal Place development."

As the reporters scribbled and the cameras clicked and

whirred, Sproat sucked in his gut and posed for a record of his first real arrest.

Nadine would be proud.

Newspapers. Television crews. Mug shots.

Raine had her picture taken more times Wednesday morning before nine than she had in the previous five years of her life. If there existed a photographer in the Seattle Metro area who hadn't shot her picture by the time she was led to the holding cell, Raine didn't know who he or she was.

It was all for the cause, and once she had resigned herself to the arrest and what it meant, she'd played it for all it was worth. They'd certainly gotten the publicity she'd once wanted and, unless she missed her mark, she'd be making the midday news on at least two stations and the five o'clock broadcast on all three majors. Of course, that created a real problem: even if she could manage to post bail, she'd never make it out of the state by the time Mason found out. She'd really like to be out of the state.

The cell door slammed shut behind her. Raine looked at the dozen or so hookers and other miscreants who were lazing sleepily on the benches and bare bunks, and raised a hand in half-hearted greeting. "Hi."

A couple of them grunted back at her.

She hadn't even had time to settle in when Zoe showed up. As they hugged, Zoe scanned the cell with a critical eye.

"If they think I'm going to pee in *that,* they can just forget it. It's disgusting."

"I'll be sure to tell the sergeant," said Raine. "What are you doing here? I thought you were just an innocent bystander."

"You didn't really think I'd let you take the fall by yourself, did you? I told them I was your publicity officer. They weren't too happy about that, considering how much publicity we just got." Zoe tapped the foot of a blowzy redhead who was taking up a whole bench. "Excuse me. Can we sit down, please?"

"Sure, honey." The woman sat up, and Raine and Zoe joined her on the stainless steel shelf.

"Thanks," said Zoe. She turned back to Raine. "You okay?"

"I'll survive."

"All you have to do is tell the cops what Arne did to you. It wasn't your fault."

"Yes, it was." Raine pulled her feet up on the bench and

hugged her knees. ''I started the whole thing, and then I let it get away from me. Arne was just doing what he thought I wanted.''

''Arne did what *Arne* wanted, and then he bailed on us. And I plan to tell anyone who'll listen what a hypocritical little chicken-shit he is. As soon as it gets out, all of Fremont is going to be behind you, you know, even with the posters. You're a martyr for the cause now.''

''Oh. *That's* why I feel like I'm tied to a stake with a lot of wood piled around my ankles.'' Raine swung her feet to the floor, then got up and paced the width of the cell and back. ''God. If I'd just talked to Mason like I said I would. I had chances, Zoe. I really did. I just didn't take advantage of them because I let myself get distracted by him and his family and the shopping and the dancing and—''

—by what came after the dancing. Her cheeks flamed and she covered them with her hands and leaned against the graffiti-covered wall.

''He's going to despise me. He probably already does.''

The tears that had first welled up out there on the sidewalk when the security guard had busted them, finally spilled over her lashes and down through her fingers. She slipped to the floor, put her head in Zoe's lap, and bawled like a baby.

''They came back.''

''I'm in the middle of a production meeting, Scott,'' Mason said into the phone. He nodded toward his senior VPs. ''Who came back?''

''Those FUSE people. They raided the warehouse again, and floated some balloons with a big banner off the roof. Plus they apparently papered every window for blocks with Going Out of Business signs that accused Canal Place of killing the neighborhood.''

''And why precisely does that make you sound so cheery?''

''Because we got them. At least a couple of them.''

''Good. How the hell did they get on the roof in the first place? Where were the security guards that were supposed to keep them out?''

''The security guard was in transit between properties, and he's the one that caught them. The leader of the group and their publicity officer are in police custody as we speak. Jake Kreutzmiller is seeing that the maximum charges are pressed."

"Fine." Mason grabbed a pencil out of the cup on his desk and scribbled a few notes on a pad. "What's the PR fallout look like?"

"That's the bad news, although I've already called Ben Pratt, and he's working on it. Reporters were on site for the arrest, and their Fearless Leader—I swear to God, that's what they call her—managed to give a very detailed statement before the police arrived. It sounded pretty convincing out of context. On top of that, the banner they floated was, ahem, a photo op in itself. We're probably going to take a pretty good hit on this. And I'm afraid they implicated you personally."

"Just what was on this banner of theirs?"

Scott cleared his throat again. "Among other things, you wielding a bloody knife. About ten feet high. It was actually a pretty good caricature."

The pencil between Mason's fingers snapped in two. "It had better be down."

"Yes, sir. We reeled it in as soon as the police finished their evidentiary photos. It's been impounded, although the men who actually trespassed to put it into place all escaped."

"I'm not sure it matters, if we have their leader. I'll talk to Kreutzmiller." Mason found a new pencil and made another note. "Fearless Leader, eh?"

Scott chuckled. "Yes, sir."

"What's this terror's name?"

"Let's see." Scott shuffled paper. "Here we are. The two women arrested were Zoe R. Levine and Lorraine M. Hobart. I'm not sure which is which."

Mason heard each individual beat of his heart, as though his pulse were being played on the office sound system. "Run those by me again."

Scott repeated the names.

"Thank you," Mason said mechanically. "I'll talk to you later." He'd heard it right: Raine, and the friend Zoe she'd mentioned.

He hung up and turned to his production people. "I'm going to have to ask you to move this meeting to the conference room. Greg, you're in charge. Here are my notes of topics to be covered." He pulled a thin sheaf of papers out of his portfolio and tossed it down in front of Greg. "I'll expect a report on my desk tomorrow morning."

"Yes, sir."

The men and women looked at each other in confusion, then gathered their papers and quickly filed out of his office.

In the silence they left behind, he turned and stared out the plate glass wall behind his desk. The day was cloudless, perfect; the water in the Sound shone glassy blue. He'd been in exactly this spot, on a day as perfect as today, when the lawyers had served him with divorce papers. The sense of betrayal had been exactly the same.

He did the same thing he had that day, almost the same thing he had done, come to think of it, the day Raine had walked out on him after he'd made love to her: he turned and hammered his fist down on the desk.

The door opened, and Chris poked her head in. "Are you all right, Mr. Alexander?"

"Get me five thousand dollars cash from my personal account," he said without answering her. "And then I want Kreutzmiller on the phone."

"Yes, sir. Right away."

He closed his eyes.

The bitch. When it came to using people, Elizabeth had nothing on Raine Hobart.

The wheels of justice freed ten out of twelve hookers and replaced them with two DUIs before Raine heard her name called.

She glanced at Zoe, then stood up. "Here."

"You're with me," the policewoman said. "Levine? You're with Officer Talley, here."

Raine followed her officer down the hall and through the doors. "Are we being arraigned already?"

"No, ma'am. Charges have been dropped."

Raine glanced back over her shoulder. Zoe was giving her a thumbs-up.

They were processed out separately. Raine received the numbered envelope with her personal items and was pointed toward a door. She started toward it and was fishing around inside the envelope for her watch when she happened to glance up and see Mason through the glass in front of her.

Her reactions were as confused as the circumstances, a mix of outright joy and the desire to ask if going back to the cell might be an option.

Her fingers closed around her watch, and she took the time to put it on. It gave her a few seconds to remind herself that their relationship was employer-employee, not lover and beloved.

"Wow, is that Moneybags?" asked Zoe, coming up behind her. She carried an identical envelope. "He's gorgeous."

Raine nodded.

When the watchband was tight on her wrist, she resealed the envelope and walked through the door. There was no visible change in Mason's expression when he saw her, while she stood there with her heart in her eyes.

"Mason. I'm sorry."

"So am I, Miss Hobart."

So it was that way. Four feet away, and as distant as if he were on Mars.

"Are you the one who dropped the charges?" Zoe asked.

"Yes," said Mason.

"Thanks for thinking of me."

"I assure you, it wasn't done out of kindness."

"Mason, I—"

"I'd appreciate it if any further discussion could wait until we have some privacy. The car is outside. We can talk there."

She nodded. "Zoe—"

"—can wait with Paul. My driver," he added for Zoe's benefit. "You won't mind, will you, Miss Levine? We won't be long."

"Of course not."

Of course not, thought Raine. It never took long to say goodbye.

She followed him to the car, clutching her envelope, which was already growing soft with the sweat off her hands.

"Paul, this is Miss Levine. Please keep her company for a few minutes."

"Yes, sir." Paul steered Zoe away toward a shady spot under a sweet gum tree.

Mason stayed with Raine. He was polite to a fault, holding the door, standing aside while she got in the car, then climbing in beside her. It would have been easier if he'd been rude, outwardly angry, but he just sat there like a lump of bronze—cold, hard, and unyielding.

She couldn't stand it. "Say something, please."

"I was going to send my attorney," he said. "But I wanted to see for myself. Was there some mix-up? Were you arrested by mistake?"

"No. I'm the leader of FUSE. We—"

He held up a hand to stop her. "I'm not interested in what FUSE has to say. Did you agree to this . . . arrangement between us knowing who I was?"

"No. I knew your name. I didn't know you owned MMT."

"When did you find out?"

She swallowed. "The next day. When I read the newspaper."

"And you said nothing."

"I know it looks bad but—"

"Looks bad," he echoed. "I think I used similar words Monday when I was apologizing for making love to you. I can appreciate now how hollow it sounded, or rather, how hollow it would have sounded if a real apology had been necessary. I must compliment you on your dedication to the cause."

"Don't be a bastard, Mason. You don't have to hurt me to make me go away." She reached for the door handle.

"Wait." He touched her arm.

A tiny hope flared, then died as he reached into the breast pocket of his suit coat. He pulled out a thick, plain white business envelope and held it out to her.

"This is a letter stating that no charges will be filed against you or any of the other people who were with you today, provided FUSE ceases any and all action in regard to the Canal Place development. There is also the five thousand dollars I owe you, in cash."

"I didn't finish the job."

"To the people of Fremont—and soon all of Seattle and environs, if the press does what I suspect they will—I am now a knife-wielding maniac. I'd say you've done a pretty thorough job, actually. I hear the likeness was extraordinary."

"Fred's very good," she said. "For what it's worth, I didn't know anything about that banner until this morning when it was already up. I was trying to get them to take it down when your rent-a-cop showed up."

"If that's true—and I doubt it—you're a lousy leader."

"I wish I could disagree with you." She popped the door open and stuck one leg out, then changed her mind and turned back to face him.

"You know, you're a real hypocrite. You talk about rationality and how important it is, but you run on pure emotion just like the rest of us. Your feelings are hurt, so you won't even listen to what I have to say about today or about the building or any of it."

"I might have listened, if you had approached me like an adult instead of throwing what amounts to a public temper tantrum."

"Approach you? I couldn't even find out who you were."

"The ownership of MMT is a matter of public record."

"Yeah, right. Buried under umpteen layers of subsidiary corporations and evasions. I tried to do it your way, Mason. I wrote letters. I went to the meetings last winter. I tried to be rational. Your stooges blew me off like I was"—she searched for an analogy—"Samantha's age."

"I never saw any letters."

"That doesn't surprise me. You've got so many vice presidents and lawyers and personal assistants and public relations people between you and us out here that I'm surprised you even know where Fremont is. For God's sake, you're so out of touch that you think marriage is about stock options and cash flow. How many layers does it take to make you that smug, Mason?"

She climbed out of the car and stood in the open door. "Keep your money and your letter. The design of that building is a disaster waiting to happen. I can't let you put it up without a fight."

He started to open his mouth, but she slammed the door in his face as hard as she could. "Come on, Zoe. Let's find a phone so I can see if I still have a job."

Zoe was deep in conversation with Paul—flirting, probably. Raine went over and grabbed her by the elbow. "Come on, you're ruining my grand exit."

"Sorry." Zoe took a couple of steps with Raine, then stalled to look back at Paul. "You're really cute. Are you taken?"

Paul nodded. "Yes, miss. I'm afraid I am."

Zoe sighed. "Oh, well. No harm in asking. Come on, Rainey. Grand exit. Stage right."

Eighteen

Angus stood back and watched Lyle Tucker drop a putt for an eagle on the eighteenth. ''Beautiful shot. Too bad I whooped your ass anyway. That's three you owe me.''

Laughing, Lyle pulled out his checkbook and wrote the check for three thousand dollars right there on the green. ''I don't understand it. The better I get, the better you get.''

''It's pure cussedness.'' Angus slipped the folded check into his pocket and handed his putter to the caddie. ''Let me make up for it by buying you a drink.''

They tipped their caddies and hit the locker room, and a half hour later were at a table in the clubhouse bar winding up a discussion they had started on the fairways, about how Wick Technologies might be able to job out some work to one of Tucker's subsidiaries.

Angus was well into his bourbon and branch when a man walked by carrying the afternoon paper. A black and red drawing of what looked like Mason Alexander caught Angus's eye.

''Excuse me,'' he said, reaching out to stop the man. ''Can I see that?''

The fellow looked annoyed, but he held out the paper. ''Sure.''

''Holy . . .'' Angus stared at the photo. It was Mason, all right, on some kind of banner, floating above the head of that landscape designer he'd met at the Alexander house. He scanned the caption, which referred him to a story on page five. It would appear that Miss Hobart was up to something besides landscape designing.

"Ahem."

"Sorry. Thanks." He handed the paper back to the man and went straight out to the rack of papers in the lobby of the clubhouse. He had the *Times* open to page five by the time he got back to the table where Tucker waited patiently.

"What was that about?"

Angus pulled the outside sheet off and handed it to Tucker. "Front page center."

"Jesus."

"Looks like the boy's got his butt in a sling on this one," said Angus.

"Yeah, I'd say." Tucker shook his head, then tapped the picture with a forefinger. "Isn't that the girl he brought to the Wilmott dance the other night?"

Angus folded his paper and laid it down. "Say what?"

"I could swear it's the same girl," muttered Tucker. "I don't remember those freckles, but—" He blocked off the mop of blonde hair on the photo with his hands. "Yes, that's definitely her. Alexander must be fit to be tied."

"I'd say so," said Angus. Hog-tied and horsewhipped, the little upper-crust sonofabitch. If he thought he could two-time Caroline whenever she left town, he had a lesson to learn.

He tossed back the last of his drink. "Lyle, I hate to say goodbye, but I have a few things to take care of. Have your people call mine and we'll see if we can't make this deal go."

They shook hands, and Angus headed for his car. As soon as he locked the doors, he pulled his cell phone out and dialed the international operator.

"Singapore, please, darlin'," he said to the voice that answered. "Raffles Hotel."

Raine was wrong. He wasn't running on pure emotion. He wasn't feeling anything at all.

There was just a hollowness, like the sound the car door made slamming in his face. Mason knew it well. He'd run on it for years after Elizabeth. It made decisions incredibly easy, because he could base them on facts, with nothing in the way. It was a good way to work.

So he worked, diving with relish into the reports and the minutiae of running a corporation. The notes on the morning production meeting arrived from Greg's office just before five, and he went over them and got enough ideas to generate a dozen memos. He was still at work on them at seven P.M. when Miranda walked into his office unannounced.

"I sent Chris home," she said when he looked up.

"I need her for another hour."

"No, you don't." She crossed to the desk and perched on one corner. "I saw the news."

Mason hit a button to save his work on the computer and leaned back in his chair. "How bad was it?"

"Oh, about like this." She pulled the late edition of the *Times* out from behind her back and tossed it on his desk.

He hadn't seen any photos yet, and it was probably just as well. His face, or an approximation thereof, snarled out from the front page just above Raine's frizzy blonde head. The rest of the banner was an abomination of gore and hyperbole.

"Why didn't you call us?" Miranda asked. "We had to find out from Kate McMullen when she picked Sam up."

"Did Samantha see this grotesquerie?"

"No. And I warned Kate to keep her away from it. She's spending the night with Adeline."

"Good. And thank you."

"I don't think I'm the one you want to thank." Miranda wandered behind him and looked out the window over downtown. "Have you talked to Raine?"

"I bailed her out. Or rather, I went down and dropped the charges. We spoke briefly."

"Did she give you any excuses? Explanations?"

"She claims she didn't know about the banner."

"You don't believe her."

"She's head of that outfit."

"Why would she lie?" Miranda walked around the other side of the desk and headed for the couch.

"The same reason she lied to me for the past week and a half, whatever that was." He pulled the *Times* off the desk and tipped it into the wastebasket by his feet. "That's one thing I don't understand. She had me as a captive audience for all that time, and she never tried to take advantage of it. She never said one word about Canal Place or *feng shui* or any of it."

"Yes, she did," said Miranda. "One of those first nights at

dinner, when I asked her about what she did besides landscaping. She specifically mentioned *feng shui*. Tish and I even talked about it the next day.''

''All right, once,'' conceded Mason. ''But you would have thought she'd try to win me over or something.''

''How could she?''

''Simple conversation.''

''Talking to you about things out of the mainstream is never simple, Mason. You get snappish when someone mentions what you define as nonsense.'' Miranda kicked off her shoes and curled her feet up on the couch. ''She probably figured that much out when you blew up at Tish for daring to bring up witchcraft at the table, then decided it wasn't worth losing her head.''

''I'm not that bad.''

''Yes, you are. I'm used to it and you still startle me sometimes.''

''Nothing startles you.'' Mason rose and walked around the desk to join his sister on the couch. ''Speaking of witchcraft, the good news for you and Mother is that you don't have to worry about reversing the love potion anymore.''

Miranda went beet red and started spluttering. ''What are you talking about?''

''Stop it, Miranda. I knew from the beginning. The iced tea tasted like the bottom of your cauldron. That first kiss on the terrace was a spur-of-the-moment attempt to get you and Mother to stop screwing around with my life. When it didn't work, I looked up Miss Hobart and hired her to date me, to teach you and Mother a lesson. I offered her five thousand dollars, although she didn't take it, as it turned out. At any rate, it was all a ruse.''

''No, it wasn't. I watched you two. That potion worked. You were in love with her. And now you're not, because of the counterspells Tish and I worked the last two nights.''

''We were acting. It was a con. And the only reason we're not still acting is because Miss Hobart was conning me at the same time and got caught. It has nothing to do with spells or counterspells. Your witchcraft does not work.''

''I'm not going to argue with you. But I know you, big brother, and you sure as hell didn't sleep with that girl as part of some con.''

''No. I'll admit there was a certain level of physical attraction that we followed through on.'' And the reaction of his body at the thought told him that, given half a chance, he'd follow through on it again, despite what Raine had done to him.

"That's all you think it was? Chemistry?"

"Of course. Although it was exceptionally poor judgment to act on it, as it turns out. Do you suppose she'd have a case for sexual harassment?" he asked dryly. "Or is sex presumed to fit in the job description of paid love interest?"

Miranda took his hand. "She really hurt you, didn't she? I'm so sorry, Mason."

"I'm fine. You're much more disturbed by this than I am."

"I know," she said. "And that makes me worry for you."

"Don't concern yourself. I'm fine. The game is over, that's all. Caroline will be back next week, and after I explain all this to her, we will continue down the merry path to joint venture and marriage. But let me warn you, if you and Mother so much as think about a love potion again, I will personally burn you at the stake before I move out of the house and out of your lives. Do you understand me?"

Miranda nodded. "Perfectly. And now, since you don't appear to need me, I will go off and waste another evening on my whirlwind social life. Should I tell Tish to expect you anytime soon?"

"I'm not sure. My mind is exceptionally clear and focused right now. I think I'll take advantage of it." He brushed a piece of lint off the back of the couch. "Would you mind leaving your car and having Paul take you home? That way I can take him off the clock."

"Sure. I parked on Level A." She handed him her car keys, then leaned over and kissed him before she got up. "Don't let your heart get too hard, Mason. You'll miss out on the good things."

"I'll phone down and have Paul meet you out front. Good night, Miranda."

"Good night."

She let herself out, pulling the door shut behind her with a firm click that left Mason to his memos and his empty, silent office.

She understood perfectly, all right.

Miranda waited downstairs until Paul pulled up, then met him at the curb.

He opened the door. ''Good evening, miss.''

So he was back to calling her Miss instead of Miranda. Why not? She'd avoided him since Saturday, not knowing what to say. She sighed.

''Is there something wrong?'' he asked.

''Oh, no. My brother's heart is broken and it's my fault, but no, there's nothing wrong. At least not if you ask Mason.''

''Miss Alexander, I'm his driver. It's not appropriate—''

''Paul, do you like my brother?''

''I like him and respect him, very much.''

''Then screw appropriate. He needs help, and I need advice, and you're the only one who knows enough about what's going on to give me straight answers. At least the only one I trust to work in Mason's best interests.''

Paul hesitated a long moment, then nodded. ''All right. But may I suggest we take the conversation somewhere other than the sidewalk in front of his offices?''

''Make a suggestion.''

He pulled the door wider, and she got in. ''Just sit back. I know the perfect spot.''

Miranda let her mind wander as they drove, and they were at the Highlands gate before she realized where he was taking her.

''I'm not really interested in having my mother in on this conversation.''

''She won't be.''

Miranda raised an eyebrow, but said nothing.

A few minutes later, Paul drove past the main house and down to the carriage house. After parking, he let her out, then reached back into the driver's compartment to retrieve a computer case before he started for the stairs at the side of the building.

''Your quarters?'' she asked.

''Privacy, convenience, and all the comforts of home,'' he said. ''Do you mind?''

''Oh, why not. My reputation could use a little spicing up.'' She shook her head and followed him upstairs. Expectation fluttered through her nerves, and she had to remind herself that nothing was going to happen.

He took a moment to pull the computer out of the case and set it on a desk covered with books and stacks of papers.

''I need to charge up,'' he explained as he unwrapped the cord and plugged it into a power strip. He pulled off his uniform jacket and hung it over the back of the chair, then pulled off his tie and rolled his sleeves up. "I have green tea, black tea, and orange juice."

"Black tea is fine."

"I'll put the water on." While he tended to that, she looked around the apartment. She'd been up here many times as a child: her father's old driver, Dawson, had been married to a woman who made the most outrageous chocolate chip cookies and had no compunctions about overstuffing the boss's daughter.

Things had changed, though—probably several times over. The walls, for instance, were a mellow sage color instead of the eggshell white they'd always been. She recognized a couple of pieces of furniture from her mother's flirtation with Japonica. They seemed more at home here than they had in the conservatory. Intrigued, Miranda looked around. Paul appeared to have his own collection of Oriental art, including a handsome trio of terra-cotta Chinese scholars on the bookshelf. She padded over and picked up one as she read the titles on his shelf.

"That's fifteen hundred years old. Please be careful."

Miranda spun around guiltily. "Caught red-handed. Now I'll never convince you I'm not an inveterate snoop."

"You won't anyway. I've watched you for six years. It runs in the family."

"Oops. Time for a new driver." She nodded toward the books as she set the statue back. "Most of these sound pretty arcane."

"Interesting choice of words, considering you're a witch. It's research material. Dissertations have to be arcane these days. There are way too many of us in the world."

"I think there might be too many witches in the world, as well. By at least two."

"What have you and your mother been up to?"

Good. He was disapproving, but not shocked. She could work with that. Miranda went to sit on the old leather couch that occupied one side of the living room. "We cast a spell on Mason. On both him and Raine, actually."

She explained the whole thing, from the decision to dose Caro with the potion to the second attempt to reverse the spell on Mason, which had taken place in the glen just last night despite her qualms. She even told him why Mason needed to marry Caroline, although discussing family finances with the staff went way over the line of propriety. Somewhere in the middle, the teakettle whistled from the stove and Paul excused himself and came back with big mugs of tea. Otherwise, he gave her his full attention and refrained from laughing aloud.

"You probably think I'm terrible," Miranda said when she had finished.

"Misguided, perhaps. Not terrible. A terrible person wouldn't be so concerned about the repercussions of what she'd done. But I'm curious, why did you repeat the counterspell last night, when you're not certain about what you're doing?"

"I figured we needed to get things back to where they were before we started. And then Raine went and pulled this stunt this morning and now Mason claims he never was under the spell to begin with. But he's hurt, Paul. He's hurt so deeply that he's not letting himself feel anything at all, not even anger. He should be furious at her, but he's joking about it. What am I going to do?"

Paul got up and walked across the room to look out the window. "You're going to do what's right."

"But what is that? I don't know anymore."

"Yes, you do."

"We need the Wickersham money. Saving the company is everything to Mason. It's what he wants."

"Probably." He turned and looked at her. "But what does he need?"

She closed her eyes and called up all the times she'd seen Mason look at Caroline, and all the times he'd looked at Raine, and there was no comparison. It all came down to his face the night of the Wilmott Foundation dance and again the other evening on the terrace when he was watching Raine with Sam. He needed to look like that all the time. Tears leaked out the corners of Miranda's eyes as she swallowed at the lump in her throat.

"Oh, God, Paul, he needs Raine and I've just spent the last two nights doing my best to make sure he doesn't have her. What am I going to do?" She sobbed.

He came back to the couch and sat beside her and quietly put one arm around her shoulder to pull her close. The unexpected tenderness made her sob harder.

"You're going to fix it," he said. "And since I contributed to the situation, I'm going to help you. Miss Hobart's friend told me some things this morning that I think you might find very enlightening."

• • •

There was nothing like a lively business meeting to keep one's interest engaged, and the meeting in the AI board room on Thursday afternoon was nothing if not lively.

The main topic of discussion was, of course, the FUSE protest and its possible repercussions, the board's guests being the chairmen of the various companies that had committed to move into Canal Place. Mason, Jake Kreutzmiller, and Scott Johnson spent the best part of an hour reassuring all concerned that, as yet, there was no significant fallout that would delay start of construction.

Scott was into the six or seventh recounting of his conversation with a member of the planning commission when the door opened and Caroline walked in.

"Surprise, I'm home."

"Caroline." Mason stood automatically, and the others followed his lead.

"Oh, gentlemen, sit down, please," said Caroline as she strolled the length of the conference room, working it as though it were a runway in Paris. "Except you, of course, darling. I missed you."

She walked straight into Mason's arms and kissed him without preliminaries.

She'd never been so public in her affections before, and it was such an obvious claim to possession that Mason went from stunned to irritated in a heartbeat. He put his hands on her waist and disengaged her. "It's good to see you, Caro, but I am in a meeting."

"Oh, no, I got lipstick on you." She pulled the handkerchief out of his breast pocket and dabbed at the corner of his mouth, then artfully tucked it back in his pocket and fluffed the corners. "I'm sure these gentlemen don't mind a quick kiss. And anyway, they might as well get used to it. There's no telling when I'll pop in, once we're married."

"Married?" boomed Kreutzmiller. "Mason, you dog. You never said a word."

Handshakes and congratulations were forthcoming. Mason accepted them mechanically, wondering why he didn't feel some sense of relief or triumph. He'd been waiting for Caroline to say yes; now she had. There should be an "Hooray" in there somewhere.

Someone buzzed out to Chris, who quickly appeared with two

bottles of champagne, chilled, though not on ice, and some plastic cups.

''Congratulations, Mr. Alexander,'' she said. She looked a bit confused.

Well, she might be, but the business heads in the room certainly weren't.

Every man and woman there knew the value of a Wick-Alexander business combine, and Mason could practically hear the cash registers ring as they toted up the numbers.

He frowned, then chided himself.

Why shouldn't they? He'd done it himself for months. It was a hell of a prospect.

The champagne was guzzled, and the meeting broke up. Caro and he were the picture of the power couple as they accepted a final round of congratulations and said good-bye, before they walked back to Mason's office.

Caroline stepped away from him as he closed the door, and went to stand behind his desk as though she belonged there in his place. She wore a navy-blue silk suit and a cool smile that said she owned the world. She probably would soon, Mason reflected.

''You haven't asked me why I came back early,'' she said, scanning the items on his desk.

''Not because you missed me?''

''I got a phone call from Daddy yesterday morning—no, this morning. When was it? I'm so jet-lagged I'm not even sure what day it is here. Thursday morning Singapore time, whenever that was.'' She leveled her pale gray eyes right at Mason. ''He said your attention might be wandering. That you had taken someone to the Wilmott Foundation dance.''

''Did he?''

''I suppose it was my fault, in a way. I was enjoying teasing you about your proposal. Letting you dangle. But I always intended to say yes. Surely you knew that.''

Mason made a neutral, ''Mmm.''

''Anyway, I made arrangements to come home right away and clear things up with you.'' She reached for her purse. ''And then he sent me this fax of the woman you'd been seeing.''

She pulled out a piece of paper, unfolded it, and laid it on the desk. Mason recognized the photo immediately, even in black and white, from ten feet away, and upside down. His stomach clenched at the sight of Raine's flyaway hair streaming across his caricatured face.

''Am I mistaken,'' asked Caro, biting the words, ''or is this the little piece of garden trash that ruined my Ferragamos with her fish crap?''

''It's not fish crap, Caroline. It's fermented fish by-products. I'd think you'd appreciate the difference, since you were wearing so much of it.''

Caro's expression went flat. She was not amused.

''Don't get smart with me, Mason. I'm too tired and pissed to find you funny. You need to understand a few things. I don't mind if you get your thrills elsewhere, even by slumming, but I won't have you jerk me around in public. And I won't have you humiliating me by sleeping with someone who's crossed me. If you want my money—and we both know you do—you'll keep all that in mind.''

''Take a look at that picture. Do you think I'm seeing her anymore?''

''Good,'' she said, reaching for the top button on her blouse. ''And now, in the spirit of celebration, I think it's time we take this agreement to the table, so to speak.''

She unbuttoned in a quick striptease as she walked toward him, tugging the creamy silk open just as she reached him. With a shrug she slipped her straps down, then took his hand and pulled it to her breast inside the lace cup of her bra. Her nipple was flaccid against his palm, not like—

He pulled his hand away.

''This is neither the time nor the place, Caroline. Not to mention the fact that I feel like a fire hydrant you're marking.''

She started buttoning up with no apparent ill will. ''As long as everybody knows you're mine, darling. Including you.''

''After your announcement, I think my status is extremely clear to all concerned.'' He glanced at his watch. ''And now, if you'll excuse me, I have a dinner meeting.''

''There's nothing on your calendar. I looked.''

''It's last minute. My roommate from Harvard. I would ask you to come along but you really do look exhausted. Get some sleep and I'll talk to you tomorrow. Good night.''

He pressed a quick kiss to her cheek and made his exit while she still had two buttons to go. As he passed his secretary's desk at a brisk clip, he said, ''Chris, tell Paul to meet me out front, and make sure Miss Wickersham has transportation."

"Yes, sir."

By some quirk, the elevator was empty. Mason breathed a sigh of relief.

The ex-roommate was a fiction. He'd just felt a need to escape Caro's clutches before he got any more disgusted with her, or with himself.

He couldn't afford to get disgusted. The preliminaries of this quarter's financial statement were in his top drawer, and they were not pretty. Without money from Wick, AI was going nowhere, and the power cell might just as well be another of his father's pipe dreams.

Paul pulled up just as he hit the front door. Mason signaled him to stay put and let himself into the car, and they pulled into the rush hour traffic with barely a pause.

"Where to, sir?"

"Someplace quiet. The mountains. Up toward Mt. Rainier." That would take several hours, especially at this time of evening. Caro wouldn't be able to track him down. The car phone rang and he hit the power button to turn it off without answering. He'd call Sam later, before bed, to explain, and they'd make it up this weekend. Maybe he'd take her sailing. They could stay out overnight. A tall ship and a star.

Paul took a left when he should have gone right.

"You're going the wrong way."

"Traffic, sir. I heard a report earlier. We'll avoid some trouble by taking another route out of downtown."

"Fine."

Tawdry. The word kept going through his head. St. Audry, the old English market where shiny, cheap baubles could be had for a few pennies and which had given its name to worthless trash. He felt tawdry.

"I like driving through downtown, don't you, sir?"

Paul's voice startled Mason. It wasn't like him to chitchat. "I suppose."

"The buildings are so interesting. Have you ever wondered why one end of downtown is so successful while the other isn't?"

"I suppose it's a matter of history."

"Maybe," said Paul. "But Seattle started down at the Pioneer Square end, and yet that part of town always seems to attract the destitute instead of the successful. Even in the old days.''

''People with money have always moved up on the hills. It's the castle mentality. That and getting away from the swamps and the fever. It's instinctive.''

''Instinctive. And yet it's almost as though it's the area that generates the success.''

''Is there a point to this nonsense, Paul?''

''Just making some observations, sir. There are areas in Hong Kong that seem successful, too. And yet occasionally, that can change. One of the most interesting cases I heard of involved a new bank that came into a district. The other businesses in the area—mostly large companies—had been very successful until this new building went up. Then they started failing, but only those along a specific line. It seems the new building had been designed with a sharp corner and lots of windows, so it was like a sort of shiny knife. Most of the businesses that failed faced the edge of the knife. Isn't that interesting?''

''That's crap. I know what you're doing, Paul, and I don't appreciate it. And where the hell are we going?''

''North on Aurora Avenue.''

Toward Raine.

''You're fired.''

''Yes, sir. I assumed I would be. Please sit back and try to keep an open mind.''

Mason didn't have much choice, at fifty miles an hour. He sat back and fumed, waiting for the chance to jump out of the car.

To his surprise, when Paul pulled off Aurora Avenue, he turned away from Raine's house. Instead, they went down past the Adobe building, under the bridge, and along the waterfront to the Canal Place site. Curious, Mason forgot his plan to jump out.

Paul's personal car, a nondescript red hatchback that had seen better days, was sitting in front of the old warehouse. As the Rolls pulled up, Miranda stepped out of the hatchback.

Stubbornly clinging to the last bit of control he had, Mason sat in the car until Paul came around and opened the door. He got out and straightened his tie.

''He's all yours,'' Paul said to Miranda.

''What the hell is going on?'' Mason demanded.

''Did you soften him up?'' asked Miranda, ignoring him.

''He's not very receptive,'' Paul answered.

She sighed. "Mason, Mason. You need to expand your horizons." She put her hands on her hips. "*Feng shui.* That's where you need to start."

"I don't need to start anywhere."

"Yes, you do. You see, I'm going to the planning commission as a friend of FUSE. I will speak out against Canal Place as designed, so unless you do some research, you're not going to be able to debate me. And you know how vocal I can be."

Mason spluttered.

"It's all right, darling. I've made it easy. Paul?"

Paul walked to the back of his car and opened the hatchback. Miranda joined him and crooked a finger toward her brother. "Come on, Mason. That's a boy."

"Quit talking to me like I'm in diapers," he said. He took his time getting to the car.

Miranda pulled out a fat three-ring binder. "I've put together the materials for you. This is a collection of articles I found."

She pushed it against Mason's chest, so that he had no choice but to take it. She reached for more. "Here's an assortment of books. And these are the architectural drawings for the current plan." She piled it all into Mason's arms.

He dumped it back into the car. "Thank you very much, but I know all I need to know about this site."

Miranda shook her head and looked at Paul. "You're right. Resistive. And pigheaded and narrow-minded, not to mention blind. I love you, Mason, but you need to get a clue."

She pulled down the hatchback and turned around and dropped the keys into Mason's jacket pocket.

"Paul and I are going to go now. We're leaving you his car so you won't stick out too much—we don't want you to get carjacked or anything—but you'll probably want to pull up onto Thirty-fourth before it gets too late. It'll give you a better view of the site and the neighborhood anyway."

"What makes you think I won't leave as soon as you're gone?"

"Because, despite being pigheaded, you're not stupid. Before you decide to drive off, walk around. See what we could destroy with too much arrogance. And then decide whether you're going to at least read a few pages. You have everything you need to sit here for a while and match up what you read to the plans. I had Cook pack you dinner and a Thermos, and there's even a flashlight and one of those reading lights in case it gets dark.''

She hugged him, and despite the circumstances Mason found himself chuckling. ''All right. I'll read your silly papers. But don't expect a lot. This stuff is pretty far out there.''

''All I expect is that you'll take a look.''

She and Paul walked back to the Rolls. Paul held the door, and they drove away, leaving Mason to be enlightened.

He snorted and got in the car and drove off.

Nineteen

"Do you suppose that will actually work?" asked Miranda as they drove north on Greenwood. Traffic was heavy, and it was taking forever to get anywhere.

"Only if he really wants to see Miss Hobart again."

"If Mother and I didn't screw that up for him." She sighed. "I'm sorry he fired you."

Paul met her eyes in the rearview mirror. "I'm not."

"I thought you liked working for us. For Mason, I mean."

"I do. Did. But there are advantages to not working. Or at least to not working for Mr. Alexander."

"Like what?"

"I can work on my dissertation full-time and do my defense this fall instead of waiting. It will put me in the pool for tenure-track positions next spring when the universities are hiring."

"I didn't know you wanted to be a professor."

"Actually, I had hoped to go to work for Alexander Industries for a few years first, but that doesn't look like it's going to pan out."

Paul slammed on the brakes as a fool on a motorcycle cut in front of the car.

"That was close. I thought I was going to see evolution in action," said Miranda. "You said advantag*es*. What else?"

"Well." He slowed the car to a stop at a light. "One of the

major ones is that, since I'm not an employee, I can ask you out."

Miranda sat stunned, until Paul turned around and grinned at her, at which point she realized how stupid she must look with her mouth hanging open.

So she closed it and opened the door to run up to the front passenger door while the light was still red. Paul popped the lock and she slid in next to him.

"Are you serious?" she asked.

He nodded as he accelerated through the intersection. "What do you think, Miranda? Can an Alexander even consider going out with an unemployed graduate student?"

Tears hung just beneath the surface. Miranda nodded. "You know, don't you, that I'm about half in love with you?"

"Good," said Paul quietly. "Because I've been all the way in love with you for years."

"Oh." She had to put her hand over her mouth to catch the sob of relief. "Oh, Paul. Why didn't you say anything?"

"You weren't ready to hear it, and I wasn't in the position to do anything about it. The chauffeur doesn't ask out the boss's sister."

"No. Probably not." The memory of all the men she'd had in the car since her divorce made her wince. She reached out, almost touching his cheek. "You drove me on dates."

"I waited outside apartments on a few of them, too," he reminded her, without accusation. "It was never easy, but after Saturday night I realized that any more would be impossible. If you hadn't given me an excuse to get myself fired, I would have had to quit. My letter of resignation was in the computer when you got in the car last night."

"So now what?" she said.

He hit the turn indicator, swung over to the curb, and turned the engine off. "Now we find out if this is going to work."

He kissed her, and it was what she had known it would be, fiery and sweet and erotic all at once, and more satisfying than any dozen kisses she'd had in her entire life. His broad hands went around her, holding her head and waist while he gently teased her mouth open. With a groan she pressed toward him, exploring the lines of his face with her palms, lacing her fingers into his wonderful, thick hair.

"I think," murmured Paul, "this indicates definite possibilities."

They necked like teenagers for a long time, each one pushing things a little further, as though they were in a contest to see who could do the most damage in the shortest time. Finally, it was either stop or make an exhibition of themselves for the neighborhood kids, two of whom were hanging out on a retaining wall trying to act casual while sneaking peeks.

"Oh, my," said Miranda, straightening her blouse. "We are out of hand, aren't we? We'd better move on before someone calls the police."

Paul started the car and pulled back into traffic. They drove a couple of blocks in silence. He occasionally glanced her way, then grinned and shook his head as though he couldn't believe it.

For her part, Miranda just watched his face, absorbing the wonder of it all. In the six years he'd worked for them, she had never sat next to him like this, where she could really watch him. His hands were strong and capable on the wheel of the Rolls, like they had been on her body a few minutes ago.

Six years, and she had so much to get to know: where his family lived, if he ate red meat, whether he had hair on his chest, how many children he wanted. All the details, none of which really mattered because she knew what kind of man he was and he loved her and the rest would work out.

"We should go up to Mt. Rainier," he said.

"What?"

"That's where your brother wanted me to take him. What do you think? We can stop for take-out along the way."

"Only if you promise that we'll find a quiet spot in the woods and crawl in the back to see if we can find some fun ways to eat it."

Paul laughed and took her hand to kiss it. "And me without my chopsticks."

Raine sat bolt upright in bed, her heart pounding in rhythm to the knocking on her door in the next room. The luminous dial of her clock read one-forty-seven.

No one should be at her door at almost two A.M., which left two possibilities: she was being robbed by a polite burglar, or Mrs. Perlmutter was sick.

She scrambled out of bed and groped around for her robe. She couldn't find it, and then she remembered where Bugsy had deposited his hairball last night and decided it didn't really matter. Anyway, if it wasn't Mrs. P. out there, a robe would just slow her down.

She crept out into the living room cautiously, picking up her baseball bat as she passed the umbrella stand. She peeked out the window. It was pitch black outside, the nearest streetlight having burned out a couple of nights back. She couldn't make out much more than a dim shadow.

It was a man, not Mrs. P., and whoever he was, he knocked again, more persistently. She checked the chain and raised the bat, then flipped the light switch and opened the door a crack.

Mason. Her pounding heart stopped, then restarted again with a painful squeeze.

He just stood there looking at her through the crack, all solemn and haggard, as though he hadn't been able to sleep well the past two nights either. His hair was mussed from him raking it back with his fingers, and, while he wore a suit, his tie was completely gone, for once, and his shirt collar was unbuttoned. He actually looked rumpled, which perversely made him even more attractive.

"Go away," she groaned, but in the same instant she closed the door and took the chain off. She pulled it open and stood there staring at him, not knowing what else to do.

His quick glance sideways to the bat in her hand brought the slightest curve to his lips.

"Get dressed," he said. "I need you to come with me."

"It's nearly two in the morning." And she was in a baggy T-shirt and boxer shorts, but that didn't seem as relevant.

"They mentioned that down at the Dubliner before they threw me out. Get dressed."

"I'm not going anywhere with you if you've been drinking."

"One scotch three hours ago and a gallon of coffee. Would you please get dressed?"

He put that soft emphasis on *please* again, just as he had when he'd asked her to dance outside his room. She turned to put the bat back in the umbrella stand, so he couldn't see what that one word did to her.

"A gallon of coffee. I guess that explains why *you're* awake. All right, Mason. I will get dressed."

She left him standing on the porch and shut herself in the bedroom to pull on jeans and a long-sleeved, cotton knit shirt. Noises in the other room told her she was wise to have locked the bedroom door: he'd walked into the house uninvited again. After she found her shoes, she popped into the bathroom to run a brush through her hair and pull it back into a ponytail.

Mason had a flashlight out and was rifling her junk drawer.

"Gee. Just help yourself," she said.

"Do you have any spare batteries?"

"They're on the list. Sorry. Wait a minute, why am I apologizing? Get out of my drawers."

He raised one eyebrow, but shut the drawer.

"Let's go. You'd better have a jacket." He stepped around her and opened the tiny coat closet, from which he pulled her favorite denim jacket.

She resisted the urge to ask him where he was taking her, but simply locked the door behind herself as she followed him outside. Questions were harder to avoid when he led her not to the Rolls, or even his Jaguar, but to a late-eighties Japanese hatchback that had seen better days, but she bit her tongue. She wouldn't give him the satisfaction of asking.

The ride was short, and ended up in the least likely place she could have imagined: beneath a light on the street above the Canal Place site.

"Whatever it is, I didn't have anything to do with it this time."

A puff of air escaped him, almost a chuckle. "I was kidnapped tonight."

"Mason! By terrorists?"

"Not unless my sister has joined the IRA. She and Paul conspired to bring me here against my will, where they forced me to trade the Rolls for this aesthetic wonder—it's Paul's, by the way; I know you've been dying to ask—and drove off. They left behind that." He gestured over his shoulder.

There was a large file box in the backseat, and Raine reached over and pulled the top item into her lap. It was a binder, which she opened. As she flipped through the pages, she grew more and more astonished.

"It's some sort of dossier on *feng shui.*"

Mason nodded. "History, modern schools, opinions pro and

con, what little scientific study has been done—and it's pretty specious, I'll tell you up front."

"This is amazing, And remarkably complete," said Raine, flipping back and forth. "Although there's a lot more that—"

"It's probably in the back. They left me books, charts, magazine articles, computer printouts." He stared out the window toward the lights on the bridge. "They told me to read it all. Of course, when they left, I drove off. I was going to go up into the mountains and clear my head. Try to forget the last few days."

"The mountains are a good place for that," said Raine. "Were you successful?"

"I never made it. There was a hellish accident on the 520 bridge right ahead of me and I sat there for nearly two hours. I don't sit well without anything to do, and since Miranda and her accomplice had driven off with my briefcase and my cell phone, as well as my car, I was left with no option but to read what was on hand." He reached over and tapped the binder cover. "That."

"And?"

"*Feng shui* is archaic, illogical except in the most primitive way, and has no rational scientific basis whatsoever."

"Oh."

"It's also fascinating. The anecdotal evidence is as compelling as it is occasionally outlandish. I found myself wishing it worked." He met Raine's eyes. "I never felt that way about witchcraft, crystals, totem spirits, or any form of chanting."

"It does work. I've seen it work. Shoot, I've made it work."

"So I understand from the letters you sent Scott Johnson. Miranda somehow got her hands on them. They're in one of those files in that box." He pushed his hair back again, and then reached into the back for a couple of big rolls of paper. "Grab the flashlight."

He got out and Raine followed, meeting him at the front bumper.

"These are architectural drawings for the new building."

"I know," she said. "I have a set of my own."

"How did you—? Never mind." He unrolled the site plan that showed the layout of the building and laid it out on the hood of the car, turning it to orient it properly to the site. "Show me what it is you see when you look at this."

"I—But—You—" She took a deep breath to collect her

thoughts. "It's complicated, Mason. I'm still a student."

"You were confident enough to make your conclusions public."

"After I checked them with a master. I have all of this at home, all worked out. It would be easier if—"

"I want to watch you go through it. If you had your work checked, then you know it's valid. Just show me the basics."

"It's pitch black. You can't see the lay of the land, which is where I need to start. I don't even have my compass."

He held up a finger. "Wait here."

In seconds, he produced a topographic map of the area along with both a regular compass and a *luo-pan*, the traditional compass of the Chinese geomancer. "Miranda didn't leave either of us any excuses."

"Mason."

"Please."

She sighed. "You're as bad as a two-year-old. You think *please* is the magic word that makes people do what you've already told them to."

"Pretty please?"

"Oh, geez, sometimes I hate you." She walked away from the car to get a good reading, then went back and smacked her hand down in the center of the topographical map and spun it so that north on the map matched north on the compass. A quick shift about twenty degrees counterclockwise compensated for magnetic declination and brought the compass rose on the map more or less into line with true north.

"Hold this," she said, handing him the flashlight. "You are here. Canal. Queen Anne Hill."

She pointed out the landmarks one by one, then took the fountain pen out of Mason's pocket and sketched in lines to show him how they fit together. She showed him how energy passed down the Ship Canal with the water and took her time explaining how the Chinese had named the landforms and how they were associated with lines of energy, positive and negative.

"There are three major lines in this area," she said. She sketched them in as she had calculated them. "Here, here, and here. See how they meet roughly in the center of town? It's that energy that makes Fremont what it is and attracts the creative people to the area."

''Maybe it's because this is where the bridge crosses,'' he countered.

''Ballard has a bridge. Can you picture the Seattle City Council proclaiming *Ballard* as Center of the Universe? Anyway, you plan to put your building here.'' She slashed a big *X* through the site; her marks cut off two of the lines of energy before they reached the junction. ''You'll stagnate the energy flows. Fremont will die a slow, painful death.''

''There are several old buildings in this area. Why don't they affect Fremont the same way?''

''They probably do, but to a lesser extent. They're wood, which is more organic, and they have a smaller footprint, so there's more open space for the energy to flow around them. In general, they're just more integrated into the area.''

She could tell from his face he was having trouble with this, but he managed not to sneer.

''Okay. Assuming I buy all that, what about the design of the building? Your letters say that the design is bad. Why?'' He flipped the map out of the way to reveal the building layout. ''What's wrong?''

''What isn't? Just from a commonsense standpoint, it's too tall and shiny.'' She lifted the plan to show the architect's concept drawings of the facade. ''Look at this and then look around here. It doesn't fit into the neighborhood at all. People already resent you for cutting them off from the water, and you haven't even started construction yet. I can't believe the planning commission let you get away with this design.''

''They're anxious to get rid of these old firetraps and get more productive use out of the waterfront.''

''And kill Fremont in the process.'' She was starting to get cold, so she stepped past him to get into the car for her jacket and slipped it on. ''From a *feng shui* view, Canal Place is a disaster. Those sharp corners''—she pointed—''will be like poisonous arrows into the businesses across the street. All that mirrored glass will reflect energy away from the whole area.

''*Feng shui* is about the relationship of humans to their environment, Mason. Most of the time that means the natural world, like the hills and the water. But sometimes it means to other humans. It all has to work together, or none of us will be well.''

He stood there, looking out over the site, absorbing her words.

"The Dubliner's one of the businesses that would be affected, isn't it?"

"Definitely."

"I used to go to an Irish pub like that in Boston. A big, shiny, angular office building went in across the street and, six months later Sean was out of business."

"And everyone claimed it was bad business judgment on his part, I bet, ignoring the fact that he'd managed to stay in business for twenty or thirty years before the *ch'i* was fouled up."

"Or it could just be that the stockbrokers didn't like stout and displaced his customer base. That's the problem with anecdotal evidence, Raine. You can make suppositions, but you don't *know* what happened because it wasn't a controlled study. It could just be coincidence."

"Then there are an awful lot of coincidences. I've done studies and corrections on fifteen houses and a half dozen businesses in the past year or so. All but two owners came back to me saying that their health was better, or that they'd come into unexpected money, or that business was up."

"Okay. So tell me what you did. Even the two that didn't work."

"All of them? That will take a while."

"I'm not going anywhere."

So she told him, about the house with the heavy beam over the owner's bed, and the business with the T-junction in front of it, and all the other cases, straightforward or subtle, that she had helped or tried to help. Mason asked a thousand questions, made her draw things out and justify her assumptions, and generally aggravated her, but to Raine that was the clearest sign he was listening, and after so many months with no one listening, it was such a relief that she wanted to dump everything from her mind into his.

At some point, about the time the flashlight batteries ran down, the summer night got too chill even with jackets. She and Mason crawled into the car and turned the engine on to get some heat while they worked under the dome light. A couple of drunks stumbled by on their way to some secret sleeping spot, but otherwise they were left alone until a patrol car shined a spotlight into the car.

Hands held up where the officers could see, Mason got out to talk with them. When he came back he looked confused.

"What the devil are submarine races? He wanted to make sure we weren't going to them."

Raine swallowed a chuckle. "That's what we used to call it back home when couples would go parking—watching the submarine races."

He still looked blank.

"Up periscope," she said, slowly uncurling a forefinger until it pointed skyward. As understanding dawned across his face, she burst out laughing.

"Oh, lord," said Mason, and then he broke out laughing, too, and they laughed until tears ran down Raine's face and she wasn't sure if it was because it was so funny or so sad that the officers had been that far off the mark.

As their laughter faded, Mason handed her his handkerchief to dry her cheeks and sighed.

"I can't stop the building, Raine. MMT is the one part of our business where we have any pull left with the banks, and that's because of this property. If Canal Place goes, I can parlay it into cash flow down the road that won't be reliant on Wick funding. If I back out now, I'm out of options."

"You don't have to back out," she said. "The building can be built, it just has to be different. Lower. A lot more neighborhood friendly. And there has to be some way for the *ch'i* to flow through—glass block walls or a breezeway of some sort. Maybe you could put in a sculpture walk, which would also give you lots of points with the neighborhood if you included local artists. You can even make it so there's better access to the waterfront than there is now, like Quadrant did for Adobe over on that side of the bridge. There are good architects who design in accordance with *feng shui* principles. It can be fixed."

"You're talking a complete redesign. That costs a fortune."

"Then I guess what it comes down to is how much Fremont is worth on your balance sheets."

The sense of futility that had faded over the course of the night washed back over her. She stared out the windshield at the lightening sky.

"I'm exhausted, Mason. And if that's right"—she tapped the analog clock on the dashboard—"I'm due to get up in forty minutes anyway. Could you please take me home so I can shut off my alarm and take a shower?"

They rolled up the plans and dumped all the papers back into

Miranda's box, and Mason started the car and drove her home. He walked her to the door, stood there while she unlocked it, and followed her in, all without saying a word.

"Mason, what do you want?"

"I'll take you to breakfast," he said. "Go on and have your shower. I'll wait out here."

The rational part of her—the part he claimed she didn't use—wanted to say no. Breakfast sitting across from him would just be too hard to deal with, and her heart wasn't up to it. Unfortunately, she didn't have the will.

"All right," she said. "Do me a favor and make yourself useful. Slap together a couple of peanut butter sandwiches and fill up my water jug. Lots of ice, please. It's supposed to be hot again."

She took her time in the shower—after all, she wasn't even supposed to be up yet—then dinked around with sunscreen and her hair until she couldn't find any more excuses.

When she walked into the living room, she found Mason crouched down in front of her bookshelf reading titles. "*Feng Shui for the Home*. *The Elements of Feng Shui*. *Feng Shui for Beginners*. I looked at your bookshelves last week. I don't remember seeing all these. You must have twenty or thirty books here on *feng shui*."

"I had them in the closet," said Raine. "I didn't want you to figure out who I was until I had a chance to lay some groundwork."

"*The Way of the Warrior*," he read. "*Zen and the Art of Motorcycle Maintenance*. You must have hidden these, too. Oh, God—*Women Who Run with the Wolves*. You don't have any desire to actually own a wolf, do you?"

"It's allegory, Mason."

"Not at my house." He stood up and stretched, then rubbed his back. "That car of Paul's could stand better seats."

"That car could stand better everything. You should pay him more. Come on, if we're going to eat, we've got to get moving." She grabbed her backpack off the knob of the closet door and started for the kitchen to toss the sandwiches he'd made into it, along with a couple of oranges. Not fancy, but filling.

"Just a minute." He stepped into her path, blocking her. "Down there at the site, you said that sometimes you hate me. How do you feel in between those times?"

She wanted to turn away, but he hadn't left her any room to maneuver. "It's not relevant. Caroline will be back soon and you two—"

"She's already back," he said. "She walked into the board-room yesterday and announced our engagement."

"Oh. Congratulations." She started to brush past him, but he held his position.

"You still haven't answered my question. How do you feel about me?" He put his hands on her waist. "Tell me, Raine. Please."

"There you go again, telling me what to do, then saying please like I'm . . . I love you, you idiot. Why do you think you can make me so mad?"

A slow, deep smile lit his face, but he turned back to the bookshelf and continued reading titles while she stood there with her chest locked so tight that she thought her ribs would crack.

When he reached the end, he shook his head. "Doesn't it just figure. I fight for years to get my mother and sister to give up this New Age nonsense, and then I go and fall in love with a woman who apparently reads nothing else."

Her breath came in a shudder and tears clung to her lashes, threatening to spill over. "I do, too. The Shakespeare and Kafka and Raymond Chandler are on the shelf right below that. Next to my welding manual."

Mason stood up and gently touched one of the tears as it trickled down her cheek, then held the droplet up like a single diamond on his fingertip. " 'O father, what a hell of witchcraft lies, In the small orb of one particular tear.' It's going to take a lot of love, Raine."

"I won't be your mistress, even if you do know the sonnets."

"Good girl." He kissed her on the cheek. "Did I happen to mention that even before I got caught in that traffic jam last night, I had decided that Caroline Wickersham was the last person I would ever marry?" He pulled back a little and put on a prissy look. "She makes me feel so cheap. Besides, I'm going to marry you, Lorraine M. Hobart."

Her heart stopped and restarted again. She took a deep breath. "I don't have any money. I can't save your company."

"But you can save me." He kissed her cheek. "And Sam." The other cheek. "And Fremont, too, because as a wedding present I'm going to have the damned building redesigned."

"Oh. Oh!" She flung her arms around his neck and peppered kisses over his face. "Yes, I'll marry you. Even without the building. But I want the building. Oh, Mason, I love you so much."

The last two miserable days vanished at the touch of his lips against hers and all that was left was the glory of kissing him and touching him and knowing it was, finally, truly, all right to be with him. That was all she wanted, to be with him, and as close as possible.

Mason pulled her into the bedroom and it was Saturday night all over again, the two of them stripping away each other's clothes until they stood there, skin to skin in the morning light. His hands played over her skin possessively, lighting tiny fires wherever he touched, and he touched everywhere, making her ready.

When she was more ready than she'd ever been in her life, she tried to pull him toward the bed. He stopped her.

''I haven't seen you,'' he said. ''Not really. Let me look at you.''

He backed way, leaving her there in the middle of the room. His eyes never left hers as he turned on the lamp beside her bed, and then he slowly, very deliberately, let his gaze wander the length of her body.

She closed her eyes and stood there, taking it, melting from it, until she couldn't stand it anymore.

''My turn,'' she said, her voice shaky.

He nodded, and stood for her while she looked to her fill. He was very male, all angles and sinew, as beautiful as an ancient statue minus the fig leaf. He was aroused, and she found herself staring as though she'd never seen a man before. When she thought about it, she never really had, not a man like this, who loved her, and whom she loved and wanted so badly.

She stepped forward and, with a boldness she'd never suspected, curved her hand around him.

He shuddered, then wrapped his hand over hers and showed her what he liked as he kissed her.

She was going to drive him crazy, Mason thought, and he encouraged it for as long as he could bear it and then wrapped his arms around her and spun her down onto the bed.

And then something about lying there on top of her made his brain reconnect with a thought.

"Raine."

"Hmm?"

"The other night, I . . . Were you a virgin?"

She got very still, and he kicked himself for asking the question, but it was out there between them and he couldn't take it back.

"No," she said. "I wish I had been."

"It doesn't matter."

"Yes, it does. To me." She looked away from him, toward the wall. "When I first got to Claremont, I went a little nuts. You know, small-town girl away from home for the first time. One day I wised up and promised myself I'd never sleep with any man I didn't love and who didn't love me. I kept my promise, too, until you came along. I was pretty sure I'd messed up with you."

"You hadn't. I just didn't know yet how much I needed you and loved you. Raine, whatever has made you who you are, I'm glad. I only asked because I was concerned that I had hurt you. You screamed."

"It had been a long time. A very long time." She looked up at him, and the mischief was back in her eyes. "But that scream had very little to do with pain. Want to see?"

She wriggled beneath him and Mason felt himself grow more taut.

"Very much so. However, while I'm still capable of rational thought . . ." He rolled off her and found his coat on the floor. He pulled a small package of condoms out of the pocket and tossed the jacket over the back of a chair.

"You have condoms in your suit?"

"Presumptuous, aren't I? I found an all-night drugstore before I came to get you. I knew if I touched you it would be all over."

"You had those on you the whole time we were down at the site?"

He nodded.

"And you strung me along and let me think you still hated me?"

"I never hated you, Raine. I was furious at you and the circumstances, but I never hated you. And as for stringing you along, I didn't intend to, but I had to be certain it wasn't just lust. I had to know that I loved all of you, the way you are, even in those areas where our minds will probably never meet. And most of all, I had to be certain that you loved me."

"Well, I do, and boy, are you going to get it for making me wait. Get over here and let me take out my frustrations before you make me late for work."

He got, and her frustrations were mighty. She teased him with mouth and hands and body. Even putting on the condom became part of her revenge. She managed to drag that one simple act out for five minutes, until he vowed he'd had enough, and he rolled her over and pinned her to the bed.

Then it was his turn to torment her, and he took his time about it, lazily kissing and tonguing his way down her body until she began to thrash and beg for him to put an end to it.

He shifted up onto her, and the weight of him, hot and solid and crazed with the same passion she knew, was so intense that the first touch of his entry pushed her right up against the edge. As he moved in her, the tension coiled tighter and tighter until with one more thrust, it uncoiled in a rush and left her shuddering and moaning his name. He slowed, allowing her the full measure of her orgasm before he pushed on to his own. His shout mingled with the last of her sighs, and they collapsed together in the tangled, damp sheets.

"Sometime," said Raine, yawning, a few minutes later, "we ought to try this when we're wide awake and don't have to be somewhere else. I've got to get to work."

"Call in sick."

"Fine corporate leader you are. Anyway, I can't. I already missed most of Wednesday. They'll fire me."

"So?"

"It's my job. I like it. And besides, we're not married yet, and I have bills to pay." She yawned again and snuggled against him. "But maybe just a few more minutes."

A few minutes turned into much longer as her breathing quickly settled into the slow, regular rhythm of sleep. Still feeling the effects of all that coffee, Mason lazed beside her, watching her sleep, debating whether to wake her or to just lie there enjoying her warmth and let her get fired so he could keep her in bed late anytime he wanted.

He decided on a compromise and slipped out of bed when she was soundly asleep. He pulled the bedroom door shut behind him and lifted the phone off the cradle to punch in his office number. It was much too early to expect Chris to answer, but he left her a voice mail message saying he wouldn't be in until late, if at all, and leaving Raine's number in case of an emergency. Chris understood exactly what an emergency was: something or someone broken, bleeding, or on fire, not a relative with an ax to grind.

Next he dialed information for the number for Johnson's Landscaping.

"Mason Alexander," he identified himself when Mrs. Johnson picked up the line. "I have a special project I'm working on and I need one of your people today. Raine Hobart."

"I think that can be arranged," said Mrs. Johnson. "As soon as Raine comes in I'll send—"

"As a matter of fact, I've already taken the liberty of contacting Miss Hobart directly, and she's on her way now. I told her I'd follow up with you. Just send the bill to the house. You have the address. Thank you. Yes, all day."

He hung up, one day of hooky neatly arranged. His third call was to the house. Lawrence answered—thank goodness, the fellow was a paragon of discretion—and Mason asked to speak to Samantha on the QT.

"Hello."

The sound of her voice took his breath away. Two days, and she already sounded older. "How are you faring, squirt? Did you have a good time at the McMullens'?"

"Yes. I'm way taller than Adeline now, but she plays the piano better. When are you coming home?"

"I'll tuck you into bed tonight, I promise. And we'll spend a big chunk of the weekend together. I'm sorry I didn't see you last night. A lot of things happened."

"Good things or bad things?"

"Mostly good. In fact, mostly very good."

"Did you really fire Paul? He's packing his books and stuff, but he says he can't leave until you bring his car back. Why do you have his car?"

"It's a long story. I'll tell you all about it when I get home. I have some news especially for you, but I want to tell you in person. I've got to go, squirt. You can tell Gran I called, but don't tell her anything else, okay? I need to do the talking."

"Okay. I love you, Daddy."

"Me, too, squirt."

A quick raid of the fridge for a glass of milk, and he was ready to crawl back into bed next to Raine.

She was beautiful lying there, but Mason understood that it was more than quenched physical desire that had filled the unholy emptiness he'd felt. Raine had brought light and love back into his life when he'd stopped believing in either. She had a talent for simultaneously accepting and giving with her whole heart, and an ability to roll with the punches while laughing at whoever threw them, which was rarer than stardust and more valuable than any combination of capitalization and stock options that the Wickershams could put together.

He closed his eyes and buried his nose in her hair, and inhaled. The scent of her mingled with the slightly bleachy smell of the sheets and the fresh morning air coming through the open window, and for the first time in ages, the world was truly good and he felt a sense of hope. They'd be all right: Alexander Industries and Sam and all of it would be fine, somehow, because of Raine. Much as she did with her decorating, she would take all the detritus of their lives and somehow make it work together. For all that he disdained witchcraft, he was going to have to thank his mother and sister for making this particular piece of magic possible.

The next thing he knew, he was being punched in the arm, and the light coming through the window was the brilliant white of high noon.

"You let me fall asleep, you creep." She crawled over him—an enticing sight, naked—and dashed to the dresser to start pawing through drawers. "I've got to call Mrs. Johnson and try to keep my job."

"Slow down. I took care of it." He explained the call he'd made.

She wasn't quite as thrilled as he'd thought she'd be. "Gee, thanks. The saving grace in this is that Mrs. J. doesn't have a nasty thought in her head. But the guys on my crew are a different matter."

"You can show them your engagement ring Monday morning."

"Oh, big help that will be." She stepped into a pair of white panties—cotton, Mason noted, but with high, French-cut legs that made him want to slip his fingers under the edge. "They'll see a ring and they'll *know* it was no special project."

He rose and walked up behind her and proceeded to indulge his whim, taken by the thought that from this day forward, he could indulge all of his whims where loving Raine was concerned. He ran his hands up along her waist and rib cage to cup her breasts. Her nipples hardened against his fingertips, and his desire flared again, a little less desperate than before. And that was good, too.

"It doesn't matter what 'the guys' think. Your time is mine today, and I intend to get my money's worth. Come on." He took her hand and led her back to bed. "You said you wanted to try this when you were wide awake. And besides, I want another taste."

Conscious, lazy afterglow was even better than Raine had expected. Not much could beat lying in bed next to Mason memorizing whiskers and playing with his chest hair in between long, drugged kisses.

They finally crawled out of bed sometime after three, and while Mason was in the shower, Raine proved she could cook, too, by whipping up a batch of soda biscuits from scratch and scrambling some eggs with ham and the one green pepper that hadn't died yet.

"I hope you made a lot," he said, buttoning his shirt as he walked out. "It's been a long time since those peanuts at the bar."

She eyeballed the pan and reached for the last two eggs in the carton. As she cracked them on the edge of the bowl, she asked, "Whom do we tell first?"

"Samantha," he said without hesitating. "And then Mother and Miranda."

"What about Caroline? Shouldn't she be first?"

"Technically," he said. "But I may need tactical support to handle her and Angus. She's going to be a handful. She'll probably threaten to emasculate me."

''She'd better not. Those are my toys now.'' Raine abandoned the stove to demonstrate her protectiveness.

His eyes twinkled as he removed her hand to safer territory. ''Don't start anything unless you plan to follow through.''

''You're no fun.'' She went back to the eggs, whisking the new ones and adding them to the skillet. ''Anyway, right after Caroline, I'm calling Bemidji. I can hardly wait to tell Mom and Dad.''

''We'll fly there in a couple of weeks. I want to meet them.''

''Not just them. Brothers, sisters, cousins, cousins of cousins. We're a big clan. And I'm the only one that's moved away.''

''I'm glad you did.''

They devoured the food the way they had devoured each other, without much talking, then Raine took a shower while Mason checked his voice mail. She smoothed her wet hair into a chignon and put on another of the outfits she'd bought on his account, a conservative, tailored dress in ashes of roses that made her look more like she belonged on the society pages than in mug shots.

She was working on her makeup when Mason walked in and pulled his neatly rolled tie out of his jacket pocket.

''You look like some odd new flavor of sherbet,'' he said.

''According to color analysts, pink is supposed to make you likable.''

''You already are likable. Mother even likes you,'' he said, shaking out the tie and looping it around his neck. ''She just doesn't think I should marry you. And even that will change once she realizes I'm really in love with you and not the victim of her misdirected magic.''

Raine stopped with her lipstick half on. ''Are we crazy, Mason? We've only known each other two weeks, and if that potion really did—''

''It didn't,'' he said firmly. ''I may be willing to concede that *feng shui* skates on the outer edges of feasibility, but witchcraft? Not a chance. Are you having second thoughts?''

''No.'' She finished her lower lip, put the top back on the lipstick tube, and turned around to him. ''And that's very odd, if you think about it. Everything in my life is about to change. No Mrs. Perlmutter. No neighborhood ball games. No kids in the alley. Yet I'm as certain that marrying you is right as I am that if I look up right now, I'll see a dead president.''

He stopped in midknot. ''I beg your pardon?''

She pointed at the ceiling. "See. The crack makes Abraham Lincoln's profile."

Mason stared up. "My God, you're right. I'm glad I didn't know about him two hours ago. Sex and Honest Abe—" He shuddered. "Not in my mind. Are you about ready? I'd like to make a stop on the way."

She nodded and reach for a tissue. "Just let me blot."

The stop was at the family jeweler, a shop that wasn't at all on the way to the house. However, Mason enjoyed Raine's reaction so much that the minor misdirection was worth it. Together they picked out an antique emerald and diamond ring that suited Raine better than the brilliant cut solitaire diamonds and modern settings the owner showed them first. The ring was a bit loose, but as a temporary measure Mr. Fussel fitted it with a spacer and told them to bring it back first thing Monday to be resized.

Back in the car, Raine kept polishing the ring on her dress, then flashing it in the light. "I love it, Mason. Thank you so much. When I was a kid, I picked out a picture of a ring in a magazine and told my mom that was going to be my engagement ring one day. I swear, it looked just like this."

"Good. It's beautiful on you."

She waggled her fingers. "It is, isn't it? I'll have to figure out something to do with it when I'm working, though. I don't want to scratch it up or knock a stone loose or something. Maybe a chain."

She chattered on about weddings and honeymoons and the other cheerful details of impending matrimony on the way home, but Mason was preoccupied with rehearsing his speeches.

The security guard at the Highlands gate gave the car odd looks, but cleared them without comment. A few minutes later they turned into the drive.

They both spotted the car at the same time: a black stretch Cadillac sitting off to one edge of the carriageway.

"Company," said Raine.

"Angus," said Mason. He slowed and stopped at the edge of the trees. "Damn. I'll give you twenty-five to one that Caroline is with him and they're all cozied up with Mother on the terrace."

"Wow. What now?"

"We have two options. Tell all of them at once and get it

over with in one messy scene, or take off and have dinner somewhere while we wait for them to leave. I can talk to Caroline tomorrow.''

''Neither way seems very fair to her,'' said Raine.

''I don't know. She—''

The front door burst open and Sam came running out. She looked at the stopped car, then yelled and waved.

''I think your options have just been reduced,'' said Raine.

Mason released the hand brake and they rolled the rest of the way down to the parking area.

When they got out, Sam looked from Mason to Raine and back again. ''I'm confused, Daddy. I heard Caro tell Gran that you two are getting married.''

''Well, she's partly right,'' said Mason. He glanced toward Angus's car and dropped his voice so the driver wouldn't hear. ''*I'm* getting married. Remember I told you a couple of days ago that you'd be the first to know when you were getting a new stepmom? Well, you're so first that even Caroline doesn't know yet.''

''You're going to marry Raine?'' asked Sam.

''I certainly am.''

''Yay.'' She hugged her dad, then gave Raine a quick squeeze, too. ''I like you better. You make Daddy laugh, and I never saw Caro make anyone laugh.''

''Thanks, kiddo. I like you better than Caro, too.''

Sam giggled.

''Just out of curiosity, is Mr. Wickersham here, too?'' asked Raine, as they started for the door.

''Yep,'' said Sam. ''He and Gran and Aunt Randi and Caro are all out on the terrace. Are we going to tell them now? I want to watch.''

''Not a chance, squirt. This is a matter strictly for adults. Actually, strictly for me.'' He took Raine's hands. ''Do you mind going into hiding for a bit?''

''No. As much as I'd like to see the look on Caroline's face when I walk out there, it wouldn't be very kind. I don't see any reason to humiliate her more than necessary.''

He kissed her on the cheek. ''Which proves which of you has more class. Sam, *please* take Raine upstairs with you.'' He glanced at Raine and grinned. ''Maybe you two can think of something fun to do this weekend. I'll come get you as soon as things are settled, so we can share a toast."

"Champagne?" asked Sam. "Can I have some?"

"One tiny sip," said Mason.

"Goodie. Come on." Practically dancing with excitement, she led Raine upstairs.

Mason shook out the tension in his arms, then straightened his tie, and walked out to face the music. A lively conversation stopped cold as he walked out on the terrace.

"Mason." His mother looked pleased that he was alone, as did Angus, while Miranda looked stricken.

Caro just looked like Caro, cool, collected, in charge—the same as she had in his office, and probably the same as she would in bed after sex. He suddenly couldn't remember why he'd ever thought that was tolerable, much less appealing.

"Good evening, everyone," he said. "Caroline."

"Mason." One precisely shaped black eyebrow arched up. "How was the evening with the old college roommate?"

"Wonderful. Don't let me interrupt. What were you talking about?"

"Your little friend," said Caro.

"I was just explaining to Caroline and Angus what happened while she was away," added Tish.

"Were you?" asked Mason. "And what would that be?"

"This way." Samantha led Raine down the hall and through a door into a room done in shades of lavender and gray. She crossed straight to the windows and carefully drew aside the heavy draperies. Sunlight poured into the room.

"This is a very grown-up room," said Raine, looking around.

"It's Aunt Randi's."

"Samantha—"

"It's okay. She showed me a secret. Come here and be really quiet." She reached beneath the pale lavender sheers and silently opened the window.

The voices from the terrace below came drifting in, faint but clear.

"We shouldn't be in here," whispered Raine.

"Don't you want to know what happens?"

"Of course, but I'm trying to be the adult." Except she didn't want to be. She wanted to hear. She leaned forward to see.

Through the sheers, the tableau below had the hazy look of an old Italian movie, and she knew she was going to watch how it played out. "Fine stepmom I'm going to make."

"Shhh. Listen."

"They hexed you, son," said Angus, with such total conviction that Mason wanted to laugh. "Your mama and sister. They mixed up some love potion for you and Caro, and you and that Hobart woman drank it by mistake. Tish says she's a witch of some kind—apparently a pretty good one, if she can get you to put so much at risk over a landscape designer."

"Is that what she told you she was?" asked Caro. "She's a gardener, Dad. A very dirty one, when I saw her." She glanced up at Mason. "I'm still not happy that you took her out in public, but at least I understand what happened now."

Mason looked to his sister. "You didn't tell them?"

"I figured you'd want to," Miranda said. "Unfortunately, it looks like it doesn't matter."

"Tell me what?" asked Tish. "What doesn't matter?"

"Later, Mother. Caroline, I think you and I should talk in private."

"I don't think that's necessary."

"Tell me what?" repeated Tish.

"I knew about the damned love potion all along, Mother. It never worked."

"Of course it worked, darling. You were head over heels for that girl until Miranda and I started reversing the spell."

"I still am head over heels."

"You are?" said Miranda. She started grinning.

"It's because we haven't been entirely successful," said Tish quickly. She reached out to touch Angus's hand and assured him, "It will be fine next week."

"Yes, it will," Mason said. "But not for the reasons you think." He looked at Caro and Angus. "I can't believe you two bought that crap."

"Don't dig yourself back in, boy," warned Angus. "Your mother has us inclined to forgive and forget."

"Forgive, anyway," said Caro.

A feeling of deep sympathy made Mason offer again, "You might want to reconsider that private conversation."

"We already did that, Mason. You know my position." She

leaned back in the chair, folding her arms and crossing one leg over the other. ''Besides, I think everyone is going to enjoy this. I know I am.''

Mason shrugged. ''Have it your way.''

He proceeded to tell the story, starting with the kiss on the terrace, right through the five thousand dollars and bailing Raine out of jail.

''So you're saying it was all pretense?'' interrupted Tish. ''No. I don't believe it. I saw you two. You were under that spell. We just need to reverse it, and you'll see what a state you've been in all this time.''

''He already sees, Mother,'' said Miranda.

''For the first time in a long time,'' added Mason.

''But—''

Angus tugged at his cuffs. ''You mean to say, you were pretending to be in love with that girl?''

''Initially, yes. But somewhere along the line it turned real.''

''Aha,'' said Tish.

''So, you are in love with her,'' said Caroline.

''I am,'' said Mason. ''I'm sorry, Caroline. I know this is not the way this should have been handled. I intended to approach you later, alone. And I did try to warn you.''

''Well,'' she sniffed. ''It doesn't really matter. She screwed you over, and you told me you're not seeing her anymore. It may be harder to ignore since I know you actually developed a *tendresse* for the creature, but the rules haven't changed. As long as you don't see her again, we can operate under the terms we discussed at your office.''

''Now there's the problem,'' said Mason. ''It took me a while to figure out, but I don't like the terms. You see, Caro, I intend to be faithful to my wife, which is apparently a concept that's foreign to you.''

''Then be faithful. I don't care.''

''Exactly. You don't care because you don't love me. And that's fine, because I don't love you, either.''

''Mason, don't,'' warned Tish.

He ignored her. ''Caroline, you are a beautiful and brilliant businesswoman, and our companies can probably make several billion dollars together over the next ten years with that power cell, but as a couple, you and I . . .'' He searched for a word, and found inspiration in the video arcade, of all places. ''As a couple, you and I suck big-time. A marriage between us would never work, and it would be best if we don't even try. I withdraw my offer.''

''You *what*?'' Caroline, Angus, and Tish all came up out of their chairs.

''The engagement is off.''

''Good boy,'' said Miranda.

''Don't be stupid, Alexander,'' said Angus. ''It's just hormones.''

''Damn it! If I hear that one more time, I'm going to become violent.''

''We'll fix it,'' Tish said. ''Just give us a few more nights and we'll have the moon in—''

''Mother, listen to me. I'm in love with Raine, and it has nothing to do with love potions or hormones, and everything to do with finding a woman who knows that life is for living. I'm going to marry Raine. Next week, if possible.''

''You bastard.'' Caroline stepped past Tish to get right in Mason's face. ''I've told people. I've already hired a goddamn wedding planner.''

''I'm sorry. I'll reimburse all costs, of course, and you can tell your friends anything you like about why you broke it off.''

''Like your airhead mother and half-wit sister? Or should I say half-witch?''

''I never!'' said Tish.

''Look, you bitch.'' Miranda came up out of her chair.

''Caroline.'' Angus took his daughter's arm.

It was as though he had touched a trigger. Caroline jerked away from her father, screaming. ''No one screws me over like that. No one.''

''Caroline! Get ahold of yourself.'' Angus stepped between her and Tish. ''There's no need to run down the ladies.''

''Ladies? *Ladies?* It's their damned dabbling in witchcraft that's the root of all this. Three stupid bitches are screwing things up for you, Mason. I'm giving you one last chance. Tell me it's a bad joke.''

''It's no joke,'' Mason said, sounding remarkably calm considering how close he was to throwing her bodily over the cliff. ''I'm marrying Raine.''

''Then I hope she's worth it, because that little slut is going to cost you a fortune. You can forget ever seeing the development money for the power cell. *You* may feel alive, but I guarantee your company won't be by next year. You pathetic bunch of inbred—"

"That's enough, Caroline," said Mason.

"It certainly is," said Angus. "Time to leave, honey."

He took Caro's arm again, but this time he held on and marched her out the door, with her sputtering and squawking all the way.

The silence after their departure was deafening. Mason looked at the stunned faces of his sister and mother.

"And that was the woman you wanted me to fall in love with."

"Oh, Mason, darling, I'm so sorry. Your marriage would have been a disaster and you would have had no way to get out of it. Thank goodness you didn't share the potion with her and get tangled up in some god-awful situation."

"I'll second that," he said.

"I'll third it."

Mason spun toward the voice and saw Sam and Raine as they came around the end of the house. They must have come down the circular staircase and out by his room. Sam rushed into his arms. He spun her around once, then set her down so he could do the same with Raine. "I love you."

"Me, too."

"Caro's not very nice," said Sam. "I'm glad you picked Raine."

"Me, too. Wait a second—how much of that did you hear?"

"All of it," said Sam. "I took Raine to Aunt Randi's room."

Raine looked at Miranda and shrugged. "I'm sorry. I just followed her."

"It's no problem," said Miranda. "I understand the temptation. I've been known to listen there myself."

Mason turned to Raine. "I can't believe you let Samantha listen to that diatribe."

"What can I say? I wanted to hear, too. But I did cover her ears when it got too bad." She demonstrated, and Sam started hollering.

"See, I can't hear anything, Daddy." She lifted Raine's hands away and spun off. "I'm so happy."

Raine slipped her arms around his neck and gave him a long kiss. "One down, one to go. How are *you* doing?"

"Amazingly well, considering the future of Alexander Industries just walked through that door."

"It's okay, Daddy," said Sam, spinning by. "I'd rather have Raine than a bunch of Caro's nasty old money, anyday."

"So would I," said Miranda.

"It's too bad we can't have them both in one," said Tish. She sighed. "However, if we get right down to it, I'd rather see you happy with Miss Hobart than miserable with Caro's money."

"Thank you," said Raine.

"I knew it," said Mason. "Now you just have to start calling her Raine." He kissed his mother, then kissed Raine again for good measure.

The sound of someone clearing his throat made everyone turn. Angus stood just outside the French doors, looking harried and uncomfortable.

"I want to apologize for my daughter," he said. "The girl went way off the deep end on this one."

"She was angry," said Tish.

"She was rude and disrespectful, Titania. You didn't do anything to hurt her, other than try to help your own flesh and blood. She had no call to speak that way. Not that she wasn't right to be mad at *you,* Mason."

"I know, sir."

"You played fast and loose with my baby girl. It makes me long for the days of buggy whips." He glared at Mason and let the words sink in. "However, there's personal and there's business, and it sounded to me like Caro just might have the two confused. Is that power cell of yours any good?"

"Yes, it is."

"I want to look at the specs on it."

"Caroline has them."

"I'm going to go around her on this one. You get them to me directly, and we'll see if it's worth me overriding her or not."

"First thing Monday morning," promised Mason. The sky seemed three shades brighter, despite the setting sun. He squeezed Raine's hand and she beamed him a smile that made Samantha giggle and spread to Miranda and Tish.

Angus walked out onto the terrace a few steps and, to Mason's surprise, his mother went to him.

"Thank you, Angus."

He dipped his head. ''There's no use letting personal problems interfere with making money.''

''I suppose not,'' said Tish.

''Just like there's no reason to let Mason and Caroline's problems interfere with our going to that concert next week.''

''No use at all.'' She reached out and touched his cheek. ''You're a very sweet man.''

Angus blushed, all six feet, two inches of him. ''Good night.''

He disappeared back through the house.

Mason looked from his mother to Miranda.

''Don't ask *me,*'' his sister said.

''Mother?''

Tish looked at him as though he were the silliest child on earth. ''We're going out again. We had a good time and decided to see how far it goes. Really, darlings, you need to grow up. See how well Miss—pardon me, *Raine* is taking the news.'' She beamed at Raine. ''You really are a charming thing, you know. I just was trying to do what I thought was best for Mason. I hope you'll forgive Miranda and me.''

''I already have,'' said Raine, and Mason was certain she meant it. ''So you really don't mind that I'm not rich or the right class and all that?''

''It would be lovely if you were, of course. But other things are more important.''

''Like what?'' asked Miranda.

''Love, of course, darling.''

''Oh, of course,'' said Miranda. ''I knew that. And while we're on that topic, sit down, all of you. I have something to tell you about Paul.''

Epilogue

All of Fremont turned out for the dedication of the new Canal Place building, drawn by great weather, a hot R&B band, and enough free bagels and iced lattés to sink a lifeboat. Tish moved through the raucous, happy crowd on Angus's arm, letting him maneuver them up near the speakers' platform, where some city official was already at the microphone.

"Oh, no, we missed Mason's speech."

"It's what we get for coming late," said Angus under his breath. "I told you we should have skipped the hospital until later."

"We'll go back later, too. Those are my granddaughters, and I'm going to see them every chance I get."

"Miranda's timing was sure off."

"Twins come when they come," said Tish. They were such beautiful little things, with the perfect mix of Paul's features and Miranda's. She could hardly wait for them to be big enough to come home.

The official finished speechifying, and Mason stepped forward to introduce a woman from the Fremont Business Alliance.

"I have a great privilege today," the woman said. "I get to present a community service award to a young woman who represents the finest ideals of our neighborhood. When she realized the negative impact of the original design of this development, she took her concerns to the parties involved, and when that didn't work, she took her efforts to the street.

"Some of you may remember the 'Berlin Wall' of a couple of years ago." A murmur of amusement rippled through the crowd. "Well, I have it on the highest authority—Mason Alexander's—that the Wall, and the efforts of the woman behind it, led directly to the redesign of Canal Place. Without her, we would not have this beautiful sculpture walk, or the breezeway and stairs, or the fountain, or any of the other features you've enjoyed today. Canal Place might have ended up an ugly, ordinary office building, completely unsuited to Fremont. Instead, we have a beautiful addition to our community, and the Alliance wants to recognize the efforts of the woman who made that possible.

"Ladies and gentlemen, I give you Ms. Raine Alexander."

Tish beamed and applauded with the rest of the crowd as Raine stepped to the podium to accept her award.

Angus leaned over and put his mouth close to Tish's ear. "I've been thinking."

"About what?"

"With Paul's dad being dead, those babies need a grandpa. What do you say, Titania?"

"Are you asking me to marry you, Angus Wickersham?"

"Yes, I am, ma'am." He took her hand and led her off behind a life-sized sculpture of a Chinese maiden balancing the world in her graceful hands. "I love you, and that's not an easy thing for me to say. We've been seeing each other for over two years. Marry me."

"Caroline will not be happy. I can hardly picture her as Mason's stepsister."

"She's mellowed out some since she saw last quarter's profits on the power cell. Anyway, the hell with Caroline. This is about you and me. Do you love me, Tish?"

"You know I do."

"Then marry me. If the kids fight, we'll send them to their rooms."

"That's a deal. Yes, I'll marry you, Angus."

As they kissed, it passed through Tish's mind that the destiny set in motion that day on the lower terrace had finally played itself out.

Mason and Raine, Paul and Miranda, and now her and Angus. Three couples, bound by one common thread.

The Threefold Law of the Craft had held true after all: Love sent out had returned Love, three times over.

A Note from Lisa

Discovering Raine and Mason lurking around Fremont has been one of the great pleasures of my life. I included bits and pieces of this wonderful Seattle neighborhood in my book, but if you're ever lucky enough to visit the Center of the Universe, you'll discover that I also made up a lot, especially about the "Canal Place" site—this is fiction, after all.

If you're curious about the matchstick puzzles Raine plays with the Alexanders, I'd be happy to provide you with the puzzles and their solutions. Just send me a note, along with a stamped, self-addressed envelope, and I'll mail you a puzzle sheet along with information about forthcoming books.

Lisa Hendrix
c/o Berkley Publicity Department
Penguin Putnam Inc.
375 Hudson Street
New York, NY 10014

You can also visit my website for news, games, and previews of future books:
http://www.lisahendrix.com

If you enjoyed
RAZZLE DAZZLE,
you won't want to miss

The More I See You

BY LYNN KURLAND

Coming in October from Berkley Books

One

Jessica Blakely didn't believe in Fate.

Yet as she stood at the top of a medieval circular staircase and peered down into its gloomy depths, she had to wonder if someone other than herself might be at the helm of her ship, as it were. Things were not progressing as she had planned. Surely Fate had known she wasn't at all interested in stark, bare castles or knights in rusting armor.

Surely.

She took a deep breath and forced herself to examine the turns of events that had brought her to her present perch. Things had seemed so logical at the time. She'd gone on a blind date, accepted said blind date's invitation to go to England as part of his university department's faculty sabbatical, then hopped cheerfully on a plane with him two weeks later.

Their host was Lord Henry de Galtres, possessor of a beautifully maintained Victorian manor house. Jessica had taken one look and fallen instantly in love—with the house, that is. The appointments were luxurious, the food heavenly, and the surrounding countryside idyllic. The only downside was that for some unfathomable reason, Lord Henry had decided that the crumbling castle attached to his house was something that needed to remain undemolished. Just the sight of it had sent chills down Jessica's spine. She couldn't say why, and she hadn't wanted to dig around to find the answer.

Instead, she'd availed herself of all the modern comforts Lord Henry's house could provide. And she'd been certain that when she could tear herself away from her temporary home-away-from-home, she might even venture to London for a little savings-account-reducing shopping at Harrods. Yet before she could find herself facing a cash register, she'd been driven to seek sanctuary in the crumbling castle attached to Lord Henry's house.

There was something seriously amiss in her life.

A draft hit her square in the face, loaded with the smell of seven centuries of mustiness. She coughed and flapped her hand in front of her nose. Maybe she should have kept her big mouth shut and avoided expressing any disbelief in Providence.

Then again, it probably would have been best if she'd remained silent a long time ago, maybe before she'd agreed to that blind date. She gave that some thought, then shook her head. Her troubles had begun long before her outing with Archibald Stafford III. In fact, she could lay her finger on the precise moment when she had lost control and Fate had taken over.

Piano lessons. At age five.

You wouldn't think that something so innocuous, so innocent and child-friendly would have led a woman where she never had any intention of having gone, but Jessica couldn't find any evidence to contradict the results.

Piano lessons had led to music scholarships, which had led to a career in music, which had somehow demolished her social life, leaving her no choice but to sink to accepting the latest in a series of hopeless blind dates: Archie Stafford and his shiny penny loafers. Archie was the one who had invited her to England for a month with all expenses paid. He had landed the trip thanks to a great deal of sucking up to the dean of his department. He didn't exactly fit in with the rest of the good old boys who clustered with the dean and Lord Henry every night smoking cigars into the wee hours, but maybe that's what Archie aspired to.

Jessica wondered now how hard up he must have been for a date to have asked her to come along. At the time he'd invited her, though, she'd been too busy thinking about tea and crumpets to let the invitation worry her. It had been a university-sponsored outing. She'd felt perfectly safe.

Unfortunately, being Archie's guest also meant that she had

to speak to him, and *that* was something she wished she could avoid for the next three weeks. It was on the flight over that she'd discovered the depth of his swininess. She made a mental note never to pull out her passport for anyone she'd known less than a month if such an occasion should arise again.

But like it or not, she was stuck with him for this trip, which meant at the very least polite conversation, and if nothing else, her mother had instilled in her a deep compulsion to be polite.

Of course, being civil didn't mean she couldn't escape now and then, which was precisely what she was doing at present. And escape had meant finding the one place where Archie would never think to look for her.

The depths of Henry's medieval castle.

She wondered if an alarm would sound if she disconnected the rope that barred her way. She looked to her left and saw that there were a great many people who would hear such an alarm if it sounded, but then again, maybe she wouldn't be noticed in the ensuing panic. Apparently Lord Henry funded some of his house upkeep by conducting tours of his castle. Those tours were seemingly well attended, if the one in progress was any indication.

Jessica eyed the sightseers. They were moving in a herdlike fashion and it was possible they might set up a stampede if she startled them. They were uncomfortably nestled together, gaping at cordoned-off family heirlooms, also uncomfortably nestled together. Lord Henry of Marcham's home was a prime destination spot and Jessica seemed to have placed herself in the midst of the latest crowd at the precise moment she needed the most peace and quiet. She had already done the castle tour and learned more than she wanted to know about Burwyck-on-the-Sea and its accompanying history. Another lesson on the intricacies of medieval happenings was the last thing she needed.

"—Of course, the castle here at Marcham, or Merceham as it was known in the 1300s, was one of the family's minor holdings. Even though it had been added to during the years and extensively remodeled during the Victorian period, it is not the most impressive of the family's possessions. The true gem of the de Galtres crown lies 150 kilometers away on the eastern coast. If we move further along here, you'll find a painting of the keep."

The crowd shuffled to the left obediently as the tour guide continued with his speech.

"As you can see here in this rendering of Burwyck-on-the-Sea—aptly named, if I might offer an opinion—the most remarkable feature of the family's original seat is the round tower built not into the center of the bailey as we find in Pembroke Castle, but rather into the outer seawall. I would imagine the third lord of the de Galtres family fancied having his ocean view unobstructed—"

So could Jessica and she heartily agreed with the sentiment, but for now an ocean view was not what she was interested in. If the basement was roped off it could only mean that it was free of tourists and tour guides. It was also possible that below was where the castle kept all its resident spiders and ghosts, but it was a chance she would have to take. Archie would never think to look for her there. Ghosts could be ignored. Spiders could be squashed.

She put her shoulders back, unhooked the rope, and descended.

She stopped at the foot of the steps and looked for someplace appropriate. Suits of armor stood at silent attention along both walls. Lighting was minimal and creature comforts nonexistent, but that didn't deter her. She walked over the flagstones until she found a likely spot, then eased her way between a fierce-looking knight brandishing a sword and another grimly holding a pike. She did a quick cobweb check before she settled down with her back against the stone wall. It was the first time that day she'd been grateful for the heavy gown she wore. A medieval costume might suit her surroundings, but it seemed like a very silly thing to wear to an afternoon tea—and said afternoon tea was precisely what she'd planned to avoid by fleeing to the basement.

Well, that and Archie.

She reached into her bag and pulled out what she needed for complete relaxation. Reverently, she set a package of two chilled peanut-butter cups on the stone floor. Those she would save for later. A can of pop followed. The floor was cold enough to keep it at a perfect temperature as well. Then she pulled out her portable CD player, put the headphones on her head, made herself more comfortable, and, finally closing her eyes with a sigh, pushed the play button. A chill went down her spine that had nothing to do with the cold stone.

Bruckner's Seventh could do that to a girl, given the right circumstances.

Jessica took a deep breath and prepared for what she knew was to come. The symphony started out simply. She knew eventually it would increase in strength and magnitude until it came crashing down on her with such force that she wouldn't be able to catch her breath.

She felt her breathing begin to quicken and had to wipe her palms on her dress. It was every bit as good as it had been the past 139 times she had listened to the same piece. It was music straight from the vaults of heav—

Squeak.

Jessica froze. She was tempted to open her eyes, but she was almost certain what she would see would be a big, fat rat sitting right next to her, and then where would she be? Her snack was still wrapped, and since it really didn't count as food anyway, what could a rat want with it? She returned her attention to the symphony. It was the London Philharmonic, one of her favorite orchestras—

Wreek, wreek, wreeeeeek.

Rusty shutters? Were there shutters in the basement? Hard to say. She wasn't about to open her eyes and find out. There was probably some kind of gate nearby and it was moving thanks to a stiff breeze set up by all the tourists tromping around upstairs. Or maybe it was a trapdoor to the dungeon. She immediately turned away from that thought, as it wasn't a place she wanted to go. She closed her eyes even more firmly. It was a good thing she was so adept at shutting out distractions. The noise might have ruined the afternoon for her otherwise.

Wreeka, wreeka, wreeeeeka.

All right, that was too much. It was probably some stray kid fiddling with one of the suits of armor. She'd give him an earful, send him on his way, and get back to her business.

She opened her eyes—then shrieked.

There, looming over her with obviously evil intent, was a knight in full battle gear. She pushed herself back against the stone wall, pulling her feet under her and wondering just what she could possibly do to defend herself. The knight, however, seemed to dismiss her upper person because he bent his helmeted head to look at her feet. By the alacrity with which he suddenly leaned over in that direction, she knew what was to come.

The armor creaked as the mailed hand reached out. Then, without any hesitation, the fingers closed around her peanut-butter cups. The visor was flipped up with enthusiasm, the candy's coverings ripped aside with more dexterity than any gloved hand should have possessed, and Jessica's last vestige of American junk food disappeared with two great chomps.

The chomper burped.

''Hey, Jess,'' he said, licking his chops, ''thought you might be here hiding. Got any more of those?'' He pointed at the empty space near her feet, his arm producing another mighty squeak.

Rule number one: No one interrupted her during Bruckner.

Rule number two: No one ate her peanut-butter cups, *especially* when she found herself stranded in England for a month without the benefit of a Mini Mart down the street. She had yet to see any peanut-butter cups in England and she'd been saving her last two for a quiet moment alone. Well, at least the thief hadn't absconded with her drink as of yet—

''Geez, Jess,'' he said, reaching for her can of pop, popping the top and draining the contents, ''why are you hiding?''

She could hardly think straight. ''I was listening to Bruckner.''

He burped loudly. ''Never understood a girl who could get all sweaty over a bunch of fairies playing the violin.'' He squashed the can, then grinned widely at the results a mailed glove could generate. Then he looked at her and winked. ''How'd you like to come here and give your knight in shining armor a big ol' kiss?''

I'd rather kiss a rat was on the tip of her tongue, but Archibald Stafford III didn't wait for the words to make it past her lips. He hauled her up from between her guardians—and a fat lot of good two emtpy suits of armor had done her—sending her CD player and headphones crashing to the ground, pulled her against him, and gave her the wettest, slobberiest kiss that had ever been given an unwilling maiden fair.

She would have clobbered him, but she was trapped in a mailed embrace and powerless to rescue herself.

''Let me go,'' she squeaked.

''What's the matter? Aren't you interested in my strong, manly arms?'' he said, giving her a squeeze to show just how strong and manly his arms were.

''Not when they're squeezing the life from me,'' she gasped. ''Archie, let me go!''

"It'll be good for research purposes."

"I'm a musician, for heaven's sake. I don't need to do this kind of research. And you are a . . ." and she had to pause before she said it because she still couldn't believe such a thing was possible, given the new insights she'd had into the man currently crushing the life from her, "a . . . philosopher," she managed. "A tenured philosophy professor at a major university, not a knight."

Archibald sighed with exaggerated patience. "The costume party, remember?"

As if she could forget, especially since she was already dressed à la medieval, complete with headgear and lousy shoes. And it was an afternoon tea for the vacationing faculty of Archie's university. Whey they had chosen to dress themselves up as knights and ladies fair she couldn't have said. It had to have been the brainchild of that nutty history professor who hadn't been able to clear his sword through airport security. She'd known just by looking at him that he was trouble.

If only she'd been as observant with Archie. And now here she was, staring at what had, at first blush, seemed to be one of her more successful blind dates. She could hardly reconcile his current self with his philosophy self. Either he'd gotten chivalry confused with chauvinism, or wearing that suit of armor too long had allowed metal to leach into his brain and alter his personality.

"I'll carry you up," Archie said suddenly. "It'll be a nice touch."

But instead of being swept up into his arms, which would have been bad enough, she found herself hoisted and dumped over his shoulder like a sack of potatoes.

"My CD player," she protested.

"Get it later," he said, trudging off toward the stairs.

She struggled, but it was futile. She thought about name-calling, but that, she decided, was beneath her. He'd have to put her down eventually and then she would really let him have it. For the moment, however, it was all she could do to avoid having her head make contact with the stairwell as Archie huffed up the steps. He paused and Jessica heard a cacophony of startled gasps. Fortunately she was hanging mostly upside down, so her face couldn't get any redder.

"I love this medieval stuff," Archie announced to whatever assembly there was there, "don't you?"

And with that, he slapped her happily on the rump—to the accompaniment of more horrified gasps—and continued on his way.

Jessica wondered if that sword she'd seen with the armor in the basement was sharp. Then again, maybe it would be just as effective if it were dull. Either way, she had the feeling she was going to have to use it on the man who chortled happily as he carried her, minus her dignity, on down the hallway to where she was certain she would be humiliated even further.